I0782128

Calhera

The Legend of Sander Helmglade

By

Corrie Pereira

Table of Contents

Prologue

In the Kingdom of Luna, there were two brothers, Sander and Fergus. Their father was the King; unfortunately, the Queen died giving birth to Fergus. The brothers lived in the same dark, dreary castle for sixteen years. Sander was firstborn and next to inhabit the throne, but he didn't want to become king, he desired to be an adventurer and travel the great seas. However, his brother wanted to become king. Fergus was taught diplomatic strategy and combat while his brother, Sander was taught to rule the kingdom and trained for close combat with a sword.

Days passed since their father's assassination, and it was time for Sander's coronation, where the Prince would become King. His curiosity led him to visit the tower of knowledge which was located on the right-wing of the castle containing the castle secrets and the history of the kingdom. When Sander entered the doorway, he saw his brother, Fergus examining the book of war and destruction. Fergus asked Sander if he knew that the castle was built to secure the city of Luna from evil demons and them completing their destiny? Sander said, "What was the demon's name?" Fergus stated that he didn't know, and the book mentioned the General of Wrath. Fergus reminded Sander of the big day to follow. "I know tomorrow is my coronation," Sander replied, "I just wanted to see the book before I become the King and learn more of the castle's hidden secret." Fergus implied, "I think its magic is holding the castle together."

"Well, Fergus, I guess we should go to bed."

"Sander, make sure you don't die before then."

"Who would want to kill me, Fergus?"

With that, the brothers bid each other a good night.

As Sander slept, Fergus put his plan to kidnap him, in place for that night. Sander was awoken to a violent blindfolded attack with someone grabbing him from his bed and taking him to the Dark Pit right outside of Sinia. The next morning, Sander woke up feeling the chilly air near the edge of the cliff as he glared into an abyss of darkness; far in the distance, he saw Fergus. "Fergus, what's going on?" He demanded. Fergus replied, "I'm sorry, Sander, but all you know is war and death. I can lead our people to greatness, but you show a lack of leadership potential for the future."

Sander insisted, "But I'm the firstborn, I have to be the King no matter what!"

"You're nothing but a scholar, Sander! There are many ways to fight," Fergus yelled, "Economics and diplomacy are mine, but you never saw the future, you're just an ignorant person."

"What are you going to do, Fergus, kill me?" Fergus said calmly.

"That's exactly what I'm going to do!"

Fergus kicked Sander off the cliff, he fell into the Dark Pit. Later that day, the advisers figured that the prince was dead, as they saw the splatters of blood in his room.

They appointed the next of kin, his brother Fergus, within three days, and all was good in the Kingdom. What they didn't know was that Sander still lived, but was on the verge of death.

Chapter 1

The Deal of Revenge

(Three days earlier)

Day One

Sander fell in the dark pit; he hit his head on multiple rocks, knocking him unconscious. As he woke up, he realized that he could not move his legs and was unable to reach out to a crimson-eyed shadow over his left shoulder. With absolute horror of the red-blood-shot-eyes demon, Sander started to question, "Who are you?" It responded, "Who am I? The real question is who are you?"

"My name is Sander Helmglade." The Shadow Demon knew the name Helmglade. "Well, Sander, how did you get here?" Inquired the Shadow Demon. Sander replied, "I was betrayed by my brother, Fergus. He kicked me into this hole."

"Well, Sander, you're almost to the brink of death," proclaimed the demon. Sander pondered about who this Shadow Demon could be. Speaking aloud, Sander asked, "Hey, who are you anyway, and why do you ask so many questions? What can you do for me? I'm going to die. At least identify yourself," Sander requested.

"Just call me R," instructed the Shadow Demon. "So, you think that you are going to die, you say? He smirked. "I can help you, you know."

"How so?" replied Sander.

"Well, I can offer you a deal, but you must give me your word to give it some thought."

"What's the deal?" Sander queried.

"The deal my mangled, crippled friend is to allow me to fuse into your body, we will become one and you will become whole again." Sander stared at the red-blood-shot-eyed demon as the demon informed him that it would be weird at first, but that he will get used to it.

Sander could feel the rage of revenge whirling up inside of him accompanied by a hatred he had never known before. Feeling the evil intent and the energy of hatred, R encouraged Sander to accept the deal, however, there was no going back, and you could seek revenge on that no-good brother of yours. Sander informed R that he would accept the deal if it guaranteed that he would regain his full health.

Sander accepted the deal.

"You will feel some sharp pain, this part may hurt a bit, but you will also feel a strong amount of invisibility." Sander and R started the fusing procedure as their souls intertwined into one body. Sander felt a rush of warmth that covered his body, he began to see red, he saw a light from the top of his head to his feet and a fire started to light up all over him. Then Sander passed out.

<u>*Day Two*</u>

Sander woke up to the sun rising on the horizon. He could walk and figure out that his wounds were healed. Not only was he healed, but he felt stronger than ever. He heard someone talking to him but knew that he was alone. He recognized the voice and remembered that it belonged to R. Echoing from within, "Are you finally awake, how much sleep do we need?"

Sander questioned the voice, "Where are you? Where did you go, and why do I hear your voice?"

"I'm in your head, Sander," said R.

"Oh, my Lord, Sander, when we fused my soul, combined with your soul which means that I'm in your head and I can take control of your body if I so desire. The good news is that you acquired all of my super strength, super speed, and the ability to see from ten miles away, and we can light up like fire. We also share some other abilities such as having wings, but you are not yet ready to take flight until you know how to use all of the other gifts."

"Wow! I never knew we had that much power," said Sander.

"Let's get to training so that I can use these powers. Do you see that giant rock?" commanded R, "I need you to pick it up, extend it over your head, and run two miles down out of the cave."

"First, why should I do that?" Asked Sander.

"Because you need to get used to our strength and speed, if you just run out there and do things without training, you will die. I have to train you and get you fit. Understand something, Sander, if you die I die. I don't want to die over this stupid sibling war between you and your brother. If you want to learn how to use these powers you need to get used to them."

Being a fast learner and an athlete, Sander could gain full use of his new powers within twelve hours. But R was not convinced of his abilities and continued to insist on training him. "I want you to jump upward as high as you can. What I want you to do is jump."

"Jump, why would I need to jump? Right, let us do this." Sander jumped as high as he could, reaching two hundred meters upward. However, not knowing how to land caused him to create a large hole resembling a sinkhole.

"Try it again, land lighter, and do not make any more holes," R instructed, "How that's it, next, we will study flying."

Day Three

Breaking the Barrier

Sander sprang from side to side bouncing from wall to wall within two thousand meters he made it, plunging through the barrier from the top. Alright, Sander, you met the challenge and now it is time to build an army, but before you do that you must return to the castle and study the layout. "But I know the castle," Sander said. "Yeah, but do you know the kingdom," R said calmly. R continued to express to Sander that he might have known the castle but not the kingdom as a prince was only given minor information to protect the kingdom's security.

"We will leave for the castle at day-break." Sander shared a great concern about being recognized. "They will notice me," Sander exclaimed. "Not if we go at night, my dear friend, we have the power of lurking in the shadows. By nightfall, we will transform into shadow, and be hidden from our adversaries, they will never even see your face."

"Is there anything else I should know?"

"Well, you can do a little of this and that with fire."

"FIRE," cried Sander. R encouraged Sander to practice using his gift of fire and warned him that without control of this power, he could die, especially in the daylight. "Nighttime is where we can use our powers for an unlimited amount of time. Now think of the tree burning and let it burn, let it burn!" Sander rejoiced in his newfound powers, almost forgetting his brother's betrayal.

"Good job it is almost nightfall, focus on the gate of the castle, now the walls behind the gate, we are almost there, let's get behind the guards. Our shadow powers are working great!"

"This shadow wrath power is really hard to get used to."

"I am going to train you, we will not strike until then," R instructed Sander to focus on the power and allow it to flow through him. Sander said that he learned fast and was ready for his training.

Chapter 2

The Break-In

Sander became more and more skillful, almost to the level of being invisible within shadows or shades. "Next, we have to go on a quest to examine a couple of kingdoms and their inhabitants. First, the kingdom of Orcuhan."

"What? What is Orcuhan? The kingdom of Orcs." Sander wondered, "Do orcs exist?"

"Yes, Orcs exist, you didn't know that?" He said. "In this kingdom, the races were demons, Elves, dwarfs, and humans." Sander realized how isolated he was and understood that the open trade with the elves in the kingdom of Elmus was only a small part of the world.

"Wait, I already know the shadow wrath power, why don't I just go to the castle."

"You need to see where you are going. You think you are ready, Sander, but you are not!" echoed R.

"Sander, do you see that sword over there? It is the entrance of the kingdom. Once we share full power you will be able to wheel many mystical swords, but Sander you're not ready yet!"

"Aren't you supposed to give me advice? Not tell me what to do," said Sander. "It's time for me to enter the throne room, I know that I have to wait until dark. I'm doing this and ending this now." As Sander entered the throne room, disguised in the shadows, he saw Fergus, and the mage of the house of Helmglade appeared.

However, it was very dark and hard to identify many objects in the room. "Use magic to light the candles and torches around the throne room," a voice bellowed. As he illuminated the room, he was noticed and quickly surrounded by Lunian soldiers with spears and swords drawn on him.

"Do you see what happens when I don't tell you what to do?" R scolded Sander, "You just get us in trouble."

Fergus was overwhelmed to see that Sander was not dead and quickly accused Sander of killing his father to gain the throne, but ran away once he feared that he would not get away with it. "Take him to the dungeon," he yelled, "Everyone knows, Sander."

"Knows what, Fergus?   It was not me, Fergus! It was you who killed father first, then tried to kill me because you wanted the throne. Yu are a monster, your greed caused you to kill father! I will get you for this, it is not over! I came here to take back my birthright to the throne and to prove to the people how crooked you are!"

"Do you think anyone will believe you, brother? How did you get in here? Why did we not see you enter the castle, what kind of black magic are you involved with? Are you a demon?"

There were many mystics with King Fergus, Altinar, a lead magician, used a spell to sense the energy of the demon inside of Sander. "My King is correct, Sander is evil. He has a demon in him." Altinar shot a knockout spell and Sander fell into a deep sleep. R talked to Sander from within, "I feel a presence in that crown, something I felt over a thousand years ago; a force that is almost as great as I am!"

As Sander was awakened, he repeated, "Fergus, you won't get away with this. I will get revenge for what you have done to me."

"Well, you have a dreadful night in this dark, dingy dungeon, as I sleep comfortably in my warm, cozy chambers," Fergus boosted.

Sander communicated from within, "R, why would you lie to me?"

"I didn't lie to you, I just didn't tell you the truth."

"You are a demon. This makes so much sense now the dark pit. It is all true you wanted to wreak havoc in the world."

"That's not what I was going to do. I was never supposed to hurt the other factions. I just wanted to hurt one."

"And what faction is that?"

"The celestials," R said with a hurt emotion.

"So, you just wanted to kill all the celestials and then what? Us? Are we next?" Sander pondered.

"No, I wanted to kill the celestials for a reason."

"Tell me the reason."

"I don't want to tell you."

"Well, we're both are here in this dungeon and probably going to get executed!"

"No, we are not, Sander, we have powers."

"Okay, but these are my people. I'm not fighting my way out because I don't want to kill anyone else, just Fergus."

"Well, we have no choice but to get out of here and put together an army and return. The humans, your people are already corrupted by him. So, let's get out of here."

"Wait, R, what? Tell me your real name."

"My name is Riker."

"Good, now we can go. But wait one more question. You said you felt a strange presence. What was it?"

"It was something I felt a thousand and two hundred years ago. It was a celestial presence. But that's impossible, celestials were never seen in Sinia for five hundred years. So that's impossible."

"Okay, let's go."

"Wait I feel it again. I know who it is."

"Riker, what are you doing?"

"I'm taking control, so I can take my revenge." Riker stopped. "NO! Galatin," Riker said in anger. Riker lit up in flames but it wasn't normal flames, it was red flames and the bars in the dungeon started to burn around him as he broke down the door.

"Get him," the guards said as Riker burned the guards into a crisp.

"Galatin, I'm coming for you," but Riker ran from the dungeon to the throne room and the guards tried to stop him. Each guard that got closer was lit up in flames and died. "GALATIN, GALAAATIN," Riker screamed in anger as he entered the throne room and saw Fergus sitting on the throne. "I know about you, Lord Riker. General of Wrath, you wanted to kill the celestials and you wanted to destroy the world."

"Whatever he said isn't true. All I wanted to do was get my revenge."

"Hey, Riker," Galatin said calmly. "Why are you in Sinia?"

"Because I heard you escaped the dark pit, so I came here, for Fergus, you are just a bonus. Fergus wants Sander dead and I want you dead. So, it's a partnership, the partnership only ends when the deal is done, it happens to both sides." Riker grabbed the sword from the knight's dead body and ran at Galatin, "I'm going to kill you for what you did to her.

"She was your sister, Galatin."

"Yes, however, my sister was a traitor plus I know all you wanted to do was to just make the abomination joining both the celestial and demon worlds. That's something that should not be born."

"Shut up!" Riker swung the sword at Galatin. As soon as he swung at Galatin, he blocked the attack, and the sword shattered in pieces. "What the hell? Wait I know that sword is the sword that helped win the war against the humans. I thought they were all destroyed."

"Yeah well, I guess this is the end of you," said Galatin. Riker was slashed with a sword as the light came out and knocked Riker through the castle wall thousands of feet into the air. "Riker," Sander said. "Wake up!" Riker began to start falling, "Wakes up!" Said Sander in fear of dying. "Oh, screw this," then Sander took control of the body.

Corrie Pereira

"Crap I don't know what to do," as Sander started to light up in flames as he fell.

13

Chapter 3

The Sprout

Sander fell through the air, he was concerned that he was headed back into the dark pit. "Riker, what are we going to do? Are going to die or get trapped? Wake up Riker, Riker! I got to use the shadow wrath power, but I don't know where to go." Then, Sander pictured a forest, and all of a sudden, he was no longer falling but gliding through the air to a nearby forest. There was no pressure as falling felt like sawing through the air. Sander opened his eyes, I never knew that I could fly. "Their wings! Riker, wake up. I need you to wake up." Sander saw a forest and tried to land there, "Alright now, to stick the landing. Oh crap," Sander lost control over them and fell into the forest.

Sander started to get up and walk east to a nearby Elven town and yelled, " Hello, is anyone there?" Sander noticed the houses were burned and destroyed. "Hello, anyone there? Can someone tell me what happened here? Anyone?"

"Help me," cried a wounded scout.

"Who said that and where are you?" Sander looked around and saw the wounded Elven scout.

"Hey, hold on, stay with me, soldier. What happened here?"

"Goblins, Orcs, and three giants came and attacked us," said the wounded scout.

"Why would they do that? I don't know they just wanted something. I think my people."

"Why would they want your people?"

"I am not sure, maybe for food. No, not for food, possibly for something worse."

"I got a bad feeling about this place," said Sander to himself. "Do you know where they went?"

"Yes," he pointed towards the north side of town.

"How can I help you? I have some medicine in my bag. Take it; it will make you better." Sander asked the wounded scout his name.

"My name is Elijah. I'm a scout captain of the Kingdom of Elmus. Thank you, I owe you!"

"You're an Elven soldier?" Sander asked.

"Yes, I am," the wounded scout replied.

"Okay, thank you for telling me where the bandits are at."

"Wait," said Elijah. "What's your name?"

"My name is Sander."

"Sander, I think I've heard that name before, or who knows it might be me. Also, Sander. Are you going to take on all those bandits alone? Before they took my people. I counted thirty-nine orcs and fifty-seven Goblins plus three giants."

"Hey, I didn't even know those guys exist, but I'm all you got against them." He heard a woman warrior from afar and began to hide. "Well, good luck there, Elijah, hang in there, backup will arrive."

"Good luck Sander, on trying to rescue my people."

"Good luck with staying alive, Elijah." Then Sander disappeared north into the forest, at that time, Riker woke up from his slumber. "Sander, I see you grew wings," said Riker.

"Oh, now you woke up?" Sander laughed. "I cannot believe that you were knocked out like that. Have you ever fought someone with the same power as yours before?"

"Yeah, I have about one thousand years ago."

"Okay, is that how you get into the dark pit?"

"Alright now. It's time to do something painful."

"Wait, Riker, what do you mean?"

"It's time to cut off your wings."

"Why the hell would I do that?"

"So, we can look more human. Want me to do it?"

"You know what, yeah, you do it."

"Ok, I will do it." Riker took control of their body. "Do you realize that it doesn't matter who takes control, we will both feel the same pain?"

"Dammit. Wait, Riker how are you going to chop the wings off with a broken human sword?"

"Yeah, you're right. It's not like I have super strength. Oh crap." Riker grabbed the two sides of the wings with both hands and used his super strength to rip them off. "Aaaaaahhhhhhhh!" They both screamed. Riker let Sander take control as the wounds heal instantly. "See, it didn't hurt that bad. We can heal," said Riker.

"Yeah, I know we can heal, but didn't you think it will hurt?"

"Well, after two thousand years, you kind of get used to the pain."

"Well, let's get to Orcuhan."

"Why would we go there?"

"Because we need an army to take the kingdom."

"No, we need to help those elven farmers."

"It's not our business."

"Yes, it is if you had a chance to save your people, would you?"

"No. why? Have you met my people they would most likely try to kill you and get your soul before helping you?"

"Oh, as a human it is in our nature to help others in need. If you want to help the elves, go help the elves."

"At night. And I will take control and eat the souls of the bandits."

"Why would we do that?"

"To get more power!"

"That makes sense."

"The more souls the more power and the better our revenge."

Riker and Sander heard a woman in the distance. "Okay, quickly burn the wings." Sander burned the wings; "Come on, let's go." Sander and Riker went to a nearby cave and started to talk. "We're safe for now," said Riker. "Now! Riker, what happened at the kingdom, how did you lose the fight against Galatin? Just tell the truth, Riker. What's going on? Who is Galatin and why do you want to kill him so badly? And who is her? You mention her in a fight. Was she of any importance to you?"

"Yes, she was. But this all happened a long time ago."

"How long?"

"Before your kingdom was even built. It all started when three realms opened."

"Realms?"

"Yes, realms. Sander, there are celestials and reapers, you know, right?"

"Wow, I got a lot to learn."

"Yes, you do. So, the three realm doors opened. All of us were peaceful. Until my father said these people killed one of our guys. Then the celestials tried defending their people. So, my father said if you're not going to take action on your people then we're going to have to go to war. Thus, the war against the celestials and demons began. The war was long-lasting for one thousand years. Until I met someone causing me to lose contact with my army. And it was just me in the forest, and then she came and caught me off guard. As she approached me, we fought and fought. Then we talked and fought again. Until she and I concluded that both of our armies were not coming to help us. So, we worked together in that forest, it was nothing but evil. She and I fought our way out.

"What was her name?" Sander asked.

"Her name was Crystal. She had a beautiful voice, dark hair that flowed down her back and around her face and the body of a goddess. When she and I left the forest we decided to join forces and stay with each other. We built a wooden cottage in the forest where we fell in love. We loved and enjoyed each other for three hundred years, in perfect harmony. Then she came to me with good news that she was pregnant with my child. It would have been half-demon and half-celestial. The first of its kind! It could have united both of our races in peace and a harmony that only I understand. Until I felt the presence of my kind nearby. So, I told Crystal I will be right back. She also told me she was in contact with her brother and talking to him. When I met my kin, they knew I was alive and my father decided to throw a party. I went to the party, but I never really stayed. When I arrived at the cottage, I saw Crystal with her brother and four Syboli, the royal archangel guards. She was a princess and I was a prince, but from two different realms," sadness overwhelmed him. "Her brother, Galatin, without hesitation killed her right in front of my eyes. He yelled at her in anger saying that she was a traitor and was supposed to die because of her marriage to a demon. I got so angry that my flames burnt in the sunlight, a curse among us demons, and yet I did not feel weakness from the sun. The two royal guards started to fight me, I killed them both, but when I lunged after Galatin, he ran away along with two other guards. So, Sander, you see why I hate remembering my past, it is just too painful. I tried going to my father for advice and assistance in seeking my revenge but the second he knew I was entwined with a celestial, he banished me from the demon realm. I couldn't go back. I made a proposition to my generals to schedule a secret ritual in Luna that would take away the sun for seven days causing death to all celestials there. Then your human race got in my way and because the celestials were scared of what I would do, both the celestials and humans blocked me! Your race was never supposed to intervene in this fight. Now, Sander, that's why I got angry and took over the control of the throne room. You have my word, Sander Helmglade, that everything I just told you is true."

Sander started to feel an overwhelming feeling of sadness. "Wow, I never knew you fought for love and revenge," said Sander. "Do you miss her?"

"Every single minute of every single day," replied Riker.

"Hey, it's been a long day, it's time that we start to get moving." Sander started to walk northward towards the evil bandits. "Let's rest at that cave over there."

"Alright. So, Sander you have a plan."

"Nope."

"Well, we got to make one." Sander and Riker started to plan until they were interrupted and caught off guard by a mysterious woman.

Chapter 4

The Mysterious Women

"Who are you, Sander?"

"Just call me S," said the mysterious woman.

"Alright, what's with everyone and the dam initials."

"The name is Sofia," she responded in an aggressive tone. Riker told Sander that we were surrounded. "So, Sofia you think surrounding us with nine of your men is a good idea."

"I don't know what you are talking about."

"I sense three on the east with longbows; three on the west with longbows, and two on top of the cave ready to ambush us when we get out of the cave. You think I am stupid or did you think that you would get me with you and your warriors?"

"Alright, you got us; guys show yourself," Sofia said. Two guys jumped down from the cave entrance, with their swords drawn along with men branding longbows as well.

"Let's just say that you are not one of the bandits who attacked the village. I don't think there are three giants, thirty-nine orcs, and fifty-seven goblins who would accept me in their crew: Due to me being a human and all."

"They think humans, elves, and dwarfs are weak. So why would they want me to be in their little group?"

"I do not know, maybe it's magic keeping you from your true form," said Sofia.

"Look Sofia, I know where they are and do not need a small crew of scouts and warriors to help me. I got this!"

"Oh right, and you didn't even tell me your name, mysterious man, so how would I know you are not one of them?"

"For the last time, if I was one of them I would have run, or killed every single one of you. I believe that as a woman you would have been violated if they found you alone. But I am just saying a woman warrior out here alone is dangerous. Also, the name is Sander."

"Sander is not going to tell a lady the last name," she replied. Well, you did not tell me yours first. I will say ladies first. Well, anyway I am going to keep tracking the bandits."

Sofia chuckled and said, "Yeah no, you are not going to win."

"Why have you been there? No, but I can tell that humans are not as good at tracking, as you all believe. I know where the bandits are and can tell you where, but it is up to you and your men to decide if you can handle the inevitable."

"What do you mean? It's not like you can handle those bandits on your own."

"I can handle those guys just fine," sneered Sander. "Trust me."

"How, with some kind of magic?" Sofia laughed.

"Something like that," Sander replied with a mystical look.

"Well, my guys are trained and so it's our duty to go and help those in need."

Sander smiled and said, "If it's your duty don't you think your King can send more than nine soldiers?" It's eleven now. Elijah and one of my men are coming to us."

"Wow, does that mean that we are a team?"

Sofia finally signaled the six bowmen to come to the cave after shaking hands and making an allegiance to each other a bond of trust was formed. Sander stated that this was all they had against those bandits and they must attack at night. "Alright, you can take the lead, Sofia, but I know the number and where they are."

Sofia interrupted, "I know that my men are not going to charge in there. Do you have a plan?"

As he was about to go with his plan, Elijah and a soldier came to the cave. "Hey Sofia, I am here," bellowed Elijah. "You finally came, since we have all our men we can get it moving."

Sander started to lay out a picture of the blueprints of the bandits' camp in the sand and went over the plan giving instructions. "We are splitting into three teams; Elijah you and a soldier will rescue the people in the cages on the left; you will get support from three longbows in the back, the same goes for you, soldiers on the other side, and the three archers have to watch over them."

"How about me?" Sofia said, "What am I going to do?"

Sander told Sofia that she was not going to fight. Sofia replied, "Uh, excuse you! I can fight."

"I know you can, but these are eleven scouts and soldiers. They have been taught to fight for their people and they continue to train plus you are just a woman who thinks you can fight.

She yelled, "Trust me I can fight, and who is the third team?"

"Oh, the third team is me and only me."

"I'm coming with you," said Sofia. "Fine, Sander, agrees you want to do something; how about you watch my back? Got it? Ok, now guys let's move."

However, the soldiers do not move. Sofia commanded her men to do exactly as he said. "Ok, let's move." The soldiers then swiftly headed toward the bandits' camp, she looked at Sander with a victory smile.

Chapter 5

The Rescue

"We have arrived, Sander and the elves are on a hill observing the hideout. Remember the plan, there are cages on the left and right. There are kids in the middle."

"Kids," said Sofia, "Why would they want kids?"

"Because kids' souls are innocent and less corrupt, "replied Sander. "The magic is strong. I can sense they're using magic."

"Magic?" said, Elijah.

"Yes magic, but not just any magic dark magic, soul-stealing magic. The less corrupted souls are, the more powerful the magic," said Sander. "Elijah, get your men and go on the left."

"Yes sir," said Elijah. Elijah left with his team to the left of the hideout. Then Sander commanded the other soldiers to go to the right. "Yes sir," said the soldiers.

"Now, Sofia, you stay right here."

"Wait, there is a cave with green lights emerging from it."

"What kind of cave is that over there? Go check it out. then tell me what is causing that light."

"Alright, there's the entrance." Sofia crept slowly to investigate, before her there were three large figures, "giants," she pondered.

Sander did his thing and he looked at the four watchtowers, each containing two orcs.

"Riker, what do I do?"

"Well, it's easy, we have to use the shadow wrath move." On her way back, Sofia witnessed Sander turn into a shadow and saw the shadow went to all four of the towers at the same time. Sander devoured the watchtowers, snapped their orcs necks, and cleared the middle area of the evil orcs. Now it was time to wait for Sofia. Sofia went back to Sander. "There were three giants in the cave, but they did not see me."

"Now that I cleared the middle and your men are taking care of the left and the right, let's go meet the boss and I will deal with the three giants. If I don't return in five hours you know what happened."

Sofia looked with concern, and said, "I will stay here and wait for my men along with my people."

Sander went into the deep dark tunnel. "Riker, where are the giants, and how big are these guys?" Riker began to laugh and warned, "You will see Sander." As he opened the door, he saw there were children ready to be sacrificed by three fifteen-foot giants. Riker instructed Sander to use his shadow wrath power and quickly move toward the giants as fast as he could. To Sander's surprise, he turned into a bolt of fire advancing into the chest of two giants and pierced their hearts. The sound of thunder roared as they fell to the ground, but there was one left.

Sander lunged at the third giant and entered through his ear causing an implosion from within. "Now, Sander, you must do the unthinkable." He had to devour the giant's soul to gain their strength. "One more instruction, Sander, I need you to think about your favorite food."

"Not so bad, Riker, it tastes like cake."

"Hello, my name is Sander. I am here to take you home." The children rejoiced, feeling happy and safe. They praised Sander for opening all the cages and rescuing them. Exiting the tunnel, Sander and the children met Sofia and her men rallied together.

"Sofia, I told you everything would work out, the children are safe and your men are fine. So, are all the bandits dead?"

"Yes, they are all dead," said Sofia. "Now I guess you should be getting home. Actually, why don't you come with us so we can team up?" Riker went dormant as he recognized the feeling of infatuation that Sander was feeling towards Sofia.

"Um sure? I guess I could get some drinks at the tavern for doing all the hard work." Sofia started to look at Sander mysteriously as he walked towards her. "It is a two-day walk to the kingdom of Elmus, we will stop at the closest village to set up camp."

With homes burnt to the ground, the soldiers and Sander had their work set out for them, before the people could go home the town had to be rebuilt and made safe. Sofia decided to camp here but Sander responded disrespectfully. Sofia requested, "Sander, come here, look, I do not care about your bad-boy reputation, or how cool you think you are, don't you ever, ever talk to me that way in front of my men, understood?"

"Whatever you say, my lady." In the middle of the night, Sander gets out of bed and decided to go back to the hideout. As he left Sofia, followed him, staying a reasonable distance behind. Meanwhile, at the hideout, he sought Riker. "Alright Riker, I am here at the hideout, I think I know what to do." In the hideout lurked a mysterious person. "Hello, there. What are you? A thief who came here to take my riches, sorry but I don't know who you are." Sander's eye began to turn red. "But you might want to get out of the way."

"Relax the name is Lumeria."

"Ok, what do you want?"

"I am here for a good reason," he replied, Sander got angry and demanded to know, "Why are you here and do not play games with me, I know that you are a demon!"

Lumeria laughed, "And what are you, an angel? Sorry, but I don't see your wings." Lumeria informed Sander that he was not an angel nor a demon, but that he was a reaper. "And I am here to reap souls for the afterlife. Sander became irritated and replied, "Sorry, but I cannot let you do that."

"Look, this is my job, to reap souls for the afterlife and I know what you are thinking," Sander informed Lumeria that he was not just a demon but also a human. Lumeria was disgusted and stated that a fusion was forbidden in the rarefaction council. "We both may agree but the thing is that my friend doesn't care." Sander showed him his eyes, instantly Lumria recognized the demon. "No way, it's Lord Riker of Wrath, the Prince of the demon realm. Look, I am sorry I do not want any trouble!" He said as he quickly ran back to his realm.

Finally, peace. Sander started to suck all the dead bandits' souls into his body, with each soul, he got more and more powerful. "Finally, now I can seek my revenge on Fergus." Sofia saw Sander getting the souls and safely returned to the village and stayed and waited for Sander. Riker awakened. "Hey, Sander does not charge in yet; we need to go to the Kingdom of Drogogon, home of the dragons." Sander pondered, "Wait Riker, why would we need to go there?" "Because there is something special over there." Sander walked to the village when he saw Sofia standing there waiting for him.

"Are you on the watch?"

"I am always on the watch. It's my job that I watch," she stated. Sander and Sofia started to walk to the edge of a cliff. Sander started to look out over the cliff. Sofia also admired the view along with him. Sander stated that the land was beautiful; Sofia agreed, "Yes, the Kingdom of Elmus is one of the prettiest lands in the Land of Sinia."

"It's good that you helped your people Sofia, usually, the kings don't care about their small villages."

"You speak as if you have some experience in the matter," she replied.

"Well, sorry, Sofia that is a story of another time." Sofia asked Sander to tell her who he was and to stop playing the games. Sander flipped the script, "You question me on who I am, how about you tell me who you are. What I do know about you is that you are a monster." She pulled out the sword and struck at Sander. He blocked, spun around, grabbed her sword and put it against her throat. "What do you think you are doing?" He yelled.

"Getting rid of evil." She flipped Sander and pushed him off the cliff. As he fell, he got angry and beheld his winds, appear lit up in burning red flames. This time his ability to use his wings was remarkable; he was able to glide and move about with ease. He flew back up and landed right in front of Sofia. "I will not die too easily," he said.

"What are you?" Sofia said with fear. Sofia screamed, "Tell me what you are?"

"Please sit down, I will not hurt you, I am going to tell you what I am but you need to relax." As she began to calm down, Sander explained, "I was pushed into a dark pit and left for dead by my brother. In that pit, I met a demon who saved my life and fused his soul with mine."

"A demon," she replied, "Now you are just messing with me."

"No, I'm not," he replied.

"But demons haven't walked in Sinia for a thousand years." Sander explained that in the kingdom of Luna they were locked up in the dark pit.

"Who are you truly? My name is Sander Helmglade, the firstborn son of King Daniel Helmglade."

"Your brother is the King of Luna, right now?"

"Yes, Fergus Helmglade and his soul is fused with an archangel, he is not a bad person he just lets greed control him. I wanted my revenge for putting me in the pit, but he's not evil. Now that I know about the archangel, I believe that he might have been corrupted by Galatin."

"I believe you," said Sofia.

"You believe me just like that?"

"Well, yes, that explains the fire and the wings," Sofia replied. "Your brother is pushing a war with the dwarfs, and we have to stop him because he is causing a once peaceful Luna to be corrupted."

Sander was surprised and questioned Sofia, "Wait, Fergus is going to war with the dwarfs?"

"Yes, the dwarfs are dealing with a horrible plague and along with that a war." Sofia encouraged Sander to go and become the rightful heir to the throne. Sander explained that he could not return because the people of Luna think that he killed his father to gain the throne and they all knew that he had demonic powers and abilities. Sofia questioned him again, "Then what are you going to do, stand by and watch your brother go power-hungry?"

"Riker has instructed me to go to Drogogon to seek the power. I need to fight this battle and then to quest to Orcuhan to gain my throne."

"Why do you need to go to the land of the Orcs?" asked Sofia. Sander let Sofia know that he needed to build an army and take back his kingdom. Sofia became excited believing that if Sander became the king, he would be able to stop the war and bring peace to Luna. She stated, "You will become a king and a hero! Keep fighting on what you're fighting for."

As the sun was rising, both warriors realized it was time to return to camp. In the bustle back to camp, Sander turned and looked at Sofia, "Wait, you never even told me your name!" stated Sander.

"You are correct, I am Princess Sofia Crimsonblade, the second daughter of King Alexander Crimsonblade," she responded.

"Well you never told me you're a princess," said Sander. Princess Sofia told him that he never needed to know who she was. "We have quite a journey to Elmus, you will continue on your quest to Drogogon and finally, Orcuhan."

Sander and Sofia headed back to the village to see the soldiers getting ready to travel to the kingdom of Elmus.

Chapter 6
The Two-Day Journey

Sander ordered Elijah to take the same men and scout ahead and everyone else just stayed around the villagers. "Sorry, Sander," he replied, "I don't take orders from you anymore."

"On whose orders?" Sander questioned.

"Sofia's orders," said Elijah. Sander turned to Sofia, "Do they know your real name?"

"Oh, they know my name, but not the villagers."

"Okay, can you please order Elijah and his squad to scout ahead?"

"Why? Do you sense anything?"

"No, but it's safer. You should keep these people safe."

"I know all about you and yet you still want to act as if you are human."

"Do you not remember the conversation? I'm half-human; I just have the powers of a demon." As Sofia and Sander talked, the villagers entered the road to Elmus. Sander insisted that Sofia ordered a squad to look ahead. Sofia agreed and ordered Elijah to go and scout with his men.

"Yes, My Lady," Elijah replied.

"There. Are you happy now, Sander?"

"Yes, My Lady," Sander replied with a smile on his face as they go back to their duties.

Sander quickly moved away from the groups and flies and got a better idea of what was ahead of them. "I see that the sun doesn't hurt me as much in the air. Riker, you once said that there is a limit, am I right? Riker? Are you there? That's odd." Riker had not responded. "Oh well, let me continue. Sander flew back down to the forest behind the villagers. "Sofia, I think we should set another camp by sundown."

"Why?" Said Sofia.

Sander replied, "Because evil usually comes out at night." Sofia with a quick jab stated, "Now that I know what you are, I will take your word for it, however, there are two hours later till sundown."

Before sundown Sofia ordered everyone to set up camp. "Have your rest because tomorrow we're going to the forest." The group set up camp as the soldiers took shifts on the camp. "Sander, look everyone is safe nothing is coming our way, Sofia said with sarcasm.

"Sofia, you are not a patient person, things don't just happen so quickly."

"Well, Sander, I will check on the children. You do you," replied Sofia. Sander heard a howl in the middle of the night; it was close and sounded enormous. Sander used his super-hearing and detected that it was a horde of animals. Sander felt that they were coming fast in the direction of the camp.

"Sofia, something is coming fast, large animals. There are wolves but abnormally large ones." Sofia ordered her man to gather around the villagers. Within minutes, Sander no longer heard the sounds of large animal, but heavy breathing. He estimated that they were about two hundred yards away. The night went quiet, an eerie silence took over the camp, even the crickets were not cracking. Sander heard a growl and then within minutes there was silence, the giant wolves began to attack the villagers. As the elves fought back, Sander realized that there was something different about these large beasts; they had both animal and human instincts.

Sander quickly tried to light up his fire, but he could not fire up. "Sofia, cover me," said Elijah. Sofia quickly pulled an arrow from her quiver and shot a giant wolf with a poisonous arrow to the eye. The wolf quickly got up on his two legs and ripped it out, grabbed Elijah, and dragged him into the forest. As Elijah was abducted and dragged into the forest as Sofia screamed his name, "Elijah!" Sander quickly picked up two kids and ran to a nearby cave and thirteen villagers escaped into the woods. Sofia led two of her guards and three kids into a nearby cave where Sander was; the kids were scared, so Sofia decided to sing a song to them, her soft, gentle voice calmed them.

Sander heard the sound of the elven soldiers being slaughtered and saw villagers running. Sander started to feel sad as he saw people from miles away being ripped apart limb from limb.

"What is your name, soldier?"

"I am Leonard," he replied.

"Well, Leonard may I have your sword?" He handed his sword to Sander. "What are you doing?" Leonard questioned in confusion. Sander replied, "Do you think I am going to stand here and do nothing?"

"What are you going to do?" Leonard was even more concerned. Sander closed his eyes as he experienced a power from within rushing through him. he opened his eyes and both were colored a crimson red of wrath. Just like that, he became a demon.

"Sander, are you there?"

"Sofia, don't worry about me, I can handle myself, worry about the enemy." Sander looked and saw an elven soldier running from two wolves. Using his powers, he instantly ran to the rescue, grabbing a sword and slashed the wolves' head off. Another wolf attacked Sander, enraging his anger and causing him to fire up. He looked with rays of fire leaving his eyes inflaming the wolf and turning it into ashes.

Four wolves were heading towards Sander's location. "Quick, go to the cave with Sofia," said Sander to the elven soldier. He grabbed his sword and ran at the wolf ahead of him and sliced his body in half. Then he went to attack the other wolf. The wolf then blocked Sander as they emerged into a fight. The wolf retrieved Sander's sword and snapped the sword in half in front of his eyes. Sander looked at the children then at Sofia to ensure that nothing happened to them. Sander stood to his feet, surrounded by wolves, he closed his eyes and experienced flashbacks of Fergus hurting innocent people – this made him angry. The rage from inside caused Sander to light up into blue flames, when the wolf went to attack; Sander grabbed his arm and threw him across to the other side of the cliff. More wolves attacked, but they were no match for Sander's fiery infernal. He turned and lit the wolves on fire. By then, the wolves were frightened and started to retreat. Sander walked back to the cave where Sofia and the children were, he commanded Sofia to get moving because whatever those things were, might come back. Sofia ordered one of the soldiers to come with her and help her find some survivors.

As Sofia and her soldier went to find the remaining villagers and anyone who survived, Sander was stuck with the kids and the other two elven soldiers.

"Cool, what are you?" Said one of the children. "I am Sander Helmglade."

"Wow, like the prince Sander Helmglade?"

"I see, you did your research."

"Yes," replied one of the children, "I am going to be in the great Elven's library when I grow up."

"The great Elven's library?"

What is this place for, child?" asked Sander out of curiosity.

"The Great Elven's library contains secrets of the old times and events that happened five hundred years ago. And all the kings and queens that came before from all three races. And some celestial battles too, and curses from evil demons," said the child.

"Riker," said Sander.

"Yes, I want to work there so that I can gain knowledge of everything."

"Well, your dreams will come true when you put hard work into them." At that moment, Sofia came back and found thirteen villagers and Elijah in the forest. "Sander, look who survived," Elijah said to Sander surprisingly.

"How did you survive?"

"Well, when one of the beasts got me, I pulled out my sword and stabbed it in the head. It ran off but made a three-inch scratch in my stomach, but nothing that I know medically will help!" Sofia responded quickly, "As long as you are alive, we can get moving." Then she rallied the villagers and children to keep walking on the path and headed to the green forest. The people started to walk on the path to the green forest; they took a shortcut next to Fort Greenwood where the entrance was eastward. "Now that we are here we can get food and water for everyone before going to Elmus," said Elijah, "But we must keep moving. We have no time to waste, these beasts that might come back." The villagers quickly walked into the green forest. Elijah told the two soldiers that one of them should guard the left and the other one should guard the right.

As Sander wondered ahead, he saw a woman in the distance by the river. Her hair was red as paint, her eyes were blue as water, and her skin was smooth as butter. Sander started to slowly approach this woman. The woman instantly saw Sander and ran off. "Wait," said Sander. But she ran so fast, Sander lost her. Sander started to worry that he did not see her having elf ears. And he also started to think to himself if she was a human outcast.

"Sander, there you are," said Sofia. "We found the fortress's entrance. Come on let's go."

"I'm coming," said Sander as he walked to the fortress. "Is there a way in?"

"Yes," said Elijah. Elijah hailed to the gate. The guards of the gate opened the doors. "Hello, Captain Elijah, welcome to Fort Greenwood." The villagers walked inside the fort. They all went for food, water, and shelter.

"Alright, Sander where did you run off to when we were at the river?"

"Oh, it was nothing I thought I saw . . ."

"What did you think you saw, Sander?"

"I don't know, a person. it may be my imagination."

"Well, maybe a nice rest will help you."

As the sun was setting down the moon started to come up. Elijah started to dream about becoming an animal and living like an animal. And also started to sweat all over his body. Elijah woke up to go get some fresh air. He looked at the ground and thought what was going on. Sander was dreaming of the woman near the river. Sander woke up and started to walk outside. Sander saw Elijah and walked up to him.

"Can't sleep either?" Elijah said. "What's on your mind, Sander."

"I see a woman in my dream," said Sander.

"A woman? If you're thinking about a woman it means you are lonely, Sander."

"No, it's not like that. I saw her when she was near the lake while your people were walking to the fortress."

"How about this, Sander? Let's take a walk outside."

"Outside?"

"Yes, outside, Sander. So, then we can see if she is real or not." Sander and Elijah decided to go into the green forest by the river.

"See, Sander nothing is here, it was just your imagination." As soon as he said that, they saw a shadow running through the forest. Sander and Elijah looked at each other and then started to follow. While Elijah and Sander were following, Elijah told Sander to go left and he would to go right so that they could trap them when they slowed down. Sander said, "That's a good idea." So, both split up to trap her. As Elijah was running through, he failed to meet her, where she would have gone, he wondered. Elijah wondered the same thing. As Sander was running through the forest, the woman came out of nowhere and put a dagger to Sander's throat and asked, "Why are you following me?"

"And why are you away from home?"

"First of all, I was kicked from my home and I ran off and second of all, who are you?"

"The name is Ava and who are you?

"I'm Sander."

"Alright now, since we met you never answered my first question. Why are you following me?"

"Look, I saw you at the river and wanted to ask why you were there. I thought elves were in these woods, not humans.

"I'm not. Never mind." Ava put down the dagger. "And smells like animals. Hey, your friend. Do you know him?"

"Who, Elijah?"

"Yeah, the friend near you. Keep an eye out for him, he might be dangerous. I must get going. I need to go home."

"Wait," said Sander. "Where do you live?" Ava stopped for a moment to tell Sander but she didn't want him to know what she was. So, she ran off. Sander caught up with Elijah and told him he found nothing.

"Sander, we should get back to the fortress. We had a big day. So, don't tell Sofia about this." Sander and Elijah headed back to the fortress. "Sander, I can't sleep so I'ma be on watch duty. You fine with that?" Said Elijah.

Sander went back to sleep. As Sander slept, Elijah thought he saw a beast in the forest and he sounded the alarm. All the guards and soldiers woke up and went to the gate. "There was a beast right over there by the tree." Sofia was confused. "Elijah, there is no beast."

"Yes, I see it right over there with red eyes and black fur." Sofia looked at the general of the fortress and looked back at Elijah. "Hey, Elijah, I think you should go with the first convoy to Elmus."

"Why? Do you think I'm crazy, Sofia? Because I'm not! I see them right over there." When Elijah looked back, he saw the wolf was gone. "I swear I saw the wolf."

"Elijah, it must be your imagination," said Sofia. "You might have been shocked when the wolves attacked. Maybe you should go to the healers with our people."

"I think you're right, My Lady."

"Alright, General Harkon, please spare some men to lead these people to the border."

"Yes, My Lady, fifteen men already volunteered as a tribute, two carriages of the remaining villagers."

"Go in the carriage, Elijah, you must go losing it!"

"As you wish, My Lady. I will go." Elijah went into the carriage along with the convoy to the border.

"Sofia, are you worried about Elijah?" Said Sander.

"Yes, of course, I do. My father, the king, is going to wed me and Elijah."

"Wait, why is he going to wed two of you?"

"Because Elijah is born of noble blood and I'm a royal, and that is our traditions."

"Well, tomorrow we go to your castle then I can gather supplies and carry on my day."

"I guess you're right. Sander, you should stop by the tavern of Elmus."

"Why is it like I need to be there?"

"I was just saying we have a fine ale at the tavern and parties as well. I guess I will stay at Elmus for a bit three days."

"That's the max, Sofia, no more than 3 days and I'm out."

"Alright, whatever you say, it's your life."

Sofia went into the barracks to supply the next convoy for the border. Sander went to the watchtower and looked for the mysterious woman called Ava. "Where is she? Who said that, soldier?"

"Oh, nothing I was looking for, but it is not there. Let the Elves do their job." Sander carried on his day while Sofia got to the next patch of convoy ready. "Hey, Sander," said Sofia, "We leave in two hours and we need to get there by midnight."

Sander went inside the shelter house and whispered to himself. "Riker, you there? You have been quiet for some time. Riker, look, I'm sorry for whatever I did but I need your help, barely any of my powers worked when those beast attacks. Riker, please." Sofia yelled Sander's name in the background. "Fine, Riker, if you don't want to talk you don't have to but seriously contact me." Sofia walked through the door and said, "There you are. Let us go, we're going now."

"Alright, I'm following you now."

Sander and Sofia hopped on the next convoy to the border of Elmus. "Alright, we're here," Sofia said. Sander woke up from his journey. "Oh, we're here. Wait, this is your border?"

"It's only a trick. As elves, we kept ourselves hidden. Past the green forest, we have our border between two mountains."

"Oh well, what are we waiting for? Then let's keep moving. I will love to see the kingdom of Elmus."

"You want to see that you will love my father; he loves the stories of the ancient ones. Commonly, we best keep moving."

As Sofia and Sander walked past the twin mountains and through the apple garden, they looked on the far north reaches and saw the kingdom of Elmus. "Wow, the stories did say it was a sight to see."

"Yep, well, I see it all day. Come on, it's best to show you the kingdom."

Sander followed Sofia into the kingdom of Elmus. "This is the weapons forge. Where you can have weapons built. This is the armor-smith for your armor, and this is the tavern where you can stay and drink. Ohm and join us for some drinks. We have a good party here, tonight. Come on, why don't you join us? Please a treat for what has happened today."

"Fine, I will guess I will join you for a drink or two," said Sander.

"Alright, I will leave you to it."

"Wait who is that up on the balcony?"

"That's my older sister. She's not much of a sword wielder."

"Yes, but what is her name?"

"Her name is Serena. But you can call her by what I call her. A drama queen. She's not like us or any of the others. She's all about parties and fun. Even the extreme ones."

"Really? Ok, thank you and will she be at the party?"

"I guess but don't think she will come to this tavern. But anyways my father is going to yell at me so best get going. Alright, good luck with the room."

"Oh, wait, Sofia, I don't have money."

"Well, if you don't have money here." Sofia gave Sander a royal medal free of charge.

"What's this?"

"It's a royal medal. You show it to the bartender he will grant you a room."

"Alright, thank you, I owe you one."

"You don't have to owe me anything. See you at the castle tomorrow."

"Alright, see you tomorrow, Sofia." Sander looked back at the balcony and looked at Serena. Sander said to himself, 'I will remember that.' Serena then looked at Sander before Sander went into the tavern. Serena thought to herself, 'I never met a human before, hmm.'

Sander walked into the bar and ordered a room presenting the medal. The bartender glanced at the royal medal and showed him his room. "Thank you, sir."

"If you need anything, come to me."

"Yes, bartender." Sander then went to bed for a nap.

Chapter 7

An Unexpected Week

Sander woke up at night in the tavern and heard music and cheering downstairs. Sander started to walk down to see what was going on. Sander saw people cheering with cups. He also saw girls dancing on the stairs and tables drunk, and walked to the bartender.

"Hey, bartender," Sander said. "What's going on here?"

"We're having a party for the rescue of the elven village."

"But we didn't save everyone."

"Yes, but were partying for the people that have come back." As Sander asked for a cup, Princess Selena and Sofia came to the tavern to party. Selena saw Sander alone at the table and headed to go sit with him.

"Hello," Sander said. Selena also greeted Sander. "So, what is a princess of your stature doing in a tavern-like this?"

"I'm here on a royal occasion."

"What's the royal occasion about? He asked.

"It's about a man sitting alone, not trying to have fun, and with no one to talk to. Rings a bell?"

Sander took a sip from his cup as she talked about him. "Usually, I work alone. I came here to get supplies for my journey.

Thanks for the help and royal medal and seal. I can get everything for free."

"Well, that's just how my sister operates," said Selena. "You help her in a journey, she gives you the gear you need. But she carries on her mission. She lets no distraction. And since she's wedded to Elijah, she is only focused on the family and the military. Most of my people, we sometimes party and want to live our lives. But as a royal or noble your life is a diplomat. I was set to marry the prince of Luna. Because my people were sort of dying out. We have more women than men and having an elven male is rare, now."

"I see," said Sanders. You're just trying to do what's best for your people."

"Although I have never seen a human before. In Elmus, human dwarfs and other races are only to the borders for protecting our lands. But why have you come?" As Sanders was about to talk, she continued, "Well, it looks like you won't stay a while because you're going to get kicked out in two days or three days anyway."

Sander started to feel a little dizzy from the ale. "Yeah, I'm sorry, My Lady, I'm feeling a bit quiet at my limit."

"No, no, stay," said the Princess. "We still have a lot more to talk about."

Sander stayed for the kindness of her heart and listened to her. "You see, Sander, I am a woman who wants to have fun, who wants to make sure that I can do as I please. You understand?"

Sander shook his head. "Aye, I understand."

"So, what do you say you want to come on a journey with me?"

Sander said, "Yes, but first, I must go to my room and sleep. My Lady, I am sorry to say this. I will be going to see Elmus with you but I must after I get my things alright."

"Alright, Sander, as you wish. Would you mind me taking you to your room?" Said Selena kindly.

"Yeah, sure, I guess you could help me". Sander felt so dizzy, he tended to forget things.

Selena was not walking him to his room but her chambers and the next day passed. A mysterious man came into town with black leather armor and his silver ring with a wolf's skull on it. A giant silver sword on his back, a tattoo of a reaper and a wolf, and with long black hair and brown eyes. The man walks to the town center. People were scared of him thinking of who he was and where he came from. The mysterious man walked to the guards at the castle entrance and hailed to them. "Hi, I'm Gildor. I'm a hunter and I request a meeting with the king."

"The king wants no access with a human-like you. He has other things to do."

"Well, if you're not going to grant me access to them, I'ma just walk right in."

"Get back, human," the guards yelled.

"Listen, your castle is in danger and I want to help you get rid of a beast. Or maybe a pack of beasts. So, I request entrance to see the king."

"The king does not want to see you, right now."

"And how would you know that? You have been standing here and talking to me."

"Stay back, human."

"Fine, I will walk away." Gildor walked around the castle to see what he could do. 'This looked like the right place.' Gildor started to climb to the castle tower until he made it to the balcony of the tower. 'Alright, now to find the king.' As Gildor was about to find the king, he heard two guards coming from around the corner; he quickly hid. Gildor waited for the guards to pass and then continued to find the king in the throne room. As Gildor was about to walk into the throne room, he saw four guards. Within seconds, the guards attacked Gildor. Gildor quickly drew out his sword and fought all four of them. He took out the guards with his great silver sword and then walked into the throne room. As Gildor walked in, the king looked at Gildor and called for the guards. The guards rushed towards him.

Then the king ordered his guards to stop. The king got up from his throne and started to walk towards Gildor. "I know what you are and I know the reason why you are here. But before we talk, tell me your name."

"The name is Gildor Landfield, second son of Lord Robert Landfield."

"Ah, so you're born of noble blood in the kingdom of Luna."

"Well, my name is King Alexander Crimsonblade the second King of Elmus. Now since I've introduced myself let us go to the royal library where only some people know about what you do and what we talk about."

"Father, what shall we do about the case of the giant wolves?"

"That is what sir Gildor is here for; don't worry, my child, everything is going to be ok."

"What will one man do to these beasts?"

"Listen, princess, I have been doing this for quite a bit and I was trained for this," said Gildor Landfield. "Everything is going to be ok. I started hunting things like this when I was fifteen years old. I know what I'm doing."

Sofia looked at Gildor as she thought he was lying. "Gildor, let us walk to the library, it's just this way right here." As Gildor and Alexander walked to the Royal Library, Sofia went to find Sander and see where he was.

"So King Alexander, last time I heard you had a wife. I didn't see her sitting on the queen's throne. Is she alright?"

"Sadly, no she passed away about three years ago. The order of magical arts probably killed her because she was once a mage before falling in love. So, she betrayed the order, when she ran away with me." The king felt deep sadness as he walked. "Now we must go up the tower to the Royal Library in the castle."

Gildor and King Alexander walked into the Royal Library. "Samuel, get me the book titled, 'The Five Wolves of Sinia.'"

"Yes, sire." Samuel got the book, "Here we are, My Liege."

"Alright, last time I checked there were five packs or family types of wolves."

"Yes, there are the white wolves which live farther north. And there are the brown wolves who live near Lunian lands. They don't harm anything. But you guys as I saw ran into the worst ones. That's impossible. The black wolves have not been spotted in the green forest for quite some time. That's because, Alexander, the black wolves hid in caves. But now they're out. And now I believe one of your men has been infected."

"My men? Well, I can't be certain but I have to expect the worst. Gildor, how much time do we have?"

"Due to the recent attack, I will talk about it tomorrow."

"Tomorrow? Oh, no," sighs the king. "Alright, you do what you must, Sir Gildor."

"Yes, Your Highness." As Gildor was walking out of the castle he stopped and heard strange sounds and screaming from princess Selena's room. 'Whatever. She can have whatever she wants. She is going to be queen.' Gildor continued to walk outside the castle and waited for the villagers and people who survived to rally up. Four hours passed and Gildor had everyone from the journey. Gildor started to question and tell everyone to show if they have any marks from the beast. "I know this may be strange but I'm sorry, I have to make sure you're not marked by those beasts," said Gildor. Gildor continued to look and see if the villagers got scratched or bitten to the point that they survived. None got scratched.

"Hey, guards, how about the soldiers that were there?"

"There are only four soldiers who survived including princess, sir Gildor."

"Bring them to me."

"Yes, sir." The guards brought the soldiers to Gildor.

"Thank you," said Gildor.

"The princess is not coming and the king wants to talk to sir Gildor after this." Gildor looked for a scratch on the soldiers. "You guys are all cleared."

"Sir Gildor, Elijah is not here; he's at his father's manor."

"Alright, I need to go see him."

"No, Sir, the king requests access for you to go to the castle."

Gildor complied with the soldiers and headed to the throne room. "You wanted to see me, King Alexander."

"Yes, Sir Gildor. I heard that you want to see my daughter Princess Sofia's Crimsonblade."

"Yes, I need to check if she has been bitten by the beasts."

"I can guarantee she has not been scratched or bitten."

"King Alexander, I will take your word for it."

"Now King Alexander, Sir Elijah has not shown up to the meeting in the town square. I request you tell his father or anyone in his house to come to see me at once."

"Your request is granted, sir Gildor. Guards send a message to Lord Lakewoods' Castle."

"Yes, My King," said the guards. The guards and the messenger started to go to the Lakewood castle, the sun began to go down and night began to rise. Gildor found a tavern next to the castle and walked in. He ordered a room. "Barkeep, may I get a room, please?"

"Sure thing," said the barkeep. Gildor walked past a room that said Sander on it and continued to walk past his room. The next morning had passed and Gildor woke up to go to the elven throne room. As Gildor walked in, he saw nobles and soldiers gathered around.

"King Alexander, I am here. Did Elijah come to the town square?"

"No, sir Gildor, we have a guy who is here to tell you what happened." A man covered in all blood walks to the throne room.

"Are you sir Gildor?" Said the soldier. The man was frightened.

"What happened? It's alright, tell me everything you know." The man began to explain what happened last night. "The giant beast came out of nowhere and attacked me and my comrades. I barely made it out. It was so fast. His claws like swords. His teeth were like knives, I was the only one to make it out," said the soldier in fear.

"Did the beast get you?"

"Yeah, on my arm right here."

"King Alexander, please say Gildor in an honorable way." King Alexander ordered his people to get out of the throne room. "Royal guards, you may stay."

"Now let me see the wound." Gildor saw that it was a big wound.

"Hey, King Alexander, can I speak to you for a bit?"

"Yes, sir Gildor." Gildor talked to the king privately. "He's been marked by the beasts. One of the signs of black wolves is that they mark whoever is the last left."

"Sir Gildor, I know what you must do. And I grant you access to do so."

"Thank you, King Alexander." Gildor grabbed his Greatsword from his back and walked to the soldier. The soldier said, "Sir Gildor." Right as the soldier was about to turn around sir Gildor chopped off his head. King Alexander closed his eyes to pay respects.

"Sir Gildor," said King Alexander. "Find Elijah Lakewood and bring him to the castle dungeons."

"So, you're going to just let him live. He's a beast now," said Sir Gildor. "There is nothing you can do."

"Yes, he may be a beast but he's still a noble of the elven race. Sir Gildor, you may see when there is a beast, they are no longer human. But I see it as they are still human in the daytime. Maybe you should change how you see things."

"If I change how I see things, King Alexander. Then I wouldn't be here."

"Sir Gildor find Elijah Lakewood and brings him to me. That's an order."

"Werewolf hunters don't follow orders. We walk our path. For what we do, we do not stay in one place because we walk alone."

"Sir Gildor, if you harm a hair on Sir Elijah Lakewood, I will have my best hunters hunt you down and end you. Do you understand me, Sir Gildor?"

"You can try but it won't work. Because I hunt beasts who are half man and half wolf. Meaning both man and beast. So, you can threaten me all you want. But it won't work, because I got a job to do." Sir Gildor left the throne room and traveled to Lakewood Castle. King Alexander sent his best scouts to follow Sir Gildor to make sure he did not cross the line. Meanwhile, Princess Sofia was at the border, telling the border guards they saw Sander.

"Hey, Captain."

"Yes, My Lady," said the soldier.

"Have you seen a man with red eyes? Looks shady, and well, you know, human."

"Ah yes, I have seen a man like this in black leather armor."

"No not him. A human. The one I came in the border with. The man with the red eyes."

"Nope, I haven't seen him, My Lady."

"I guess I will try somewhere else." As Sofia continued to find Sander, Gildor was on his way to Lakewood Castle. Gildor stopped as he knew he was being followed. Gildor pulled out a knife, turned around and threw it behind him in the bush.

A scout got hit by a knife in the leg. "Stop following me," Gildor said. "I know you're following me. And I know you want to obey your king. But I walk alone. Meaning you cannot just follow a werewolf hunter. I have been hunting werewolves since I was fifteen. I know when something is following me. Because I hunt creatures that follow me every day. I hunt creatures with animal instinct and human instinct. So, I recommend both of you go home or I will hurt both of you."

An elite scout came out and started to help the other wounded elite scout. "Listen," said the scout. "I know you walk alone but our king gave us a mission. We don't want to hurt you, Sir Gildor. But if we have to then we will. As you're hunting a noble elf and Sir Elijah is wedded to Princess Sofia. So, we need to make sure you don't kill him and we can find a cure for his illness. So that's why, we have been assigned to this task. You need to understand, Sir Gildor, you are one man, how can you hunt a beast like that? You can't do this alone."

"I gave your king my word and I will never go back on it. So, stop following me. I have to do this alone. Because if I go alone no one will get hurt. If you continue following me, I'm not afraid to kill an elf." Gildor looked straight to the soldier's eye. "If you follow me I will kill you." The soldier looked into Gildor's eye and knew he was telling the truth. "So, go back to your king and your king has to trust me on this."

"But, Sir Gildor. . ."

"Stay away from me that's all I am saying." Gildor continued to walk to Castle Lakewood.

The elite scouts stopped following him and went back to their king. Gildor made it to the town of Lakewood and looked for a way to the castle. Sofia went back to her father and told him that she saw the demon man.

"You mean the man you told me last night?" Said the king.

"Yes, father, that man."

"My dear, I have not seen him. But I would love to meet him. Last time, I heard he was at the tavern inn. You should check there, my dear."

"Father, I did but he was not there."

"How about the border, my dear? He might have left."

"Father, I checked with the captain and he said he did not leave."

"Then Sofia he must be around then. Elmus is a big place. But when you do go find him and make sure to double your elite guards."

"Father, why?"

"Because things are dangerous." Sofia noticed that her father was hiding something from her. "Alright, my dear, I must go do some paperwork."

"Wait, father, I saw that strange man with the back leather armor going to Lakewood Castle. Is there something wrong, father?"

"No, my dear, you don't have to worry. Sir Elijah is fine."

"I never said anything about Elijah. I was going to worry about Lord Lakewood."

"Sofia, my dearest child, you have focused so much on our military. You don't have to worry about things like this. Leave it alone."

"Father, I know you're hiding something, can you just tell me?"

"No," said the king in a loud voice. "I'm sorry, my dear, I did not want to yell at you. Just leave this subject alone."

"Yes, father."

King Alexander went to his royal chambers to work on some paperwork. As Sofia went to the royal library to find anything on the giant beast. Meanwhile in Lakewood town, Sir Gildor found the way to Lakewood Castle. As Sir Gildor walked to the Lakewood castle, he saw some homes destroyed and claw marks on trees. Gildor said to himself, "The black beast has been here. I must be going the right way." As soon as Gildor went through the gate, he was stopped by guards.

"You sir, stop halt, right there," said the guards.

"I'm here to see Lord Lakewood."

"What is your business here and what is your business with Lord Lakewood?"

"I'm here to talk about his son and I'm here on royal decree ordered by the king."

"Sorry, but I can't let you in."

"Fine, I'm sorry, I'm here because a company of soldiers was attacked by a wild beast. I know what that beast is and not just that I see trees and destroyed homes. I'm guessing you know what I'm talking about." The guard stopped talking and waved to the gatekeeper. "Open the gate," said the guard. The gate opened and Gildor continued to walk to the Lakewood Castle. Gildor walked into the Lord's throne room.

"Good evening, Lord Lakewood," said Gildor. "I am here on the royal occasion of the strange animal seen around here. The company of soldiers on the way here. The strange giant claw marks on the trees and destroyed homes. I am the man to hunt the beast. I am the black leathered hunter. My name is…." As soon as Gildor was about to say it, Lord Lakewood stated his name.

"You're Sir Gildor Landfield of the House and Field."

"So, you've met my father."

"No, Gildor, I met your uncle. You are wearing the black leather armor just like he did forty years ago."

"You knew my uncle?"

"Yes, I did, Sir Gildor. And I'm guessing you're here because my son is here."

"Yes, Lord Lakewood."

"Well, I will say I have not seen him. So, if you're looking for him he's not here."

"Well, do you where he could be?"

"No, I do not. Last time I heard there was a werewolf sighting in the town. So, I think you should start there. Now if you please, I need to do business."

"Yes, Lord Lakewood."

Gildor saw Lord Lakewood as he was suspicious. Gildor walked to the town and asked questions to the townsfolk.

Sofia kept knocking on Princess Selena's door. Selena put her clothes on and walked to the door and asked why she was here. "Selena, have you seen a human from your balcony?"

"Sofia, I don't look at my balcony for boys."

"Well, the last time you did, you always had one in your room the next day."

"What are you calling me now?"

"Nothing. I just I need to find him. Well, if I knew where he was I would not tell you."

"Is he in your room?"

"No, he's not."

"Let me see."

"You're not coming into my room."

"Fine, then how would father think of you doing things to your people?" Sofia ran to the king's chambers to tell the king what Selena did in her spare time. Selena closed and locked the door and ran after Sofia.

Meanwhile, Sander woke up in Selena's chambers naked. Sander started talking to himself. 'Is she gone? Hello,' said Sander. 'She's not here.' Sander then snapped his wrist and slipped out of the chains. He grabbed the key and freed himself from the other chains. 'I guess I have five minutes before she comes back.' Sander quickly got his clothes back on and decided if he wanted to leave or jump out the balcony. 'Alright, here we go.' Sander jumped out of the balcony. As Sander was falling, he sprouted out his wings and flew to the elven forest. Sander then landed in a perfect landing. 'I'm getting good at this,' Sander said. Sander then found his way back to town, so he could get supplies for his journey. As Sander was doing his own thing, Gildor followed the trail of the werewolves' attacks. Gildor asked the Lakewood town barkeep if he saw the beast. "Sorry," said the barkeep but all he heard were rumors. And last time he knew of anyone who knew of the beast it was the old lumberjack whose house was near the woods. Gildor then asked where he could find the lumberjack house. The barkeep then replied that the house was near the Lakewood town sign. "There's a path that leads deep into the Lakewood Forest. There you will see his house."

"Are there any other houses there?" Said Gildor.

"Nope, it's the only house in the forest. And you will know it when you see it."

Gildor then left the Lakewood tavern and walked to the path that the barkeep said. Gildor made his way to the path and saw the house. Gildor went to the house and knocked on the door. "Hello, anyone here?" Said Gildor. No response, Gildor then knocked on the door again. The door opened and the man said, "What do you want?"

"Are you the lumberjack?"

"Yes, I am. I heard you have seen the wolf."

"Who are you?" The lumberjack asked.

"I'm Gildor. I hunt these types of beasts. And I want to ask if you can point to me where did you find the best at."

"How would I know you're a hunter of these beasts?"

"You see this ring; this ring is what protects me from them. This is a symbol of my guild of what we do. We hunt these beasts if they get out of hand and we walk alone. Never get help, unless it's one from our guild. We cannot love anyone unless we are passing it down to someone. This is what I am. A werewolf hunter. That beast you saw is a werewolf. So, I would like to know where you saw the beast and where it usually goes. I will even beat the info out of you."

The lumberjack then began to tell Gildor where he saw the beast. "Listen, I saw the beast in the forest around here. I don't think he noticed me."

"What was he doing?"

"He didn't attack anyone. After he left the forest he went to the mountain and looked at the kingdom of Elmus. Then he went somewhere to the castle of Lakewood.

"I know it's not much but we don't have to get rough about it," said Gildor. "Thank you, lumberjack. That's all the information I wanted to know."

Gildor was angry and he headed to the castle of Lakewood. As Gildor was walking, he was figuring out the puzzle in his head. 'That man lied to me for a wild goose chase. He knew his son was the beast. Now he can't do anything about it. Because I'm coming to the castle.' Gildor walked to the castle and when he arrived at Castle Lakewood, the guards stopped him.

"Halt there, you may not pass."

"Says who?" Said Gildor.

"Says the Lord Lakewood. He gave us orders to stop your water whenever necessary."

"Well, did your Lord tell you I know who the beast is?" The soldiers were shocked that he found out.

"Wait, you knew and got the townsfolk scared of the beast. And you all knew who he was. Well, then I have no choice. By order of the king, I say you must let me through."

"The guards will not let Sir Gildor inside the castle."

"Then I will just walk back to the kingdom of Elmus and make sure the king brings his army."

The gates opened and out came Lord Lakewood. "Don't have to start a war for this. I will go to the kingdom and say I'm the beast."

"But you're not."

"Sir Gildor, have you had a son yet?"

"No, I will say, I do not have a son."

"Well, you will understand if you were a father. You must always protect your son. Elijah is my son and he is my only child. So, if the king wants a Lakewood he will get one."

"I understand," said Gildor. Gildor and Lord Lakewood along with some guards walked back to the kingdom of Elmus. When they arrived at the gate at night, Gildor requested they should get in, and get to the royal throne. When Gildor, Lord Lakewood, and his guard walked to the castle, they heard a howl nearby.

"We best get inside quickly," said Gildor. The guards started to protect Lord Lakewood as they saw a giant wolf-like creature on the mountains. Lord Lakewood rushed straight inside the castle and Gildor stood outside waiting for the wolf. As Gildor was waiting and guarding the castle's entrance, Lord Lakewood entered the castle and went to the throne room to see the king.

"My King," said Lord Lakewood. "May you please stop this and take me instead."

"No, Lord Lakewood. Your son is infected and I wanted to find a cure."

"My King, there is no cure for a werewolf."

"Yes, there is Lord Lakewood. In the archives, I have heard of a root that can cure the wolf. But I need to find herbs to do so. Thanks to my wife's mage book."

"So, My King, you're sure that you can cure him."

"With our top physicians, I know we can cure him. Then we will capture my son."

"Yes, Lord Lakewood, let's work together to cure your son." As King Alexander and Lord Lakewood were talking about the cure, Sir Gildor got ready for the wolf.

Sir Gildor said to the guards, "I want you to leave now and leave this fight to me."

"No, sir Gildor. my position is here."

Sir Gildor stopped and looked at the guard. "Do you want your bones to be ripped apart? Do you want to get your leg a bit off? Do you want to get clawed to death? If you don't want all these things. I suggest you go inside the castle now."

The guards looked at Sir Gildor with fear when he said that and quickly ran into the castle and boarded up the doors. As the doors shut, Sir Gildor was all alone in the street. It was just him and the beast. The beast came walking with two legs. The beast stopped and sir Gildor was 20 feet away from the beast. The beast and sir Gildor stared at each other down on who was going to strike first. Princess Selena looked out of her balcony to see the fight. Selena looked with lust to the man facing the beast. She looked and thought, 'Who is this man? Why is he fighting a beast like this? Why is he not afraid?' The guards in the castle looked at the whole window, watching Sir Gildor facing the beast. The villagers were fearful of looking outside their houses. Sir Gildor gripped his weapon. Everything was silent until sir Gildor ran with his giant sword. The beast then ran toward Sir Gildor. Sir Gildor swung his sword at the beast but the beast stopped the sword and started clawing him apart. Sir Gildor screamed in pain from the clawing. The beast then started to bite his shoulder. Sir Gildor stopped screaming and died. The beast then started walking to the castle's wooden gates. The villagers looked from inside of their homes in fear of what the beast did. As the beast walked with Sir Gildor's blood dripping from his mouth and claws, Princess Selena looked from her balcony in fear. She looked at the beast as if this monster did get through the gate. What would happen? The guards looking through the holes were shocked and started shaking. The wolf stopped and heard a heartbeat. "Is that all you got, you hairy ass, piece of crap?"

Sir Gildor got up as if nothing happened.

His wounds have healed and his pain was gone. "I thought you could do better than that." The beast looked at Sir Gildor and sprinted at him. As the beast was about to strike, Sir Gildor struck the beast in the middle of the chest. The guards started to cheer Sir Gildor on. Lord Lakewood and King Alexander went up in the tower to see what was going on. When they got up, they saw the beast stabbed and Sir Gildor fighting the beast alone. Sir Gildor then pulled back the blade and reversed the beast's head. The king from the top of the tower closed his eyes for peace. Lord Lakewood, looking at his son got on his knees knowing his house has ended and knowing his son was no longer alive. As the beast turned back human, the townsfolk, guards, and princess Selena saw Elijah Lakewood dead on the ground. People started to worry and grieve.

Princess Selena wanted to thank the man even when he killed an elven hero. Sir Gildor then looked at the king, put his sword on his back, and walked back to the tavern. When the sun rose the next day, everyone started walking out of their homes. A huge crowd circled around the noble hero. "Let me through," said Lord Lakewood. Lord Lakewood closed his eyes and walked to the castle to the king's throne. Sir Gildor was sitting in his room quietly. When he heard a knock at his door, he answered the door to see who it was. It was Princess Selena.

Sir Gildor asked, "What are you doing here, princess?"

"I saw what you did. That was brave."

"It's what I do."

"So, may I come in?" Said the princess.

"Yes, you may, princess." Sir Gildor then sat on the side of the bed. "I know it's sad that he died and I will probably get punished for it. It's sad but I have to do the job. It's my destiny."

Princess Selena then asked. "How do you know it's your destiny? Because no one else will do it and this ring?"

"The reapers' ring. This is the wolf version. I can't die by no wolf if I am wearing this ring. Sorry, you don't understand."

Princess Selena then asked, "Then you can show me." Princess Selena lay him in the bed. "Princess, I can't. This is treason plus I need to get going."

"You know why I know it's not your destiny to always stay alone and walk alone?"

"Why, princess?"

"Because you make your destiny and sometimes you need to do things in your own heart. So don't think of me like a princess. Think of me as a normal woman."

The princess then kissed Sir Gildor. As love filled the room, the bartender heard strange noises coming from upstairs. As Sir Gildor was having a love for the first time, Princess Sofia heard rumors and rushed to her father in the castle. When the princess came into the castle, Lord Lakewood was talking to the King.

"Is it true?" said Princess Sofia.

"My dear, you were not supposed to know until tomorrow."

"Father, is it true?"

"Sofia."

"Answer me, father, is it true?"

"Yes, my dear, it is true."

"Why would you do that? Why would you send a hunter after it? Why didn't you just capture him? We need to get revenge on the person who has done this."

"My King, I have to agree with princess Sofia."

The king thought about it. "I will need a little more time to think about it. He's a werewolf hunter. And werewolf hunters do what is necessary."

"But father?"

"Enough, Sofia," said the King. "The decision will be tomorrow."

Sofia rushed out of the castle. "Lord Lakewood, you may stay as a guest. But once my discussion is done, it's done."

"Yes, My King. May you show me my room."

"Yes, guards show Lord Lakewood his guest room." The guards then showed Lord Lakewood his guest room. The king then took a walk to the royal library to think and read more books. Sofia ran into the forest to her secret hiding place. She stopped to see a tree where she and Elijah used to meet at. She looked past the memory of Elijah making the promise to always protect her, 'No matter what the cause, Sofia, I will always protect you.' She then flashed back to reality and saw a small hut they made together. Elijah said, "Sofia." Sofia started to cry because no one was around to see her weakness. She then went to sit near the campfire they made together when they were kids. She wept from the memory of Elijah building the campfire. "I told you I will keep you safe. Here's a fire so you can keep warm, Sofia."

"You always got me, Elijah. You always know that I acted strongly on the outside. But inside I was just a fragile soul." Sofia then sat and wept from the grief of losing her best friend.

Chapter 8
What is Love?

As Sabander was walking to the forest to see if the beast left any signs, he heard a woman crying. Sander then walked to the woman. Sofia. "What's wrong?" Said Sander. "Oh, Sander, nothing." Sofia quickly whipped hereabouts.

"Sander, tell me where you have been?"

"I was busy. I drank and was around here," said Sander.

"Are you sure?"

"Yes, I am." Sofia turned around. "I was looking all over for you where have you been when I needed you the most?" She walked to Sander and punched him in the chest. Sofia got angrier when tears started to come out of her eyes. "You were never there when it happened."

"What are you talking about?"

"You just did your thing, left, or didn't say anything."

"Sofia, what's going on?"

"Elijah is dead," said Sofia in pain and sorrow. "He died. And now I do not know what to do. I feel as if I am going to explode."

"Sofia, this is called to grief. I know because it happened to me when someone I knew died." Sofia then hugged Sander, putting her head on his chest.

"Who was that someone who said it?"

"It was my father. He told me I would be a good king one day. That was the last thing he said before he died."

"How did he die?"

"He died from assassination in his sleep." Sander looked at Sofia. "Come on, let's sit." Sander walked with Sofia to sit on the ground near the fire.

"So, did he build this?"

"Yes, he did. We were nine years old when we used to come here. Ditch our guards and come and play. It was me, him, and Jake."

"Wait, who's Jake?"

"Jake is a common folk. He was the son of our best blacksmith. We called him the legendary blacksmith. His weapons were of pure power. And his arcane magical resistance was never before. But when we were thirteen, Jake got in trouble."

"What happened?"

"My father found out that Jake and I were together. And he got mad. Jake was young so his father took the blame for his crimes. The next day he was executed. Jake was given another chance before he stole food from the market. Then he was sent to prison. And when he was out he got into more trouble."

"Do you know where he is now?"

"No, my father kept him away. It was just me and Elijah. Then at age fourteen, my father decided with Lord Lakewood that we would be wedded at the age of twenty-one. At that time, he promised me. And he always kept his promise. He said I will always protect you. No matter what the cost was." Sofia began to weep as one of her good friends died. "He never gave up. He never gave up on those words."

Sander felt what Sofia was going through and he decided to share his side of grief. "I understand, what you're going through. My father wasn't always the best adviser and didn't give me any playtime. But he wanted the best for me. He wanted me to be a better king than he was. So, he put me to learn everything that he knows. He taught me how to use a sword. Yes, he didn't spend time with me a lot. There were some moments when he spent time with me, which I cherish the most. So yes, losing someone is heartbreaking. But that's the way of life. That's the way of growing up. And that's the way the world works. The only thing you have of them is memories."

Sofia looked at Sander as he looked back at her. "Hey, did anyone tell you that you make people feel better? Like you think you're all in revenge. But your heart still beats. That demon inside you does not change you. You're still the prince who lost his father." Sander looked at Sofia and she looked at him as if he was a guardian sent by the gods. Sofia was about to lean in to kiss Sander.

"I have to go," said Sander. "I need to go check on the tavern if my room is still not taken. Sofia, hold on to those memories. I must get going."

"You wanna meet here tomorrow at sunset?"

"I will be here to comfort you. But I must get going. Good day to you, princess."

Sander then left the forest to rush to the tavern. When Sander got to the tavern, he asked the bartender, Is my room still, my room?"

"Yes, of course, why wouldn't it be?"

"Ok, thank you." Sander quickly rushed to the room he was staying in. When he was in his room he lay in his bed and thought about what happened at that moment with Sofia. 'What was that? Why did I feel emotional energy? I must be overthinking. It's treason here for being with the princess. I should go see the king tomorrow. Tell him what I am or what is Riker. Maybe I should get some sleep.' Sander heard Selena's voice in the hall. 'Oh no.' Sander then went to his door and locked it. He stayed quiet.

"Well, Gildor, I'ma go tell my father not to chop off your head and give you a lesser punishment."

Sander wondered why the name felt familiar. Gildor and Selena said their goodbyes and Selena rushed back to the castle. Sander then unlocked his door and opened it to knock on the door next to his room.

"Hello, is this who I think it is?"

Gildor then answered the door. "No way, Sander. Come in. So, what's your business in Elmus?"

"I was wondering if you could ask me the same thing, Gildor."

"Well. Prince Sander." Sander quickly stopped Gildor from saying his title.

"Just call me, Sander. Why did Sir Gildor ask? Because you never heard the news, did you or the new rumors in Luna?"

"Sander, I have never been back there since I left two years ago. Why, did something happen?"

"Yes, something did. So where do I start? My father is dead."

"The king's dead." Gildor was surprised. "So why are you not there as the new king? Sander then explained what Fergus did. "Well, Fergus kidnapped me from my bedroom and brought me to the dark pit then kicked me off. And convinced the entire kingdom that I was evil."

"How did he do that?" Said Gildor.

"Well, you know of that one thousand years old fairytale that our fathers told us of. about the demons and the angels. Well, that's true. I fell in when Fergus kicked me in there and met a demon. His name is Riker, by the way. Then he went dormant. But I still have his powers. That's what happened. So, what have you been up to?"

Gildor then started to tell the truth. "Well, Sander, I'm glad you figured it out."

"Figure what out, Gildor?"

"Figure that there are monsters in this world, Sander. Monsters and beasts are made to destroy and some people need to be the caretaker or take care of what these things are."

Sander then asked, "What are you doing here, Gildor? Gildor, what are you doing here? And tell me the truth about why you're here."

"I was in the tavern one night to hear a story from one of these animal hunters. He said that there was a pack of giant wolves. Man-sized wolves. I have followed them ever since. That was a week ago."

"Wait, Gildor. Were there black man-sized wolves?"

"How did you know, Sander?"

"Because we ran across them on the journey here. That explains the bodies. So, wait, Gildor you hunt those things."

"Yes, I do. It's my job. That's why the king does not want to speak with me right now. He kinda hates me."

"What did you do to the king that could hate you?"

"I killed Elijah Lakewood."

"Wait, for what? Why?"

"Because Elijah was marked by them. And he was turning and he also was a werewolf form when I killed him."

"But Gildor, isn't there a cure?"

"No, there is not. Once you're marked and turned, you're turned for good."

"I understand. So, you had no choice but to kill Elijah."

"It's my job, Sander. Ever since we were fifteen years old, we were trained for this. We all wanted to be knights. Well, I was going to be a knight but when my training came. I had no choice but to accept it. Ever since I have been a hunter. My brother took the house name and my cast to hunt these creatures. Because three lords in Luna know secrets the other Lords don't. My house is in charge of the wolves. The other two have their duties."

"Wait, so my father doesn't know about this?"

"No, Sander. Your father does know about this."

"Well, did he know before his death?"

"I'm guessing Sander, as king would have the secrets."

"I am finding out now, am I not?"

"Yeah, I guess so."

"So Gildor, what are you going to do now?"

Gildor then stood up, went by the window, and looked outside. "Sander, I think I'm going to wait. With even a princess word to a king, I say I'm probably going to be banished from the kingdom. Unless there is a werewolf here. But in all honesty, I must get going anyway. I still need to hunt the pack. How about you, Sander?"

"Well, I don't know. The princess and I have gotten to be friends. And now she asks for me tomorrow night. I don't know, I just want to spend time with her."

"Little Sander is all grown up," Gildor said while he smiled. "Sander, this emotion is called many names. Love, lust, crushing. You're experiencing what most men want. The real question is are you going to run away from it or take it? That's all on you." Gildor then walked up to Sander and tapped him on the shoulder. "Sander, don't be like me and run. Don't give up on whatever it is on your brother and go for it. You have a second chance. So, take the chance."

"But how do you know I am planning something for my brother?"

Gildor began to smile at Sander. "Because I have known you since we were kids. And I know you and your brother never did get along then. And you surely won't know." Gildor then said, "Let's go," and said a couple of words. "Sander, if you have a chance to be happy, take it. Don't follow the darkness." Gildor grabbed his weapons and belongings and walked out of the room. Goodbye, Sander," said Gildor.

As Sander saw Gildor leave the room, he started to call out to Riker in his head. "Riker, I need your help. Riker, Riker, are you there, Riker?" Riker continued to stay dormant in Sander's head. "Riker, if you can hear me I need your help. I need you to take away my emotions. So, then I can focus on my mission." Sander still had no answer in his head. "You know what, I'ma just act on my own." Sander got up to go to the spot where he told Sofia to meet.

Gildor headed into the throne room to hear what his punishment was. Gildor entered the room and stood right in front of the throne. "You ask to see me, King Alexander."

"Enough," said the king in anger. "I hate that you came to this kingdom. Acting like you own the place. You have no right to speak. I told you to bring Elijah Lakewood alive. How dare you disobey my orders in my kingdom?" The king sat down in anger. The king looked at Gildor with hatred. "Do you have anything to say to Sir Gildor of the landfill? Say it now for this is your last."

Gildor looked around the room as he saw royal guards and nobles. He then looked at Sofia. He saw that she had fear and she was grieving for her friend and then looked at Selena. As Selena was scared of what her father would do to Gildor and Gildor finally looked at Lord Lakewood. Lord Lakewood was happy to see Sir Gildor dead. Then, sir, Gildor looked back to the king and said what he had to say. "King Alexander, the second, The king of Elmus, we both know you cannot kill me. If you kill me other werewolf families will know. And if they know, then you can forget about us taking care of werewolf problems in your land." The king looked at Gildor with even more anger. "So, you see, try and kill me. But truth be told, you can't."

The king then spoke. "If I can't kill you then I will just banish you from my lands. Now, Sir Gildor, get the hell out of my lands." Gildor then smiled at the king. "As you wish, King Alexander. Gildor then left the castle and the land of elves.

Sofia told her father. "Hey father, remember the man I told you about, the one I wanted to bring here." The king then looked at her daughter. "What do you mean, my dear? Are you talking about the man you were telling me about? The man that helped save your people."

"Yes, father, that one."

"Then yes you may go get him." Sofia walked to the place where she met Sander. When Sofia arrived, she saw Sander and asked him to follow her. Sofia said, "Sander."

"Yes, you need something?" Sander replied.

"Yes, I do," Sofia answered with a smile.

"Are you alright about, Elijah? Like do you need someone that understands what you're going through? I can be your shoulder to cry on."

Sofia then smiles at Sander. "No, I don't want your shoulder right now. I'm here to bring you to my father. He wants to see you and know your story." Sander then began to explain to Sofia he couldn't know the full truth. "Sofia, if your father knows about me, my title… It's just that I don't want you people involved between me and my brother. I don't want to bring the elves into this." Sofia then yelled at Sander, "Sander, enough walking alone. You don't have to do this on your own. You helped us and we are gonna help you."

"I don't need your help, Sofia. What kind of a person I am to ask for help if I helped you? I'm not that person. Sofia, I did it because I am human. And now I will get going." Sander started to leave when Sofia ran in front of him. Sofia told him, "You can trust me. My father won't do anything to you and I will do what's best in my power. For him not to hurt you. I promise," As Sofia kindly explained to Sander, they both heard a thunder. "I think we should get to my father quickly before the gods interrupt us." Sander then looked at Sofia. "You know what princess, I think you're right." They quickly ran into the castle.

Gildor was on his way to the border when Selena stopped him. Gildor waited, he stopped and turned around. "Yes, Princess."

"Don't go," said Selena. "Maybe I can talk to my father. Maybe we can think of a way for you to stay."

"I can't, sadly. Look what we had in that room was just a moment. It's not loving, it will never happen. You're a princess of the elves, I'm a human. We're from two different worlds."

Selena walked towards Sir Gildor. "Fine, you may go. Try and forget what we had. But deep down I know what I felt and I will not stop until I get what I want. You made me feel as if I am myself. It might be the leather armor or the muscle." Selena stopped in front of him. "Or it might be your heart. Because deep down I know you're not to walk alone. Deep down, I know you're not supposed to be alone." Selena then kissed Gildor on his lips for five seconds. She looked at him and said, "I ask you to come back for me because I will make sure you come back for me, and if you're still banished, I will come to look for you."

Thunder roared louder. Gildor said a few words. "If I'm not banished, I will come back here. But for now, I need to continue my job as a werewolf hunter." Gildor kissed Selena one last time as it began to rain. "Even though I don't believe I will have a happy ending, I will try with you, Selena." Gildor continued to walk to the border, he turned around to look back at Selena one more time. "You should get inside, princess, if you don't want to get wet."

Selena laughed as she waved goodbye. Selena walked back to the castle, thinking of Gildor.

Sofia and Sander were running in the rain to the castle. As Sofia and Sander got inside, Sofia began to laugh. The rain came out of nowhere. Seeing Sofia smile, Sander also began to smile. "I think the gods were against us, Sofia."

"You think so because I think they were very much on our side." Sander looked at Sofia with a glaze. Sofia put her hair behind her ear as she looked at Sander. "Oh, right, Sander, I forgot my father is waiting." Sander then acted like a gentleman to Sofia. "Lead the way, my lady."

Sofia and Sander entered the throne room. Sofia then told her father who he was. "Father, this is Sander."

"Sander, my daughter has told me so much about you. That you saved the villagers. I must say, Sander, how does one know how to fight? Where were you born? And where did you live?" The king said in confusion.

Sander lied about where he was born and where he was living. "I was born in the lower sections of the kingdom of Luna. Down there it was rough and my mother did what she could do to survive." Sofia looked at Sander and wondered why he lied. King Alexander then told Sander how he learned how to fight. Sander then answered the king with a lie he created. "I taught myself how to fight. As I said, down in the lower kingdom it was rough."

The king then asked, "How did you get demonic power?" Sander stayed silent. "I asked you a question, Sander." Sander said, "I cannot say here. But somewhere in private."

The king replied, "I understand, Sander. We can speak in private. But first I want you to test your skill with a sword." The king called the captain of the royal guard to the middle of the throne room. Sander then asked the king, "Am I to get a sword too?"

The king got a sword from one of the guards and gave it to Sander. "Here you go, Sander. I want to see how good you are with a sword."

Sander got in a position. The guard then got into his position. The king then said, Fight."

Both participants fought to see who was the victor. Every time Sander swung his sword, it was with pure rage. Sander was screaming like a battle cry. The royal guard was trying to counter most of his attacks. "I will kill you if you stand in my way, Captain," Sander said with rage. Sofia stood looking at Sander as she saw the pain in his heart. The king looked at Sander as if he was using rage. But the king also saw the way he was fighting not as a peasant but as if from a noble house. The royal guard lost his grip when Sander slashed his sword to the ground and pointed it to his chest. The fight was over. Sander had one but for a split second, Sander thought of killing him.

The king then said, "At ease, Sander."

Sander gave the sword back to the guard. The captain got up and told Sander, "This was an honorable fight. Maybe we can train more sometime." Sander looked at the captain and said, "I would train with you but soon I must get going, maybe another life." Sander then looked at the king. The king then dismissed the captain. "Alright, Sander, let's just walk to the royal library. Sofia, my dear, you coming?"

"Yes, father."

Sander, Sofia, and the king walk to the royal library while talking. "So, Sander, you said that you learned as a peasant to be exact."

"Yes, King Alexander, I have."

"Please Sander, call me Alexander."

"Ok then, yes, Alexander."

"Sander, I know you're not a peasant so you can quit the act," The king said calmly. "I know you're at least part of a household for the humans."

"Alexander, with all due respect, I don't want to talk about it."

"It's alright, Sander, I understand. Every house has its dark secrets."

Sander asked Alexander, "Where are we going?"

"Well, the royal library, of course. There are secrets of the castle and everything that our ancestors have written down since before the demon and celestial war. We keep it locked up and safe in the royal library."

Sofia then began to ask her father questions. "Father, why have you kept this from us and the kingdom?"

The king responded to Sofia as he walked, "Well, my dear, I have not been keeping secrets. You just never found the idea to check and read the books. My dear, the more you read the more you become a better leader and ruler. I never stopped you from going to the royal library. It's all in what you think. What you want to do. And what truth you want to learn."

The king, Sofia, and Sander arrived at the royal library. "Here it is," said the king. "The royal library. Now, remember. This is my royal library. Whatever you learn stays between us." Sander and Sofia understood and they walked inside the royal library. King Alexander told them two to behave. "I don't want to see books where they should not be. Alright, have fun researching."

Sofia and Sander started to find the demon section of the library. "Sander, over here," Sofia said. Sofia found a book of the most powerful demons. "Sander, look, maybe this will work." Sofia started to search the book. Sander then said something and told Sofia to go back. "Wait, go back."

"What is it, Sander?"

"Go back to the destruction demons." Sofia turned the pages back to see where the destruction demons were. "Sander, is this what you want to see?"

"Yes, thank you." Sander grabbed the book and saw the name, Riker. "Sofia, Riker was the worst demon. He was the firstborn son of the demon king and he destroyed many villages and cities. He's a monster."

Sofia looked at Sander. "You think he is going to take over you?" Sander then began to defend him. "I don't think so. I feel as though he is hurt by what happened."

"Well, Sander, tell me what happened to him."

"Sorry, Sofia, it's not my story to tell. Let's just say it was not a happy ending."

Sofia then stopped talking about the demon and decided to talk about the lore of the demons. "Sander, the demons were sent to destroy this world. But it also said the celestials wanted to take control as well. It says here that the demons and celestials entered this world from their doors. Sander, don't you see. If a demon enters this world, they need to pass by the gate connected to this world."

"Where do you think this place is, Sofia?"

"It says it's unknown."

"You mean to tell me Sofia no one knows where this place is."

"No, Sander, it's like their gates are hidden." Sander looked at Sofia. "Why are you staring at me?" Said Sofia. "Oh, nothing just thought of something."

"What did you think about, Sander?"

"I thought of nothing but training." Sofia looked at Sander with confusion. "Training. Why were you thinking of training, Sander?" Sander looked at Sofia with a feeling. "I don't know but I got to go."

"Wait," Sofia said as she grabbed his hand. "Where are you going? And why are you acting so weird?"

"Sofia, it's getting a night out. I think I should go back to my room and sleep."

"Wait, Sander. Why don't you just move to the castle?"

"Sofia, I can't, it's not my home."

"Yes, but I can allow you in as a guest," Sofia begged Sander to stay. "Please, Sander."

"I will stay. But I will find what I want to find." Sander tried to find a story of what happened a thousand years ago. Sofia found a book related to it, sat down, and started reading. Sander found another related book and sat down in front of Sofia.

They both started reading until Sander stopped for a second to look at Sofia. "Why are you helping me, Sofia?" Sofia looked at Sander. "Because I know what it is like to try and find something. I see as you're trying to find answers and I see you're trying to find ways to get away from me as well."

"What do you mean? I don't find a reason to get away."

"Yes, you do, every time you're around me, you find a way to get yourself out. Instead of just showing your emotions."

"Sofia, I don't know what you're talking about." Sofia got up and slammed her hand on the table. "Cut the bullcrap. I know you feel what I feel when we are with each other. So, why are you hiding from me, Sander?"

"I'm not, I swear. It's just that it's complicated with me. I don't know what I am feeling." Sander looked at Sofia as he said that. "I'm sorry, Sofia, I never felt this way before." Sander looked at Sofia. Sofia saw that he was telling the truth. "I'm so sorry, Sander. I just thought you were playing games with me. Had you ever had any fun?"

Sander told Sofia. "No, I had no fun with a girl. I was forbidden to be with girls. My father will not allow it. Sofia, whenever I'm with you I feel as if I should be closer. As you make my heart feel warmer."

Sofia sat back down. "Come on, Sander, tell me what you feel." Sander then took a deep breath. "I feel as if you're bringing me closer. As you are a magical being. I feel as if there is a sense of energy pulling me towards you. And I feel as if I need to be around you." Sofia smiled as Sander continued, "My mind thinks of you everywhere we go. And I feel as when I'm around you it brings light and I forget about the revenge on my brother. I don't know what this is. Sofia, what is this emotion?" Sofia smiled at Sander. "Sofia, please tell me." Sofia then giggled and laughed at Sander. "Sofia, what's so funny?"

"Sander, you're an idiot. The emotion you feel is love. You finally experience life. Sander without love this world would have been destroyed. Come on, night is young, let's go have fun." Sofia grabbed Sander's hand and ran with him to the castle gardens. When they got to the castle gardens, Sofia showed Sander what was life. "Look, Sander, you need to learn how to have fun." She then asked him to catch her if he could. Sofia ran around the garden. "Come and find me," Sofia said. Sander began to run around the garden.

Sander tried to find Sofia. "Sander, come find me." Sander went around in circles trying to find Sofia. "Where are you, Sander?"

"That's for you to find out." Sofia started to give Sander a hint. "Try hearing the water." Sander stopped walking and started to listen to a water source nearby. Sander followed the water source.

As Sander was walking around the garden, Sofia was playing with the water. Sander continued to walk. As Sander turned left, he saw Sofia looking at the water. Sander silently walked up to Sofia. "Look at the water. I found you, Sofia." Sofia turned to Sander with tears in her eyes.

"What's wrong?" Sander asked.

"You know why I showed you this place, Sander? It's because my mother and my father met here for the first time. I miss my mother. She was the best. If I ever needed advice I would go to her. But she passed away three years ago. Now I don't know what to do." Sofia ran to Sander. "Sander, I think I feel what you feel about me. But I feel it with you. I feel as if this is what life means: To meet the ones you love." Sofia then looked at Sander and he looked back at her. "I never felt this way for a guy before. You might be the first."

"It's funny, Sofia because I feel as though you might be the first." The moon was full and the stars were shining. The water was calm and the wind was whistling. Sander then gently kissed Sofia on the lips and they both closed their eyes. After a two-minute gentle kiss, Sander opened his eyes.

"Is this love? Is this what I should be feeling? I have been asking myself one single question." Sofia smiled at Sander.

"What is it? What is the question?"

"The question was what is love? I found it now." Sander went in for another kiss. The wind whistled even more. The leaves were blowing with the wind. Sofia grabbed Sander by his hands and took him to her room. When Sander and Sofia entered Sofia's room, they both started to see the love they shared for the first time.

As the moon started to shine upon the room, the two souls shared their energy. The night lasted long and the beauty of them made it feel like a once-in-a-lifetime experience. The moon went down and the sun began to rise. Sofia woke up with her arms wrapped around Sander. Sander was still sleeping. Sofia put her hand on his chest and talked to herself. His heart still beat. For someone who had a demon inside him, he sure still had a heart. "I wish I could stay like this forever." Sofia put her head on Sander's chest and started to daydream. Sander woke up. "Sofia, you awake?"

Sofia then looked at Sander. "I have been awake. How was last night?" Said Sofia.

"It was new. It was like the world was surrounding us." Sofia kissed Sander.

"I'ma go get dressed," Sofia said with a smile. Sofia got out of bed and went to get dressed. Sander then got up and looked out the balcony and saw the sun rising in the sky. Sander smiled and then went to get dressed as well. Sofia walked to Sander. "I got to go to work."

"A Princess who works. Since when does this happen?" Sofia looked at Sander.

"Since I was born."

Sofia walked out of the room smiling. Sander sat down and thought about Sofia. As Sofia was walking out of her room she ran into her sister. "Hello, Selena," she said calmly. "Oh, Selena what are you doing here?"

"Why else, Sofia? I live here. Why are you acting strangely now?"

"I'm not acting strangely," Sofia said with anger. Selena then smiled. "What are you hiding, Sofia? Did you finally find someone to play with like me?"

"I'm not like you, Selena. You're a person who does not follow rules."

Selena then smiled and continued to go on her day. Sofia then looked at Selena before she went and walked to the garrison. Sander stopped thinking of Sofia and looked outside the door to check if it was all clear.

Sander walked his way to the royal library, and when he got there, he had a flashback of what happened last night. Sander thought of a way to get good flowers. Sander then asked the royal librarian. "Hey, do you know a flower that grows in Elmus?"

"Yes, I am sure I do. There is a flower that grows by the lake of Elmus."

"What's it called?" Sander said to the librarian. The librarian then got the book about flowers that grow in Elmus. "Yes, this is it. The golden bloom flower. It seems this is the right day when it grows. You see, the golden bloom flower grows around 30 years. So after today, it won't sprout its magical energy."

Sander then asked the librarian what would happen after today. The librarian began to explain, "You see, young sir, this flower is special because on this very special day, every 30 years it sprouts magical love energy. Meaning love is for you for one day. But it will only work if the other person is in love. The flower has a special kind of magic. So be careful. Make sure you give it to her when the sun goes down or it will be a failure. And then the flower is as useless as the others. So, Sander?"

Sander looked at the librarian surprised, "I know your name, Sander. You better not be caught around with the princess. Can make you put in jail." Sander started to get angry.

"Relax, fellow, I won't tell. Here in the library, we keep things quiet. So, my lips and my eyes are closed." The librarian sat back down. "Best for you go now by the lake. It grows there."

Sander quickly ran out of the royal library and bumped into Sofia. "Hey," Sofia said to Sander in a surprised tone. Sofia smiled as she pulled him back cutely. "Sofia, I can't right now, because I'ma go get something special for you."

Sofia smiled as she said, "What it is?"

"I can't tell you, it's a surprise. You're going to have to find out by the end of the day." Sander then left to go find the flower around the lake. Sofia entered the royal library and talked to the librarian about what Sander was looking for. The librarian told Sofia it was a surprise. Sofia then went on with her day as a Princess while Sander walked by the lake looking for a golden bloom flower. He saw many flowers but not the golden bloom. Sander started to walk around the lake. "Hey, Riker you there? I need your help." Riker stayed quiet and dormant. "Riker, are you there? I need your help". Riker continued to stay dormant.

As Sander was walking and trying to reach Riker he saw a field of golden flowers. "There you are." Sander walked to the golden bloom flower and he saw a light passing by through the sky. "What the…" Sander then saw another light pass by as the other one was chasing the white light. "Weird. What is that?" Sander then continued to pick a golden bloom flower until he was stopped by an elf. "Um, don't touch those flowers," said the elven woman.

"Um, relax I'm only here to take one."

"Leave it alone," said the elven woman.

"Listen lady, I'm here to get one flower and leave."

"I'm the protector of these flowers."

"What makes you the protector?"

"Because I was born here."

"You being born here doesn't make you the protector." The elven woman looked at Sander. The elven woman told her about her father. "My father was the caretaker of this lake. He would come every day to the lake. He would take care of the flowers. Every single one of them. Until he met my mother. I never met my mother. But my father told me things about her. My father took care of the lake's flowers. My mother loved animals. She took care of all the animals close to the lake." Sander listened to her story. "Later, they had me. And my mother passed the next day. My mother would heal the creatures with magic and my father would feel the plants as if they were his own life."

Sander then asked a question that shocked the elven woman. "So, you have magic?"

The elven woman then sighed. "Yes, I do. I can heal creatures. And I can control and listen to the trees."

"Wow, so you know when I'm going to pull this flower out of the ground."

"Yes, I know when I see it. I never really practice my natural magic. But I have healed creatures before."

Sander then asked what her name was. "My name is Kiana," said the elven woman.

"Well nice to meet you, Kiana, I'm Sander. So, where's your father now, Kiana?" Kiana then stayed quiet as Sander said that. "You know what, never mind, it's not my business."

Sander then got up to walk to the castle. "Wait," said Kiana. "Here, take the flower." She then picked up the flower from the lake's ground. "Here," she said with kindness. "A gift for not treating me like a commoner."

Sander then took the flower. "Thank you," said, Sander." By the way. I never did ask. What is this lake called?"

Kiana then said, "The golden lake. Famous for its flowers. So, who's the special girl?"

Sander then got nervous. "It's kinda a secret."

"Well, whoever it is, I hope she feels the same as you do. Because you're the fifth person I gave a flower to."

Sander then said goodbye and walked back to the castle. As Sander was walking back, he looked one more time to see what she would do. But the elven woman was gone. Sander then continued to walk back to the castle. As Sander entered the castle, he walked to Sofia's room and put the golden bloom flower in the vase on top of her table. Sander then waited for Sofia to come into her room. As Sander was waiting Selena saw Sander doing everything he could to love Sofia. Selena felt jealous that Sofia found love but she didn't.

So, she quickly rushed to her room to think about what new strategy she could make. When Sofia walked into her room, she saw Sander waiting for her and noticed a golden flower about to bloom.

Sander then grabbed the flower and gave it to Sofia. "Here, I got this for you. It's called the golden bloom flower. It grows by the golden lake, every 30 years." Sofia smiled at Sander. "Thank you." Sofia then took the flower and kissed Sander on his lips. As the moment hit, the golden flower bloomed – bloomed into a magical love sense. Both Sofia and Sander smelled the flowers around them. Sander since he had demonic magic, was seeing the aura surrounding him and Sofia.

On that day, love was born in Sander, and Sander saw as he found peace. Sander and Sofia then kissed. It felt as if Sander was having to meet his fate and for this moment when he was with Sofia, he found nothing but peace. He forgot about his brother. He forgot about what he wanted to do and most importantly, he forgot about the deal. The two souls felt free in that room. Sofia and Sander never left the room for the rest of the day. They stayed there until the sun went down and stayed all night long. On that day, love was born in Sander's heart. But something always went wrong for a time like that. Selena was hearing this happen. Selene felt jealous and decided to go call the guards. When morning rose, Sander woke up next to Sofia and he saw ten guards with spears pointing at him.

Sander was then dragged out of the bed and forced to put on clothes. The guards then took Sander to the fort dragon's teeth. When Sander was walking in the gate, he saw it as a normal fort. And felt no danger until he got in. As Sander was walking to his dungeon cell, he saw a man. Sander was pushed into the cell. He saw people losing their minds, but when he looked at the man on the corner, he saw he was enraged. Sander felt this man. The guards then told Sander. "You will die in the next ten days for your acts. As you will be killed for high treason with the Princess." The guards then went back to the castle so they could move on to their duties. Sander walked up to this enraged man and sat down next to him. Sander then talked to the man, "So who are you and why are you the only one I see so far not losing his mind?"

The man began to talk to Sander, "Because I grew up here and I know more about this place. My mind is strong and I will find a way out of here." Sander then looked at the man and continued talking to him, "Hey, my name is Sander. What's your name?"

The man told him his name. "I'm Jake. Jake Presley."

Chapter 9

The Escape

Two days had past and Sander saw no way out, they wanted to make people think there was no escape. Sander tried to see if there was a way out as he had something he was fighting for the outside. "There's no escape," said Jake, the angry prisoner. "Trust me I know. The only escape you have if they take you out of the cell. But fighting those guards is a death wish. You would want to be killed. These guards walking around with those swords are trained by the legendary swordsmen. He's a man who lives in the monastery up north on the frozen mountains and he does not live alone. If you do get past the guards trained to guard here or go on special enemy missions. Such as assassination. If you get passed. That's an if. You have to deal with the archers. And they're not normal archers. They were also trained by a legendary fighter. And it's not the same of the swordsmen. He is trained as a marksman of archery. There are about 9 legendary weapon masters. And three are in this fort. Now if you get past the archers. That's good. You made it past two out of three of the weapon users. Then you have to deal with the dragon. A friend of the elves and he is about five centuries old. That's if you're taking the outside out. If you're taking the tunnels underground, you're gonna need to be one hell of a swordsman."

Sander started to wonder who this man was. "Who are you and how do you know this much information?"

Jake, the angry prisoner, started to tell him the truth about himself. "My father was a legendary blacksmith before he died and I was supposed to be his successor. But that's another story for another time. So, there is a way out. But it's a death wish both ways."

Sander asked, wondering, "So how long have you been here, and how do I know you're not lying about your father? How do I know you're not a person who is a murderer?"

"You don't. You just gotta trust me." Sander looked at him with suspicion. "Oh right, forgot to mention. If we do escape they are allowed to make a purge to us. So, they can kill us whenever they want," said Jake, looking at Sander.

Sander then began to pace back and forth in the dungeon cell. "Wait, you said there were three legendary weapon users. What's the third? Sander asked.

"The third was spear weapon users. There are the ones near the gate and yard outside. They are masters of the polearm and they are not to be taken lightly."

"So you said your father was a legendary blacksmith, right?" Said Sander.

"Yes, he was," Jake replied with a little sadness. "

So, then you can tell me what swords, bows, and spears they are using?" Sander said with a thought of escaping in his mind. Jake then explained to Sander. "Listen, both ways out is a death wish. And I can tell you the plan. But our chances of leaving from the yard alive onto the lands is sixteen percent. And in the tunnels are eight percent. This fort was made to keep prisoners here. No one is allowed to escape. The people who tried have failed. You're no different," said Jake with a straight face.

Sander then walked to Jake, "Fine, I'm desperate."

"Any plans you got? Because we can work together to get ourselves out of this prison."

"Wait, Jake, why don't we disguise ourselves as the guards?"

"But you're going to have to knock them out," Jake said with confusion. "That's if you knock them out." As Jake was about to say something two guards walked by and opened the cell. The guards then took a prisoner as the prisoner was being transferred to another cell. The prisoner was screaming as if he was going to hell. They then closed the cell door and dragged him to the lower cells. Sander looked at the guards dragging the man with fear. Sander then looked at Jake. "Where are they taking him? What's going to happen to him?"

Jake then replied to Sander. "It must be his eighth day. When the eighth day hits, the prisoner is transferred to an isolated cell. There the guards torture him for information or sometimes when the guards are bored they do it for fun. It's a cruel way but it's how they act. On the ninth, they just put him through suffering pain and act like they are wild boars in a cage. Sometimes they make each prisoner fight. Whoever wins stays alive and whoever loses, dies the next day. This is what hell you're in. These are the ways of the elves when you're not in the outside world. Welcome to Fort Dragon's Teeth, Sander. This is where dreams die."

Sander asked, "Wait, how many days have you been in here, Jake, and do you think you have an escape plan?"

Jake answered Sander with no fear, "I have five days left in here. And my plan is when they take me, I will die and I will then move on from this life."

Sander then told Jake, "What if I have a plan?" Jake then looked at Sander. "What is your plan?"

"My plan is when I am taken from my cell I will attack the guards. I will grab the keys and give them to you. When you get the keys, you open the cell door. Now that's not just you got to open the rest of the cells as well. When people are fleeing, they will do a massive purge. It will be harder for us to get detected." Jake then looked at Sander as if he was going to follow up on the plan. "That's a good plan, Sander. But what way are we taking? The tunnels or the gate."

Sander looked at Jake with a smile. "We're going to take the gate."

Jake said, "Are you seriously losing it now? There is a dragon outside this fort. If we step out we die by fire or we get eaten."

"Relax, Jake. We knock two guards and then when we take their armor and weapons we get out." Jake then looked at Sander with surprise. "Wow, never knew a human was this smart."

Sander then told Jake, "This human is not only just human and has a lot more surprises."

"Let's wait for the night out," said Jake. "It's the perfect time to strike."

Jake and Sander waited for the night as time went by. Jake talked to Sander, "Hey, if we make a fight out now then we can get the guards' attention. I can mock the guards and get them inside to fight me and then this whole cell can jump the guards and knock them out. The whole point of this plan is to get the guards' attention and make sure we set everyone free. So, we have a better chance of escaping."

The sun went down and night arrived. Sander picked a fight with another prisoner. They both got into an argument and shouting and all the other prisoners in the cell started cheering. Sander threw the first punch, making a striking blow on the guy's face. The other prisoner got mad and fought back with Sander. Sander and the prisoner went at it. Jake looked around to see any guards coming around. The prisoners got louder and louder to see who was going to win the fight. Four guards came rushing from the corners to see what was going on. The guards then stopped as they wanted to see what was going on or they just wanted to see who killed each other first. Jake began to annoy the guard as he started to talk trash and made fun of how they acted. The guards got angry at Jake, opened the door, and walked in. The prisoners stopped fighting when the guards came in and started to fight against the guards. The guards tried to pull out the weapons but there were too many prisoners to fight. Sander and Jake teamed up on one guard and took him out once and for all. One guard managed to escape and went to the garrison to warn the others. Sander grabbed the keys and started to unlock the cells next to his cell. Sander then gave the keys to the other prisoners so they continued to break more men out before the garrison got to them. Sander and Jake went back to the knocked-out elven swordsman. They took off the guards' clothes and armor and disguised themselves as guards. Jake and Sander then patrolled the halls of the fort. "Alright, Jake, you know more about this fort. Show me the way."

"Sander, I'm sorry but I don't know every part of the fort. I know the fort information. Just not that much about in the fort. Company will go down and take over from here."

The guards then walked past Sander and Jake and went down to the lower basement. "Wait, Sander. I think this is the first basement and we were in the second basement. If we want to make a bigger distraction. We would need to prison-break this entire basement. So, we can slip away. And the ones about to get executed we need to set them free too. So, then the dragon has a lower chance of taking us out."

"You're right, Jake. But where are we going to find the keys to this cell?"

"Where else, Sander? The garrison upstairs. Follow me. I have been here before just not down there."

Jake led Sander to the stairs of the first floor of the fort. When Sander and Jake walked through the doors coming from the first basement, they saw the mess hall where they saw all of the guards, skilled watchers, and polearm guards. "Wow," said Sander. "I never knew it was this much. I always thought they were scattered everywhere. Once those guards come back up they will start to purge the entire prison."

Jake looked at Sander. "We got to hurry to the garrison."

"How about this, Jake? I stay here in the mess hall to see if anything is suspicious. And you go get the keys."

"No," Jake said. "I need a person with me in the garrison. Let's go." Sander and Jake rushed to the garrison of the fort. When they entered, they saw about thirty guards. Sander and Jake were walking around the garrison when they saw the first basement cell keys.

"Alright, Sander. I will get the keys and you will distract the guards."

"Wait, Jake. Why do I have to distract the guards?"

"Because have you ever stolen anything in your life? Like anything. Anything for you to survive on the streets or anything."

Sander stayed quiet. "That's what I thought." Jake continued and got the keys as Sander found a way to get the guard's attention. Sander figured why not a drink for all the guards of the Fort Dragon's Teeth? Sander hailed all the guards for their attention. "To all the guards listening to me." Sander made a name from the top of his head. "I'm Lucius. I am a guard here at Fort Dragon's Teeth. "So, I say we all have one cup of ale. For all of us. And the duties we do for keeping the cruelest prisoners in our cells. For the Fort Dragon's Teeth and its protectors." Sander grabbed a cup and poured some ale. "For Fort Dragon's Teeth. Here, here," Sander cheered the cup in the air and drank the cup of ale. The other guards looked at him and also grabbed a cup as well as they celebrated with Sander, on whatever he came up with from the top of his head.

Jake was grabbing the keys from the garrison and putting them in his back pocket. Sander put the cup down and continued to go find Jake. Jake went back to Sander and tapped him on the back.

"Alright, now Sander, let's go."

Sander and Jake walked out of the garrison and went to the mess hall. When Jake and Sander got there, they saw a guard beaten down and they also saw the six guards from the first basement. Sander and Jake knew they were in trouble and they hid from the crowd. Sander and Jake heard the man speak, "They jumped me in the cell. I lost three of my comrades in that cell. We need to get back down there and find their bodies." The six guards then talked about the people that came from there. The first guard told them that they must be prisoners in disguise. The guards all started worrying and decided to raise the alarm. Sander and Jake decided to walk outside the courtyard.

"Sander, we must go to plan B."

"What is that, Jake?" Jake looked at Sander. "Sander, we run." Jake bolted through the gate running as fast as he could out of the fort. The watchers saw Jake running. Sander decided to run with Jake through the gate. The polearm guards decided to chase after Jake and Sander as they ran for their lives. Sander caught up to Jake.

"Jake, what's the plan after we run?"

"What part of plan B do you not understand, Sander? They're going to kill us if we stop. We need to keep running until we head to the border."

"Yes, Jake thank you, that's easier said than done. Are you forgetting there are border guards as well?" Sander and Jake stopped for a second and when they looked behind them they saw the guards stopped chasing them. "Good, we outran them, Jake. Now we can rest."

"We can't say that," Jake said with fear.

"Jake, what's going on? Are you ok? Listen, we got away from them."

"No, Sander, we got away from the soldiers. You're forgetting one of the most important things about Fort Dragon's Teeth. That a dragon is going to hunt us down." Sander and Jake looked at each other when they heard a roar in the sky coming from behind them. They heard a large horn that sounded like it summoned a legion. Sander said to Jake, "Yes, Jake. We need to run now."

Sander and Jake looked to the sky and saw a dragon coming for them. His whole body was armored. "Jake, you didn't tell me this dragon had body armor."

"My people don't know things that go on in that fort as much. Sander, let's go."

Jake and Sander kept running. They ran because their lives depended on it. The dragon caught up to them and landed right in front of them. Sander and Jake fell to the ground. "Who do you think you are? Running from the prison. Committing crimes. And then escaping to have more crimes. Who do you think you are? The dragon said with a deep voice.

Sander stood up. "I'm Sander. And who am I? I am the man who was betrayed by my brother. I am the man who is trying to get my revenge. And I am the man who was put in jail for falling in love with a royal. So, if you're asking who I am, I am just a human who has a heart. That's who I am."

The dragon began to relax. "I guess you may be right, Sander. As you are human. But humans lie and deceive. So, how do I know you're telling the truth?"

Sander looked at the dragon. "You don't, that's the thing. You believe what you believe. And I believe what I believe. That's how this world will work and only this world will work."

"Well, I'm sorry, young Sander, I am bound to kill any prisoner that escapes the Fort Dragon's Teeth."

"Screw you," said Jake. "You're a dragon. Protecting my type of people. What's in it for you? Why do you protect the elves when they lie? When they kill my father for protecting me?" The dragon looked at the elf. "I'm sorry but this was a young elf that I must do. As I have been doing it for five hundred years." The dragon began to build up flames inside his throat as he was going to blow them at Jake and Sander.

"Jake, get behind me."

"What? Are you insane, Sander? He is going to destroy both of us. That's dragon flames."

"Just do it, Jake, and trust me." Jake got ten feet behind Sander and Jake closed his eyes. "Alright, all-mighty dragon. Give me what you got," said Sander with pride. The dragon then opened his mouth as fire came out of the dragon's mouth and hit Sander, he closed his eyes. Jake opened his eyes to feel the heat but he did not feel pain. When he opened his eyes. he saw Sander in front of him absorbing the fire like swimming in water. Jake fell to the ground in fear of what this human was. Sander then opened his eyes to see fire pushing towards him but not hurting him. The dragon closed his mouth and was shocked to see that the human and the elf were still alive. Sander then closed his eyes again. Riker came back to Sander's head. "Sander, I see you found out we resisted the fire. Fire cannot burn us. Dragons cannot affect us. Depending on the dragon."

"Riker, you're back."

"Yes, indeed, I am Sander. And I will always go dormant for some while but I will always be here in your body and I see, you got used to using my power while I was gone."

"Yes, Riker, I have."

"Good, you're going to need to get used to it. It means you're getting stronger. Sander, what you used was fire absorption. You can absorb flames and reflect them at me."

Jake looked at Sander as if he was insane. "Now Sander, we need to get out of here," said Riker.

"Wait, Riker, wait, no I need to go back to Sofia."

"Sander, you cannot be here for too long. You must finish your deal."

"No, Riker, I must follow my heart." Riker in Sander's head decided to sign. "I knew you were going to say that, I'm sorry for this." Riker erased Sanders' memories of Sofia in his head.

"Ahhhh!" Sander screamed in pain. Riker took control of Sander's body and he mentally knocked Sander out. "Who are you to say the dragon with rage? Huh. I have never seen a dragon in one thousand years. May I ask what your name is? I said who are you," said the dragon with anger. "Who are you and how did you get through my flames? My flames are ancient-level magic. Born with me to use against anyone. The only ones who can reflect my flames are demons. But they have not been seen in Sinia for a thousand years. So mortal. How did you get that magic and who are you?"

Riker, who took control of Sander's body, decides to speak. "I'm Riker, son of the demon king. Heir to the demon realm and the most powerful demon here."

The dragon started to fear the name, Riker. "That's impossible; he has been trapped in the dark pit. He is not a threat. You're lying," said the dragon in fear.

"No, I'm not lying, I'm telling the truth. I'm Riker and I fused my soul into this young man's body because he wanted revenge on his brother and I'm going to finish that deal. Because I am a demon of my word. So, if you do not let me pass. I'm going to disintegrate you. Now lizard, are we done here?"

Riker turned around. "You must be Jake. I will help you the way out. Just follow me. And we will get to the border."

"Not so fast humans."

"I told you I'm not Sander." Riker got angry to summon blue fire around him. "I told you to move, dragon. Get out of my way," Riker said with anger.

The dragon began to fear Riker. "Listen here, dragon, I can smell your fear. So, best to leave or die." The dragon didn't want to die from a demon. So, the dragon flew up and went back to the Fort Dragon's Teeth.

"Alright, Jake. Sorry about this." Riker put on a flame himself and around him and walked to Jake. "Sorry, Jake, like again we can talk after." Riker punched Jake so hard that he knocked him out with one punch to the jaw. Riker then picked up Jake and sprouted his wings. "It's been a while since I had an old friend. Let's just fly out of the border." Riker flew up to the sky carrying Jake. He went over the elven border and a couple of miles away from the elven border. Riker landed with his wings and put down Jake near a hill. "Now, we're alone. There is a town nearby. We should go there at the right time." Riker then waited overnight until Sander and Jake woke up. Riker sat down and stared at the sky rethinking old memories.

Chapter 10

The Slaughtered Village

The sun went up as a peaceful night ended. Jake woke up from the sun in his eyes. As he saw Sander sitting near him, looking at him with red eyes. "Sander, what happened last night?" Said Jake as his head hurt.

"I'm going to tell you once, Jake, the elf. I'm not Sander. I'm the demon friend inside him. The one who gave him this power and I saved you because you helped Sander get out of the ruined fort. So, I thank you for letting Sander out. So, you are free now so you should get moving. I'm going to wait for Sander to wake in my head so I can let him take control." Riker lay back on the tree. "So, Jake, where are you going to go?" Jake then looked at his red eyes.

"What are you, and are you going to kill me?"

"No, I'm not going to kill you. You saved Sander so I'm going to let you live. If you were a threat then I would kill you. But you're not, so you don't have to worry. Now you never answered my question. Where are you going now, Jake?"

Jake calmly said, "I'm not going anywhere and I don't know where to go. So, I'm just gonna stick with you. Plus, you might need my help in the future." Riker then looked at Jake again.

"What will I need your help for? What use will you come to help me? You know what never mind. You can come but you have to try and keep up. Ok, so Jake, there is a village near this forest, it will take a while to get there. So, let's start heading there now. Maybe we can find somewhere to relax and get some help." Riker and Jake got up to walk to the town nearby.

"So, what do you think this town is anyway?"

"You expect me to know," said Jake.

"Yes, I expect you to know, this is still an elven territory."

"So, just because I'm an elf I know every town and every village along with every person and every place," said Jake with frustration.

"Well, if you don't know, and only know the kingdom passed the border. I say you were isolated and you don't know much about your people," said Riker as he walked to the path to the town.

"Do you know your people, Sander?"

"Listen, it's not Sander, it's Riker, and I don't know everyone. But I know my realm and I know who is in charge and who to trust and who not to trust." They both then stayed silent until they headed to the sign with the village's name on it. They arrived at the sign. "Oh, would you look at that? The sign is chopped off. It's just el. The village is just el. Let's go to Jake's village." Riker patted Jake on the back and walked into the village. Jake followed Riker.

"Oh crap," said Riker with surprise. Riker stopped and so did Jake.

"What is it?" Jake walked next to Riker to see. Dead bodies everywhere. Jake puked as he witnessed a man ripped apart.

"Jake, this town has been raided."

Jake stopped puking, and said, "What type of monster can do this?" Fear was evident in his voice.

"Jake, you can relax. They are half-monsters. This is the work of a werewolf. But one werewolf would not have done this. This is the act of a pack of werewolves.

"How much is a pack? Riker, I ask you a question, how much is a pack?" Jake calmed down.

"A pack is three or more. But this is not the act of three werewolves," Riker said with no emotion.

"How do you know?"

"Because my father and I were the ones who cursed man and turned men into werewolves."

"Your race was the one who made these monsters?"

"It was made during the war on the celestials and we need more people to fight for us. Creating a beast like that made us have a bigger advantage. Along with vampires."

"Wait, vampires exist?" Said Jake in a shocked voice.

"Yes, vampires exist. Now we can stay here all day talking about what my people did or what I did one thousand years ago or we can see where these wolves went. Your choice, Jake." Jake agreed to go on with Riker further into the village.

"Let's go, Riker." Jake continued walking through the village. As they walked, Jake looked around, shocked to see what werewolves could do. He saw a man's organs out of his body. He saw another man's limbs ripped out and severed from his body. Jake tried not to puke himself again. Riker stopped to use his powers to see if he could sense any wolves nearby. Riker closed his eyes and relaxed.

"Wait, what are you doing, Riker?"

"Relax, little elf. I'm trying to concentrate and see if there are any werewolves nearby."

"So is there?" Said Jake, worried.

"I need peace, please. So, in that meaning, Jake, shut up." Riker began to hear two men waking up. The first man said not again. And the other man covered in blood was freaking out. Riker opened his eyes.

"Alright, Jake, there are two people left alive. One guy is, I got a feeling of knowing what he is and the other guy has to be a werewolf. The man covered in blood walks out of his house and walks to Riker and Jake.

"Hello," said the strange man. "Who are you and what happened?" Riker turned around and was going to tell the man the truth if he was not interrupted by Jake.

"So, if you see, your village has been attacked by..." Jake told Riker to shut up and Jake asked the man what he remembered from last night.

The man explained the horror he witnessed, "It happened so fast. I was in my house with my wife. We were relaxing and peacefully, talking and all we heard was screaming. We heard as there was a stampede of horses traveling to us. People started screaming. We believed it was bandits. But then we realized a large howl. I look outside my window to see a giant seven-foot wolf ripping apart my neighbor. They were everywhere. Wait, where's my wife?" The man asked with weariness. Jake told the man she might be alive.

Riker then said, "Or she might be dead. She's possibly dead." The man fell in shock as he thought his wife was dead. Jake tried to calm him down.

A man with black leather armor came out from the fields. The man carried a giant sword on his back. The man saw Sander and began walking to him.

"Sander?" The black-leathered man said.

Riker spoke, "I'm not Sander. Well, I am. But I'm not him."

The black-leathered man then noticed. "Oh, you're the demon inside him. Sander told me what happened. Don't worry, I'm not going to tell anyone."

Riker replied, "I must thank you for not spreading the word and my name is Riker."

"Nice to meet you, Riker," said the black-leathered man. "I'm Gildor. And I'm a werewolf hunter."

Jake then asked, "Do you know what happened to this village?"

"Yes," said Gildor. "I will tell you what happened. Black werewolves attacked the village as they were hungry. I have been hunting these wolves for quite some time and they end up here. I tried to help. But I'm just one werewolf hunter. So, I managed to kill two. But they killed me and now I'm here."

"Wait," said Jake, "If you died, how did you come back?"

"Oh, my ring," said Gildor, "It's hooked with a deal from the reaper and man and the blood of a werewolf and some reaper magic. They made this to balance the odds. The werewolves could not be stopped. So, one hundred rings were made to stop the werewolves. So, my family has carried the ring ever since. I'm one of the families who has it. So short story short, I passed by here and I'm guessing they're heading north to the village near the river. So, now I'm going to continue hunting the werewolves until I kill all of them."

"Now, he is a survivor," Jake then answered Gildor.

"Yes, he is a survivor." Gildor pulled out his giant sword. "Good," said Gildor as he swung his sword on top of his head and sliced half of his head. Gildor then put the sword on his back as it was not a big deal.

Jake freaked out. "Why would you do that? He was an innocent man. He was just worried. It's not like he was lying about the werewolves." Riker then shut up Jake.

"Listen, Gildor knows what he's doing."

"Listen, kid," said Gildor, "Those black werewolves that attacked have a code type thing. Every time they attack they kill everyone but one. They leave the one alive. Because they marked it and that one will turn into a werewolf. That man who was left alive will join the hunt. Think of it as mind control and listen elf, I have been hunting werewolves for six years. I think I know what I'm doing. But this type of werewolf shows no mercy unless you're the last one."

"But isn't there a cure?" Asked Jake.

Gildor then sighed. "I'm sorry but there was no cure when they were intentionally made. So, there is no cure for a werewolf. I'm sorry."

Riker then looked at Gildor. "Sorry, but you're wrong, Gildor. There are two cures. One is killing werewolves in human or wolf form. Which you do, I'm guessing." Gildor agreed on that point. Gildor then asked what the other cure was.

Riker said, "It's not a journey. It's not a magical artifact. But it is magic that makes the cure. There is another but it's not a cure but it's better."

"How do you know all of this?"

Riker looked at Gildor. "Because I'm one of the demons who made the werewolves. I'm the man who made the beast. But let me finish my part. The second cure is magic. I have to do it to perform the spell. Because I'm the guy who created it. But the werewolves are supposed to be cannon fighters. But I thought the celestials would have killed them all. But I guess they didn't. So, Gildor sorry for going off-topic. I will help you get rid of these werewolves. May you show us the way." Gildor then looked at the guy next to Riker.

"We will go if he's up for it." Jake agreed to go with Gildor and Riker to follow the werewolves.

"Alright, let's go," said Gildor. Gildor, Jake, and Riker in Sander's body went to follow the werewolves and put a stop to their bloodshed.

Chapter 11

The Hunt

"I know when someone is lying." Riker looked away from Jake and took a long stroll along with the village. Jake went to each village house and told everyone that the wolves went away and it was safe to come out. Riker strolled as he continued to sense the archangel's energy.

He then said in his head, "Why is this person still here? Why does he want to be here? And why does he think that I don't sense him? He should back away. But maybe I should play it safe. Let's see what he will do when the sun comes up. I also need to question why those werewolves I used the spell on did not turn into men again. I need to research more on that. Maybe Gildor along the journey with Sander and me is useful. I'm going to ask him if he wants to join us on this journey." Riker continued to walk from the village into the forest.

The strange man then made it to Gildor's dead body. "Damn, you have probably been through worse." The strange man then sat next to Gildor's body and waited for him to wake up.

Jake was running to the village elder's house. Jake knocked on the door. "Hello, the beast was driven away." No one answered. Jake knocked again. "Is anyone there?" Jake then went around the house to see a hole the house. When Jake walked in he saw, the village's elder and his wife's bodies. He saw it as a horrible and tragic death.

Chapter 12

The Aftermath

People came out of their houses. Everyone was joyous as there were no monsters or beasts around anymore. Jake went back to the bell and sat on a chair. Jake looked at the ground as he saw a monster. Later on, the sun began to rise. It was peaceful for a little bit.

Until someone screamed. The villagers then saw a couple of people dead in their houses. Gildor was awakened from death by the wolf. Gildor woke up as if it was a dream.

"Finally, you're awake," said the strange man.

Gildor looked at the strange man. "Who are you? And why are you here?" Said Gildor in confusion.

"Well, if you did not know from last night. I'm a werewolf hunter just like you. And I came here because I was hunting the same pack as you. I suspect you're Gildor, the werewolf hunter. Black leather armor. The giant silver magical sword on your back. Yep, you're Gildor, alright. Listen, Gildor the werewolves of all packs, all five werewolf's species have gotten worried. They all have different names. The black wolves have one name carved in their homes and their travels. The black wolves carve the name cronovus, every time the black wolves move or stay. I don't know what it means. But the five species of werewolves carved a different name. But the black werewolves only carved cronovus. So, do you know what it means?"

Gildor looked at the man. "First of all, I don't know your name. Second of all, I don't know what you're talking about, and third of all, why are you acting like this is normal? Meeting another hunter is rare. How is this normal to you?"

'The strange man started to answer Gildor's questions, "Ok, Gildor I'm Walter, the silver swordsman. Your second question, I cannot answer, that's why when I saw someone with the same ring as me, I thought you would have answers and your third question is how am I doing this normally? Well, you're the fourth werewolf hunter I came across. This ain't my first time. And I have more good stuff to tell you about our rings, what powers it can give us, and what benefits it may bring later."

Gildor then started chatting with Walter, the silver swordsman. "Alright, so Walter, what do these rings even do? They bring me back to life from any werewolf attack. But what do they also give?"

Walter then explained what the rings could do. "They all don't match each other. Depending on the user and his personality, the rings will act on their mindset. So, I may have the power to see into the future attack of a village or group from the werewolves. But you may have the power to increase speed or have a stronger wielding ability. They all act differently. Like for example, Gildor, the last werewolf hunter I came across with the ring had the power to kill a werewolf. But every time he killed a werewolf they would light up on fire. You may know him as Pyro, the beast killer. His name ain't Pyro. But he goes by the name because of the power he uses. So, you see Gildor it's all on your personality. Do you know any power you may have from the ring?"

Gildor stopped and thought about it. "Well, there is one, but it does not make sense. Sometimes when I'm on a journey or hunting, I feel like I'm being followed. There's like a voice or some type of warning telling me to watch out. It mostly works a lot. And I catch people following me. Do you think that's a ring power?"

The strange man told Gildor more about the ring, "The ring has one thing in common with the rest of the rings. It brings you back from werewolf attacks. But at the same time, you get two more powers. Mine is visions and being brought back to life. Pyro got bieng brought back to life, killing werewolves and burning them. We all have different abilities. So, make sure that sense you have is one of your powers. Now, if you don't mind Gildor, I need to find more answers. If I can get it from any other werewolf hunter, then I will go to find a mage to take me to the order of magical arts. So, I say good day to you, Gildor."

Walter, the silver swordsman, got up and walked out of the village, and disappeared into the forest. Gildor then got himself up and walked to the middle of the village thinking of what the other werewolf hunter said. Riker continued to walk into the middle of the forest. Riker stopped to see seven werewolves burnt and dead. Riker put his knee on the ground and looked at the beast's eyes. Riker saw they were blinded when they were fighting. Riker talked to himself in his head. "I knew it. It's not any normal celestial angel. It's an archangel and he is following me. This work is the work of an archangel. But my real question is who. Who is stubborn to try and sneak up on me like this? This is a perfect time to attack me. So, why isn't he doing anything? This is going to be a long one." Riker then turned back and made his way back to the village. The people of the village continued to stand around the middle of the village, trying to get answers from the village elder. Jake still looked at the ground as he was in shock at what happened to the elder and his wife.

Gildor came up to Jake. "Hey, Jake are you alright?"

Jake stopped staring at the ground and looked at Gildor. Gildor looked at Jake, and asked, "What's wrong, Jake? What's going on? Are you ok?"

Jake pointed at the elder's house. Gildor looked at the elder's house and tried to open the door. "I can't get in. Maybe there's a back door." Gildor went around the house to check for a back door. Gildor saw hole in the house and walked into it. When Gildor walked in, he realized he did not save everyone. He saws the elder and his wife ripped to shreds, and blood was everywhere. That was why Jake was shocked. He never saw this happen to someone. That poor boy.

The people of the town started to get worried about why the elder was s not showing for an explanation. Gildor walked out of the house and into the middle of the town.

Riker came up to Gildor. "So, how is everything going so far?" Gildor told Riker what happened in the elder's house. "Hey, everyone." The town stopped talking and looked at Gildor. "The beast has been driven back. You guys are safe now. But some people did not survive. I am sorry to say that your town elder, your leader and his wife had been killed in this event. I am sorry for your loss, but we did what we must do to keep the beasts out. I say we grab all the bodies and burn them. For a sign of respect. Let's hope the gods give them a better life in the next. So, let's get wood."

Gildor and Riker went to gather wood. As the town gathered the people who were killed and put them in stacks. The people then put the bodies in the field. Gildor and Riker arrived with the wood to put together a fire. Riker went to Jake to talk to him while Gildor put together the fire.

Riker sat next to Jake, "Listen Jake I know this is probably your first time seeing a werewolf finish off its attack. But hey, you got to put it past you. You gotta keep moving forward. Look, there are worse things like werewolves than werewolves. And I know you have not been seeing things like this, you have been caged. You never know what is on the other side of the border. But now you do.

What I'm trying to say is, loss is not easy. I know, you never knew him. But you need to know that you gotta put your head up and keep moving forward. Now follow me, Gildor should be done putting the fire together."

Jake then looked at Riker. "Why are you so nice? Aren't you a demon? Aren't you supposed to destroy the world?"

Riker looked into Jake's eye. "Listen, I was going to try and conquer the world. But I met someone who showed me something better. I fell in love long ago. She showed me the light. She showed me light in my dark heart. This person showed me the world can change, if I can change then my people can change. There's hope in everybody. Now let's give them a good pass on." Jake and Riker got up.

"Alright, let's go." Together, they walked to the fields.

The entire village started to go to the fire and pray before lighting the fire. Gildor started to talk to the people, "Listen, I know I never knew the elder, but I see he was a good leader. I see he was a man who wanted to protect the village. That man and the people who died should not be punished for their horrible actions. But should move to the afterlife. To live forever with the gods. It's a good day today. But it's also a sad day. To see people dead it's never a good thing to move on. But you guys should let these folks pass to the afterlife. No matter the horrible things they did to you. You should remember your fellow villagers for the good times. Now, that's all I have to say. But after this, let's not focus on the past and push forward toward the future." Gildor then walked out of the center of the area. He watched as each villager spoke about the elder, his wife, and the people of the village. After everyone was done with their speeches, Riker summoned fire on the wood. The village then watched the people who died burn into ashes. Jake felt what the villagers were feeling – grief. Gildor quietly looked at the fire. But Riker looked at the fire as if it was nothing. Riker heard a voice crying from the forest. The voice was of the souls that died. The voice was crying about why they were killed.

Riker heard this but he did not say anything. The village was quiet for about two to three hours. Some villagers started leaving their homes and carrying on their lives. Riker, Jake, and Gildor started to group up next to each other.

"Alright, it's time to get going," said Riker.

"I agree with you," said Gildor.

"Wait, how about the fire? Said Jake. "We're just going to leave the fire burning?"

Gildor put his hand on Jake. "I'm sorry but by the next morning, the fire will be gone. We must get heading out now. I need to know more about werewolves from Riker and I need to know why Sander is going," said Gildor.

Jake then turned and looked at Gildor. "Fine, I guess we can go."

Gildor, Riker, and Jake made their way out of the fields and into the forest.

"Now, Riker, where are we going?" Said Gildor.

"Well, Gildor was going to Drogogon. Where my sword is so I can claim it or Sander can claim it? We can have material to fight against Galatin."

"Well, then what are we waiting for? Let's go."

Jake asked, "What's Drogogon?"

Riker explained to Jake what Drogogon was, "Drogogon, Jake, is the land of dragons. But it's not like any land. It's a mountain full of dragons. They're like monks. They're peaceful. But we're going under Drogogon. But I will explain that when we get there. Now, let us go. It's a long walk to Drogogon."

Gildor, Jake, and Riker started to make their way to Dragogon.

Chapter 13

House Gladstone

Two days have passed and Jake, Riker, and Gildor wanted to stop and get some rest. Jake said, "May I rest first because I'm really tired?"

Riker told Jake he could rest. "I will take watch," said Gildor.

"No, you may rest, Gildor. I can take watch," said Riker. "I cannot sleep. And demons and celestials don't sleep unless in our realms. But I must stay awake as I am a demon. I will know who is coming from miles away anyway. So, I will take this whole night's watch."

Gildor and Jake agreed. Gildor and Jake made a fire and slept on the ground by the fire. Riker then patrolled around the camp to make sure nobody was coming. Riker leaned to a tree, looked at the sky and said one word, "Crystal," Riker said with sadness in his heart. Riker continued to think of Crystal until he detected an archangel's energy nearby. Riker telepathically talked to the archangel that was following him. "If you're going to follow me and think that you're not detected, you are off by a long shot. I knew you were coming when Gildor was feeling as someone was following him. Your first mistake is going after me. You are forgetting that I am the firstborn son of the demon king. I have more abilities than any other demon except my father and mother. You know the only one who can kill me is Galatin, three birds, or the heir to the reaper realm. But other than that, we never saw the three birds around. The heir to the reaper realm is usually never in this world. And Galatin is in Fergus's body telling and whispering to Fergus on conquering the world. So, I may ask if you want to try and kill me, go ahead. But I can show you what will happen if you do. If you want to talk, let's talk. So, come out and show yourself."

The archangel then walked next to Riker and looked at the sky. "How did you know I was behind you?" Riker heard a soft voice and turned his head. "Wait, you're a girl. Who is an archangel? How is that possible?" The soft voice of the archangel then told Riker who she was but did not give a name. "Well, since you're here I can tell you who I am. I am the youngest child of the celestial kingdom and the youngest daughter."

"Wait, but there should be one daughter of the celestial king. What time were you born?" Said Riker with a curious face.

The archangel lady then told Riker how long she had been in this world. "I have been here for about five centuries. After the evil demons have been annihilated. My brother Galatin is a hero in the celestial realm for killing the person who killed my older sister. My older sister was Crystal. She had the power to make anyone of her race or any of the races equal to us. Tell the truth. She also had the power to read minds and telepathically talk to anyone across the world. Her power was amazing. And her elemental powers were light and water. She was a good leader and a good sibling. Sadly, she died in the world by your sword. That's why, I followed you here. Because I want to get my revenge on my older sister. The one you killed." The archangel lady then looked at Riker as if she was going to kill him.

"Listen, I may not know your name. I would not care. But I never killed your sister. If you want to see the truth I can show you. She did not die from me. She did not die from any of my demons or my race. She died by one of your races. If you want to know the truth, I can show you. You also got to know this now. How do I have her power? How did I telepathically talk to you? Think about that. Whatever Galatin said or did, you guys believe him but you're forgetting one thing. If he said he killed me, how am I still alive? If Galatin told you that I'm dead, how am I still alive?"

The archangel lady then looked at Riker. "If my older brother is lying to me and my people. What will happen? What would I do? I'm the youngest and weakest of them all. I stand no chance against Galatin or my older brothers. And I don't have as good a reputation with my people. Galatin is like our hero. To tell you the truth, you may be lying and when I turn my back, you'll kill me. So, what do you have to say?"

Riker looked into the lady's archangel's eyes. "I won't kill you unless you want to kill me. I'm only in a vessel. If you kill me, you kill the person who owns this body. So, you might want to turn back and leave me alone. Because every time I think of Galatin or any celestial, I think of Crystal."

She got angry. "Why do you speak of my sister as you knew her? Who do you think you are?"

He replied, "I don't want you to know much. But I knew Crystal. We were more than friends. I'm her lover and she is mine. We had a life together. We had a child. But I will tell you this, I did not kill her. It was not me who killed her and my child. It was Galatin. I saw my people get closer to our area. I went to my people and told them the celestials were the other way. Crystal and I would not be caught together after the party. After all, my people were drunk. I went back home and saw Galatin. I will let Gelatin tell you that story, now, I know you won't believe me. I can show you my memory. But you have to trust me."

The archangel lady took a back step. "Sorry, but all my life I heard of your stories of what you did. I don't trust you. And I will never trust you. So, deal with it."

Riker then started to walk away. "I will deal with it as I have no problem with it and I only have a problem with your brother."

"Wait," said the lady, "Why are you walking away? Don't you think I will kill you? Don't you think I might stab you in the back?"

Riker then turned around and said, "No, I know you won't stab me in the back as you're not even prepared to fight me. I'm stronger than you and you know it. I suggest you go home now. I had enough of talking to you." The lady archangel then dashed at Riker. Within a blink of an eye, Riker was behind her. "Wait, I thought you were in front of me."

Riker then whispered in her ear. "I am going to kill you if you keep trying to attack me. I am stronger, faster, and smarter than you. So, go home now. Because I won't warn you again."

Riker showed her a small vision of what would happen in the next five minutes. The lady then got scared and flew off. Riker watched her fly away as she got afraid of what Riker showed her. Finally, she was gone. Riker looked at the sky to see that the sun was coming up. Riker then went back to camp to wake up Gildor and Jake. When Riker arrived at the fire, it was turned to ash. "Hey Gildor, Jake, wake up now. The sun is up."

Gildor woke up and got ready for the journey. "Hey Jake, wake up," said Gildor. Jake woke up and then yawned. "Why do we still have to keep going?"

Riker then looked at Jake. "Because Jake we need to go to Dragogon. Now, it ain't that far from here. If we walk now, we will get there. So, let's go." Jake then got up and got ready for the journey.

"I'm ready," Jake said.

Gildor, Riker, and Jake then continued their journey to Dragogon. As Riker, Jake, and Gildor walked along, they saw five tents ahead. "Wait, get down," said Gildor. Gildor pushed Jake down. Gildor looked at its noble banner. "I don't recognize that banner from a thousand." Gildor stared down a banner. "I know what that banner is. It's of House, Gladstone's."

Riker looked at Gildor, "What are you talking about?"

"Sander is Gladstone. House Gladstone was made forty years ago. To round it up, it was the brother of the king. So, if Sander is in which body you are in and Fergus dies, Sir Kevin, son of Samuel Gladstone will take the throne. He is next in line if Sander and Fergus kill each other."

"Ok, are they friendly?" Said Jake.

"What are you scared of?" Gildor said while smiling.

"No, I just don't know you, humans, as much. So, I want to know if he does not like elves. Sir Kevin is one of the noblest and nicest in the land of Luna."

"Trust me," Gildor said with confidence as Riker was about to go. Sander awoke in his mind.

"Riker, what happened?" Said Sander in his mind. Riker then talked to Sander in his head. "Finally, Sander, you're awake, now take the wheel. Riker, let Sander take over control of the body."

"Gildor, Jake what did I miss?"

"Wait, Sander, is that you? Wait, where's Riker? We need his help."

"I'm still here but Sander you're gonna have to talk on my behalf."

"He said I have to talk on his behalf. I am the guy who's showing the way, well, both Riker and I are."

"Sander, what is Riker telling you to do now?" Said Gildor. "What is that house Gladstone banners?"

Sander started to walk to the tents, "Screw it," said Gildor. Gildor and Jake followed Sander toward the tents.

When they got to the tents, Sander stood in the middle of the camp. When his cousin came out of the tent, he said, "No way, Sander, is that you?" Said Kevin Gladstone. Kevin ran to Sander and hugged him. "I thought you were dead. That's what they said in Luna. Where have you been?"

Sander then explained what happened. "After the small fight between Riker and Galatin, Riker was knocked out of the castle and into the air. I grew wings and I flew and crashed into the green forest. Went to a village. Saw a scout. Killed some bandits. Then after all that got attacked by werewolves. Met the king of Elmus. Long story short it was a very big journey until I got here. I can explain it to you later. But right now, we're on our way to Drogogon."

"Do you even know what's going on in Luna now?" Said Kevin. Sander shook his head no.

"Well, Fergus got us marching towards the elven kingdom and the dwarven kingdom. He wishes to marry one of the elves. He wants to conquer the dwarfs. There is a reason. If he conquers the three dwarven kingdoms, he will have access to the mines of all three. If he marries the elves he will know the elves. He's moving fast. That's why I'm trying to find Drogogon as well. Because they have all the answers and all the history dating back one thousand years ago. I want to challenge Fergus to a battle. But Fergus has magic now and now he's strong. So, if you guys are on your way to Drogogon, then I am going with you," said Kevin.

"Wait, Kevin, why are there five tents?" Said Sander. '

Kevin then told Sander that he brought four of his bodyguards with him. "Yeah, so I didn't want to bring so much attention. Just acting like I'm going on a hunt with my bodyguards. Anyway, who is this guy?" Kevin then points at the elf.

Sander then explained how he met Gildor and Jake. "I met Jake in a prison. We escaped together. I met Gildor at Elmus. But the demon was taking most of the control."

"Wait, so you do have a demon inside you?" Said Kevin. Sander shook his head in yes.

"Enough talking, we gotta get moving. Are you coming with us?" Said Gildor.

Kevin shook his head yes and decided to get ready, while Gildor, Sander, and Jake waited for Kevin to get ready. They got surrounded by his four guards with his swords out.

"Stand down," Kevin said, "They are with me."

The four guards then put their swords away. They packed up tents and were going to Drogogon with Jake Riker and Sander. Within a few miles, the group stopped at a sign.

"I don't understand the language," said Gildor.

"It must be the language of the dragons," said Kevin.

"It says if you are not a dragon or have any wings, you must walk up this mountain path to come to the mountain city of dragons," said Sander. Wait, how did I just read that?"

"Because I know the dragon language," said Riker in Sander's head. Sander then explained how he knew the language to the group.

"Let's walk up the path, let's leave the horses here." Kevin and his guards left their horses near the path and the group to walked up the mountain pass.

Chapter 14

The Mountain City of Dragogon

The group finally made it to the top of the mountain to see a city on a mountain. The group walked until two dragons came from the sky and landed right in front of them.

"Who are you, people? Why do you walk the path to Dragogon? State your business," said one of the dragons.

"My name is Kevin Gladstone. Son of Samuel Gladstone. I wish to enter Dragogon for answers to challenge the King of Luna," said Kevin with courage.

"How about you, with the red eyes?"

"I am Sander Helmglade, the rightful King of Luna. I am here to pick up a weapon that is protected by the dragons."

Sander then turned his head to Gildor. "I am Gildor Landfield and I am the second son of the Landfield. But I am a werewolf hunter. I wish to find answers for the ring I am holding right now."

Gildor then turned to Jake. "I am Jake Presley. I wish to enter Drogogon for more knowledge of materials." The group stands together with might.

The two dragons then looked at each other. "Very well, we will let you pass. If you try anything funny, we will gladly turn you into dust. Alright, now follow us down this path to the mountain castle." The two armored dragons then walked and took the group to the mountain Dragogon castle. As they walked to the castle they started talking.

"So, Mr. Dragogon, may I ask, why are both of you wearing armor?" Said Kevin.

"Well, human child, both of us are what you would call a soldier. We have many dragons here that are soldiers. Some read ancient books to help them with magic. Some like to fly and spread peace to the land. But most of the time when we are not here, we go into human form. To not scare away the common race. We're peaceful dragon folk. But that's if you choose to challenge us, we have no choice but to make you go, poof. But you look like a group that will not challenge us. Now, we're gonna let you enjoy the walk. Enjoy the view."

The group finally reached the doors of the mountain castle. "This is how far we will go. You may enter and see the master." The two dragon soldiers then flew up in the air and started patrolling in the sky.

The group then walked into the mountain castle to see dragons on the second floor with golden armor. The group continued to walk down the castle. One of the golden armored dragons told the group to go to the throne room. The group followed what the golden armor dragon said. While walking to the throne room, the group was amazed by what they saw in the castle.

"Guys, look at that," said Kevin. The group then walked to the statue. "It's like this dragon is their god."

"Sander, this is not their god, it's their mother," said Riker in Sander's head. "Their mother founded the Dragogon thousands of years ago. Every Drogogon area has one of the dragons. There are ten Drogogon places and right now you're standing on one of them. The statue you're looking at, Sander, is the great dragon, Myra. She is why we are here, Sander."

The group then walked out of the throne room. The doors in the throne room then closed shut.

"Riker, you did not tell Sander all about the sword. Does he even know its name? You need to tell everything about the sword to Sander to control it," said the golden dragon.

"Wait, why do I need to know the name? Why are you speaking as if the sword is alive?" The golden dragon stayed silent.

"Because it is, Sander," said Riker in his head. "The sword is the last of its kind. The celestial race destroyed its brothers and sisters along with its creators. The sword is a sword but it has a mind of its own. It can take control of the person wielding it as well if the person is weak. You must have the rage and a vengeful spirit. Like mine to Galatin. The sword's name is Soul Absorber. The sword is a living sword. So, you must build a relationship with it."

"So, Riker, this sword is alive."

"Yes, Sander, it is alive."

"But wait, Riker, why do you call it the Soul Absorber?"

"I'll leave that to the golden dragon to tell you. As he is listening in our head."

Sander looked up and he saw the golden dragon looking down at him. "Wow, Riker, I didn't know you would realize I'm hearing the conversation of you and Sander," said the golden dragon telepathically talking in Sander's mind. "Sander, the Soul Absorber's name was given to him for a reason. It was made for Riker. The heir to the demon race. The creators did not like the celestials and so they created the swords. But the celestials found out. So, the creators tried hiding the swords but they were too late. The celestials came and destroyed all of the swords and their creators. But one survived and was not destroyed. When Riker came to claim the sword, the sword, and Riker had the same enemy. So, Riker and the sword were good friends. Riker, later on, started getting revenge for Crystal. The sword started getting revenge for its brothers and sister along with its parents. Every time the sword killed a man or any race killed the sword itself. The sword will absorb its soul into energy. Later, the people around started calling Riker's sword the soul absorber and that's how it got the name. So, Sander that is the word you're trying to acquire. So, be careful. Now, I must let you go. I have other things to do in Drogogon than talk to you about the sword. I must go talk to Gildor, Kevin, and Jake about their things. But I will say these last words, do not let the Soul Absorber try and control you. Alright, now let the others in." The doors opened up and the dragons let the rest of the group in.

"Alright, Gildor, if you seek knowledge of the ring, we can help you with our library. Kevin that same rule that goes to Gildor applies to you. Jake, what do you need?"

Jake then spoke to the dragon, "I want to find more knowledge of forging armor and weapons. More knowledge of what my father tried to teach me."

"Well, Jake, I will also give you access to our library. Anything else?" Said the golden dragon. The group then shook their heads and said no. "Then I will let you guys with the knowledge and I will give you guys two days to prepare yourself to meet the great dragon, Myra."

"Wait, two days?" Said Kevin.

"Oh, right I'm sorry, I forgot to explain this to you. Sander and Riker are here to find the great dragon, Myra. So, I expected you guys wanted to see her as well. I'm sorry if I did not tell you guys earlier. I'm almost up to my life span. I'm old."

"How old are you exactly?" Said Gildor.

The golden dragon started to sit up straight. "I'm exactly one thousand three hundred and thirty-two years old. Yes, I lived at that time when Riker was put away."

"Wait, I thought dragons lived up to one thousand years," said Gildor. "How are you over your life span or was I wrong?"

"No, you were not wrong, Gildor. We, dragons, are different. The dragons you see with metal armor or being a soldier are dragons who live up to one thousand years. It goes for most of the dragons in this place, but us golden dragons live an extra five hundred years. That's what we dragons do. But there is another kind of dragon who lives up to three thousand years old. Twice as a golden dragon. But they are in different places. It is very rare for a dragon to be here. But those dragons you won't learn about until later. But along with that, you must take two days to prepare for the great dragon, Myra. As she is ready to see all of you. Now, I must let you go and get ready. I hope you can see our knowledge help you. If you think about stealing a book, Jake, we will have no choice but to make you go poof. If you don't know what that means then I can just say you burn to death if you think that Riker will stop the fire. Then you know they will come, Riker."

"Sander, make sure they didn't cross that line," said Riker in Sander's head.

Sander then told the group not to make the dragons cross that line. The golden dragon then continued, "Alright, now that I've warned all of you, I will let you have full access to the mountain city Dragogon's library. I will let you be off now."

The giant doors opened behind them, the group then turned around and walked out of the throne room. When they walked out, two dragons were waiting for them. "Follow us and we will show you to the library." The two dragons started to walk to the library. "Let's go, fellow heroes," said the two dragons. The group felt as if the dragons were making fun of them but they just let the dragons do what they did. The group finally got to two giant silver doors. The two dragons opened the doors. When the group walked in, they saw so many books, they couldn't even count them.

"How many books are here?" Said Kevin.

The two dragons laughed at Kevin's question. "There are about around five hundred thousand books here. Books that contain magic and books that contain histories of five thousand years ago. But we have people watching everywhere, so you don't steal. If you need help to find the books, we have the librarians over there. So, have fun now we got business somewhere else." The two dragons walked out of the library closing the doors shut. The group then walked the long path down the library. The group kept walking down watching every sector of the library until they reached the tables and librarians. The group finally reached the librarians.

"Wait, what the hell? You're human. Are humans allowed here?" Said Sander. The librarian told Sander she was not human.

"Yeah, you are. You're a human being," said Sander.

The librarian went into an open space. "Would you prefer this form?" She said. She then turned into a dragon to show them she was not human. "Now, you prefer this form. What books do you need, Jake Presley, I assume?"

"How do you know my name?"

The librarian dragon then started to look at Jake. "Because I know you're Jake as you're the only one here that has pointy ears."

"How did you know our names?"

"The master told us. All of us every single dragon. We're all connected. Now, what do you need Jake, the elf?"

Jake then told the librarian what he wanted. "I would like books of materials all around Sinia. I would want books on armorsmith making. I want books on weaponsmith making."

"Very well on your way." The librarian told one of the dragons to get those books. "Now, Jake, you wait patiently over there away from the group, I don't want you talking. Now Kevin, what do you need?"

Kevin asked for a book to challenge the King of Luna. Then Kevin asked for a book on what his sword meant. The dragon looked at the sword, and said, "I can get you those books."

The librarian told another dragon to get the books of human challenge and the book of angelic weapons. "Now Kevin, go sit over there, away from Jake. Wait for your books."

Jake and Kevin sat at the tables away from each other. Kevin's guards then walked to Kevin and sat next to him.

"Gildor, what do you need?" Gildor showed his ring. "I want to know more about the ring and anything that has the name Cronovus in it." The librarian asked the third dragon to get Gildor the book of hunter rings and the book of the original werewolves. "Now Gildor, you may sit." Gildor then walked to one of the tables and sat and waited for his books.

"Last but not least, Sander, what do you need?" Sander asked about the Soul Absorber. He also asked more about the great dragon, Myra. The final thing he asked was about the celestials and demon war. The librarian then told Sander to go and have a seat. The librarian went to get the books that Sander requested. Sander sat at a table and waited.

Chapter 15

The Cave of the Great Dragon

The group waited eight hours until the dragons came with the books. When the dragons arrived carrying the books, the group got up from their tables. The dragons then put the books on the tables. Gildor's instinct started reading about his ring and what it gave him. Kevin started to read about the challenges of humans dating back three thousand years ago. Jake started reading every material he could read in the book. And Sander started to read about the celestial and demon war. The group began reading what they could read for the whole day. Later, after the day was done, the group was sleeping in the library. They read all night and they did not take a rest. When the librarians woke up they saw them sleeping in the library. The librarians then let them sleep as they went to go get them food.

"Hey, Sander, wake up," said Riker in his head. Sander woke up from his nap. "Riker. what's going on?" Riker told Sander to finish reading the books. Sander continued to read the book on the Soul Absorber. As Sander was reading, he saw its origins and why it hated celestials.

After reading the books, Sander got up from his table and grabbed the books to return them to the front desk where the head librarian sat. Sander then woke up the group so they could continue their reading. "Hurry up, we got one more day until we have to go meet the great dragon, Myra." As the group was reading, the dragons came back and brought a cooked cow.

"Lunchtime," the dragons said.

The group was looking at the cooked cow-like meal they had never seen before. The dragons put the meal on the table while carrying on their duties. The head librarian stayed to make sure they ate the meal. The group did nothing and just stood there.

"Why aren't you eating?" Asked the head librarian. "Don't they have cows where you're from?" The head librarian stood there looking at them.

"They have cows where we're from. But we don't have one giant cooked cow."

"You prefer it a little more black?"Said the head librarian.

"No," said Gildor with a loud yell. "This meat is just fine. Let's eat, guys."

The head librarian then turned around and carried on her business. The head librarian went into human form and grabbed the books that Sander put on her table. "I will go put these away." The head librarian put the books away in the mountain Drogogon library. The group then began to eat the cooked cow that the dragons got for the group. Jake grabbed the meat and went back to his table to continue reading.

"Gildor, what did you learn about your ring?" Said Sander.

The group then listened to Gildor as he spoke about his hunter ring. "My ring gives me power. It brings me back from the dead. But it gives me two more powers."

Riker then told Sander to take control of the body for a couple of minutes. Sander then trusted Riker to take control. "Gildor, listen to me. Remember when you said someone was following us when Jake and I were hunting down the werewolves? Well, truth be told you were right. We were being followed. We were being followed by an archangel. But she was born after the war and after I was trapped. She was born after Crystal died. We were being followed, I can't tell you the details. Gildor, I know you're powerful, and the reason why I know you're powerful is that I have that same power as well. The power is called sensible; meaning you can sense anyone nearby. It's a good type of power that gives you a heads-up on everything. So, you are aware of even an arrow. It's good for power, sorry for lying to you about someone being followed. It's just I wanted to know who was stupid enough to follow me. But your second power, Gildor, is what you need to find on your own. That is all, I have to say about, Gildor. And Kevin I'm going to tell you something about your sword. Your sword is special. It was made one thousand years ago. The reason why it was made was to stop the demons from pushing forward. Galatin and what was left of his battalion gave the humans the weapons that were used to kill a demon. The sword you're using cannot kill a demon like me or a higher-power demon. But it can kill a demon knight and below. That sword is important because not many were created. The sword you have right now, with enough training, you can kill anything with that sword. Even a dragon. The sword you have is powerful. So, keep that in mind, we have one more day until we meet Myra. Jake, I know you're trying to read. But there is a secret in your family name that every legendary blacksmith is allowed to do. But we can help out with that. You guys have one more day so make it count. Now, I'm going to let Sander take control of the body." Riker then let Sander take control of the body.

"Wait, why did you say Myra like you already knew her? I feel as if Riker is hiding stuff from us," said Kevin.

"He probably is. But what can you do?" Sander then got up to take a walk around the mountain Drogogon Castle.

The group then ate and started to continue their reading. Sander was walking through the halls to see another statue of a dragon. Sander then went to the statue of the dragon. When Sander was looking at the statue, he had a flashback of a golden and black dragon. Sander saw a dragon killing humans. The dragon then went against a demon and fought with him for two days. The demon was then injured and the dragon flew back to the mountain city of Drogogon. Sander then blinked his eyes twice.

"What was that? What the hell was that?" Said Sander.

"It was one of my memories," said Riker in Sander's head. "It's the price of me and your souls merging. Normally, I think. But what you just saw was my brother fighting against the black and gold dragon. I never knew his name but he was a strong dragon who could injure the second son of the demon king."

"But why did he kill the humans?" Said Sander with fear.

"Because those humans were killing his people. By the looks of it, he is probably a hero dragon."

"Well, where is he now?"

"He is probably dead." As Sander was talking to Riker, the golden dragon walked next to Sander. "I see that you are done with your research. You need any more assistants?"

"No, thank you," said, Sander.

"Ay, yes, Colinborn. One of our strongest fighters back then."

"What is his name?" Said Sander.

The golden dragon told Sander what his name was and what the dragon did. "The dragon you're looking at is Colinborn. He was a dragon back when the time celestials and demons went to war. He made sure none passed our border. He was a good soldier. But after the war, he was never to be found."

"Is he dead?" said Sander.

The golden dragon looked at Sander. "I don't know if he is dead or not. He just disappeared. He was able to live for five thousand years. The only one of his kind. But follow me, Sander." The golden dragon then began to walk on a bridge with Sander to a giant tower. Sander and the gold began to walk as they talked.

"Sander, you have Riker in you right now. To tell you the truth, soon in a century, I will die. But another will take my place. Your friends are not ready for the journey they are to embark on with you."

"What do you mean by the journey?" Asked Sander in confusion.

"Sander, Galatin wins by killing Riker. The fate of the human race and all of the races will be dead. The celestials will finally conquer the world. So, what Riker is doing is saving the world. My mother, Myra just said that you and your friends will meet new allies along the road to your vengeance, but you and your comrades now, you guys are going on a journey to save the world. You, Riker, Jake, Gildor, and Kevin will go into the cave. But don't worry, your friends think you are going to fight the great dragon, Myra. You're not! You're going to be taught everything you can in a week." The golden dragon stopped and started looking at the sun as it went down. Sander then looked at the sun going down as well. "Sander, this journey is not only a journey of your revenge but a journey to save the world from being conquered. Riker, I know you're hearing me. Mother Myra has something you thought you lost in her cave. You and your group of comrades are ready for the cave. Tomorrow morning, you and your comrades will meet me at the dragon platform. We're going to fly to the cave. Now, Sander, you should get some rest. See you tomorrow morning."

"But I have more questions to ask you."

The golden dragon then looked at Sander. "Your questions will be answered when you meet my mother. Now get some rest, young hero. You have a big day tomorrow."

Sander then walked back to the library. When Sander was walking back, the dragon said something to his head. "Colinborn, I know you're alive and I know you don't want to intervene but your destiny is to help these young heroes. Mother wants that. Colinborn, your new destiny has been chosen." The golden dragon then started to walk back to his throne room. When Sander arrived at the library, he saw the group was done with their books and ready to go. Sander told the group what the golden dragon told him.

"Hey, guys, we go tomorrow morning. We meet the golden dragon at the dragon platform. He says we must get some rest. Now if you don't mind, I'm going to sleep." Sander walked to a table and slept on top of the table. The group then put their books on the head librarian's table and started to choose a table and floor to sleep. When the group started to sleep, Sander in the middle of the night started to dream of the celestial and demon war.

Sander was witnessing Riker's memories of the celestials and what they had done to the other factions. Sander then saw Riker ripping off the wings of the celestials and burning their wings. Sander saw Riker murdering the celestials in cold blood. Sander saw

Riker slaughtering anything that got in his way of revenge. Sander woke up in the middle of the night sweating and in fear of what Riker did to the celestials during the war. Sander looked at the group as they were sleeping. Sander then went to the books on the librarian's table. Sander began to read the books to pass the time. The sun began to rise. The group was still sleeping. Sander finished reading the materials and forging books. Sander then began to wake the group up from their sleep.

"Guys, we need to go to the Drogogon platform." The group yawned, and walked slowly through the library. Sander and the group walked out of the library.

When they walked out, they saw two dragons waiting for them.

"Young heroes, we will show you to the Drogogon platform. Follow us." The two dragons then started to walk and show the group of heroes to the Drogogon platform. When the group arrived at the Drogongon platform, they saw the golden dragon and eight other dragons ready to fly them to the cave of Myra. The heroes each got on one dragon and flew.

"Hold on tight," said the golden dragon. The dragons then flew down the mountain and through the large redwood forest. The dragons then landed next to a giant cave.

"We're here now, young heroes." Sander and the group then walk to the cave. The golden dragon told them to keep going into the cave. "Once you enter, the torches will light up. Now, begin your journey, young heroes." The group then walked through the barrier of the giant cave. Sander looked back and saw the dragons were gone.

Sander then continued to walk down the cave.

Chapter 16

The Great Dragon, Myra

Sander walked down the cave as more torches lit up.

"Hey, guys," whispered Kevin. "You think she is a normal-sized dragon or is she bigger?"

"Hey, Riker, can you tell us what she looks like?"

"I'm not going to tell them, Sander," said Riker in Sander's head.

"He's not going to tell you he said. You will find out from now I guess."

"Shhhh," said Gildor. "Let's stay quiet. She might hear us. Let's move and stay quiet." The group then started to see a light from the other side of the cave.

The group walked to the light and saw a waterfall with some green grass and some trees. It was like Springfield here. The group then saw a tunnel that kept going down.

"Guys, I think we need to go deeper." The group went even more down the tunnel. When they arrived, there was no deeper tunnel. Torches started lighting up and down the giant cave. The group saw a large giant white rock.

"Guys, look at that rock. It's white. It looks like marble." The group noticed two ways up. The left side of the cave, the right side of the cave, and in the middle was the large giant white rock. Gildor and Sander walked on the left top-up. Jake and Kevin walked on the right side of the cave. The four guards followed Kevin as their job was to protect him. The cave was quiet. There were no birds. No rocks were shaking. It was a peaceful cave.

"You guys, find any other cave over there?" Said Jake loudly across the other side of the cave.

"No," said Sander.

"Oh, I found something," Kevin said. "I found a sword," said Kevin out loud. Sander ran around the entire cave to Kevin. When Sander and Gildor were almost there, the ground began to shake.

"Hang on to something," Sander said, "It's an earthquake."

The earthquake stopped five minutes later.

"Is everyone alright?" The group agreed they were fine except for Jake. Jake was looking at the middle of the cave.

"Jake, you alright?" The group tried calling out to Jake if he was alright. Jake then pointed slowly to the middle of the cave.

"What's wrong?" Said Kevin. When Kevin said that a giant dragon head popped right from the middle, the wings stretched out to the cave. The great dragon then breathed out, black smoke coming out from her nose.

"Hello, Sander and Riker, I know you guys will come for the sword. Gildor, I see that you have questions about the ring you have. Jake is a young legendary blacksmith. Last but not least, Kevin Gladstone. You want questions on the celestial blade you are wielding. I see you all come far. I see you all come to get answers."

The group decided to run out of the cave. That was when they saw the exit the rocks close together like the wall was made of magic. "You cannot escape your fate. You cannot escape your destiny. You guys were destined to meet each other."

"Who are you?" Kevin asked.

"I am who you seek. I am the great dragon, Myra."

"You're the great dragon," said Jake. The great dragon then relaxed her wings and started to turn around. When she turned around another cave had opened.

"Are you controlling this cave?" Said Gildor.

"Indeed, I am, Gildor Landfield."

The great dragon told them to follow her down the giant cave. As the group followed the great dragon, Myra they smelled saltwater. The great dragon Myra came to a stop. The group saw an underground forest and grassland.

"Now, here is where you're going to train." The group saw a lake and river near the grassland.

"Gildor, your power on your ring will activate more every time you kill a werewolf. The soul of the beast, not the human soul, the beast's soul will go into your ring and give the ring power. You already have the second stage. Now you must get to the third stage. A couple of werewolves will enter this cave. Now werewolf hunters go hunt those beasts down."

"How many are there?" Said Gildor.

"There are about two hundred of them."

"I never hunted that much in my life," said Gildor.

"Well, I guess you should start hunting now, Gildor."

Gildor entered the underground forest. Within a couple of hours, Gildor was gone.

"Where did he go?" Sander asked.

"That is not of your concern," said the great dragon. "Now, Sir Kevin Gladstone. You need to learn how to activate that sword. Those words have the power of light. The sword you wield can give you power on the battlefield." The great dragon Myra summoned four golems on the grassland. "Go fight those golems." The great dragon opened a small cave, and said, "Go to Jake."

When Jake entered the small cave, he saw ancient blacksmith equipment. Jake was shocked by the blacksmith equipment.

"How did you do?"

"You're not the first young legendary blacksmith I have come across with."

"But how am I going to get materials?"

The great dragon opened another cave next to the blacksmith equipment. "This is a cave of all materials in the world. But you must be careful of some materials. You four guards of Sir Kevin, you can help the blacksmith. Now carry on your duties and train. Jake, your training is to make Kevin, Sander, and Kevin's guards, the armor they can use."

"How can I do that?"

"You researched the materials. Just tell them what ores they need to find. Now Sander, follow me back to my hibernating place." The great dragon then left the giant cave with Sander to go back to the hibernating place. "Now, the sword you're about to wield is powerful. It can take control of you. But you are lucky that you have Riker. Riker can help you with the sword. Now, the sword you see up there is a copy. It's a fake. I made it for anyone stupid enough to come into my lair. The real one is right over there." The great dragon Myra then opened a cave on the wall. Sander walked over to the sword before being stopped by Myra's tail. "Riker, I know you hear me. You have not seen Soul Absorber in one thousand years. So, be careful what you are going to do. Sander trusts Riker for this mission. Sander, you will be with that sword's mind for seven days. Try and make sure you don't die." The great dragon Myra then removed her tail out of the way to let Sander get the sword.

"Wait, what do you mean don't die?" Said Sander with a confused face.

"I thought you read the book," said the great dragon, Myra.

"Sander, you're going to be fine you have me," Riker said in Sander's head. "I guess I'm ready," said Sander. Sander then went to the sword and interacted with it. When Sander interacted with the sword Sander fell to the ground.

"Hmm, that will keep him busy." The great dragon Myra then walked back to the giant cave and watched what the group was doing. "So Jake, have you figured what armor you're going for," said the great dragon, Myra.

Jake shook his head yes. "I'm going to have Sander with silver mixed with red crystals. It will be red crystal silver then mix the red crystal silver with black iron. Then I'm going to have Kevin's guards have emerald steel armor. Sir Kevin will have sapphire steel mixed with iron. I will have silver mixed with iron." Jake tried to explain to the great dragon what he said about the materials.

"I already know what you mean," said the great dragon, Myra. I have been in this world for four hundred thousand years. Now, all you gotta do is make it perfect." The great dragon Myra went to check on Kevin. As when the great dragon Myra was watching, Kevin struggled to activate the sword. The great dragon, Myra then told the golems to stop. "Kevin, you're trying too much. Feel the sword. Feel as you and the sword are one. Once you feel as if you and the sword are one then you will have the sword activated. You're just trying to force it out. Now, keep practicing." The great dragon then went back to her hibernating place and closed her eyes. When the great dragon Myra sat down and closed her eyes in her hibernating place, she saw Gildor running. She then telepathically talked to Gildor.

"Do you need my guidance?" She said in Gildor's mind.

Gildor then told her no. She then let Gildor hunt the werewolves as she watched him fight the wolves. He saw three werewolves coming from the right side. Gildor then began to kill the werewolves. The great dragon, Myra then watched Gildor get ripped to shreds by a werewolf. The great dragon, Myra then opened her eyes. She continued to watch the young heroes train to their full potential. While Sander was knocked out in the sword's mind.

"Where are we?" Said, Sander. Riker showed his true form in the soul Absorber's head.

"We're both here, Sander. We are in the Soul Absorber."

"What do we do, Riker?"

"Sander, it's simple why we are here. We're being tested. The Soul Absorber must deem us worthy to wield his power. Here time is different. We will be here for seven years. But out in the real world, we will be knocked out for seven days. Seven days for this test. As all the others have their potential to fill, we have our mission and potential."

Riker turned around and saw a stairway up. Sander then tried to smell the area of a way out. "Sander, there is no way out. We can hear but there is no smell. After all, we are in a mental state. Let's go up these stairs, Sander. Get our first quest to deem us worthy."

Sander then followed Riker up the stairs to the first quest. When Riker and Sander were in their minds, Jake was finding a way to perfect his armor skills. Jake had found an emerald crystal and sapphire crystal and began to melt the crystals separately in a different metal bowl. Sir Kevin's guards began to keep mining in the cave next to the forge. Jake and the guards tried to make good armor for the team. Kevin was trying to master the way of the angel sword. Kevin sliced and cut the Golems but the Golems kept coming back.

"Work, you damn sword," said, Kevin. "Why aren't you working? You're supposed to be giving light. Not wasting my damn time."

Kevin forced the sword to give him power. As in the forest next to the grasslands, Gildor woke up from his death and began to pick up his giant sword to continue his hunt. Gildor tracked the wolves' footprints.

As Gildor was tracking, he felt as if he had gotten more power and was used to his sensing power where he could track the sense of the werewolves. Gildor saw from his tracking sense he was surrounded by werewolves. Gildor then chose another werewolf and began to hunt it down. He slashed and killed every werewolf he saw. As Gildor fought and hunted, knowing it was training, he continued to kill anyone that hit him. The great dragon, Myra sadly wept as she wanted to find her son. The great dragon thought of Colinborn. She sat and looked down with water in her eyes. She lay down and thought of her son, weeping quietly.

"Colinborn, why don't you come to visit me? The young heroes would love to need you right now."

The great dragon then stayed quiet.

Chapter 17

The New Journey

Four days passed in the dragon's cave. The heroes were still training to reach their full potential while Sander and Riker were still stuck inside the worlds of their minds. Gildor was still trying to kill the werewolves inside the forest. Kevin was still trying to activate his sword. And Jake was still trying to find the materials to perfect the armor. The great dragon was still thinking of Colinborn while she was watching them in her head. She then thought of a good idea for Kevin. She got up from her hibernating spot and walked to the giant cave. She looked at Kevin as he was tired and sat down. She then made illusion magic of the one he held dear to his heart.

"Help me," said the illusion of Kevin's love.

The golems then go for the illusion of Kevin's love.

"How are you here?" Kevin was stuck on decisions. Kevin shook as he felt he couldn't do anything. There were goosebumps on his body. But as Kevin was shaking he finally got up, not knowing what to do. He ran towards the golem who was picking up the sword and slashed everything he got on the golem standing in his way. The golem then melted in front of him. He then ran to the next golem without a mind to save the person. When he ran, he saw a light coming from the sword. When he struck the golem, the golem then melted into the dirt. The illusion then faded away.

The great dragon spoke to Kevin, "I knew it. You were struggling with a sword because you were trying to force it. When you should have been thinking of the lives that are at stake. You are a noble young man, Kevin Gladstone. You put yourself in front of other people. You are the man who acts as a shield when people are in danger. That's why the sword reacts. It reacts to who you are. Not of what the picture looks like. Not as a knight. As a man who puts people first instead of his own. You have completed your training. But if you wish to train more with the sword you have, I will not mind. Just remember your father, your mother, and your younger brother are counting on you. People in your house and land are counting on you. When Sander disappeared, the kingdom was at war. The people are scared. There is no longer peace when Fergus is on the throne. That's why you went out to find answers to dethrone him, but you have passed your test to be ready. A gift from me to you. This will represent that you have met a higher power and succeeded in the test I gave you." The great dragon, Myra then gave Sir Kevin of House Gladstone a stroke of pure white hair. Kevin then started to train more with the sword to get used to it. The great dragon, Myra went back to the hibernating spot to watch Sander's test. When she arrived, she closed her eyes to see if he was doing his test. As Riker and Sander were in the mind of the Soul Absorber. They were still doing the test.

"Hey Riker, we walked upstairs. We went through a forest. Where are we going now? What test even is this?"

"Patience. The Soul Absorber has not seen me for one thousand years and not just that just like you have a bad story in your life, the Soul Absorber has one too. We will talk later about his story. Let's keep moving."

The great dragon then stopped watching Riker and Sander. She began to telepathically talk to Colinborn from afar asking him for help. "Colinborn, I won't protect him when they die. I need you to watch them. After Galatin is dead, come and see me. It's been a while." Two days passed in the cave. The great dragon waited as she heard nothing from Colinborn. The great dragon went to the large training cave for the heroes. When she arrived back at the cave, she saw Sir Kevin training harder with the sword. She then watched Gildor when she closed her eyes. She watched Gildor reach his final power. Gildor ran into the forest. When Gildor reached deeper into the forest, he sensed fifty werewolves behind him.

Gildor stopped and turned around. "I'm not running anymore. I will stand and fight. Let them hunt me. I will stand my ground." Gildor got a flashback when his uncle taught him to stand his ground. Gildor then pictured the faces of the ones he lost and loved.

He pictured his uncle's body from coming back from a war. He pictured his father sending him to his first werewolf hunt. He pictured his brother and mother. He pictured the people who died at the hands of werewolves. "Enough running. I will stand my ground and I will just head for them." Gildor waited as the werewolves came to him. He heard the growls from a mile away. He sensed the ground shaking as the wolves ran at him. He felt the wind blowing through his ears. He took one breath of air. He blew out and got ready to attack the wolves.

Within those seconds, he closed his eyes and took another deep breath. He then opened his eyes, what was once a dark forest, was now a clear forest. He saw the wolves in the dark coming at him. Fifty werewolves were coming at him, the first wolf that came in contact got a striking blow through the head. And after the first, he just swung more and more until all of the werewolves were dead.

The great dragon, Myra then started to seek her eyes in Sander's mindset with the Soul Absorber. Sander and Riker then saw a cave inside the Soul Absorber's mind.

"Sander, here is the test. It's not of our mind, it's of his."

"What's this cave to me?" Riker then explained to Sanders the meaning of the cave. "Sander, this cave means who the Soul Absorber came from. From its creators and its brothers. You will find out his story. Let's go, Sander." Sander and Riker walked into the cave. When Sander and Riker entered the cave, they saw a giant forge in the cave. Sander saw two shadows doing magic.

"What are they doing?"

"Just watch," Riker said. "Stop asking me questions and watch."

"Wait, Riker, do you smell that? It smells like fire. But it also smells like nature as well." Sander and Riker saw the two shadows create thirteen swords with fire and iron. Sander and Riker saw nature magic enter into each one of the swords. The swords then raised, levitating above the ground. The two shadows appeared to be happy. Sander then walked around the forge looking at the shadows and the thirteen swords. They were amazing, and they were alive. Sander then saw five white beings come and look as if they were going to attack the shadows. The five white beings attacked the two shadows. Sander and Riker watched as the two shadows were murdered in cold blood. The thirteen swords began to fight back. Sander then saw the thirteen swords fight the five beings. Sander and Riker both watched the five beings destroy the swords with strong blows. A sword flew across the forge, falling underneath a table. Riker and Sander then continued to see the five beings murder and destroy the sword. When all swords were destroyed, the five beings then destroyed the forge and burned everything to the ground. The five beings then walked out of the cave, never to be seen again.

"Riker, what was that?"

"It's the sword's story."

"How is the sword here if all were destroyed?"

"Not all of the swords are destroyed." Sander saw the sword underneath the table. The sword looked to be alive and dead at the same time. Riker and Sander saw the cave crumble to pieces. Sander and Riker woke up in an empty black void.

"I see you have seen my story."

"Who said that?" Said Sander.

"Sander, that's Soul Absorber. He is talking to us."

"I have been in the cave of Myra for one thousand years. After being taken away from Riker. But I already know why Riker is here. But why are you here? Human, you may speak for yourself."

Sander then began to speak. "I am here because Riker needs you in these times, and I need Riker's full power to destroy and get revenge on my brother, Fergus Helmglade. But there were some complications. When I got to my brother, he wasn't the same. Riker saw another being inside a Fergus. So, I asked Riker who he is."

The sword then asked Riker who Sander was talking about. "Riker, tell me what he means. I do not understand humans."

"Soul Absorber, he is talking about my lover's brother. The man who commands the celestial race. And ordered your brothers and creators dead. Galatin, he is talking about Galatin."

The sword spoke again, "I'm sorry, I never got your name. What is your name, human?" Said the Soul Absorber.

"The name is Sander Helmglade. But you can call me Sander."

"Sander, you and Riker are telling me that your brother, Fergus has Galatin inside of him and you and Riker need my power to kill Galatin and killing Galatin will also kill your brother, Fergus."

"Yeah, to sum it up, that's setting it all up."

"Sander, you, me, and Riker are going to be the best of friends. Any enemy of Galatin is a friend of mine. Riker, you will get my power back, and Sander, I'm guessing you're taking the wheel as well. I will give you my power. And Galatin and all celestials will fall by me." The sword then gave his energy to Riker and Sander. They saw a golden energy flow around him.

"Now, awake, Sander." Sander woke up from the Soul Absorber's mind. Sander then got up and grabbed the sword. "I feel nothing," said Sander.

Riker talked in Sander's head. "It enhances our super speed. Our superstrength and our powers."

"Hello, Sander," said the Soul Absorber.

"What the hell?" Sander said.

"Oh, right, Sander, you know how I am in your head."

"Well, he is now in your head as well. So, now it's me and Soul absorber along with you. Ok good now since we're done with our test let's go check on Jake and see what he is doing."

"Glad you're awake," said the great dragon, Myra. "I see now that you have survived. If you and the Soul Absorber were not to agree, you were to fight him. And if you were to lose, you would have died. But I'm happy you survived. But to tell you the truth, Sander. There was another path that you would have to fight the Soul Absorber. But now since you passed, it's the wait on Gildor." The great dragon Myra entered the giant cave with the grasslands and forest. Sander followed the great dragon Myra to see if anyone was done with their training. When Sander and the great dragon entered the cave, Sander saw Kevin sitting down.

"Kevin, are you done with the training?"

"No way, Sander. Where have you been?" Sander and Kevin talked about their training.

"Kevin, I have been in a soul's mind for six days. It would have been seven if I had to fight him. But I am happy that it was six. But now since I have the sword, Riker said our power is enhanced. After the cave, we move to the second step of our journey. But I will tell you that when we are all done with our training. So Kevin, how is your sword? Did it work?"

Kevin then told him what he experienced in the past days, "My sword is a celestial blade, so for days, I thought I had to force it to work. But the great dragon, Myra used an illusion spell. And I saw Kayla Garland. And without a thought, I rushed in, picked up the sword, and started to try and save her. The sword does not react if I am a knight, or if I am a noble. It reacts not to what I look like, but it reacts to who I am. To fight with a celestial blade, you must fight with your true self. Of who you are. But yeah, that's what happened in my training. Now, I'm just waiting for Gildor and Jake to be done with it."

Sander then told Kevin to check on Jake. "That's a good idea, Sander." Sander and Kevin went inside the forge to check on Jake.

When they entered inside the cave forge, they see Jake making his sixth armor.

"Good, Kevin, you're here." Jake picked up the armor and gave Sir Kevin the sapphire steel armor mixed with iron. Sir Kevin went to find a safe place to wear his new armor. Jake then finished up Sander's armor. Jake then put the armor in a water spot, it released steam from the heated armor and smoke filled the room.

"Sander, when that armor cools down, you can wear this crystal silver mixed with black iron. Now, if you don't mind I need to make my armor. Sander, may you please leave the forge." Sander left the forge to wait and talk to Riker and the Soul Absorber. As Sander left the forge, Kevin came out with his sapphire armor. Kevin to patiently waited for Jake's armor to be complete. While he was waiting, he thought of Kayla Garland. The day had passed. Gildor had not come from the forest. Sander was still talking to Riker and the Soul Absorber. Sir Kevin was still thinking about Kayla Garland. And Jake was finishing up with his new armor.

"Sander, come here, I need you."

Sander walked into the cave forge and looked at the red-crystal armor he was waiting for. "Alright, Sander, go put that armor on." Sander grabbed the armor and went to a private place to get his armor on. As Sander is getting ready with his armor, the guards started to get their new armor on. Jake then grabbed his new armor and got it on. While the team was suiting up with their new gear and armor, the great dragon, Myra heard a voice back from her head. She started to talk telepathically to him.

"You were calling for me, mother," said the voice.

"Colinborn, you finally talked back. I am happy to know my son is alive," said the great dragon, Myra.

"I have just been sleeping for five hundred years," said Colinborn. "I have also met my father. You were right about him. He is an idiot. But hey, I can't do anything to change that. Ever since the war, I have been exploring. It looks like the dragons don't need a protector. So, I heard your voice. And I was wondering if I was to talk to you or not. But if you were to call out to me asking for help, it must be important. So why did you call out to me, mother? I'm in Finsera with Aunt Gab."

The great dragon, Myra talked to her son, "My son, I have missed you for a thousand years. Hearing your voice makes me happy. I call out to you for help. Some new young heroes are willing to stop Galatin. I'm asking if you want to join these young heroes to help them stop Galatin. But here's the thing, Riker is with them. What do you say, my son?"

Colinborn replied, "Mother, I do not like Riker. And I don't like Galatin either. But if I had to choose, Riker changed and fell in love. Galatin took that away from him. If I have to choose, Galatin is a tyrant. I'm coming home to my mother. But it will take me a month to fly there. Looks like I'm coming home to my mother. Where do you think the heroes are going?"

The great dragon, Myra then told Colinborn where their next destination would be. "To attack humans, you need an army. Colinborn is going to Orcuhan to gather an army. Alright, mother, I'm coming home to stop Galatin on this world. And mother, after this is over, I'm coming back to you. I have missed you for a long time." The great dragon, Myra and Colinborn said their goodbyes. The great dragon, Myra told the group they were ready for their new journey. The group came out with their new armor. Sander had red crystal-like armor with black iron. The guards came out with emerald-like armor. Sir Kevin with his blue sapphire armor. Jake came out with silver and iron armor mixed.

"It looks like your group is ready for the journey ahead of you."

"Yes, we were just missing Gildor," said Kevin. As Kevin said that, Gildor walked out of the forest.

Everyone started to look at Gildor. "Gildor, you're alive," said Kevin.

"Guys, look at his eyes," said Jake.

Gildor had blood all over his body. His black armor was tainted with blood. And his eyes were as grey as silver. Gildor then walked to the group. "I'm ready for the journey ahead of me."

"Gildor, what happened to the werewolves?" Said Kevin.

"I killed them all, every last one of them. And I acquired my third power."

"What's your third power?" Asked Jake.

"My third power is night vision. I can now see like a bat."

"Now, what are we waiting for?"

"We're waiting for where we need to go next." The group then looked at Sander. Sander asked Riker where they needed to go next. Riker told Sander that they needed to go to Orcuhan to get an army. The group asked what was Orcuhan.

The great dragon, Myra told the group, "Orcuhan is a land of orcs. The orcs are of barbarians state-like matter. There are about eight to ten feet tall. Every clan has a chieftain. And the man who rules over the land is not a king. They call it a warlord. The land is not like the elves or humans. Or like the dwarfs. So, be careful. And after you leave the cave, you will have to listen to Riker. As he knows where the land is at. Now if Riker goes dormant in Sander's head, then here is a map. The great dragon, Myra then magically makes paper and makes a map to Orcuhan. The great dragon Myra makes the places onto Orcuhan. Now, prepare to go on the new journey. But wait." The great dragon Myra used magic to take the blood out of Gildor's black leather armor. "Now, you are ready." The great dragon Myra then opened up the exist of the cave. She walked to the hibernating place. The group began to leave the cave of the great dragon. The group walked to the exit of the cave. As the group was walking out, the great dragon, Myra turned back into a giant marble boulder and then the light disappeared in the cave.

The group walked to the near top of the cave to see the grass, trees and some nature underneath the mountain. The group saw a baby golden dragon walking around.

"Come on guys, we need to get going." The group then walked out of the cave. When the group reached the exit of the great dragon, Myra's cave, a paper flew to Gildor's feet. Gildor picked up the paper, it was a note from Gildor's vampire hunter friend. Gildor then read the note out loud to the group.

Note: Gildor I know this is an odd time. You're probably hunting some werewolves. But I need you. There is a coven of vampires in this castle. The stories call it a Black Brick Castle. But the vampires and the castle are not the problems. The problem is they have a pack of werewolves patrolling the castle. I don't know how they have those werewolves patrolling but that's why I came asking for you for help.

Sincerely, your great friend Raymond.

"Guys, we need to help my friend."

"But we have to go to Orcuhan," said Sander.

"Wait, what direction do we need to go right now?" Said Gildor.

"We need to go north."

"Good because of the Black Brick castle is in the north. If we help him maybe he might join the fight against Fergus." The group then agreed with Gildor.

"Sander, he's right, the more people, the better."

"Alright, fine," said Sander. "Let's go help your friend."

The group then set off north to castle Black Brick to help Gildor's friend.

Chapter 18

The Town of Inthra

A dreadful week had passed as Sander and the group headed north towards the town of Inthra. Sander, Jake, Sir Kevin, and Sir Kevin's four guards did not know much about the town of Inthra or why it was created by a faction. Gildor stopped and told the group what the town of Inthra was about.

"Guys, the town of Inthra is not a normal town in the land of Luna or Elmus. It is what they call a neutral ground where there are no kings or queens who rule this land. It's run by a governor, and it is turning into a city. I want you guys to be careful. In the tavern, there are lots of strange men and bounty hunters. So, you guys with bounties on your heads beware. And anyone who wants to get their hands on gold would definitely go along with that. The guards there are highly trained and have about twenty ships ready for fleet combat. So, please do not do anything stupid."

Gildor sensed wolves. "They are nearby, but they are normal wolves, not werewolves. Let's go hunt them! There are about six of them. Also, I heard of the Black Brick Castle's vampires before and their coven is strong. Raymond knows I will be here waiting for those vampires."

As Gildor was talking, Riker was telling Sander he sensed a strange thing that he hadn't felt in a thousand years. "Sander, there is a strange sense I am feeling but we need to get closer to the town to figure it out. Keep an eye out for that."

Gildor then told the group to go hunt for a pack of wolves. The group went and found a den of wolves. Gildor led them to the den as he tested his new sense of power. When Gildor arrived at the den, he saw six wolves.

"I was right," said Gildor.

"How did you know it was six wolves?" Said Jake with silver armor mixed with iron.

Gildor explained to the group and Jake that he knew because of his werewolf hunting. "It's because of wolves. You see, I sense danger but this danger felt a little more passive than the others. So, I guess when I'm being hunted by werewolves the sensing power of these wolves doesn't branch off that much. So, that's how I know it's wolves."

"Guys, I know this is a good thing to explain but I think we need to fight those," said Sander, worried.

"Sander, relax, they're in their cave," said Gildor. Gildor turned around to see wolves looking at him. The group then pulled out their weapons and attacked the wolves as the wolves attacked them back. After a two-hour battle against wolves, the group killed the wolves.

"Alright now, what do we do?" Said Jake.

"Have you not been hunting before?' It's simple," said, Kevin. Kevin and Gildor began to cut the meat out of the wolves and lay them on their empty backpack. "We can sell half of the meat we got for the coin. That could give us around five hundred silver coins. But if we skin the pelts we can use these pelts to sell for gold coins. Which is a thousand silver each. So, we can get three coins each. So, I would say we get about, maybe eight to ten gold coins. So, let's get to work."

"Kevin, I want you to get the meat and I will skin the wolves." Kevin and his guards began to get the meat from the wolves as Gildor began to skin the wolves. After another hour, Sir Kevin had two and a half backpacks full of wolf meat. Gildor had all perfectly skinned six wolf pelts with him.

"Alright now, let's go to the tavern to sell the meat. And let's go to the leatherwork to sell the pelts."

The group then set off to the town of Inthra, where they were stopped by the guards. "Halt, who dare enters the town of Inthra." The guards then stopped and recognized Gildor. "Gildor, we did not know it was you. I am sorry. And who are these folks?" Gildor then told the guards these were his friends. "Oh sorry, Gildor, we will let you pass it's just vampires and werewolves have been seen here in this town." Gildor then said, "Listen, Raymond told me that vampires are somehow working with werewolves so that's why I am here to help Raymond."

The guards understood and let Gildor and his friends into the town. When the group entered the town, it was a beautiful sight to see. They saw the bright blue sky and the smoke coming from the blacksmith. They saw the townsfolk wondering and the kids playing in the fields.

"It's a good town," Kevin said. "It reminds me of Luna when Sander stole bread from the bakery and almost got killed by his dad."

"Hey shut up, we don't want to speak of that," said Sander. The town was as happy as a fly.

"Wait, how are they happy if there are werewolves outside?" Said Jake.

Gildor then told the group the guards were not werewolf hunters but they had a division that handled werewolf attacks and that they also had a division that handled vampire attacks as well. So, the town was very safe. Gildor then told the group to split into two groups. Sander, Kevin, and his guards decided to go to the tavern to sell the meat and get a drink. Gildor then went with Jake to the leatherwork to sell the pelts. Sander, Kevin, and Kevin's guards decided to walk into the tavern. When they walked into the tavern, they saw a lot of shady people inside the tavern. It was like the atmosphere changed when they entered the tavern.

The barkeep asked them, "What do you guys need?" Sander, Kevin, and his guards walked to the barkeep and sat at a table. "Hey, we heard you like to take meat." Kevin gave him a backpack full of wolf meat. "This is wolf meat we got earlier. It's fresh and ready to be cooked." The barkeep then counted and felt the pounds of the meat and gave Sander, Kevin, and his guard a full five hundred silver. "Would you like a drink?" Said the barkeep. The group said yes and they all decided to have one nice good drink. Sander Kevin and Kevin's guards were having a drink while Gildor and Jake found the leatherworking area. Gildor walked to the leatherworking where he would like to sell you pelts.

The leatherworker then asked, "What pelts?"

As soon as the leatherworker looked at the Gildor, he said, "No way, Gildor, the black leather werewolf hunter. What do you have for me this time?"

Gildor then showed him wolf pelts. "Ah yes, I would like to give you three gold pieces for each and one of those." Gildor gave him the six wolf pelts.

The leatherworker gave Gildor eighteen gold pieces. Gildor and Jake started to walk away until they were told to stop by the leatherworker. "Wait. I want to ask you something here." Gildor and Jake walked inside. As the leatherworker closed the door, he then asked Gildor if there was any way he could get him five werewolf pelts.

"How am I going to do that, leatherworker? Most werewolves are turned into werewolves. You're asking me to kill five purebloods," said Gildor. "I will try and want it for myself."

The leatherworker said, "I will give twenty pieces of gold to each werewolf pelt." Gildor instantly took up the task as if he completed it he got one hundred gold pieces. Gildor and Jake walked out and headed to the tavern to go see the group.

"Let's go celebrate," said Gildor. Jake and Gildor smiled as they walked to the tavern. When Jake and Gildor walked into the tavern, they saw Kevin with five hundred silver.

"Hey, bartender, can me and my friends get a good meal, please?"

The bartender said, "Yes, Gildor."

"Wow, Gildor, you're a regular here. Half of the town knows you," said Jake. "When we were at the leatherworker even that guy knew him."

Gildor then told them why they knew him. "Listen, the reason why they know me is because, at the age of fifteen, I was sent into werewolf hunting. When I left my father two years later, I went to this place, lived here for a year, and did some things now and then. That's why the town knows me."

The bartender then gave Gildor and his friend the meal to eat. The bartender then started to talk to Gildor. "So Gildor, you were here because Raymond probably called you. There are werewolves in Black Brick Castle. I'm guessing the vampires are controlling them." Gildor then asked what werewolves they were.

"I don't know what werewolves they are." Gildor's group ate the food as they never ate it in their mouths. They said these werewolves blended into the trees as they were camouflaged with the green. There was no way he escaped that prison.

Riker said in Sander's head, "Hey, Sander keep quiet but when we get out of this, I need to speak to Gildor with your voice." Sander and Riker talked in their heads.

"But Riker, what is it?"

Riker told Sander what he was talking about. "Listen to werewolves, vampires, and dark sirens. I have created all of them for the celestial and demon war. But the werewolves were supposed to be cannon fighters until we figured they could turn things. Then we have eight original werewolves. Long story short. We kept three locked away and these three ones that we locked away are the strongest. The other five escaped and now it's the world's problem."

Sander then screamed in his head. "You created those things."

"Yes," said Riker. "And now I'm going to tell Gildor everything I know. Ok but for right now we need to hear what the bartender has to say."

"So yeah, the guys couldn't even see the werewolves in the forest. So, we're hoping you can kill those werewolves. It must be brown werewolves," said Gildor. "Don't worry, I will settle the wolves down." Gildor then continued to eat his food as he knew what to do with brown werewolves. The barkeep stopped talking to Gildor and continued to do his job. The group talked about the brown werewolves to Gildor expecting Gildor to know more about them and see what they could do.

"Alright, best I say the brown werewolves are smarter than the black werewolves. You see the black werewolves rip anything apart and leave one alive. But the brown werewolves make sure there is no escape. And then they choose randomly. But they at least leave five alive and kill the rest. The brown werewolves are bigger than the black werewolves. So, if it's them, we got to play smarter than an animal and human mind. We need to be prepared for them. Because by the sound of it, they got a big pack."

Sander told Gildor later that he needed to talk to him. "What do you need to talk to me about it?"

"Not now, later maybe by the lake or in my room in the tavern." As Sander and Gildor were talking, a strange man appeared, carrying two longswords on his back, holding orange leather armor, and a ring with a skull with fangs with a reaper's mark next to it on his hand.

Sander thought to himself. "He has the same ring as Gildor but with a skull with fangs. Who is he?" Sander said in his mind. Gildor turned around to see his friend, Gildor at the door. The strange man sat down and greeted Gildor.

"Who are you? Kevin asked.

"Guys, this is the man I have been talking about or seeing. This is Raymond. He is a vampire hunter. So, Raymond what do you say about the journey?"

Raymond decided to explain his story of a journey. "Well, I walk to Black Brick Castle. You know what people call the Black Brick Castle. And I heard rumors of a vampire coven being there. So, I decided to try and check inside. Until I see man turning into wolves. But these weren't brown wolves. Or black or white or the ones we see commonly. These were green werewolves. So that's why I found the quickest mage and sent a message to you."

Gildor then looked at Raymond. "Do you know what they are?"

As Gildor was about to speak, Riker took control over Sander's body. "Gildor, listen to me, I know who is the original werewolves and I know everything about vampires and werewolves. But I will explain to you upstairs about the green werewolves. But they're mostly used and called the forest wolves. Back in my time. I say we go now to see the castle."

"That's a good idea," Raymond said. "But I need to ask what are you?"

Riker told Raymond, "He's a human." As everyone stayed quiet for the lie.

Gildor said he was going to rest at the inn and they should go in the morning. Sander then took over the body. The group then grabbed a piece of silver to each get themselves a room. The group went up but Sander stayed to keep his eye on a girl. Sander looked at her and made sure he did not show it. A girl with purple and white hair. Her body was as sexy as a princess. She sang to the tavern and the people like an angel. Sander felt happy when she sang.

Chapter 19

The Strange Women in Tavern

Sander continued to hear the strange girl sing. Sander saw another man leaning on the wall smiling at her singing. He carried a black and sapphire-looking spear. "That's a strange spear," Sander said in his head. Sander then stopped looking at him and looked at the singer. When she sang, he seemed to be at peace. He felt as if he was a child playing with his friends in Luna on how to become knights of Luna. When the singer stopped, Sander got emotional. The singer then walked up to the spearman and decided to leave. They quickly ran out of the tavern and into the fields. Sander quickly followed as it looked suspicious. When he got to the fields near the lake, he saw the two folks were gone. Like they just disappeared.

"Sander, I've felt this presence before. It feels as if there is dark magic or a feeling I felt during the war. It must be my powers acting up. Sander get some sleep I may not sleep. But you're still human. Your soul is still human. So, let's go."

As Sander was leaving, he felt as if someone was watching him. Sander went to his room in the tavern. He saw Gildor waiting for him.

"Alright Sander, spill. Let Riker talk to me." Riker took control.

"Alright, I'm going to tell you about a time when we the demons were being pushed. This was when we owned twenty-five percent of Sinia. We were almost out to die. So, I saw humans willing to risk themselves to take back their land. There were eight tribes. So I decided to give the eight tribes a primary color of hair. I made it so to have man turn to beast. To be used as cannon fighters in the war against the celestials."

"But wait," Gildor thought of what Riker said. "You said there were eight tribes. But there are five species of werewolves. What do you mean there are eight tribes?"

"Gildor, you have been hunting species of five werewolves. But there are actually eight werewolf species. Lucky, we helped put away the red, green, and blue werewolves. The red werewolves were the most aggressive ones. The blue werewolves were mostly for defensive. The green werewolves were used in the trees and forest as camouflage. The sand werewolves were for the dessert. The black werewolves were for night attacks. The brown werewolves were for dirt road attacks. The white werewolves were for snow attacks. And the grey was for mountains. We gained fifty percent of Sinia for that attack. The werewolves gave us an advantage. But we had to store the alphas away. They were too dangerous for humanity. The eight stayed in prison as the rest started to do their job for us. I'm sorry, Gildor but the green werewolves are one of the smartest and stealthies in the green forest or anywhere. And there is one of the three werewolf species that can control their real form. So, Gildor, I say we need to be careful on this journey."

Gildor looked at Riker in anger. "So, it's your fault that the beasts are terrorizing the folks. It's your fault that I have to kill them and not fall in love. It's your fault I have to watch people die." Gildor then walked out angrily and went to his room.

Riker let Sander take control. Riker went dormant as he felt the guilt of making monsters. Sander went to bed to sleep and dreamt of him falling off the cliff as Fergus pushed him. Sander dreamt of darker moments. He dreamt of the moments of his father saying to him and lecturing to be king of Luna. Sander woke from his nightmare to see it was grey outside. Knowing the sun was about to come up, Sander then walked downstairs to the tavern. He told the bartender to get him breakfast. Sander then sat and waited patiently for the breakfast. As Sander was waiting, he heard footsteps coming down the stairs. He saw Gildor. Gildor grabbed a chair and sat next to Sander. They both started to talk about their dreams.

"Sander, I don't know, what's going on but I dreamt of a giant wolf. The size of a giant. It was black with red eyes. And claws ready to destroy anything in their path. You think it's one of Riker's creations?" Sander nodded yes.

Sander drank a sip of his water and talked about the dream he had. "Gildor, it was not a dream but it was. It felt as if I was in my own memory space. Watching me fall into the dark pit. Watching my father talk to me to be king. It was a nightmare. Because it made me angry. The memories of my father and me." As Sander was talking, the strange woman came in and said hello to the innkeeper. Sander then turned his head to see the strange girl and the man with the spear again. As Gildor was trying to get Sander's attention, Sander felt an emotional connection with the strange girl.

"Hey Sander," said Gildor. Gildor snapped his figures at Sander. Sander then looked back at Gildor. "Don't you dare use that prince's charms. You know we're going to be heading out soon. When everyone wakes up, we go. So, don't you dare use your charms. We're leaving soon."

Sander told Gildor to relax. "I'm only going to go meet her and greet her. Just in case we come back I want to see her again. So, relax Gildor, it's not like I'm trying to have sex with her."

Gildor looked at Sander as if he was a stupid-minded idiot. "Alright, Sander, you do you. I will continue to eat. And hey are you going to eat your breakfast?"

"No," said Sander.

Gildor then grabbed Sander's plate and began eating as Gildor basically stole his plate.

Sander went up to go ask the strange girl her name, "Hello," said Sander, "What is your name?"

The strange girl with the purple and white hair turned around. "Oh hello. The name is Duvessa."

As he was talking to her, he looked on his left shoulder to see a man with an angry face looking at him. "Um, is he your boyfriend or are you wedded to him or something?"

She looked at her friend. "Oh no, that's my brother."

He then walked to Sander and said, "Hi I'm Darius." He then walked away and leaned on the wall and it looked as if he was observing Duvessa. "Hey, I know you may not know me and I looked to be a strange man. But your singing helped me look at the old strange ways of my family. But it was the happy moments. Not the bad moments. You have a gift, why don't you go to the kingdoms and sing for the kings and stuff? You will make really good money doing that."

She smiled at him. "But hey, let me show you something, I practiced the art of magic. Would you like to see a trick?" She then told Sander yes. When Sander said fake words and summoned fire from his hand. Darius grabbed his spear and pointed it to Sander's neck.

"Step back from my sister," he said. Sander slowly backed away from his sister and went back to go sit with Gildor.

As he sat down, Gildor laughed at Sander. "Wow, you totally scored that one."

"No, it's just Gildor she has a way of singing to men, I feel it."

As Sander was talking about her, Riker came to his mind. "Hey, Sander, I know why I feel the strange presence. It's been a while but I believe the magic is dark sirens. I made them as well. But sirens lead men with a song then they kill them. But since she is well known here we need to catch her off guard. But you also need to watch out. They can control water. All of them can. It's in their blood. So be careful now, if you don't mind, I'ma go dormant now. Also, when you hold the sword, Soul Absorber comes into your head, he's not in your head right now. But just to point that out there. You're not in any danger so whatever." Riker went dormant in Sander's mind. Sander in his head thought to Riker, "What the fuck did you just leave me for?"

Sander got up to walk to the lake. Sander sat by the lake looking at the water, trying to recognize that humans, elves, and dwarfs were not the only race in Sinia. He thought of why there were more races. And why Luna did not give the kids a reason for why there are more races and factions out there. As Sander was thinking by the lake, Gildor was eating breakfast as another one of the groups walked downstairs. Jake walked downstairs, he came and asked Gildor questions about werewolves and how he could be a werewolf hunter. Gildor kindly told Jake he could not because he needed the mark of the reaper and the ring of the wolf's skull. "I'm sorry, Jake but you cannot be a werewolf hunter."

Jake tries to convince Gildor. As he was convinced, Sander was still at the lake looking at the water from afar. He then saw Duvessa and Darius going into the water and disappearing. "What the hell?" Said Sander. "Who are they really?" Sander kept to himself as he walked to the tavern with his suspicion of Duvessa and Darius. As Sander went upstairs to talk to Riker privately, Kevin and the group came downstairs to get breakfast and sat down and chatted with Gildor. The group talked to Gildor about what was to do with the brown werewolves. Gildor put down his cup and told the truth to the group about Riker's creation of the werewolves. When the group realized it was all Riker's fault for making the werewolves, the group fell silent.

Kevin decided to give them an open eye." Look, I know Riker has done a lot of things in the past. But you also got to know the good things. That he cares for us even though he does not show it. If he wanted us dead, he would have not told us about this werewolf stuff. And if he really wanted us dead he could have just burned us alive in pain. What I'm trying to say is, we all have done bad things in the past. So. why don't we give him another chance?"

The group then agreed with Kevin and decided to go up to Sander's room. "Alright listen, if we're gonna forgive him, he needs to tell us what else he created that we're going after."

The group knocked as Sander let them in. The group then crowded around Sander. "Alright, Sander was here to talk to Riker about his creation." Sander then let Riker take control as everyone settled down.

"So, Gildor, I'm guessing you told them," said Riker. Gildor nodded at Riker as he began to speak.

"Alright, Riker, they want to know everything you created that we might face right now."

Riker then decided to sit down as he was about to speak. "You might want to sit down for this."

As Riker was about to speak Raymond walked through the door. "I heard what Gildor said downstairs. I have questions."

Riker told everyone to at least sit down. Everyone sat down except Gildor and Raymond. Riker then explained the werewolf story to the group. After he explained the story of dark sirens and vampires to the group. Giving the group every detail of the dark creatures he had made. After Riker was done with his speech on the dark creatures he made, everyone was ready to go on the journey to Black Brick Castle. The group then looked at Riker in silence.

"Now everyone, let's pack up some food, water, and things to go to Black Brick Castle. Riker, let Sander take control and tell him to go downstairs to the tavern."

When the group started to get things ready for the gate meeting, Sander decided to wait for Duvessa to sing him a song downstairs. Sander waited for about two hours until Duvessa and Darius decided to walk through the tavern door. Sander smiled at Duvessa knowing he had an emotional feeling for her. Sander then watched her sing to the tavern. This song was called 'song of safety.' She then began to sing a song about sailors coming home and being on safe travels. The song ended with a nice tune.

"Riker, I feel drawn to her somehow. Her voice is amazing. I'm going to go talk to her." As he got up, Riker decided to tell Sander to wait. "I know why I feel this strange feeling. They're somehow related to dark sirens. The creatures I created. We will come back for that later, right now let's go to Black Brick Castle and help out with the green werewolf problem," said Riker in Sander's head.

Sander then went to go grab his things and headed to the gate of Inthra. When Sander got there, the group was waiting for him.

"Good now that everyone is here, let's go to Black Brick Castle," said Raymond. The group then ventured off through the forest and near the entrance to the dark forest.

Chapter 20

Black Brick Castle

The group stopped to see giant black trees and no leaves in the forest. It was like death was straight ahead.

"Am I the only one who sees no animals and life here?"

"Come on guys, we need to pass through the dark forest and we will reach Black Brick Castle." Raymond went into the forest and liked it was nothing as Gildor followed.

"I thought I took all the magic out," said Riker in Sander's head. "But I guess this is where great grandpa is at." Sander made a confused face as he started to walk into the forest. The group walked into the forest, they heard nothing but silence. The only thing they heard was their footsteps.

"Guys, this is weird." As they walked into the forest the sun began to go dimmer and dimmer. When they reached the end of the forest, they saw a castle on a mountain with clouds hiding the sun from it.

"There it is, guys, the Black Brick Castle," said Raymond. The group just started talking about the black trees.

"Wait, what was that forest?"

"Oh, nothing just the dark forest. Relax it won't attack you unless you have dark magic in your possession. And well as long as you don't spend the night there. Now enough talk. I want to get back by sunrise." The group then decided to walk up to the mountain castle. When the group reached halfway there, they saw the sun going down. The group decided to keep running and climbing up the mountain to reach Black Brick Castle. When they reached the top, they saw men turning into werewolves. They saw seven men turn into werewolves and run at Gildor and his group. As they attacked, the group of Kevin's guards got dragged into the castle. Gildor managed to fend off the group with the green werewolves.

"Alright, me, Kevin, and Jake are going into the castle to deal with the werewolves. Sander, along with Riker, Kevin's guards is going to look for the werewolf. And Raymond, go have fun."

Raymond then pulled out dual-wielded longswords and ran into the castle. The group then split up and went into the castle. As the group split up, Gildor saw a hall of werewolves inside. Shit. The first group of Gildor, Kevin, and Jake ran into the hallway to kill the werewolves. Kevin activated his sword to attack the werewolves. Jake ran at the werewolves wearing silver armor, sliced, and tried and kill them. Gildor grabbed his great sword to go and attack and kill the werewolves. While they were killing the werewolves, Sander and the second group were trying to find the guards.

"Where do you think he has gone? Said the guards.

"I don't know, maybe he might be dead," said Sander. Sander continued to find the guard around the castle with Kevin's guard. Meanwhile, Raymond was having the time of his life, killing turned vampires and aristocrats.

"You vampires really think you can hide from Raymond. Come out, come out wherever you're hiding." He then saw a group of vampires and decided to kill them all. Meanwhile, Gildor finished off the werewolves in the hallway.

"Everyone alright?" Said Gildor.

"Yes, I'm good," said Kevin and Jake getting their heads straight.

"You do this all your life?" Said Kevin.

"Yeah, of course. This is nothing. Wait until there's a pack of fifty in one area." Jake and Kevin looked at each other with worry.

"Relax," said Gildor. "There is not going to be fifty. I think." Gildor then walked off with a smile on his face. Kevin and Jake caught their breaths and followed Gildor as Gildor proceeded on to find more werewolves. Sander found a room full of vampires and the guard. Sander did not move and just stood there looking at the vampires. Sander was about to grab the Soul Absorber, when Riker said, "Wait, Sander, don't you see that man?"

"Yes," said Sander in his head.

"Well, Sander that guy is one of the original werewolves. We need Gildor to be here to fight him. And even though Gildor has a forty percent chance to live if Gildor kills him and I fuse the magic in his ring, Gildor will be strong enough to kill the others. But we need Gildor here."

"Who dares enter my castle? And who dares kill my people in their name? I do not allow you to do this. These are my people and we do not harm the human race or any of the races. State your name."

"Wait, are you a queen?" Said Sander in the throne room.

The vampire said, "Yes. I am the lady who owns this castle. But I am no queen. And yes, I am a vampire. I am a pure blood. I have dark magic. And I will use it to protect my kin and my people."

The vampires then started to line up side to side as if they were about to fight.

"Sanderm the original green werewolf disappeared but don't worry we will kill him one day. Now, Sander, we have bigger things to worry about." Riker then told Sander to get ready for a fight. As soon as Sander was about to be ready, Gildor Jake, and Kevin walked inside the throne room.

"We're Raymond," said Gildor. The lady of the castle then told the vampires to stand behind her.

"You dare send Raymond, the vampire hunter, after us. You have no soul. Your race thinks vampires are bad, that we're only evil. But we have been drinking animal blood and kept hidden for quite some time. And now you try and kill us and our children." As she spoke, Sander turned his head to see little eyes looking at him. Sander then patted Gildor on the shoulder and pointed to the child on the left side of the throne room.

"Gildor, they're just trying to live. And I don't think it's bad. Because then I would have felt a feeling of my power telling me that they were lying. They're, telling the truth," said Sander.

As the group put their weapons away, they heard yelling from the hall to the throne room. "I'm going to kill you." Raymond then burst through the door telling the vampires it was their time now not the humans. "You may have killed a group of soldiers. But not here, I'm here to kill you." Raymond then rushed at the lady and killed her, stabbing her through her back into the heart. He then sliced and diced his way through her, and tried to run at the vampire. But then he stopped.

"Mommy," said a random child. The child then ran at her mother who was slaughtered on the ground. Raymond raised his sword at the child. Raymond then decided to put his swords on his back and walked outside the castle. As Raymond walked out, the group was shocked by what just happened. The vampires started to get angry as their pure-blood leader died at the hands of a vampire hunter.

"You humans. Your races are all the same. You think we're monsters just because we suck blood. You guys are the monsters. There are good ones and bad ones. The bad ones traveled somewhere. And left the blame on us. Your friend is dying but even though you killed our pure blood. We will heal him. By turning him into an aristocrat." The aristocrat looked at the pure blood. "My dear, it's time you show us your training. And you people get out of the throne room and wait in the hallway."

The group then walked to the hallway as Sander stayed to tell the vampires about Riker and him. As the group went into the hallway the doors shut.

"What are you still doing here, human?" Said the aristocrat vampire.

"I'm not only human. I was born as a human. But a couple of months ago, I fused my soul with a demon. How old are you, sir?" Said Sander.

The aristocrat said, "I am around seven hundred years of age. And the pure blood your friend killed was a thousand years old. And this is its only child. You monster. And humans can't fuse with demons, they have never been shown for a thousand years. Plus, what demon did you so-called fuse with?" Sander told the vampire its name.

"Riker, the demon is Riker."

"That's impossible," said the vampire. "We have not seen him for over a thousand years." Sander then showed him the eyes of Riker. "He is in me and I know he created the original vampires. Now if you don't mind, I'm here to see how you will heal him." The aristocrat bowed down, along with the other vampires and their children. As all vampires knelt to Sander, "We're sorry for not knowing your master."

"Sander, they call me master because I created them. But this is not what I want on this journey. One vampire will do. That's what they're going to do to Kevin's guard. They're going to turn him into a vampire. Tell them Sander that we want you to heal him."

Sander then listened to Riker and decided to tell the vampire to heal him. The vampire told the pureblood what to do and told her to heal him. The pureblood then pulled out her fangs and bit him. With her nice silver eyes, the pureblood was turning him into a vampire. As she turned him, Kevin's guard fainted as he was being sucked dry. The pure blood then took part of her magic and some of her blood and gave him to drink it. When she was done, she then sat next to him.

"How old is he?" Said the girl.

"He's around Kevin's age. Somewhere by the looks of it seventeen to nineteen." The girl told him that he looked handsome.

"Is he a knight?" Asked the girl. Sander then told her that he could not answer and that only Sir Kevin could.

"Who is this you call Kevin?"

"He is standing in the hallway."

"Well, he will wait then." She then ordered the aristocrat to take him to the underground. She then turned around to look at Sander. "I do not know much of Riker. All I know is he is the creator of werewolves and vampires. But most werewolves do not get along with us. But it does not matter." She told her vampires to go and guard the hall to the throne room and patrol the castle. She then told them to leave her and him alone. The other vampires bowed down and decided to go and do their duties as aristocrats and normal vampires.

"Sander, may you please bring me Kevin? I need to speak to him." Sander did what the girl said and decided to leave the throne room to go and get Kevin. When Sander left, he told Kevin to go inside the throne room.

When Kevin entered and closed the door, the girl said, "You wanted to see me." She then walked and touched Kevin slowly on his back and then slowly walked around him. "So the guard who helped you, do you know his name? Or where he came from?"

Kevin then answered the questions, "I do not know him. But I heard stories about him. He is a great swordsman. Along that his name I do not know, you have to ask him. And where he came from is from the north part of Luna. The part where its always snowing. That is where my house is. Gladstone. And he is the son of one of my other guards. That is all you need to know. Now, where is he?"

He demanded to the pure blood girl. She then smiled and told him. "You have a noble heart I see. But I'm sorry, he is saved but he cannot be along the journey with you no more. He needs to learn how to control his thirst. We had to turn him into a vampire. So, then he can live longer. That's how we saved him. For now, he is a normal vampire so the sun will weaken and kill him. So, I might have to keep him for a while. He will return back to you. Where is your group headed?" She asked with concern.

Kevin told her some place called Orcuhan.

"The kingdom of the orcs, the land of the barbarians. You must be careful there. They're very threatening. Now you must leave me and I will not return him unless he is fully recovered to go to Orcuhan. You may leave." She then went to the throne and sat on it. Kevin then bowed to her and decided to leave the throne room. In the hallway, the group decided to walk out of the castle to meet Raymond, the vampire hunter. When they found Raymond, they saw Raymond was sitting by the edge looking at the sun as it came up.

"Raymond, you alright?" Said Gildor.

"I almost killed a child, Gildor. I would never expect me to walk that path. I let the death of my sister take a hold of me. She died by a vampire. And ever since then, I walked to find something to stop these monsters. I looked to them as they're monsters. And all I saw today here was a race that is protecting their young. I must give up this ring."

Raymond then looked at Gildor. "What do you think, should I deserve to die in this world?" The group all started to sit with them.

"So, what is your group of friends headed off to, Gildor?" Gildor looked around.

"We're headed to Orcuhan. Wanna come with us?" Said Gildor with a smile as he stuck out his hand.

"You know, I will go with you to the ends of the world." Raymond shook Gildor's hand. The group then added a new member, a vampire hunter. The group then decided to head back to the town of Inthra.

"Wait, Kevin, how about your guard?" Kevin looked at him as if he was dead and it was too late. The group shook their heads in sadness, looked to the sky, and started to walk to the town of Inthra.

Chapter 21

Duvessa's Secret

A day had passed and the group entered back into the town of Inthra. Sander quickly headed to the tavern and ordered himself a room. He then rushed downstairs to see Duvessa happily ready to sing. He then saw her brother Darius waiting for her to get going later. Sander then sat and watched her sing to the people in the tavern. The people in the tavern looked peaceful at her as they relaxed. Sander started to notice something weird about this same song. Riker's power kicked right in at the right time for Sander. He started to notice that other people in the tavern fell into a deep sleep and a deeply relaxing state. What was going on? Duvessa realized Sander was not feeling anything. Sander then got up and walked to the lake to sit by the lake and look at the water in the lake. Sander thought about what just happened in the tavern. As Sander was thinking, the group came back empty-handed without werewolf skin.

"Oh crap, I forgot to get the werewolf skin. But wait none of them were purebloods. So maybe another time."

Gildor got himself a room and headed upstairs to take a nice rest. The group got a room and looked around the town for a safe passage to Orcuhan. As the group was trying to find a way around, Sander finally came across a tale that swam past his eyes. He looked closely to see a man with a blue tail in the darkness of the lake. "What the hell?" Sander quickly got up to walk to the tavern.

"Riker, what is that?" Sander said in his mind.

"That was a siren."

"Tell me more about sirens, Riker."

Riker told Sander about siren's ranks and how they lived off the last time he encountered them a thousand years ago. Sirens also had a voice in which they sang to make men bend to their will.

"Riker, you don't think Duvessa is a siren."

Riker told Sander to go ask her if she was a siren. Sander then walked over to the tavern. When he entered, he saw Duvessa was gone along with Darius. Sander began to ask around in the tavern if they had seen a girl named Duvessa. The tavern people said they didn't even notice when she left. Sander then went out of the tavern to run around the entire town to find and ask about Duvessa. Sander found nothing about Duvessa; the townsfolk didn't even know such a name. Sander then headed to the lake to see the siren again. When Sander got there, he saw no siren. He took off his armor and his weapons to go for a dive into the water.

He jumped and entered into the water diving fifty feet down. Sander stopped and looked around the water to see a tail; it shocked him. Sander swam back up to the top of the water. When Sander reached the top of the water he swam to shore. Sander then decided to wait for Duvessa. He decided to stay the night out on the shore. Sander stayed overnight, put on his armor, and waited. Sander noticed Duvessa going on shore on the other side of the lake. Sander saw her turning human-like; it was a force of energy swishing around her. Sander then saw Darius following behind her with his black spear. Sander then headed back to the tavern to see if she was going to sing in the tavern. Sander got into the tavern and decided to take a seat. When Sander took a seat, Duvessa and Darius walked through the door. Darius took a seat with his spear in his hand. And

Duvessa went to the middle of the tavern and began singing to the tavern people. As she started to sing, Sander paid more attention to what she was going to sing to the people in the tavern. When she started to sing the song of sailors, the tavern became quiet, like calm waters – as if they were in a trance. Sander then realized that she had to be a siren. Sander waited for the song to be over. While Sander waited, Gildor woke up from his bed from a soft voice singing downstairs. Gildor headed downstairs to sit next to Sander.

"Hey Sander, isn't she beautiful? Her voice makes me feel the time when I was a kid. Before all the werewolf hunting." As Gildor continued to talk to Sander about Duvessa, Kevin and the rest of the group headed downstairs to listen to the soft voice. Everyone in the tavern was at peace except Sander. Sander thanked the demon soul he had now as it could resist the song of sirens.

The song ended and everyone was ready for sleep except Sander. The group started to go upstairs as they were being mind-controlled. Sander then grabbed his sword and headed outside to wait for Duvessa. Duvessa and Darius then went outside.

"Hey, Duvessa," said Sander, "Can I talk to you for a second?" He grabbed Duvessa's hand and headed to the ally between the tavern and the cottage. She told Darius to wait for her.

Duvessa then said, "What do you need?" With her purple majestic eyes, she looked at him at what he was about to say.

"Listen, tell me the truth because I will know when you are lying."

She then smiled and stroked her hair back. "What is it, Sander?"

"Are you a siren, Duvessa? And tell me the truth, are you a dark siren that has dark magic and that makes people get killed in the waters?

Duvessa looked at Sander with anger. "Are you calling me ugly and mean and that I would want to kill you?"

"No, I'm just asking you, Duvessa, are you a dark siren?"

"I thought you were going to ask me something different, you fucking asshole."

She then slapped Sander in the face and told him that she was not a dark siren. She walked away.

"Wait, I'm sorry. I saw you with a tail. So, the closest thing I knew was dark sirens."

She then walked back to him to tell him that she was not a dark siren. "I'm not one of the evil ones. I'm a siren but not a dark siren. I do not have dark magic. But I can control water." She then grabbed Sander's hand to make him follow her to the lake.

"Now I know you might go and tell the others of who I am. And I might have to run away. Or swim away. But look at the true forms of who we are." She then told Darius to go into the water. Darius and Duvessa entered the water showing their true forms. He saw the purple and blue tails swim around the water of the lake. Darius then glowed in the water as he was happy swimming. They then stopped and looked at Sander. Sander told them to not be afraid of him as he had a secret too. Sander then showed Duvessa fire without using a spell.

"Wait, you already showed us your fire magic. Why is this a secret?"

"I have a demon inside me. He is the original creator of the dark sirens." Sander then told them that he and his group of friends all had secrets and to not be afraid.

"Listen Duvessa, I know this is a big secret. But would you and Darius care to join us on our journey to Orcuhan? It's a place of orcs. You get to see the rest of the world. Now come with us."

He lifted his hands out to Duvessa asking her to come along with him on the journey. Duvessa reached out and shook Sander's hand.

"Maybe Duvessa and Darius, you guys can show me and my friends how sirens are really."

They both smiled and they began to go to the surface to go with Sander. Sander then took them to the tavern and bought them a room as Sander just got another two people in the group. The people of the group then went to sleep. The very next day, the group went downstairs to discover more breakfast. The group then began to ask if there was anything new. They said that they heard from another person a ship had entered port, they heard they were sailing north.

Gildor told everyone, "This is a good chance for us to go to Orcuhan. We can stop north then head south or head even more north."

"Gildor, how do you know it's going north and there are not pirates trying to put us into slavery?"

Gildor then replied, "Because if they were pirates we got a werewolf hunter, a vampire hunter, two new people, a blacksmith, another knight, three of his guards, oh right, and Sander who has a demon inside him. I think we can handle our own."

Gildor then went to the docks to see if he could strike a deal with the sailors. As Gildor was going to get them a ship, Sander introduced Duvessa and Darius to the group. "I'm glad you guys came to our group. We all have secrets but it would be nice to have a soldier and a singer on our adventures." Duvessa started to hum silently to herself as she was shy to tell everyone who she was.

Darius then spoke, "I'm Sir Darius, commander of the second legion of the sirens of Astra."

Everyone was shocked at what Darius said.

"Why? Is everyone ok?" Said Darius.

"No, we're fine," said Raymond. "We're just surprised we got a commander on our journey. What made you leave your kingdom if I may ask?"

Darius replied, "Well, I left because my brother died. And I knew I could not go back on it. He died in a battle in my arms. It was not joy when we won the battle. So now I traveled here. To the great town of Inthra. And now I meet up with a group. But I would like to hear from you guys about what you guys do."

The group then told Darius and Duvessa what they did and who they were. As they were talking Gildor came through the door, out of breath. He caught his breath to tell the group that he found out where they were going. "Alright, they're headed north to Orcuhan to set up trade there for the orcs owning the port."

"That's awesome, it made our journey easier. Come on guys, let's pack," said Sander. The group followed Sander to go and pack for the journey. Duvessa and Darius went and got their clothes ready for the journey. Three hours passed, the group met up at the docks.

"Alright, you guys ready to go," said Gildor with a smile on his face.

"Wait for a second, what's with that glove?"

Duvessa replied, "Oh, it's for our new journey." Darius looked at her with the strange spear.

"Tell me later what that is," said Darius.

"Alright," whispered Duvessa.

"Alright, whatever, let's move it along; we got a week's journey to Orcuhan." The group then paid the people on the dock to climb on board to Orcuhan. As the group was climbing on board, Gildor went to go talk to the captain as the rest of the group went to the cabin on the ship to settle their things. Duvessa got nervous around people as she walked by the crew. The crew looked at her in a dirty way as they were going to do something harmful to her. Darius with a scary face started to go in front as a shield for her not to get uncomfortable.

"Alright, this way, Duvessa."

Everyone entered the cabin to put their things inside and get themselves settled. The ship started moving.

They heard the captain said, "Up next, Orcuhan." The group then set sailed north as they were not entering the high seas.

Chapter 22

The First Day at Sea

A day passed and they were now at sea. It was their very first day at sea. The group then decided to talk more in their cabin at sea. The waters of the sea were so calm that you could not make a sound to make the water flow into waves.

"Wait, it's too quiet," the captain said.

"Is there something going wrong?" Said Duvessa. "Why is the captain going into caution?"

Gildor replied to Duvessa, "It's probably nothing. Maybe it's just a captain's thing.

"Over there, captain," said a crewmate on the top of the deck. The group looked out the window to see a giant squid heading towards the ship.

"What the heck is that?" Said Sander. "Riker, do you know what that is?" Riker told Sander he had no clue about what Sander was seeing.

"Guys, what is that?"

Darius looked at the window of the ship to know exactly what that was but Darius did not say anything. "Hey, Duvessa, can I speak to you privately?" Darius took Duvessa to a private room on the ship.

"Hey, Duvessa, I know what that is. It's called a Kraken. Trust me, I know what it can do. It's a dangerous creature. Although this one is smaller than the last one I fought."

"Wait, slow down," she whispered in the cabin. "What do you mean when you last fought one? You mean to tell me you fought one like this before?"

"Yes, I have Duvessa but it was with nine others." Duvessa then tried getting more answers before they got out and went back to the group. "Wait, oh whatever." She then headed up to the deck to see the giant octopus up close. It had eight twenty-five long tentacles. Duvessa was shocked by what she was seeing for the first time. The group then headed up to the top deck carrying their weapons. Duvessa looked at the group with their weapons, she then went and got her glave. She then ran back up to see even the group and crew were in shock.

They all started to fear as their weapons on the ship were not working against the monster.

"Lads, we're dealing with a Kraken. Grab the ballistic," said the captain.

The crew then started to put in the work to defeat the Kraken. A crewmate got lifted and eaten by the Kraken. Sander's group started to put in some work as they did not want to die. The ship started shaking as more tentacles started to come from the water.

"We're surrounded," said Kevin. "We must fight it." Kevin then pulled out his sword and started to attack the testicles on the ship. Gildor then went to the wheel of the ship to start steering. Raymond headed downstairs to go shoot the harpoons. The rest of the group neither attacked nor shot the harpoons with Raymond.

The ship was under attack by a sea monster. Darius grabbed Duvessa and decided to go talk to her downstairs.

"What do you need, Darius?"

"Listen Duvessa, we need to fight that Kraken. Or I need to. Not you. You're too weak against that Kraken." Darius then grabbed his spear and decided to go and dive into the ocean turning into his siren form and attacking the Kraken. Duvessa with her glave then chased Darius and tried to fight the Kraken as well. As on both sides, the crew of the ship and Sander's group started fighting the Kraken. They saw a blue glow in the water. They saw a tentacle go down as it was chopped. The Kraken then got even more aggressive. Duvessa thought she could play hero, so she swam to attack the tentacle. As she was about to attack, she got hit and knocked to the edge of the ship. She was dizzy after the attack and headed back to the ship. Darius continued to fight the beast head-on and recklessly. When Duvessa headed back to the ship, she made sure she was not seen by the crew and the group – to make sure her secret was kept.

Duvessa then told the captain that she read a book about Krakens. And that she should let the blue lights under the water deal with them. The captain had no choice but to follow as he had no experience with Krakens. She prayed to a God that she did not know. She prayed to the water god for Darius's safety. As she prayed, the water got more light blue and lighter. The crew then stopped as they saw multiple tentacles go down as he just lost his limbs. The water got even lighter, it felt as if a god was in the water. The Kraken then made a roar as it started to sink to the bottom of the sea. Meanwhile, in the water, Darius was fighting the Kraken. He stocked all of his tentacles. Afterwards, he swam as fast as he could activating the water knight mark, enhancing his speed of swimming. Then he pointed his spear straight and dashed through the Kraken's heart. Darius then looked and secretly went behind the other side of the ship to make sure he was not spotted in the waters by the other races. Darius made it to the deck of the ship. He then started to act as his name was, Darius again.

"What I missed?" Said, Darius.

Gildor started to explain to him while the group headed back down to the cabin. Duvessa looked at Darius with a face. Gildor then explained to him what happened to the Kraken. "Where were you when it attacked the ship?"

"Oh, I was trying to find a piece of bread I was hungry."

Gildor laughed and then patted him on the back. "Let's head back down to the cabin and talk about what creature it could have been or something. And what to do when it attacks again."

The ship then continued to sail north as it was with the wind. "Wow, not even the first day out and we ran into a sea creature. Why do you think it attacks? Rumors say Raymond is reading a book on sea creatures. That the Kraken will fall if the heart is killed. That's probably why the blue light did. It killed the heart. Wait, it also says a Kraken has fifty-five-foot tentacles. That one we fought was like a child." Raymond continued to research the Kraken as the group was in shock that there were bigger things in the ocean than fish.

"What are we going to do against a sea creature like that?" As they were talking in fear about the sea monsters, Sander stared a bit at Duvessa as she should know. But she silently said no to him and pointed to Darius.

"Hey Darius, can I speak to you for a second?" Sander and Darius went to speak somewhere on the ship alone.

"So, what was that thing?" Said Sander.

Darius then explained what Sander was referring to.

"All right, that was a Kraken. It was to be a child. But it is led by dark sirens to attack the surface ships."

"Oh, next we are expecting sirens?"

"At least a small group of them. They will attack the ship because the ship scared the Kraken. But I won't know what they're sending. So, let's just be prepared about this."

"No, Darius, this is what you're going to do," Sander replied in a little bit of anger. "You're going to tell the group what you and Duvessa are. Or it will be worse for them to find out. So, it's best now."

Darius refused the offer and went back to the cabin to the group.

"Alright, so Raymond," said Darius. "What do you have on that monster book of yours?"

"Well, there are dark sirens," replied Raymond. "It says here they are half-man or women with black tails. Or dark-color tails. They can control water. So yeah. There are also a lot more sea monsters." Raymond then turned around, found a desk, and started reading.

"Wait, Raymond, are you going to read that whole book?" Raymond looked at Gildor.

"Yes, if we run into more sea monsters I will know their weakness." Raymond then carried on his duties. Gildor got up to go ask captain a question. As Gildor and Raymond got busy, Kevin went upstairs on deck with his guards to go help out with the ship.

Duvessa pondered out the window on what she was going to see on land next. Darius went to the bottom of the ship with space and practiced the wielding of his obsidian spear. Jake began to read more on materials and ores he may forge in the future. The group carried out the journey and their duties on what to do when they get on land or meet another monster. Sander then went to the front of the ship on deck and talked to Riker.

When Sander got there, he talked to Riker for guidance. "Hey Riker, what do you know about dark sirens?"

Riker replied in his head. "Well, dark sirens were originally sirens. I gave them dark magic to fight with me in the war. They had the ability that I made them get dark magic. Water is strong but they had dark magic of blood magic. And they controlled the seas if the angels were sailing or coming from the sea. They would kill them. These dark sirens had their purpose. But I do not know what happened after the war. Or what happened to the other siren race. But all I know is Duvessa and Darius are a siren race but not dark sirens. I'm guessing by the way of how Darius acts. The sirens are at war with the dark sirens. But that's between us. What we should do is pay attention to our next journey to Orcuhan, Sander. As you need an army to kill Galatin and get into the castle. That is the day where you will kill your brother. And I will kill Galatin. Once and for all."

The group then continued sailing through the winds and to the north to Orcuhan as it would be a peaceful day at sea. But what they did not know was the race that sent that Kraken was coming for them.

Chapter 23

Dark Sirens

It was a night out. The moon was shining in the waters. The black cold waters made a swish sound every time they hit the ship. Duvessa went down to the bottom of the ship deck to see Darius training with his obsidian spear. She then grabbed her glave to train with him.

"Hey, Darius, can you see if you can use my weapon and show me how to use a polearm?"

Darius then grabbed her glave and started to swing it with two hands. "Duvessa, this blade is heavier than a spear." Darius then wielded it with two hands as he knew what he was doing. "It's a good blade but it's not my style. Are you sure it's yours, Duvessa? Maybe you should carry a lighter one."

Duvessa refused Darius's proposal. "Alright then, it's your weapon," said Darius. "I will let you have it." Darius gave the glave back and continued to practice his form of fighting. Duvessa asked for some tips on using the glave. Darius accepted the glave and taught her how to use it. Darius taught her some ways of using it and how to grip it right. She then told Darius to give it back when Darius went up to the deck to see what was out at sea. Devussa continued to train.

Darius was going to check on the crew up on the deck. Raymond and Gildor were learning more about sea monsters in the book they found on the ship. "You guys are boring me," said Jake and he went up the deck to look at the water. As Jake looked in the water, for a split second, he saw a black tail that swam really fast under the ship.

"What was that?" Jake said. He went to go look for Kevin while Sander continued to look out the ship as he was thinking of something.

Sander thought about what his father said to him before he died. Sander recollected the memory. "Sander, you will become king. Stop acting like an arrogant fool. You're not a knight. You are not a soldier. You're not a pheasant. You are the future king of Luna. You understand you cannot be an adventurer. You must become king. Your brother Fergus has no right to the throne. You do. Why do you act like an idiot? You cannot have fun no more. You must join me in war meetings and join me in diplomatic meetings. And stop acting like a child. Act like a future king of Luna."

"But father," said Sander. "I wish to not be king. Why can't we just let Fergus be king? I need to know why we must follow the firstborn rule. Why are you hard on me?"

"Because you're my son," replied Daniel Helmglade. "And you should know that the future king is you. Look, follow me." Sander followed his father. They made it to a balcony. "This kingdom. You will have this one day. And you will learn that it's not all about you. It's not all about the king sitting on his tush, you may call it. It's all about ruling a beautiful kingdom. From the peasants to the middle class. To the high class of nobles and lords. They all have their part. Even you. Now you know I have to punish you now." They both giggled.

"How about not using the sword for a weak?"

"Understood, father." Sander and the king walked away laughing. Sander then went back to life as he was staring into the water. "I miss you, father," said Sander with sadness filling his heart. Sander then stopped looking at the water and went downstairs to see Gildor and Raymond on what they read. When Sander entered the room, he heard a beautiful voice coming from the winds of the sea.

"Stop the ship," said the captain. Darius went downstairs to talk to Duvessa. As they got to talking, the songs got louder and louder. The crew and Sander's group started to fall into a trance. When they all walked to the top of the ship, they saw beautiful women in black tails trying to tell them to get in the water. Raymond tried to refuse but the song was so strong it made Raymond want to get closer to the women in the water. The crew was silent the whole time. In the night, the women in the water started to sing to them to get closer to the water to meet them. Half of the crew jumped in the water and decided to swim to the beautiful women in the water. As soon as they were doing that Darius and Duvessa stopped talking.

"Wait, Darius, why isn't it loud? It's quiet. Wonder what's going on?"

"Dammit," said Darius. "It's dark sirens. But how were they affected and we're not?" Because sirens are not affected by music from other sirens. Or dark sirens. We have to move before the crew gets into the water. Darius and Duvessa headed up to see Sander about to hop in the water. The rain started to pour when Sander woke up from what he was about to do. He saw the crew members in the water.

"What the hell?" Said Sander.

Darius ran to Sander. "Sander, it's the dark sirens."

Sander yelled from the top of his lungs, "Black sirens!" The crew then woke up from what they were about to do and they all started to get on their stations. The captain woke up and started ordering his crew to prepare to fight. Sander's group started to help out the crew. The rain started to get even more intense as the crew and the group had no chance against water-controlling fish. Sander then looked to Duvessa and Darius.

"Enough acting like Darius, Ares. It's time you show them who you really are." Ares started to refuse Sander and stayed back. Duvessa then started to get flashbacks of what happened to her parents when they disappeared.

"You may be a coward," said Duvessa. "But I'm not."

She began to glow light purple as if she was enchanted. She walked to the edge of the ship and yelled as loud as she could, making waves towards the dark sirens. The crew and the group then stop to see the women with the controlling water.

"She is a black siren," said the crewman. Duvessa then got scared as he got PTSD and got angry about what was about to happen.

He then felt as if blood was on his hands. Ares started to lose control. He then got his spear and started to glow light blue. His markings started to glow as if they were alive. Duvessa moved out of the way when she saw the true side of him being realized. He then headed to the edge of the ship making a shocking rage of anger. His eyes started to glow hazel as he was starting to feel like his old self. The symbol of a water male holding a spear, battling a Kraken started to glow more than usual. He gripped his spear as the water poured on him. He yelled again even louder than his normal yell, making the rain stop. He looked at the giant group of sirens. He jumped and dived into the water revealing his true form, his tail started to glow like a blue star. He cut through and sliced through with his rage killing dark sirens in his way. He dashed as his mark of the spear Kraken started to glow brighter. The symbol of Astra. Speaking the words underwater, "I am a water knight who serves the people of Astra in time of distress. We stand against the dark sirens and we fight for the evil in which they stand against us." He got louder and started to battle it out with their leader. He clashed as the waves started to go out of control. As peaceful as it was up in the ship, it was fierce on the waters. The ship started to shake. Ares was battling to save the people on the ship. As he battled it out, the people on the ship saw black sirens coming all around him, surrounding him as they were going to finish him. All of a sudden, another blue light came from the north of that position and attacked the black siren. He was helping Ares fight back against them.

"Who is that?" Said Sander. Sander looked at Duvessa, thinking she knew. She then looked back shrugging like she did not know. The waves started to clash as if there were gods in the water. In a moment of truth, there were no more black sirens. And all there was one blue light fading and one light shining. The night was dark but they shone in the waters.

Duvessa freaked out as she dived into the water going to grab Ares. When she reached Ares, she saw another man. A man with a blue tail. Chest ripped as he was carrying a building. Blue hair and silver eyes. She wondered who this person was. She then asked for his body to swim him back to the ship. He looked at her with a strange look.

"Why do you want to see, my master?"

"Who is your master?" She said with confusion.

"I'm holding him," said the strange man. "He's the man who taught me how to fight."

"Are you his brother?" Said Duvessa. "If you are, I do not want to quarrel with you."

"I'm not a prince, I'm just a noble warrior," replied the strange man.

She looked at him, and said, "But you look like a kid. Like me. So, why are you saying you're a man?"

"Allow me to introduce myself," said the other blue-tailed stranger. "I am Scorpius of the kingdom of Astra. And I came here looking for my master. The one who trained me. Now I'm here to help. But if I may ask who are you?" Said Scorpius.

Duvessa then introduced herself, "I am Duvessa. I have the power to see into the future of sirens. But I'm not able to control it."

Scorpius then told her to help him out with Ares. She helped out with Ares and swam with Scorpius to the ship. When they arrived at the ship, they hopped on and went to the lower deck. As Duvessa was dragging Ares there, Scorpius started to learn how to walk. The crew was still in shock and feared for who they were. Duvessa picked up Ares and put him on top of a bed. She then started to nurse him with first aid. As she nursed him, Scorpius came down, trying to see if he could help fix his master.

Duvessa asked what could make him faint or fade. Scorpius then told her of the water knight mark. "That is so ancient. It's able to enhance siren warriors, strength, speed, and senses but does not work on their energy."

So, this is what happened when he said the sirens were protecting something." She then asked who was Darius. Scorpius then told her who Darius was. "Darius or King Darius of Astra was a good king. He was the older brother of Ares. But he sadly died at one of the Astran borders. After that, next in line was Ares. But Ares was afraid of his destiny to be king and he ran away. And I guess he found you. An oracle." As Scorpius told her that, he knelt to her as if she was of high importance.

"Why are you bowing down to me?" Said Duvessa.

Scorpius rose and began to guard Ares and Duvessa. The crew then started to yell at each other to decide if they were going to keep them or not. As they argued, Sander and his group came down to hear an explanation of what just they saw.

"Alright, enough with the lies, Duvessa, if that's your real name. Tell us the truth about who you are."

Duvessa would basically explain that she and Ares were not really siblings and that she found him when she was about to go to sleep. Thanks to him, she learned the truth about sirens, how there were two types of sirens, true sirens and the corrupted ones.

"Long ago, sirens while solitary, still interacted with humans and other land beings but it was few and far between. Most of them were in small pods or tribes and then the giant war broke out. Sirens wished not to get involved if it didn't involve them as they didn't want to harm their kind or choose a side they didn't believe in. So many went into hiding only for an evil land being to have found a group. Using some sort of corrupted magic, the being corrupted a group of sirens. These became the first corrupted or dark sirens. The dark sirens attacked their own kind along with those on land, starting the legend of sirens. Sirens banded together forming kingdoms in hiding to keep the people of the land away as they were the cause of the corruption. It was also because of the corrupted ones that a curse was placed on all sirens. If a siren became corrupted by their own emotions they would turn into a dark siren. Because of this, young children were forced to grow up quickly and everything became basically military."

Duvessa admitted that she had siren blood. She discovered her powers and worked to master them after her family died and had to teach herself. "Ares realized this and taught me how to properly use them once we met. We pretended to be long-lost siblings and family ever since."

The group then realized she was only protecting herself and Ares. Raymond was still confused, so he asked, "Who is Ares?"

The group looked at him, and said, "Darius. Darius is Ares."

"But Ares is his real name," said Gildor.

"Oh, that makes sense now. I'ma go up the deck and see if we can find the solution." As Raymond found the solution, and the group then focused on who was the other guy.

"Hi, I'm Scorpius of Astra." He then bowed down and said he was only there to serve his master Ares. The group welcomed him to the group as a companion. The group just settled their new companion and truthfully, they began to carry on and fix the issue up the stairs on the deck.

Chapter 24

Abandoned Ship

The crew began to continue arguing for three days at sea trying to decide if they should stay. Suddenly, they stopped and they decided to go and kill the sirens. The crew and the group came downstairs to talk to the sirens about chopping off their heads.

The captain came and said, "You may have to leave or die."

Sander and the group stood in front of the sirens. "If you're going to kill or throw them overboard then you will have to get past me and my group," said Sander.

The group then drew out their weapons and so did the crew. "Wait, wait, wait, we can all talk this through without causing an outbreak."

The captain then offered Sander a deal. "Look, listen I only have half of my crew from those dark sirens. Now I'm not saying the dark sirens help us. But if you want them to stay, your group must help us on the journey to Orcuhan. It's only fair and we won't hurt anyone in your group."

Sander accepted the deal and everything went well on the ship. The crew began to go on their days on the ship. Raymond hid from the group to read more about sea monsters. As he read, Sander and the rest of the group started to help around the ship. The ships sailed for a while until clouds came hovering over the seas, delaying the time they were going to get to their destination. As they were sailing in the hardcore rain, thunder struck near their ship. They heard birds striking the lighting. They heard the birds fly past them. The lightning sounded like cannons of war. All of a sudden, a crewmate saw a giant snake-like figure roll through the water. He saw the eyes of the figure for a second, shocking him. In fear, he started to panic.

"Captain," the crewmate said. "Sea monster."

The crew looked on the edge to see nothing but heavy waters. The crewmate started to panic so much that he began pushing everyone out of the way to sound the bell. The captain ordered his men to stop the man. There was a big fight going on, Sander began to look at the water, as he believed what the man was saying. When Sander looked out of the ship, he saw a giant snake as well in the water. The snake was so big it could destroy the ship if it charged.

Sander then hailed to the captain. "Captain, you must turn the ship around. The crewmate is speaking the truth. We need to turn around."

"Who dares command, my crew?" The crew started to turn against Sander. Sander's group then had no choice but to fight. They all pulled out their weapons to attack each other as they were sailing through the hard rain with lightning and the sound of cannons. As they were fighting the crew, Sander's group heard a roar from the waters. Everyone then stopped fighting to see what this roar might be.

"What the hell is that?" Said Jake. Everybody started to notice the giant snake. The crew started to get to their battle stations to get ready to fight. Jake looked into his eyes to see the fear within himself. Jake ran under the deck to hide. He then ran to Ares to wake him up.

"Leave him alone," said Duvessa. "He is trying to heal."

Scorpius then grabbed Jake and put him on the wall. "Leave the master alone."

"Get your hands off me. Listen, there is a giant snake-like slithering thing out in the water."

"What do you mean?" Raymond got out of hiding and asked what did it look like. Jake explained to Raymond that it looked like a giant snake in the water. Raymond scrolled through the pages to see a word.

"Does it look like this?" Raymond showed Jake the drawing. Jake then shook his head yes. Raymond then began to read more about what it was. "Ok, it's called a basilisk. It is a venomous creature and it's about three ships long. Weakness unknown. Wow, I guess we're going to die," said Raymond.

Jake started to shiver out of fear. Sander's group came down to get Jake.

"Wait," said Jake. "Listen to what Raymond has to say. There is no way to stop it, its weakness is unknown."

Raymond told them that Jake was telling the truth. The group then realized it could not be stopped but they had to abandon the ship. Sander then agreed, that to save the group's lives, they would abandon the ship. Sander ran with Gildor, Kevin and his guards to go get them out of the ship and save their lives. Sander knew in his mind the boat was not big enough for the group so he would rather risk his life and save his friends. Sander got the group to the boat. As he got Ares and Duvessa, Scorpius told them to go on without him. And one of Sir Kevin's guards told him that he would not leave. The group then held Kevin back as the boot got in the water. They then came to the safe land as the waves crashed.

"Hold on tight." Duvessa controlled a bit of the wave to make them go safely through the waters. Scorpius then got his spear and dived into the water going to battle the giant snake. Sir Kevin's guard got on the ballista and started to shoot the giant snake with big arrows. The crew was also trying to man the ship as much as they could.

Sander went to the captain, and said, "What do I do? I have fire magic." Sander then released the Soul Absorber. Sander felt the power that the Soul Absorber was giving him. Sander then grew his wings and flew straight to the giant water dragon snake. All of a sudden, the giant snake jumped out of the water trying to eat Sander. Sander missed it but the snake then found a new target on the ship. Sander started using demon fire on the creature as it was affecting the creature. But it was not effective enough.

"Why are my powers not working?" Sander continued to fight back with his flying. As Sander was fighting back under the water Scorpius was stabbing and cutting deep in the snakes under the chest. Sir Kevin's guard who got left behind shot an arrow striking the giant snake's eye. The water continued to go wavy. Water ended up on the ship. The crew then grabbed buckets to throw the water out of the ship.

"Fire," said the captain. The ballista kept shooting the giant arrows. Sander then flew down like a bird and stabbed the monster on its head. Sander then held on to his dear life as it did not hurt the creature but its armor on top. Scorpius got attacked underwater, knocking him out. Scorpius then retreated to his master's area as Sander and Kevin's guard continued to fight with the crew. The ship looked to be unstable as the giant snake charged straight to the middle of the ship, breaking through the ship and making everyone drown. Sir Kevin's guard looked at Sander as he got chopped in half. Sander then released the sword with full outrage, attacking the giant snake with everything he had. The rage consumed Sander as his soul made him as powerful as the demon inside him. Giving it all, he got the snake to make a giant roar. The snake was about to retreat. Sander flew north to go back and fly south like a spear in the sky. Sander flew as blue flames started to go around him, making a sharp fire spear. Sander then pointed out his sword. The giant snake then headed straight towards Sander. Sander hit through the snake's armor. Sander hit through its armor and attacked his heart without even knowing he did. He struck all the way through the giant snake. Sander flew up looking at the giant snake sinking, looking at the ship sinking. Sander then felt weak as he lost a lot of energy. Sander then fell into the water making a big splash. Sander then began to drift wherever the water took him. The water drifted him to the land of trees, where no man ever walked and survived The ship sank along with the crew with no man hearing of what the giant snake monster had done. The screams did not wake Sander up nor did the death. As the reapers go around the ship, reaping them to where the souls should go.

Sander continuously drifted to the land of trees.

Chapter 25

The Land of Trees

Sander woke up on the beach, seeing the ocean, and remembered nothing about the last night's attack. Sander then got up with the Soul Absorber next to him. Sander grabbed the Soul Absorber and sheathed it on his back.

"Riker, you still with me."

"Sander, I am fused into your soul. I will never leave you until the deal of your brother is done. Now, Sander let's regroup."

"Alright, Riker, we can't save what happened. I only remember the ship sinking."

"Sander, maybe you need some rest. Let's go find the rest of the group and maybe they will explain."

Sander turned around to see a giant green tree forest. He saw creatures moving around the forest. Sander then questioned Riker, "What is this?"

"Sander, all I have to say is be careful. I do not trust this place. It looks too good to be true."

Sander walked to the giant tree forest of life itself. As Sander was walking, he saw the magic of auras floating around. "Wow," said Sander. "I never knew such places existed." Sander then continued to walk deeper and deeper into the forest. Suddenly, Sander felt weaker.

"Sander, I think we are poisoned," said Riker in Sander's head.

"Why would you say that?"

"Because your body is feeling weak." Sander then fainted in the giant tree forest. Sander woke up in the forest. Sander could not move his body as it was numb.

"Sander, the pain from what you're feeling will heal but it will take three days as I am new to this venom as well." Sander realized he was being dragged. He moved his eyes around and saw a naked woman with leaves all over her body, dragging him from the top of his eyes. Sander wanted to question her but he could not speak. So, Sander decided to wait until he saw where he was going. The strange lady dragged him to a cave near the middle of the giant tree forest. The auras flew all around her as if she was someone special. Sander then stopped getting dragged and was put on a wall of the cave. The woman with leaves and gentle skin then went out of the cave and into the big tree forest and disappeared. Sander got a glimpse of Deja vu.

'I wonder who she is," Sander said in his head. Sander started to question how he saw her here in this forest. He then waited for three hours to see if he had any movement going on. Three hours passed and Sander started to feel movement in his mouth. The woman came back with three more women. They then had an elixir.

"Who are you?' Asked Sander gently. They did not answer and started to show signs of motion to insist on drinking the elixir. Sander did not drink the elixir as he was scared they were going to make the poisoning worse. The three women started to touch Sander, feeling every bone in his body. They were acting like they had never seen a man before.

Sander then questioned, "What are you doing?"

The women did not speak and they continued to do what they were doing. They figured he was some type of creature. Two women then left and decided to go and get something.

"What are you going to do to me?" Said Sander. The sun shone in the forest, making it look like a paradise island. Sander asked the women more questions, who are you, why do you have leaves and why are you naked? The women then looked at him trying to understand.

The women then replied, "What are you?"

Sander weirdly looked at them as he thought they were women as well. Sander again got a strange hit of Deja vu. They looked at him as they started to examine the body.

"Listen, aren't you human?" Said Sander. "Or are you elves?"

One of the women grabbed the elixir again and decided to give it to Sander as a gift to drink. Sander then decided to take a sip. When he did, he found out that the elixir tasted awful. They were trying to give him medicine. The women then left the cave.

"Wait, come back," said Sander. They continued walking and ignored him. Sander then waited as the sun went down and the moon went up. Sander started to feel his toes and his legs started to move. As he was recovering his powers, he said, "Riker, I think you said three days, right?"

"Yes, Sander, I said three days."

"Well, why am I feeling the numbing going away now?"

"Because I think it's what the elixir or medicine they gave you. Maybe we should get out of here, Sander. I never met women like that one thousand years ago."

Sander then told Riker that he would not go and he would go thank them. Sander then got up and felt a little off. But Sander started to look for his sword. 'The Soul Absorber must be at the beach. I must go back there and get it.' Sander walked out of the cave to see glowing leaves. Green, blue, and pink aura flying around the trees and life of the forest. Sander then saw more of the women looking and nursing the trees.

"Who are these types of people?' The women then looked at Sander and started to hide behind the trees, looking at him as he walked. The girls and women started to run and looked at Sander as he passed through the forest. Sander questioned why were they scared of him. Sander tried to look for a way out to the beach. Sander tried going up to them but the girls and women kept moving back.

"Hey, listen, I need help. Do you know where the beach is at? I need to get my sword. Please I need help."

Suddenly, all the women were scared of him. One woman had more leaves on her body than leaves on trees, walked behind Sander, and spoke. "They were all shy of you and young. They do not know your kind like me."

Sander turned around to see the woman. "Kind, you say. What race are you? You look to be elves and humans together."

The woman with the leaves told him that they were not any of those races. "Come here, follow me." She then asked Sander to walk with her to a cave. Sander continued to walk. "My sisters and children do not know of your race, human. They are isolated to protect the forest. You see the reason why there are no humans, is because humans destroy the life of forests. So, we protect the forest by attacking back. You seemed to be no harm. Are you with harm?" She looked at him with her light green delicate eyes.

Sander looked at her. "I prefer you not to call me human. My name is Sander. And what's your name if I may ask?"

"Arula," she said. "My name is Arula and I'm the queen of these lands." Sander looked around to see nothing but trees.

"Where do you guys live, if I may ask?"

She then told Sander to look up. When Sander looked up at the trees, covering the sun, the wind blew against the leaves, and Sander saw beautiful women dancing in the trees. He saw the beauty in which they were controlling the roots and the sticks of the trees as if they had nature's magic itself. Sander got a Deja vu of what in Elmus of women of such stature. Sander then looked at queen Arula again.

"What are you, if I may ask, Arula?"

Arula told Sander to continue walking. "So, you people control the forest."

She then giggled a bit and replied to Sander, "We do not control the forest. We simply nurture it. We help plants, trees, and the aura surrounding them. We bring water to the roots itself. And thanks to our creator who is in a different land. But she has soldiers and her daughters are here to protect us from humans with an army."

"And who is your creator?"

"Well, she's also a protector and she has the special gift of knowledge. All of the writing of the dragons' rules and what they do comes from her. She's called the great dragon gab. And she is like the great dragon Myrvus. You, other races know little of what we know." She then stopped at a ginormous tree bigger than the other ones. It was like that the tree was king itself.

"This is my home, my tree."

Sander looked at her in confusion. "What do you mean?"

"Sander, I'm older than the demon inside of you. And yes, I can sense his magical energy. I am exactly over one hundred centuries old. Yeah, I'm ten thousand years old. And my race, we control nature and help nurse it. We do not want war. We want peace. We helped you, now I must show you the way to the beach."

She then showed Sander as they walked back to the beach. Sander and Arula then went back and started to talk more about their creator. "So, your creator gab is a creator of nature?"

"No, you fool, she created us to help the forest. She also created the elves and some of the creatures in Calhera."

Sander looked at her with confusion. "What is Calhera?"

She then explained to Sander, "Calhera is a place on the soil which you stand on. The world that you like to call Sinia. That is Calhera. Calhera is the forest the plants the water. The sun. The moon. That is Calhera. Gab is our crater and we pray to her every day. And her sons and daughters protect us."

Sander then asked, "But her sons and daughters are dragons then."

She then shook her head yes. "They're all around you, just hidden in camouflage. They are nature dragons. They have no fire but wind magic. Now just up ahead there is the beach." Sander looked forward to run to the beach. "We can continue this conversation when I get back. Just let me get my sword." Sander ran to the beach to grabbed the Soul Absorber. When Sander arrived at the giant forest, they were gone. Like they all disappeared. Sander questioned where they went. Sander then saw a giant rock that looked like a bush of emeralds. Sander walked to it. Sander looked at it closely as green eyes opened up. Sander pulled out his sword, ready to fight it. When he did, a black dragon told the emerald dragon and Sander to stand down. The black dragon with partly gold on his body came down. The green dragon then bowed to him as he was of such importance. Sander then remembered quickly who he was.

"Wait, there was a statue in the mountain city of Dorgogon. There was a memory of Riker's that you attacked his brother. You're Colinborn, the protector of dragons."

The black and goldish dragon replied, "Yes, i am Colinborn, the protector. The dryads have told you enough of them and now they're back to tree form."

Sander looked confused about what he was saying.

"And the dragons are the protectors of the forest. Well, gabs' kin, of course. Now, I have been across the world and I will say the nature dragon will show you the way. I'm just here to introduce myself. I'm going to go find a place to meditate. I will be back in three days but it's nice to meet you, Sander."

Colinborn then flew up and went to a nearby mountain in the far north.

"Follow me, human, demon," said the nature dragon.

Sander followed the nature dragon as she led him out of the forest of giant trees. "Now, this is how far I can go. Your friends must be north. Before heading to Orcuhan, there is a border there. You must find another way. As the orcs are brutal, they want to put you in slavery. They act really barbaric. Now, that is my advice to you, human. Go now and find your friends."

Sander looked back to see the dragon walk away in the distance. Sander looked back as he put on a face as he was ready. Sander walked on the path to Orcuhan and hoped he saw his friends or comrades, some of them on the way.

Chapter 26

The Grey Mountain Knights

Sander walked along the way to see a small camp in front. He realized that his friends were not there, but four other people. Sander then realized that there were two dead people and he pulled out his sword.

"Listen, I do not want to hurt you but if you let me pass, I will not hurt you. So please, let me pass," said Sander calmly.

"That's a good-looking sword there, young boy. I would love to take it off your hands. It can be gentle or forceful. Depends on who you are." The group of strange people started to laugh. Sander realized these people were bandits. But Sander did not want to show his power as there was a small village of dwarfs ahead. Sander told them to calm down. As he said that a strange man with knight armor, who looked like a human but then Sander saw his pointy ears. Sander fought the two bandits as the other skillful armor man fought the other two bandits. The swords were clashing as both the strange knight and Sander knew what they were doing. The skillful knight managed to kill both of them by severing their heads. He then turned around to see Sander stab a bandit and make a critical hit to the stomach on the other one. Sander then turned around to see the knight with strange armor.

"May I ask who are you and what you want?"

The knight looked at him and quietly told Sander to come with him and follow him. He then pointed to the hill east of the position of a strange castle from afar. The knight began to walk that way.

Sander then followed him to see what he pointed at, to make him go away from meeting up with his friends. The knight then continued to walk with Sander beyond a forest and a land of hills to finally see a castle on a mountainside.

The knight finally spoke, "We're here, young boy with the strange sword. This is a grey mountain castle. We are a group of people who devote our lives to the cause of saving evil things in Sinia. Usually, when someone sees me, they run for their lives. Or they run from the bandits that are attacking me. But you stood and fought. In other words, our headmaster would love to meet you. So, now you may enter."

Sander looked at the Grey Mountain Castle and felt joy. Sander walked inside to see a small group of fifteen people with swords and with different races. He saw orcs, humans elves, and dwarves. United as if they were brothers. He then saw a picture of Gildor Landfield as Gildor was one of them. The knight then told everyone to meet at the mess hall. The entire fifteen people plus the knight went to the mess hall and told Sander to follow him. When Sander entered the mess hall, he saw the candles on the walls light up. He saw the giant windows of the castle. Sander walked to see the picture on the walls explaining the celestial and demon war. Sander then sees the knights line up in two lines, one on each side with a man with a greybeard in the middle. The knights then shifted and looked at each other. They then put their swords as the blade touched the ground while they held on the handle.

"For honor," they all said. The man with the greybeard then told Sander to walk to him. Sander walked up to the man with greybeard knowing that he did not probably want this. Sander then stopped at the man with a greybeard.

"Why am I here and why do you want me here?"

The man with greybeard told him, "I know you would be coming, Riker."

Sander was shocked that he knew the name Riker. The knights then knelt on the ground. The knights then said, "All hail, Riker."

Riker then told Sander in his head, "Wait, I need to check around the castle, why they worship me as a king."

The man with a greybeard said to Sander, "I know Riker is with you and we want to help Riker in his journeys. We are the knights of Grey Mountain. And we worship Riker to help us with revenge on this world. We read his side of the story and the celestials in the library. We know what the celestials did to Riker's people and we know they started the war. Riker just wanted revenge on his love. He is no different from the rest of us. So, we know Sander who you are. I have been gifted by Rhino, the great dragon to help me with the visions. They call me Greybeard here. And I want you to be a knight of the Grey Mountain. You devote your life to the cause. Saving the world from evil. Getting a new job to protect the world from evil itself. I call you now no longer Sander Helmglade. But Sander, the demonic wielder. Now do you accept this title, Sander?"

Sander realized these grey mountain knights had a lot to offer. So, Sander accepted the deal to become a knight of the Grey Mountain castle.

"Now, you are a brother. But first, you need to go and do us a favor. There is an arc angel. He goes by the name of Matthew, the arc angel. He is one of the brothers of Galatin. We want you to go with Riker by your side and kill Matthew."

Sander accepted the quest to kill Matthew. Sander went out of the castle and looked straight ahead, not knowing where to go. He then turned back to ask where was he last sighted. Greybeard told him that he was near the town and he was just with one of the knights. Sander went back to the village to see if he could find any clues about Matthew. Sander set off to the dwarven town to go and check for any clues on Matthew, the arc angel.

As he was on his way, he saw a giant bird with black feathers pass by him in the air. Sander looked at the giant bird wondering what in the world was that. Sander followed the giant bird heading toward the town of dwarfs. Sander continued to follow it as it might kill the dwarven citizens in the town. When Sander arrived, he saw the town but did not see the giant bird as if the giant black bird was just an imagination. Sander continued to walk to the town to find clues about Matthew, the arc angel.

"Alright, what is the first place I should check?" Sander had the idea that he should go to the tavern first. Sander decided to walk to the tavern. When Sander walked through the tavern, he saw the dwarfs with drinks trying to get drunk. He also saw a beautiful blond girl with brown eyes. Sander walked as if he didn't care who she was, he was there to find Matthew. He walked to the girls to say hello. She then replied hi. He gazed into her eyes to use his charm to find Matthew.

"Alright, so, I am here looking for someone."

"Who are you looking for if I may ask?" She said with a kind voice.

He told her of a man named Matthew. "This man is dangerous he has a gift that can kill everyone here. He's a dangerous man, that's all I'm saying. Do you know where can I find him?"

She pointed him in a direction, he then looked across the village house and thanked her. Sander walked out of the tavern and into someone's house. As he did that the beautiful girl decided to go outside of the tavern and into the mountain pass.

Sander walked in yelling, "Matthew are you here?"

Riker told Sander in his head, "Sander, Matthew is not here. I would sense his power. But I do feel a faded sense on that mountain pass. Maybe we should go there." Sander then followed Riker's advice to go up the mountain pass where he felt the energy.

"Also, Riker, was she lying?"

Riker said, "I did not know, Sander." Riker was confused as they walked up the mountain pass to go see who Matthew.

"Riker, have you met Matthew?"

Riker said, "I have met Matthew in the past. Matthew was a young arc angel when I was fighting."

"So, what do we do when we met him?"

"Well, Sander when we meet him we have no choice but to fight him and get answers on what Galatin's plan is. Sander, Galatin is not a good guy. He wants to conquer the world. As when he does that the humans, elves, dwarves, and all of the races in Sinia will be his slaves. The demons did not want that but they did want to have Sinia under their control as a vessel. In my realms, we're warriors and more. And in the celestial realms, there are also warriors."

As Sander and Riker got round the mountain pass, they saw a giant crater. They saw the wings of purity and the blue eyes. The black hair with ripped body. "Who is that?" Said Sander.

"That right there is Matthew, the stealth arc angel."

"Wait, who is that bartender with him? Is that the human girl? Is she his servant?" The human girl then switched to her angelic form as she turned into a beautiful white goddess. Her hair looked gold. Her eyes continued to stay brown and her wings the same as Matthew's, pure. Sander then got down and looked at them to see if they would make a move.

"Listen, this is what we're gonna do, Sander. We're gonna attack Matthew and kill him. Grab the girl and take her to Grey Mountain Castle to interrogate her on Galatian's plan."

Sander then released his wings, jumped off the high mountain, and flew down to the crater. Sander landed on the ground of the crater and looked at him with crimson-red eyes to see Matthew.

"Ashlaius," he said, "Stay back, Riker is mine."

"Let me guess," Sander said. "Galatin did not come alone in this portal." Ashlaius stood in fear as she did not know what to do in a situation like this.

"I'm here to kill you, Matthew. By orders of the Grey Mountain Castle."

"Listen here, Riker, I am not going to let you kill me and my sister." Matthew ran faster than the speed of sound. Sander saw him come closer in a slower way as he dodged the attack.

"What the heck was that, Riker?"

"Sander, I did not teach you this. But as a demonic super being like me against an arc angel like that. Speed and agility along with sword-wielding is a power of great intensity. He is going to attack you again now, dodge and take out the Soul Absorber, and fight back, Sander." Riker yelled in Sander's head. Sander then pulled out the Soul Absorber, enhancing his power to attack back. Blue flames crowded around Sander. Sander also moved faster, thanks to the sword enhancing his power. Sander fought back Matthew with rage and revenge for Galatin and Fergus.

"Where is Galatin?" Sander said. Matthew then never let his guard down. The two beings went at it with each other with multiple rounds of hits. The rocks of the crater and the mountain pass started to break. They took into the air, and Matthew flew up to the air along with Sander trying to hit and kill Matthew. The rounds were intense as the wind was their weapon. Gravity itself did not stop the two from murdering each other. Sander then charged up his attack like it was a muscle memory. Sander dashed with full speed faster than Matthew, and faster than the speed of light. Sander then severed Matthew's head and with eyes turned into fire.

"No," said the girl down in the crater watching her warrior brother die. As Sander with rage and anger passed his limit of control, Sander felt proud. Sander grabbed Matthew's head as he flew down and put it in a bag. Sander landed on the ground safely and looked at Ashlaius.

"You're next," Sander said with power and pride. Riker in Sander's head told him that he needed to relax as she was going to be a hostage. Ashlaius released her power of mind reading as it was her sisters as well.

Riker knew what she had. "Sander, I need you to capture her not kill her."

"Shut it, Riker," said Sander. "I will kill her."

Sander swung his sword but it stopped. Riker held him back from the power making Sander want more of the power.

"Riker, she's a celestial."

"Remember the plan, Sander, she is to be caught."

Ashlaius then started to run. Riker took control of Sander knocking him out in his own mind. Riker dashed fast behind her and knocked her out. He was so fast it was as if he teleported. Riker then put the sword on his back, and at full speed, he flew up and back to the Grey Mountain Castle carrying Matthew's head in a bag. Riker arrived at the Grey Mountain Castle and landed at the doorway. Giving the head to one of the knights, Riker carried the hostage into the dungeon, where Riker couldn't use his demonic or ancient magic. Finally, he placed her in the dungeons.

Chapter 27

The Interrogation

Sander woke up in his own body in one of the castle rooms.

"Riker, what did you do?" Sander said in frustration. "I had her. But you won't let me get her." Sander then rambled about how it was all Riker's fault.

Riker replied, "Listen, Sander, I stopped you because you got too corrupted with the power. It's not my fault, it is actually yours. Next time remember that the powers do not represent you. You are only borrowing these powers to fight against your brother and Galatin. You are losing yourself every time you use my powers. Remember, the power is not you. You control the power. Do not let the dark magic or magic control you. You are in control, remember that. If you remember that, I can give you more of my powers."

Sander understood. "Now, where is that lady celestial thing?"

"Her name is Ashlaius, Sander. She is in the dungeons being interrogated by the knights of the Grey Mountain Castle."

"Maybe we should go check on her."

Riker told Sander maybe he should not and he should wait until tomorrow. "The thing is the Grey Mountain knights are probs torturing her like the old ways. It's not like the ways you have done, Sander, where you talk and tell them to wait. This is the old ways and arc angels are fierce powerful warriors. So, it means, you need to break them. What do you guys like to call it? So they are probs breaking the soul of her right now."

"Why would you guys do that? That's so cruel," Sander replied with sadness. "Maybe I should go down there and ask her like a human being. Maybe she would answer to less cruel way."

"What do you mean, Sander?"

"A warrior of such high power and a fierce warrior who wants to kill you in battle with no mercy will be happy to answer questions nicely," Riker said sarcastically.

"Well, if you put it like that, no. But you got to understand she is a female. And last time I checked females are gentle and kind." Sander started to talk more about this with Riker as he walked to the dungeons.

"Listen, she's not human at all so she won't do what you think she would do. You're getting too full of pride about what you understand. I understand more than you as I lived over your last three grandfathers' timeline."

Sander told Riker to shut it as he entered the dungeons to see two knights in the cage with the celestial torturing her with a couple of nails and fists. "Tell us where your brother is?" The guard said demandingly as they pushed and violated her with everything they could do to get answers.

"Stop," said Sander. "Let me try my way," Sander said with anger. The knights looked at Sander and told him to leave.

"Why must I leave? Let me have a turn at her to see if I get any answers."

The knights then looked at her. They also began to look at Sander. "I see what you're doing, young knight. You're trying to get the angel for yourself with some alone time." The knights laughed as the celestial cried silently.

"Just please, knights, let me have alone time, maybe I might get some answers about Galatin and some other stuff."

The knights winked at Sander as they began to leave and lock the dungeon door. Sander walked into the dungeon with the celestial to see her in a corner, scared out of her mind.

"Does she look like an angel to you, Riker?"

"No, she doesn't. She looks like a scared child," Riker said in Sander's head.

She looked up as she cried in fear of what they did to her. Her broken arm and her torn-up wings. Her feathers were everywhere as they almost ripped her wings off.

"Listen, demons have a way of interrogating. But this was far beyond what we would do," Riker said in Sander's head.

"Hey, I'm Sander Helmglade. What is your name?" Sander tried to act kindly with the celestial as she was in fear of what the other humans and elves did to her. "Look I understand what they did to you and I'm sorry that happened. But I'm different. I want to know more about you, celestials with no harm done. So, maybe give me your name."

"You already know her name," said Riker in Sander's head.

"Yes, but it's gentler if I ask her."

She began to speak to Sander, "My name is Ashlaius."

"Nice to meet you," Sander said. "Now, are you hungry? If you are I can get you something to eat and some medical supplies for that arm and your wings." Sander smiled at her with a friendly face. "All right, look, I will be back in a couple of minutes and I will give you food and patch up that wound of yours." Sander went to the castle's top floor.

"Hey knights, I'mma need some bread and water."

"What for?" The knights said.

"For the prisoner, I think she's hungry." The knights then looked at Sander as if he was an idiot.

"Sander, are you all right? I think I did not hear what you just said. It sounded as if you wanted to give the prisoner food to eat."

As Sander bargained with the knights about what he wanted to do with the prisoner the headmaster came down to tell the knights to go get him some water and food. The knights bowed down and decided to go and get Sander the food and water for the prisoner.

"Sorry, Sander but I want to ask did you get any information about her."

Sander then replied, "Yes. I have her name. Her name is Ashlaius."

The headmaster was confused about the name. "I'm sorry, Sander, may you please repeat that again."

"She said her name was Ashlaius."

The headmaster had never heard of an arc angel of that name before. "Sander, keep trying to get information about her. "I'ma go upstairs to my library to see what her name could be. Good work, Sander Helmglade of the Grey Mountain Castle."

Sander then waited for the food and water. The food and water arrived and Sander went to the dungeon cell where Ashlaius was. Sander then opened the door and put the tray of food and water on the ground for her to eat.

"Look, I know it ain't much but I got to go again to get the medical supplies." Sander left again to get the medical supplies. When he went upstairs, he saw another group of knights.

"Hey, do you know where the medical supplies are?" Riker stayed dormant as Sander was trying to get the medical supplies. "Listen, she is hurt. The only way I got information was by being nice to her. Unlike you guys torturing her, I approached it differently. Now, please, show me where the medical supplies are." The knight pointed to where the medical supplies were and Sander walked towards that door. "Thanks," said Sander. Sander opened the door to see the medical supplies and saw shelves of medicine. He grabbed a cloth and string and headed back to the dungeon. When Sander arrived, he saw her eating the food.

Sander then gently walked over to her and grabbed her arm. She looked as she was scared of what he was going to do to her. Sander made the cloth and string into a sling. Making her arm not worse than it already was.

"All right, that should be better." Sander then walked to the dungeon door to close it so they can talk privately.

"Now, may I ask why are you and Galatin working together?"

She then replied, "I thank you for your kindness. But I don't know where my brother Galatin is. So, I'm sorry for not giving you good information. I was with my brother Matthew the whole time before you killed him. Why would you kill him? He was protecting me and I was protecting him. But you came with that strange sword and killed him. Why?" She asked with sadness in her heart. "Why would you kill him for no reason?"

Sander then told her it was a quest from those knights to save the world. "But now that I think of it, I feel bad for killing your brother. I'm sorry."

"Sorry is not going to cut it," she said with her sadness. She took the bread, walked over, and sat down to eat it.

Sander looked at her. "I will give you some space." Sander then walked out of the cell and went to the headmaster's office as he wanted to go speak with him. When Sander arrived at the headmaster's office he told her what happened in the cell. "Look, she does not look like a warrior. She looks like a normal female."

The headmaster then replied. "Listen, young boy. Celestials act like innocent people but in reality they are not. They are just people who have what we have. Free will to do whatever they want. And what they want is us to be in slavery. Look, it has been a long day maybe you should go get some rest. We will look after the cell and make sure she is not harmed."

Sander agreed and headed right out to go to his room and sleep it through. Sander walked into his room and slept. When he fell asleep, he saw the nightmares of what his brother did to him. Sander then later woke up in the night, scared and sweating through his clothes. He looked out the window to see a black bird staring at him. The blackbird looked tall as if it was a giant bird. Sander then closed his eyes and reopened them. He saw the blackbird. "This ain't a dream. Who or what is that?" The blackbird had black spurs of magic coming right off him. Like he was death itself. With his blue eyes, he telepathically called out to Sander.

"Listen to me, human. These people are not all the good things. These people even have dark secrets about what they are going to do with the celestial. I advise you, to save it. As Riker is dormant you have full control of his powers. He is there to make sure you don't die. Riker cares for you and you alone. Now, I must go. I will meet you in the town where you met her for the first time. Save her, Sander." The blackbird flew away like a flash into the air making the ground vibrate.

"What was that?" Sander looked out of the window of the castle. Thinking about what was that. Sander wondered why that thing was talking to him like a prophecy. Sander then stopped looking at the window, grabbed his gear, and began to go downstairs to the dungeon to rescue her. When he arrived at the dungeon, he opened the door to see her with her shredded wings.

"What happened while I was asleep?" He said to her, worried.

She answered to him in fear, "They came and wanted more answers and then I did not give them to them because it was not your type of kindness. So, what I stayed silent."

Sander then tried to break the chains but he realized that he did not have his powers. "I will be back."

Sander ran to the dungeon armory to go and get the chains as he saw two guards walking to the cell. He walked to the two guards telling them she was giving him information that he could not imagine and he needed both of them to tell the headmaster.

The two soldiers said, "Alright," and they went as they trusted Sander. Sander quickly rushed to the keys and headed straight to the cell to see Ashlaius again. Sander quickly unlocked all the chains to pick her up and told her to hold on tight. Sander then ran up the stairs to get out of the castle. As he got upstairs, Sander saw the guards of the Grey Mountain Castle. All of them stood and stayed in front of the door even the headmaster.

"Sander, you have Riker in you and you still save the celestial. You will not leave with her." Sander then quickly put her down as he lit up blue flames. The knights rushed. Sander used what Riker used in his castle to burn the insides of the knights' armor. Sander then closed his eyes and thought of burning trees. Sander reopened his eyes to see the guards burnt to ash. The headmaster was terrified of what Sander had.

Sander said, "I'm sorry but I'm not leaving without saving her. The great black bird said that."

The headmaster then told the rest of his guards to encumber Sander. Sander then burned the rest of the guards to ash as they went down like leaves. Sander grabbed her and picked her up with his super strength and decided to run and breach through the castle. Sander rans as he burned the headmaster to ash. Sander decided to walk to the town again where he met Ashlaius for the first time.

Sander then had a long walk as she began to heal herself.

Chapter 28

The Name is Raphael

As Sander and Ashlaius got to the town he realized she fully healed herself.

"Wait, what the?"

She then looked at him. "What's wrong, Sander?"

"Well, you're fully healed." Sander then stopped to drop her on the ground.

"Wait, why did you put me down, human?"

"You don't see how this works. I'm, not your slave. You should have told me you can heal yourself."

"Well, all rarefactions heal faster than humans. So technically that's your fault for not knowing that."

"My fault? I still need to regroup and find my friends. I got a little distracted from the Grey Mountain Castle. So, may you please just leave this and we can move on. Or if you want to go your own way you can. I need to regroup with my friends." Sander then continued to walk. She gave him a mean look and decided to follow him wherever he went.

"So, exactly where are we going?" Ashlaius asked rudely.

"Well, mean lady, I'm going to this town to just get settled and to show me the right path. Once then I will see where I can go."

Sander then continued to walk and talk to her as they went into the town. "Listen if you're gonna follow me, don't be annoying. I need to complete a mission."

"What's the mission?" She said.

Sander then stopped and told her what his mission was. "My mission is to kill my brother, Fergus Helmglade. And guess who is in Fergus, Your dam brother, Galatin. As I have Riker in me," Sander said, enrage.

"That's not true, you're lying," she replied. "Riker died by Galatin one thousand years ago. The battle was fierce in Luna but our hero, our prince, our next king killed the evil demon. Riker, the general of wrath." Sander opened his eyes in shock at Riker's true title. "So, you see you can't have Riker in you as he is dead. So, human, stop, you lied."

Sander then looked at her in her eyes as she looked back into his eyes. Sander closed his eyes to reopen them, showing the crimson-eyed eyes. "Riker is alive. But he has been in a pit for one thousand years. And now he's out and he wants blood for what happened to Crystal." Sander then continued to get angry as he talked about Riker's past as if he was Riker himself.

"You're lying as well. Riker killed my sister. She was pregnant and she was killed by Riker. He is a true monster. And I must stop you. Riker is a horrible person."

Riker woke up from his dormancy. "Sander, grab her head and clash it with yours. The memories will be shared." Sander did what Riker said and quickly did it to her, allowing the memories of Riker and Sander be shared with her. She shed a tear as she became angry. Sander then let go while Riker went back to being dormant. Riker stayed dormant for one reason, he did not want Sander to know much of the truth.

Sander then looked at Ashlaius with sadness over what his brother did to him. He looked in the sadness of the memoirs of Riker. Sander then wiped his tears and decided to tell Ashlaius to keep moving forward. Ashlaius wiped her tears and decided to follow Sander as she had nowhere else to be.

Sander and Ashlaius finally arrived at the town. They walked as they saw a dwarf there. "You need help," Sander asked the dwarf.

"Yes, I do," said the dwarf. "I lost my ax, it's my war ax given to me by my grandfather. Will you help me find it?"

Ashlaius saw a group of dwarves walking around. She then asked, "What does the ax look like?"

The dwarf told her that it was a two-head sharp ax with a golden carving on it. "Does it look like that?" She pointed to a group of dwarves carrying the same ax he described.

"Yes, that is the ax. But I can't get it because look at them and look at me."

Sander looked at the dwarf-like being, he had no time. While Ashlaius agreed to go get the dwarf his ax. Sander looked at her and shook his head in a 'no.'

"I don't want to go get the ax face." She then told the dwarf she agreed. The dwarf thanked her like she was a woman sent by the gods.

"The name is Raphael," the dwarf said with a greeting. "So, do I wait here or would you like me to go with you?"

Ashlaius calmly said, "Wait here."

The dwarf waited quietly as she grabbed Sander's hand and made him follow her like it was a happy adventure.

"Ashlaius, wait," said Sander. "Why did you say yes? You know that I have somewhere to be."

She said, "Well, it can wait. Someone needs our help. It's neither that nor you and me duel until I get out of my head that my brother killed my sister. And killed a baby child. And not just that lied to my people that he killed Riker and he was a fraud. So that's why I took this quest. So, we can just forget about what just happened. Now let's go find those dwarves." She then walked away with an attitude.

Sander followed as he did not want her to get hurt. They kept lurking around the giant group of dwarves. At some point of the following, they saw the dwarves enter into a forest. Sander and Ashlaius followed them into the forest leading them into a cave. When Sander and Ashlaius arrived, they heard the dwarves in the tunnels drinking and cheering that they got the ax. Ashlaius then walked in like she knew what she was going to do. Ashlaius walked in there and started to demand to give the ax back to Raphael. The dwarves stared at the arc angel and started to laugh as if they were just going to give up the ax for a simple demand.

"Listen, lady with those beautiful wings. We're not going to give it up as it belongs to us now."

"Why is that, because you steel and claim it as it's yours?"

The dwarves then agreed that was exactly what they wanted to do. Sander waited patiently as it was quiet. All of a sudden, the arc angel got mad and decided to go with the action. Sander was peacefully sitting outside, waiting for her to come with the ax, when he saw a giant light flash inside the cave, along with the screams of the dwarves calling her a demon and apologizing. Sander was shocked by how scary it got for them. She started to go brighter as they screamed because of the pain in their eyes. She told them to give the ax. The dwarves gave back the ax and half of the dwarves were burnt to the ash, only five dwarves survived. The arc angel then murdered all of them so that they couldn't tell the story.

She walked out as Sander was looking at her with shock evident on his face.

Sander asked, "Why did you do that to the dwarves?"

She told him, "Well, you did it to the Grey Mountain knights for being bad. So why can't I do this stuff to bad people, as well?"

"Yes, Ashlaius you can do that. But those Grey Mountain knights were going to kill me. All you had to do was show your true power and you could have scared them. Not murder all of them with your light and torture them. That's now how we do it around here."

She then replied, "Oh well, anyway, here is the ax. Let's go give it back to Raphael."

She quickly grabbed his hand and headed back to the village, making Sander run with her. He then asked in his head, "Why is she so positive? And why is she so scary?" They then reached the dwarf who lost the ax.

"Here you go," she said with kindness. The dwarf thanked her and called her a gift from the gods.

She said, "Well my name is Ashley."

Sander on the side whispered, calling her a liar.

"What was that, Sander?"

Sander said, "Fear nothing, Ashlaius. I mean, Ashley."

Sander stopped talking and stayed quiet. "Alright, and do you know where the border of Orcuhan is? He then told her that he did know where the border of Orcuhan was. He told her that all he needed to do was get his cart and his horse and he would be ready for the journey.

"See, Sander all you got to do is be nice."

Sander looked at her, making strange faces at her. "You just murdered a whole gang of dwarves. For not giving the ax to you," he whispered to her.

She smiled and said, "Well, I forgot that this world is a lot weaker than my realm. Now, where to, Sander? Where are your friends?"

Sander told her, "There is a forest near the border of Orcuhan. I think because that's what Colinborn said."

Ashlaius recognized the name Colinborn from the books in the celestial realm. Sander then waited patiently as the dwarf came back with a huge cart of ores and equipment to sell for the orcs.

"Wait, dwarf, are you a blacksmith?"

Raphael said, "Aye, I am a blacksmith. Listen here, human."

"The name is Sander."

"Alright, listen here, Sander. I have crafted many weapons and many armor. And I would like to sell them to the orcs in Orcuhan.

So, if you don't mind, let's get on this carriage. It's a long journey to Orcuhan."

Sander and Ashlaius got on the carriage to go to Orcuhan with the dwarf they newly met, named Raphael. The carriage left the town and went into a newly set forest.

The dwarf said, "Farewell dwarves and in Farwell town, I am going to Orcuhan with new friends. Also, Sander, I see you have black wings. I never believed the stories when I was a kid. But are you a demon? And Ashlaius I know you're an angel then if he's a demon. I read many stories when I was a child."

The stroke with the carriage was pleasant enough as they made their way to a forest.

Chapter 29

Cronovus

Raphael, Ashlaius, and Sander finally made it to the forest. They saw a giant black bird talking to a black and goldish dragon in the front of the road. Raphael stopped the carriage and told Sander and Ashlaius if they wanted to go to a different route.

"Why would we want to go to a different route? I know those creatures."

The dwarf looked at Sander with a strange face as if Sander was crazy. "Listen buddy, when you went with those dwarves, dd you bump your head a bit? Because that's a dragon and it looks like a phoenix is right there."

"Great, phoenix then," Ashlaius said with excitement. "I read about those guys. They are diplomats of the celestials demons and reaper. If that the black one then that's the demon one."

"Ashlaius, that is the bird that told me to save you from the Grey Mountain Castle."

"Really?" She said with excitement.

"Maybe we should go talk to them. And I think that's Colinborn, the protector. He is the son of a Rhino and Myrvus. He is the hero of the dragons."

"I would love the meet them can we go meet them," she said with even more excitement to the dwarf and Sander.

Sander looked at the dwarf as the dwarf looked at him. "I guess we can go see them."

The dwarf whispered to Sander, "If I die, that's on you. They look like they would eat me for lunch."

"Relax, I think Colinborn won't. I do not know about the other guy," Sander said.

The carriage continued to start going forward. when it finally arrived between the two giant creatures they both looked at Sander.

"I see you saved the celestial, Sander. For that, I thank you," said the giant blackbird. "If you do not know my name. My name is Sam, the black demon phoenix."

"That was not what he was supposed to do," Colinborn said with anger.

Sander looked at Colinborn wondering why he was so mad. "Colinborn, I'm on my way to my friends and Orcuhan."

"No, Sander, you're too late. You need to go find the sirens and sir Kevin. Jake Gildor and Raymond all got captured by the orcs at the border. You need to go get them in order to go to Orcuhan. Your first need to defeat that chieftain in a duel for you to go and save your friends. Now, your friends are all around this forest. You must find them. Once you regroup with them then you go to the kingdom of Orcuhan. I will see you there if I can."

"Wait, I don't know what you mean."

Colinborn then flew up in the air and disappeared. "Well, good luck, Sander I see what I entered into."

"Wait not you to," said Sander. Sander then saw the great phoenix flew up in the air and also disappeared. The forest then went foggy after that second. Sander started to light flames to make sure they have a torch.

"Is this better?" Ashlaius then looked at Sander.

"Well, it's ok, we can try and see where we are going. As long as we keep to the road we will be fine."

Riker then woke up from being dormant. "Sander, I sense danger nearby. But it's not a normal danger. It's the things I have created. Things I have created a long time ago. I think you should tell Sshlaius and the dwarf to stay put as we need to go check the forest to know it's clear."

"Riker is right. I heard what he said, Sander, you don't have to explain it to me. But you should do that. As it was Riker's creation that stopped us from going to the land of orcs."

Sander looked at Ashlaius. "Why are you so mean to me?"

Ashlaius then replied, "Because I'm not dumb enough to make a deal with a demon even at my death."

The dwarf looked side to side as he did not know what was going on. "Ok, stop both of you. I hate it when you bicker. Now, Sander, what do you have to do? And who is Riker?"

"I will explain what Riker is later. But for now, Raphael and Ashlaius, you must stay here as I will go check out what darkness is in the forest."

Sander then walked into the fog as Ashlaius and Raphael saw him disappear. Sander continued to walk on the road. He then felt a dash of wind flash by him - like a dark, giant shadow walked by him. Sander then follows the giant shadow into the forest. Sander then lost it among the trees, he felt as if he was being hunted. He saw a dash of red eyes in the distance.

"Riker, who do you think that is, it's definitely not you. You are in my body so who is that?"

"Let me put the pieces back together, Sander. Giant shadow. Red eyes. Sander, get closer to it."

"Riker, are you insane? That thing can kill me."

"If I know what it is, you will not die since you have me inside you. Now, go closer to it," Riker then demanded Sander to go closer to the giant shadow with red eyes. Sander got closer and realized he saw claws. Riker started talking to him. The giant-like creature with red eyes and black as night looked at Sander like he was about to attack. Riker did something, the beast then turned into an elf.

"Hey kid, what did you just say?" The elf being just talked back after turning into human form.

"Wait, are you a werewolf?" Sander said, in shock.

The elf then replied, "Yes, I am the werewolf."

"The werewolf?" said Sander. "There are more of you."

The elf then started talking. "Listen kid, I spared your life. So, tell me why you said Riker a moment ago?"

"Oh, Riker, do you know the name?" Said Sander.

The elf replied to Sander. "Yes, I know the name. He is the one who created me."

Riker then told Sander, "Wait, Sander, I know him. Sander, I created him and seven others. This is Cronovus, the black night werewolf. The first of the black werewolf, Sander."

"Wait, Riker, if he's Cronovus. The werewolves have been carving their name, the black ones every time they go some were. What does that mean?"

Riker then told him that it was because the werewolves were predicting that the original werewolves were coming back.

"Wait, you said there's a total of eight. I thought they were five," yelled Sander in his head. As Riker and Sander were talking, Cronovus got angry about why sander was not answering him.

"Listen, you idiot human, I will kill you if you do not answer me. Why do you say the name, Riker?"

Sander stopped talking to Riker about werewolves and yelled at Cronovus telling him the truth of why he said the name Riker. "Listen, Cronovus, he told me your name, so don't complain. Riker is fused with me as a human. That's why I know Riker."

Cronovus then began to start laughing. "Sander, we can have this conservation later about werewolves. Right now, Cronovus has not believed you, so he is gonna fight you to test that you have a demon inside of you. We should be regrouping with my friends not doing this."

Sander then pulled out the Soul Absorber. Cronovus then turned into a giant fifteen-foot werewolf. Cronovus swung his claws, pushing Sander two miles back into the forest.

"How strong is he?" Sander said to Riker in his head.

"Well, Sander, he's the third strongest in the original pack." Sander grabbed the Soul Absorber. Cronovus, in his werewolf form, ran towards at Sander with all his might about to launch him back again. Sander held on to the Soul Absorber, cutting Cronovus and lighting up blue flames from his body.

"Stop it!" Sander said with anger and rage in his body.

Cronovus then turned back to elf form and knelt to Sander. "You do have Riker in you. I'm sorry for landing a hand on you. Master, I am here." Riker told Sander to tell Cronovus that it was ok that he did not know. Sander told Cronovus what Riker said.

"You can stand up, you know," Sander said. "I'm, not your king."

Cronovus said, "I know that but Riker is. Riker helped fight the war against the celestials. And I will serve him for that. I finally got a lot of revenge and wrath on the celestials from my family."

Riker wanted to hear more about Cronovus's back story. So, Sander sat down and Cronovus told what happened. Cronovus said he did not want to talk about it. So, Sander then asked Cronovus if he had time to show them the forest and also that he was looking for a group of humans. Cronovus said he knew where they were.

"Where are they?" Said Sander.

"There in my girlfriend's cabin."

"Wait, girlfriend?"

Cronovus said that she was a vampire and decided she wanted them as a snack or dinner.

"But does one look like the age of fifteen with two guards?"

Sander agreed that it was Kevin. "Yes, that's my cousin and his guards. Can you show me where the cabin is?"

Cronovus decided to show Sander where the cabin was. As Sander got up, he heard Ashlaius force in his head. "Wait, why is she in my head?"

"Sander, I want to warn you that vampires and werewolves are bad."

Sander replied in his head back to her. "How are you in my head?" As he walked with Cronovus to the cabin.

"Because that's one of my powers," she said calmly in her head.

The werewolf finally reached the cabin as he turned into elven form and entered. Sander continued to talk to Ashlaius telepathically. Sander told Ashlaius to shut up and that he got this. Sander thought he knew what to do with a vampire and werewolf. Sander entered the cabin and saw Kevin and two of his guards.

"Hey, Sander, how is it going? Did you find Duvessa and the other sirens?"

Sander replied with a no. "Kevin, may you please tell me what happened after Cronovus's story?" Kevin agreed as a vampire started to sit next to him and listened to Cronovus's story.

Chapter 30

The Beginning of the Werewolves

"This is my story guys. This all started long ago a thousand years ago when everything was peaceful at first. The celestial and demons were at peace. It was like a golden age for all of us. Until a demon crossed a line. The celestials then went to war with the demons. And anyone between Sinia was set to die. Or be cannon fodder or unknown casualties. It was at that time they sent their most powerful hero. Their strongest archangel to control Sinia and make their vassal. Sinia was seventy percent almost captured. Until one young boy. A young man stood against leading a handful of demons. He later gathered an army. To fight back. His name was Riker, the revengeful. Some tribes of men elves and dwarves stood by him. With dark magic on their side, it was like we were winning. Riker got a hold of some sirens and turned them into dark sirens. Making our underwater legions stand their ground. At first, it was going well. Until the celestials manipulated the other side telling them that the demons were at fault. That they are trying to conquer the land. So, Sinia, for five hundred years, was at war with itself. Until Riker made vampires. Half dead and half alive. They were smart but there were not enough. So, then he moved to us next. The werewolves. There were seven who stepped up. The reason, why I stood to fight, was that. My family was killed by the celestials. They chose not to fight with them. What the celestials did was kill my entire tribe. I fell in love with a girl. But she also died in my eyes. The celestials were just too powerful. The other seven had their reason. But one of them was half-demon and half-human. He was the red wolf, later on. Our leader in this fight had around over five thousand demons doing the ritual. As there were dead wolfs spirits and human elves and dwarves. In the ancient ruins, the magic flowed. We closed our eyes to see the brick of purgatory. But when we awake, we all felt more strongly than ever. We became faster and stronger. We were able to see for two miles. And we were able to hear from two miles as well. It felt as if we were able to fight against the celestials. So, we found a way to train. We trained for two years against demons. It was time for our first battle. The celestial had a fort. They sent us in as cannon fodder. All eight of us ran into that celestial fort being commanded by an angel. The angels are the third class of the celestial race. There were about five hundred of them. Our job was to take the castle so we could have a battle advantage. As we were taking the castle the demons were trying to attack two different areas, the celestials had a couple of my tribe into slavery. I rescued them from that fort. And murdered and killed every single one of them. The celestials were not on the good side. They were the ones who wanted to destroy, or so I thought. After that day, we became an elite group of units to attack and kill celestials. Riker later told us who was the one who was running the show. The one who wants to conquer Sinia. After that, we decided to hunt down every fort. I learned the gift of turning when I was seventeen years of age. I was fifteen when I first became a werewolf. I was the first to know about turning. It was when my tribe wanted to fight with me. There was an animal part of me who wanted to bite them. All of a sudden, when I was a wolf, I bit and started to scratch everyone in my tribe. After turning back to elven form, I see that the members of my tribe started turning into werewolves like me. They all obeyed me as they had no choice. And this was the first time the black werewolf became a species. Because of me. I told it to the rest and my comrades. My brothers. My friends. My pack. They began to do it, as well. Sooner, in like six months, we had an army of werewolves. But they were not as strong as us. They had a quarter of our power. But we had over one million total werewolves of all eight species. We wanted to go see Riker. But all of a sudden, as we were in many battles, Riker disappeared into the black night forest. For three hundred years, they were gone. Yes, we werewolves knew about Riker and Crystal, second in command of the celestials. We patrolled his land around the cottage. He told us information to attack the land. We were gaining Sinia's freedom. We had over eighty percent of the land. It was going well. Until Riker told us what happened that one day. Everyone started to gather their forces for one last assault, we called it the Battle of Luna. Until the celestials manipulated it again.

Us, eight barely escaped. And when we did, we doomed ourselves for a thousand years. But our tribes our species still lived. But we did not know what happened to them for one thousand years. A year ago, I was awoken. To see the world change. I think, I awoke the rest of my comrades. They are right now looking for their tribes.

And me, I am here looking for mine. Until a beautiful girl showed me that vampires are not all bad. And she also was about to drink my blood. She shot me with an arrow when I was in beast form. This is how I and Holie Syborn met. Then after that, I met three new people. Took them to my cabin with Holie to treat them. They barely survived an attack. Then later, I met a human who has Riker with him. Master, I hope you know after the Battle of Luna, the war continued. And we won. But the demons later retreated into the demon realm same as the celestials. And us eight werewolves along with Colinborn, the protector, know of a place of secrets. That is my story and now I will look to you guys for some answers."

The group was shocked by his story. Kevin then asked, "So why are you looking for your species?"

Cronovus then told him that it was because he could control the black werewolves and command them as he was the first alpha.

"Now, any more questions?" He asked the group.

The group stayed silent for three hours.

"So, what about your story?" Cronovus then looked to Kevin as he was ready to tell his story since the boat.

Chapter 31

Regrouping

"It all started, Sander when we were on the ship. Kevin and the group went into the boat. My guard, I think risks his life trying to make space. I am forever to show him honor. We went in the boat. Me, Duvessa, Scorpius, Ares, Jake, Gildor, and Raymond. And well, two of my guards. We settled in the water as you battle the giant snake dragon. We did see your fire from afar. We rowed to a place. It was a town. We knew you were going to Orcuhan, so we found someone to take us there. As we were on the way, we saw many things. We rescued many things. People. Leave girls and whatnot. We continued to go along the road to Orcuhan. It was around a day or two that made it complicated. Duvessa and Gildor started to think that you would not come back. I never left the faith. I stood saying that you never died. But you were gone for a long time, Sander. So, we had to come up with something. We settled to go to Orcuhan. When we got there the orcs did not let us in. So, we challenged their chief. It was a battle to the death. Ares won the battle. But kicked me Raymond Gildor and my guards out. It was like he changed. He and the sirens stayed with him. Duvessa, I think was learning now how to use a glave. And Scorpius is training the orcs. So, Sander, the truth is, you have to go to Orcuhan so that we can reclaim that you're not dead. After that, we split up. Jake was taken hostage by the orcs or Ares took him hostage. He is now forced to make armors. There really ain't much to tell but we split up. But then Gildor went his own way. He went looking for black werewolves. He is right now hunting black werewolves."

As Kevin was telling his story Cronovus was shocked that they had a werewolf hunter in their group.

"Yeah, and Raymond, I think he's hunting some vampires. They're both trying to grieve for you, Sander. But now since you're alive, we can go find Gildor in the town. He must have heard something about Cronovus." Cronovus got angry as Holie told them to get out.

"Listen, I need to find my group. We're on a mission." Sander then turned to Cronovus. "Look, I have Ashlaius and Raphael waiting for me in a carriage, I can tell them the location. They can spend the night here. But we need to find Gildor and Raymond to head to Orcuhan. Cronovus, Galatin is back and he's in my brother. If you want revenge, he is in the kingdom of Luna. But if you want to play it safe, come with us. I don't know about your girlfriend but she can come too. Now, Holie, I will warn you it might be dangerous but as long as you are part of my group, I will do what I can to not make you die. So, I will give you time to see what you can do with the decision. Kevin, you stay here, I need to go check on Ashlaius and bring them here."

Sander left the cabin as he headed back to Ashlaius and Raphael. "Guys, I found one of my friends. Well, I found my cousin. Now, follow me we're going to spend the night there," said Sander.

"No, no, no. I came here to go to Orcuhan. So, if you're not going to Orcuhan, I understand. But I need to go to Orcuhan. Ashlaius, are you coming, my dear?"

Ashlaius looked at Sander and then looked at Raphael. "Well, Raphael, maybe they have drinks there that you dwarves like."

Raphael looked at Ashlaius and Sander. "To the cabin!" He said with excitement. "You could have just led with that, I would love to have some drinks there. Sander, you lucky, they have drinks."

Sander looked at Ashlaius, wondering why would you say that to the dwarf. The dwarf then strolled his carriage to the cabin. "Well, show me the way, Sander." Sander then showed the dwarf the way to the cabin. When Sander arrived at the cabin, he entered Holie's cabin to tell her a dwarf and a celestial were part of the group, too. Cronovus got angry.

"Why is the celestial here? I will go kill her!" He said with anger.

"No, Cronovus, she's a part of our group that you will be signing up for."

Sander then tried to push Cronovus back as the dwarf and the celestial got the tents together. "Cronovus, she's with us and she was not born during the age of the war. She was born in the age after."

Cronovus then yelled at Sander, "So, is she a third-class angel or an archangel? Well, she is an archangel but she seems to be no harm. She is kinda stupid and clueless." Cronovus looked at the celestial and looked at Sander. "Oh, I see you, Sander. Looks like Sander has something going on for the celestial."

"No, that's not what I'm saying."

The people in the cabin started to laugh and giggle. Kevin got up and walked to Sander. "Look, Sander, I know you're using demonic powers. But I think you don't stand a chance. Maybe have a human."

Sander pushed Kevin. "I'm not in love or have something with her. All you need to know is that a giant black bird named Sam told me to go and save her from the Grey Mountain knights."

Cronovus got happy. "Wait, did you just say a giant black bird named Sam? You must be talking about Sam, the blackbird demon. I have known him since the war. He is wise. If he says to save her then I won't attack her. Unless she is attacking our group. That is the only time I will attack her." Cronovus then sat down.

"Now, what do we do now?" Said Kevin.

"Well, I say that we should have two for a tent. And we need Gildor to come here. And Gildor's favorite thing to do is get werewolves. So, let's get an original on the path to get Gildor."

"It's easy, Cronovus, all you have to do is wreak havoc for two days and he will come, I promise. But as long as you don't kill anyone we are ok with that." Cronovus kindly agreed and decided to go and wreak havoc in the forest. Cronovus took a trip to the forest to wreak havoc with some nearby lumberjacks. Sander told Kevin and his guards to go sleep outside in the tents.

"The night is late and we must get some sleep. We will be going in groups to the town to spot Gildor. So, let us begin this plan. After we get Gildor, we get Raymond. But Holie, you can relax because I know you're a vampire. All you got to do is not kill anyone."

"Wait, you're a vampire," said Kevin. "Wait, that's why you're being nice. You were gonna drink our blood."

She smiled at Kevin and said she was sorry and she was going to be careful. "But we're friends now so we're gonna be fine."

She then got excited as she ran towards the room. Kevin looked at her and decided to go outside to the tents. As the guards started to follow him, not stopping their duty to protect the heir to the Gladstone's family name. Sander then asked Holie if she and

Cronovus were coming to the group or not. She yelled from her room as she said yes that she would be coming to the group.

Sander then left the cabin to go and get sleep in the tent. The wind was soothing as Sander lay in night rest. The sun began to rise and everyone was swelled. Sander slept normally in the tent. Ashlaius then woke Sander up with a gentle touch telling him to wake up. Sander woke up to see a blond-brown eye person right next to him. Sander then quickly woke up telling her to go away. She then yelled at him telling him that she was just trying to wake him.

"You're a perv, you know that, thinking that I would just do that. I'm a celestial race so that means I am a warrior, too. You are just ignorant and overthinking things. This is why humans should not be in contact with celestials. You're such a pervert, you piece of crap."

Sander looked at her as he said in his head. "Omg, jeez, she needs to calm down."

"Sander, I think you need to relax with this one," said Riker in his head. "So, who do you think is going first, Sander? Who do you think is going first to the town, you, Ashlaius and Raphael, or Kevin and his guards?

"I think Kevin is going, Riker."

"Well, Sander what are you going to find to do?

"I think I might teach Ashlaius about this world."

Riker told Sander, "You know, I can feel you like her, right?"

Sander then started to feel more about Ashlaius. "I know but as long as the group does not know I am good." as he is ready to tell his story since the boat.

Chapter 32

Regrouping

It all started, Sander, when we were on the ship. Kevin and the group went into the boat. My guard, I think, risked his life trying to make space. I am forever to show him honor. We went into the boat—me, Duvessa, Scorpius, Ares, Jake, Gildor, Raymond, and two of my guards. We settled in the water as you battled the giant snake dragon. We saw your fire from afar. We rowed to a place—it was a town. We knew you were going to Orcuhan, so we found someone to take us there. Along the way, we saw many things and rescued people, including slave girls and whatnot. We continued on the road to Orcuhan. It took about a day or two, which made things complicated. Duvessa and Gildor started to think you wouldn't come back. I never lost faith. I stood firm, saying you had not died. But, Sander, you were gone for a long time.

So we had to come up with a plan. We decided to go to Orcuhan. When we got there, the orcs wouldn't let us in, so we challenged their chief. It was a battle to the death. Ares won the battle but kicked me, Raymond, Gildor, and my guards out. It was like he changed. He and the sirens stayed with him. Duvessa, I think, is now learning how to use a glaive, and Scorpius is training the orcs. So, Sander, the truth is, you have to go to Orcuhan, so we can prove that you're not dead.

After that, we split up. Jake was taken hostage by the orcs, or maybe Ares took him hostage. He's now forced to make armor. There's not much else to tell, but we split up. Gildor went his own way. He went looking for black werewolves. He's hunting them now. Kevin is telling his story when Cronovus got shocked that we have a werewolf hunter in our group. Yeah, and Raymond, I think, is hunting vampires. They're both trying to grieve for you, Sander. But now that you're alive, we can go find Gildor in the town. He must have heard something about Cronovus.

Cronovus began to get angry as Holie told him to calm down. "Listen, I need to find my group. We're on a mission," Sander said, then turned to Cronovus. "Look, I have Ashlaius and Raphael waiting for me in a carriage. I can tell them the location. They can spend the night here, but we need to find Gildor and Raymond and head to Orcuhan. Cronovus, Gelatin is back, and he's in my brother. If you want revenge, he is in the Kingdom of Luna. But if you want to play it safe, come with us. I don't know about your girlfriend, but she can come too. Holie, I will warn you, it might be dangerous, but as long as you're part of my group, I will do what I can to keep you safe. So, I'll give you time to think about your decision. Kevin, you stay here. I need to check on Ashlaius and bring them here."

Sander leaves the cabin and heads back to Ashlaius and Raphael. "Guys, I found one of my friends — well, my cousin. Now follow me, we're going to spend the night there," Sander said. "No, no, no, I came here to go to Orcuhan. So, if you're not going, I understand. But I need to go to Orcuhan. Ashley, are you coming, my dear?"

Ashley looks at Sander and then at Raphael. "Well, Raphael, maybe they have drinks there that you dwarves like," she said. Raphael looked at Ashley and Sander. "To the cabin!" he said with excitement. "You could have just led with that! I would love to have some drinks. Sander, you're lucky they have drinks!" Sander looks at Ashley, wondering why she would say that to the dwarf. The dwarf then strolls his carriage to the cabin. "Well, show me the way, Sander." Sander then shows the dwarf the way to the cabin.

When Sander arrives at the cabin, he enters Holie's cabin to tell her that a dwarf and a celestial are part of the group too. Cronovus gets angry. "Why is the celestial here? I'll kill her!" he says in anger. "No, Cronovus, she's part of our group that you'll be joining." Sander tries to push Cronovus back as the dwarf and celestial set up their tents. "Cronovus, she's with us. She wasn't born during the war; she was born afterward." Cronovus yells at Sander, "So, is she a third-class angel or an archangel?" "Well, she is an archangel, but she's harmless. She's kinda clueless," Sander says. Cronovus looks at the celestial and then back at Sander. "Oh, I see, Sander. Looks like Sander has a thing for the celestial!" "No, that's not what I'm saying!" The people in the cabin laugh. Kevin walks over to Sander. "Look, Sander, I know you're using demonic powers, but I don't think you stand a chance. Maybe stick with a human." Sander pushes Kevin. "I'm not in love with her or anything. All you need to know is that a giant black bird named Sam told me to save her from the Grey Mountain Knights."

Cronovus looks surprised. "Wait, did you say a giant black bird named Sam? That must be Sam, the Blackbird Demon. I knew him from the war. He's wise. If he says to save her, then I won't attack her, unless she attacks us first. Then I will fight her." Cronovus sits down. "Now, what do we do?" Kevin asks. "Well, I think we should pair up for the tents. We need Gildor to come here. His favorite thing is hunting werewolves, so we need to find him. It's easy, Cronovus. All you have to do is cause some havoc for two days, and he'll come. But don't kill anyone. We're fine with a little chaos." Cronovus agrees and goes off to wreak havoc in the forest with some nearby lumberjacks.

Sander tells Kevin and his guards to sleep outside in the tents. "It's late, and we need sleep. We'll go in groups to the town to find Gildor. After that, we'll get Raymond. Holie, you can relax, because I know you're a vampire. Just don't kill anyone." "Wait, you're a vampire?" Kevin asks. "That's why you were being so nice! You were gonna drink our blood!" Holie smiles and says, "I'm sorry. But we're friends now, so we're going to be fine!" She then gets excited and runs to her room.

Kevin decides to go outside to the tents, followed by the guards, who remain diligent in their duty to protect the heir to the Gladestone family name. Sander then asks Holie if she and Cronovus are joining the group. She yells from her room, saying they'll both join. Sander then leaves the cabin to sleep in the tent. The soothing wind helps him drift into sleep.

The sun rises, and everyone is up. Sander still sleeps peacefully in the tent until Ashlaius gently wakes him. Sander wakes to see a blond, brown-eyed person next to him and quickly tells her to go away. She yells at him, saying, "I was just trying to wake you! You're such a pervert for thinking I'd do something! I'm a celestial warrior. You're so ignorant! This is why humans shouldn't be around celestials." Sander looks at her, thinking, "Oh my god, she needs to calm down."

Riker, speaking in Sander's head, says, "Sander, I think you need to relax with this one. Who's going first? You, Ashlaius, Raphael, or Kevin and his guards?" "I think Kevin is going first," Sander responds. "Well, Sander, what are you going to do?" Riker asks. "I think I might teach Ashlaius about this world," Sander says. "You know, I can feel that you like her, right?" Riker adds. Sander begins to think more about Ashlaius. "I know, but as long as the group doesn't find out, I'm good."

Chapter 33

Ashlaius First Encounter with the Land of Sinia

"Alright, looks like I'm going to the town first," said Kevin. "I'll let you know if I find Gildor." Kevin and his guards start to leave for the town. As they leave, Sander thinks to himself that he should show the celestial how this world works. Sander begins to walk over to Ashlaius and asks her for a walk.

"Sure, I guess I can walk in the forest with you, Sander," Ashlaius replied.

Sander begins to walk with Ashlaius in the forest. "Look, I know what realm you came from, but this world is sensitive and dangerous," Sander said as they walked. "I know you want to help and all, but I have my own mission. And I'll tell you this—if you want to go and explore the world, then go explore it. But I've got my own dealings to handle."

He then stops to look at the sky as he watches the clouds slowly move. Ashlaius wonders why he is telling her this.

"Look, Ashlaius, you killed a lot of dwarves for not giving you axes. Wherever you come from, we don't do things like that here. I know they were mean, but still, it gives you no right to use your powers and kill them all. There could have been a different approach, like asking them for a duel."

Ashlaius responds, "Well, in my world, if you want something, you must fight for it. So, I guess I was wrong. No wonder they were screaming."

"Ashlaius, follow me," Sander says, grabbing her hand and taking her deeper into the forest. "Look at the life here. Look at the trees, the leaves blowing in the wind, the animals running around, and us talking about these things. Here, we call this life. We don't make anyone follow orders. We live our own lives. No celestial or demonic laws — just a pure life here."

"Well, if you talk about such a pure life, why did you kill my brother Matthew then?" Ashlaius asks.

Sander replies, "Ashlaius, I'm sorry for killing your brother. I thought I was doing the right thing. For that, I apologize. But the Grey Mountain Knights knew what they were doing until I found out what they did to you. Then a blackbird told me to save you."

She then gets angry. "I'm going to tell you this once. That blackbird is called Sam, the Black Phoenix. He is a wise bird. So, whatever he says, I think you should listen."

"Listen, Ashlaius, I'll call him the Blackbird, but there are other things I want to show you," Sander says as he grabs her hand and leads her to a lumber yard. "Look, that is a lumber yard. They collect wood, but there are many people in this lumber yard who have lives."

"Are the lumber yard people bad?" Ashlaius asks.

Sander begins to teach her about lumber yards and what they do to benefit the world. Sander then takes her to see the farms near the town. "Look, these are farms. They help make food for people to eat," Sander explains, continuing to tell her more about the resources of the world and how they benefit the people.

He then grabs her hand and moves to a stone quarry. "This is a stone quarry. They gather bricks and stone to make castles. Ashlaius, this world is more than life and earth. There's more to explore than you think."

Sander explains what stone can do for the people in the town. He then grabs her hand and returns to the forest. "I haven't had this much fun in a long time," Sander says.

Sander then tells Ashlaius, "So, you see, the world is not like your realm. Look at those animals over there. They're like a family."

Sander then takes a breather. Ashlaius, noticing him sitting on the soft grass, asks, "What are you doing?"

"I'm taking a breather," Sander replies.

Ashlaius, confused, asks, "What's a breather?" since she is breathing constantly. Sander tells her to take a seat.

Ashlaius feels unsure of what he is about to do, but Sander gently instructs her to sit down and take one slow breath. She begins to relax as she slowly takes a breather. "You see, Ashlaius, this is what we call fun. I forgot who taught me to have fun, but I think it was someone important in my life."

Sander closes his eyes and sees a shadow with him in the Castle of Elmus. He tries to think about who this shadow is but sees nothing. Sander begins to wonder who this shadow is as he opens his eyes and lies back. He glances over and sees Ashlaius sleeping next to him in the soft grass. Sander looks at her gentle blond hair and her peaceful face, feeling butterflies in his stomach. He tries to focus on something else and looks up at the clouds.

"Hey, Riker, do you know much about the demonic laws?" Sander asks.

Riker awakens within his system, giving Sander advice about Ashlaius and explaining the laws of the demonic realm.

"Sander, demonic laws are different from celestial and reaper laws, but some are the same. For instance, grabbing souls and eating them—that's not allowed by any race. But in the war, we had no choice. It almost escalated to the point where the reapers were going to go to war with us and the celestials for eating too many souls. So, we used them as rations. The reapers weren't happy with my actions, but they weren't happy with Galatin's either."

Riker continues, "That's the reason they made the law against eating souls. All races can do it from the rarefactions and higher, but the reaper that came was scared of me, so the next reaper will be stronger, more like a warrior. So, Sander, when you steal a soul, be careful. Leave some for the reapers to reap. Like next time, take fifty percent of the soul so they have a place to go, and you can gain some power from it. I'll teach you that later."

"Another law you need to know is the honorable law—the law of battle. If we attack anyone, we must give them an honorable death. We learned it from the samurais in a different land. When we kill our enemies, we must sever their heads from their bodies. This law was created after the samurais taught us."

Riker pauses, then adds, "But when we fight Galatin and Fergus, we cannot follow that law, as they will kill us before we can. Galatin is a cruel archangel. He's a liar and a deceiver. But he's also a great warrior, matching my fighting style. That's why people couldn't take us out. The gods and the great dragons created a balance, and that balance is me and Galatin."

"Sander, I know this is a lot of information, but the more laws I tell you, the more your mind might explode. The only law you need to follow for now is not to eat souls unless I say so."

"Now, Sander, Ashlaius will wake up soon. Explain to her why I'm in your body and why we're talking so much. She may think we're friends, but we're really not. We're just partners until Galatin is dead," Riker says as he goes dormant.

Sander then thinks to himself that Riker is lying, as he feels it.

Ashlaius begins to wake up next to Sander. "Well, hi. How was your sleep?" Sander asks.

Ashlaius gets angry. "Wait, why are you angry at me? What did I do?" Sander asks, confused.

"You didn't wake me up while I was sleeping!" she snaps.

"Look, I didn't know you wanted to be woken up. I just let you sleep. No need to hurt me for that. I was just going to ask how your rest was. Did you rest well? I'm sorry," Sander apologizes.

Ashlaius calms down. "Did you at least watch over me?" she asks with a calm voice.

"Yes," Sander replies. "No one touched you in a weird way."

She begins to get angry again. "So, did you touch me in a weird way?" she demands.

"No!" Sander responds, now scared of Ashlaius when she is mad.

"Look, let's head back to the cabin. Maybe we can calm down there," Sander suggests, shaking as he speaks.

Sander gets up, and Ashlaius follows. She gives him a kiss on the cheek to thank him for protecting her. "Thank you, Sander, for protecting me. Usually, I have guards for that, but since I'm alone in this strange world, I guess you can be my protector. Thank you for signing up to be my guard," she says before running toward the cabin, knowing the way through the forest.

Sander looks at Ashlaius in a weird way and thinks to himself, "Wait, so I protected her while she slept, got a kiss on the cheek, and now I'm her guard? Gods, she has a lot to learn. I hate that I have to teach her all this."

Sander then looks up at the sky. "If I have to protect her, what is she going to do?"

"Sander, are you coming? I need my guard," Ashlaius calls out.

Sander stops pondering and begins to follow Ashlaius. He knows he needs to teach her more about the world. Sander and Ashlaius arrive at the cabin to see the group getting ready.

"Sander, you're here! We're next to fight Gildor in the night shift, right?" the dwarf asks.

Sander agrees as the dwarf continues to talk to himself about ores. "Ashlaius, we're going to be the next shift."

"Okay, my loyal guard," she says as she walks into the house.

Sander then mutters to himself, "I'm going to hate being called that now."

As the sun starts to set, Sander waits for Kevin to return with his guards. Raphael begins to prepare the fire for Kevin and his guards, cooking food and drinks for their return.

"What are you doing, Raphael?" Sander asks eagerly.

"I'm making them food and getting drinks ready for this Gildor fellow," Raphael replies.

Sander tells the dwarf, "Gildor's not going to arrive—it's too early."

Raphael responds, "So, why did you send them out there then? You sent two giant humans with armor and a boy to get a man who probably carries a great sword? Now you're telling me that, Sander the demon man?"

"Don't call me that—call me Sander!" Sander says, starting to get frustrated as the dwarf mumbles to himself.

Sander begins to ponder while the dwarf gets things ready for the group's return. The dwarf then asks, "What about that Raymond fellow? You think he'll show up with Gildor?"

Raphael grabs another plate and fills it with ale. "It's always good to make extras for the group," he says, then heads back to his carriage to get more food for the group.

"Dang, Raphael, how much food do you even have?" Sander asks.

"I have plenty for the journey to Orcuhan," the dwarf responds. "Also, Sander, do you know how to consume fire? We need to cross the area of the Lava Titans, and you must play nice with them—they're very territorial."

Sander tells the dwarf that he'll try to consume the fire. As the sun goes down, Sander closes his eyes to think about the shadow he saw earlier. The smell, the taste of the shadow's lips—Sander starts to wonder who this shadow is, or who she might be. As he ponders, Ashlaius calls out from inside the house, "Who's that?"

The dwarf gets excited as he sees people approaching.

Chapter 34
Back On Task

"No way, Sander, is that you?" Yelled Gildor from afar. Sander opens his eyes to see Gildor waving at him. Raymond follows behind Gildor. Raphael begins to prepare another plate as he notices the new arrivals. While Raphael cooks bread and meat, gathering drinks for everyone, Gildor, Raymond, Kevin, and his guards make their way to the cabin. As they approach the cabin, Cronovus, in elf form, emerges from the forest.

"Hello, Gildor and Raymond, how are you doing?" Sander asks.

Gildor and Raymond, excited, roughly pat Sander on the back. "I'm glad you're alive, Sander," said Gildor.

"Yeah, we thought you were dead," added Raymond.

Gildor begins to recount what happened after the boat ride to Orcuhan's borders. "The group split up, Sander. Ares wanted to lead, but I said we should wait for you. But when you didn't show, we thought you were dead and we all went our separate ways. Sorry for that, but now that you're alive, we can head to Orcuhan. By the way, have you seen a werewolf around? I heard one last night. It's strange because werewolves usually don't come out this early."

Sander then tells Gildor that the werewolf is on their side. Gildor laughs, and Raymond joins in. Kevin and his guards approach Raphael to ask for food. The dwarf gladly offers them food and drinks. As Gildor and Raymond continue to laugh, Sander assures them he's telling the truth. Gildor stops laughing and gets angry at Sander for what he perceives as a mistake.

"Sander, listen to me. Werewolves aren't to be controlled—they're just ravaging beasts that want to destroy everything in their path," Gildor says angrily.

As Gildor speaks about the dangers of werewolves, Cronovus appears behind him.

"So, a werewolf hunter now?" Cronovus remarks. "I sensed you when you entered the forest. If you're looking for a werewolf, I'm here. I'm the one you heard last night, the only werewolf here—a lone wolf."

"Well, that makes it easier for me," Gildor says, drawing his greatsword.

Cronovus stops the blade with incredible speed. "How are you this fast? No werewolf is this fast!" Gildor exclaims.

Cronovus explains, "I'm the first black werewolf. Listen, I don't know your name, but yes, I'm a werewolf. Deal with it. It actually makes things easier for the group since I can control other werewolves. Every first werewolf can control their own species. If a black werewolf pack attacks, they won't need to fight—we can control them. If you don't like the idea, I guess I can let you kill me."

Gildor pauses, considering Cronovus' words, and then releases his grip on the sword. "Fine, you can come along, as long as you leave me alone," Gildor says angrily.

Gildor then joins Raphael for food and drinks. Raymond is about to follow until Sander stops him. "Wait, Raymond, I also need to talk to you. We don't just have a werewolf on our side, but also a pure-blood vampire."

Raymond begins to yell. "Are you serious? You have a werewolf and a vampire on your side? What's the vampire's deal? Can she control other vampires?"

Sander explains, "No, she can't. She's just a normal pure-blood vampire."

Raymond continues to shout, "So now what do we do? Gildor and I hunt vampires and werewolves. What happens when vampires come around? Do we just let the vampire and the werewolf handle everything? You're literally taking away our jobs, Sander."

Gildor runs over to Raymond. "Listen, Raymond, it's easier this way. If you think about it, we can be the backup plan if diplomacy doesn't work. And since I've heard she isn't an original vampire, that makes you a valuable asset if things go wrong, which they will sixty percent of the time. Now calm down, eat some food, and we'll talk about this on the journey. Trust me, this dwarf makes the best food I've ever had. Come and eat, Raymond."

Cronovus then joins the group to eat in human form. Sander goes for a walk to talk to Riker about what to do next. As he walks, he sees Ashlaius in the distance, dancing among the trees. He watches her, pondering.

"Riker, do you hear me?" Sander asks.

Riker awakens within Sander. "What do you need, Sander?"

"I have a big group now. I think we're ready to go to Orcuhan. But they also mentioned crossing the volcanic area. Anything I should expect there?"

Riker replies, "She knows what's over there. Sander, there's a lot you should be aware of. There are great phoenixes — created by all three factions. There are three in total. You may know one as the giant blackbird, Sam. Then there's Sydney, the Heartful. She's a pure white bird — you'll know if it's her. And lastly, there's Redgy, the Transporter. He's a grey bird, able to travel to Purgatory and back. You'll know him when you see him. There are also normal phoenixes, the offspring of Sydney and Sam. But the titans…"

"Hold on," Sander interrupts, "There are titans? How big are we talking?"

"Really big," Riker answers. "There are two species of titans. The Rock Mountain Titans aren't near the volcanic area. But the Lava Titans, they're very territorial. I suggest not fighting them, because you're not ready. That's really all you need to know about the volcanic area — phoenixes, great phoenixes, and lava titans."

Sander thanks Riker for his advice and calls out to Ashlaius from afar, telling her they'll be leaving soon. She looks at him, then looks away, continuing her dance.

Sander heads back to the cabin and tells everyone to pack up, as they'll be heading to Orcuhan to meet Ares and the others. The group begins packing for the journey. Sander walks into the cabin to inform Cronovus and Holie about the plans. When he enters without knocking, he sees Holie drinking from Cronovus' neck.

"Whoa, stop! What the hell are you doing? Why are you trying to kill him?" Sander yells.

Holie quickly pulls away from Cronovus and hisses. "I'm not trying to kill him. I'm taking his blood for my benefit."

Cronovus heals his neck and explains, "My blood is unique to vampires — it gives them power. She's drinking my blood because it helps her. And since you're here, I'm guessing the group is ready to go."

Sander nods, confirming they are. "Look, just don't do this around Raymond and Gildor—they might think you're planning something, or worse, trying to kill each other. They don't see you as friends, just assets to the cause. So, a word of warning—don't do this on the journey unless it's really necessary."

Sander tells them to pack up, as the journey to Orcuhan starts the next day. As he leaves, he sees Ashlaius approaching the cabin. "What were you doing?" he asks roughly.

"Wow, that was rude. I wasn't dancing, if that's what you were thinking. I was controlling my energy," she replies quickly.

"We don't have time for this, Ashlaius. We need to get the group to Orcuhan right now," Sander demands.

"Why are you so angry? Do you want to fight for leadership?" Ashlaius says, trying to intimidate him.

"All set, Sander! My carriage is ready to go," said the dwarf from the side of the cabin.

Sander replies, "Listen, Ashlaius, we don't have time for this. We need to get to Orcuhan and stop my brother before he destroys the world with that stupid archangel of his."

"So, you think archangels are stupid now, Sander?" Ashlaius counters.

"Not all archangels, just Galatin. I think he's using my brother— that's what I believe."

Ashlaius grabs his hand and pulls him into the forest, away from the cabin. "Look, I think you've fallen for me. You're using your rage to push me away."

Sander laughs, a forced, awkward laugh. Ashlaius looks at him with disgust. "That's the worst fake laugh I've ever heard."

They begin to argue back and forth. Ashlaius is about to use her power. "I have a power that makes people tell the truth," she warns. Riker goes dormant, giving Sander power. Ashlaius' eyes turn blue as she uses her truth-telling power on Sander.

Sander begins to tell the truth, despite trying to lie. "Yes, I like you. That's why I'm acting this way," he blurts out, confused by his own words. "What the heck? I have a demon inside me. Why am I telling the truth?"

Ashlaius teases him, "Good. You're telling the truth, human boy. Where's Riker? Shouldn't he be protecting you? I'm dangerous, you know."

Sander sighs, "Look, I can't date you or do whatever with you. You're an archangel, and I'm a mortal human. There's no love between us — it's a ridiculous idea, like a god falling in love with a mortal."

Ashlaius retorts, "So, you're not going to try because you're human? That's a stupid reason."

Their argument continues, as the group prepares for the road ahead. Gildor, frustrated, asks, "Why are they so loud?"

"Young love," Raymond chuckles, "They're going to fight."

Ashlaius declares, "Look, Sander, you're my guard now. It would be unprofessional if we fell in love."

"What's that supposed to mean?" Sander exclaims. "You were just talking about love a minute ago, and I didn't choose to be your guard—you made me your guard! You're literally the stupidest person here!"

"So now I'm stupid? Fine, you're no longer my guard," Ashlaius says, storming away toward the cabin.

Sander watches her give him the silent treatment. "I didn't want to be your guard anyway," he mutters, heading back to the cabin.

As Sander arrives, he sees Ashlaius packing her things and the group staring at him. "What's everyone staring at? Let's get on the road!"

The group quickly stops staring and begins packing. Once everything is ready, they load the carriage and set off for Orcuhan. As they leave the forest, Holie says a quiet goodbye to her cabin. The carriage sets off between the twin mountains.

Chapter 35

The Twin Rock Titans

The group finally arrived at the Twin Mountain path.

"Which way do we go?" asked Gildor.

Raphael then told the group, "Don't split up. Go to the left."

The group followed Raphael, as he knew where Orcuhan was. As they followed the path, the rocks started to shake as they climbed up the mountain. The group had to ride and climb as they made their way through the Twin Mountains.

"So, what are these mountains called?" Gildor asked.

The dwarf explained, "They're called the Twin Mountains."

"Why do they call them that?" Kevin asked.

"Because, my dear boy Kevin, these mountains look like twins. There's a rumor of guardians here to protect the road, but I've never found them, so it's just a legend. We'll be at Orcuhan in two, maybe three days. It will be amazing to see the Orc barbarians; they have their own culture, you know."

As the dwarf rambled on about the orcs, the group felt a short tremble.

"What was that?" asked Sander.

Raphael brushed it off, "Oh, it's nothing, just a normal tremble. We get these all the time in these mountains."

Gildor asked, "Why do they call it the Twin Mountains if there are many other mountains that don't look like twins?"

Raphael responded, "We're not at the actual Twin Mountains yet. We're still on the path to them. Once we reach the Twin Mountains, we'll head to the lava area. I don't know the name of that part of Sinia, but it's very dangerous. We must be careful. This road is narrow, so we need to move in a single line. After this road, there's another bridge, and we must be cautious. These rocks are very sensitive."

Raphael led the way with his carriage, which was lighter than having seven people on the narrow, rocky trail. Eventually, Raphael stopped at the end of the trail when he saw the bridge on the other side of the mountain had been destroyed.

"It looks like we're trapped. We need that bridge to get to Orcuhan," Raphael said.

The others reached the edge of the broken stone bridge.

"It looks like we have to turn back," Raphael said. "There's no way to Orcuhan."

As Raphael started to turn his horse around, Sander had an idea.

"Wait," Sander said. "Raphael, how strong is this carriage?"

Raphael looked confused. Sander explained, "When I acquired power from Riker, I became strong enough to carry a boulder. If Ashlaius and I carry the carriage to the other side, we can keep going to Orcuhan."

Sander began to fly and told Ashlaius to help him lift the carriage. With their celestial and demonic strength, they began to lift the carriage. As they did, the wind on the mountain pass grew colder.

"It's getting chilly here—can you hurry it up?" said Holie.

"Shut it, vampire," Raymond snapped back.

Cronovus growled in anger as Gildor pulled out his sword.

"Guys, enough!" Sander called out. "We're moving the carriage. Fighting won't help."

Sander and Ashlaius managed to carry the carriage a mile to the other side of the bridge. When they landed, they saw two mountains standing next to each other with a narrow path between them. Something stirred in the distance.

"Raphael, stay here. We need to get the others," Sander said.

Raphael stayed put, keeping watch on the dark, narrow path between the mountains. As Sander and Ashlaius flew back to pick up more of the group, they heard Raphael scream. Sander shouted something unintelligible as he picked up Cronovus and flew through the fog to the other side of the bridge. When he landed, he saw the carriage destroyed and Raphael gone.

"Go into your beast form so we can track him," Sander told Cronovus. He then flew back to get the rest of the group. After thirty minutes, the whole group gathered at the end of the bridge, and they began searching for Raphael.

"I think this is a trap by the orcs. Maybe we're in Orcuhan now," Gildor said.

"We're not in Orcuhan," Sander replied. "The borders are after the mountains and the lava area. Something took Raphael. He wouldn't just leave without a note. Someone must have taken him."

Raymond agreed, "Yeah, either that or he didn't listen."

Sander told the group, "Let's keep moving. We'll find him."

The group walked through the mountain path, searching for Raphael. Kevin asked, "Where do you think he went, Sander? The wind's picking up, and soon there'll be snow and a blizzard. We need to find shelter."

Raymond and the guards agreed.

"Sander, it would be wise to camp out until after the blizzard," Raymond suggested.

Sander looked at Raymond with Riker's red eyes.

"I'm not leaving him. I won't leave anyone — now or ever. We need to find Raphael, then we can camp."

The group, fearful of Sander's determination, agreed to continue. Ashlaius watched Sander and saw him as a hero of courage and bravery. The wind grew stronger as the group came across a large rock. The rock opened, revealing an eye. Sander backed up.

"Guys, back up. Riker told me there are titans near the lava area, but these aren't lava titans. They're rock titans."

The eye fully opened, and snow burst out.

"Who goes past the Twin Mountains?" the rock face asked.

"It is I, Sander Helmglade, true king of Luna. I'm here to find my friend Raphael, a little dwarf who's gone missing."

The rock face responded, "I am not the guardian of the entrance. My brother is."

Sander thanked the rock titan and ran back to the bridge. He searched for another rock-like face. "Guys, help me find a rock-like face—I think I know what's happening."

The group started searching, confused. Sander explained, "If the titans are this big, they should have mouths, right?"

Understanding Sander's theory, the group began searching quickly. Sander fired a fireball at a rock, and it groaned.

"Ow!" said the rock. The eyes opened, revealing another titan.

"You foolish wizard! How dare you attack one of the Twin Titans!" the titan yelled.

Sander told the titan to open its mouth. The titan refused, saying he just ate a snack. Sander, now engulfed in blue flames, threatened the titan.

The group became frightened as the air grew warmer. Sander's eyes turned red, and his power surged. The mountain began to shake as the titan emerged, causing half the mountain to break off. Sander ordered the group to grab the carriage and make it through the exit. The group obeyed in fear.

Sander, now surrounded by purple flames, grew stronger. Riker warned him to be careful, reminding him that the sun was up, but Sander ignored him and attacked the titan. The battle was fierce, with sonic waves crashing between them like gods clashing. Sander, remembering his battle with the water dragon, created a spear of flames and struck the titan's chest. The titan fell, and Sander, still enraged, used his sword to melt the rock titan into liquid.

After hours of battle, Sander found Raphael, buried under rocks.

"Sander, help me!" Raphael cried out.

Sander, now weak, put away his sword and helped Raphael. He flew him to meet the group at the end of the Twin Mountain road.

Chapter 36

The Red Werewolf

Sander flies down and lands, seeing the group behind him. He waits for them to meet him at the end of the road. The group sees Sander and runs to him, noticing he has no scratches, almost as if he was too pure to be attacked. Ashlaius thinks to herself, "He has no scratches because of the demon soul, and he's getting closer than usual. Coming to Orcuhan from Luna takes six months. The deal of fusing only works if it's under a year. If it's more than a year, then Riker and Sander will become one forever. Unless Riker hooks his soul into a weapon or armor, like my brother Galatin did."

Ashlaius asks Sander, "How far until Orcuhan?"

Sander looks at the dwarf, who begins examining the sky and feeling the ground to determine their location. As the dwarf figures out the direction, Cronovus looks ahead and spots another werewolf. Gildor notices Cronovus and gives him a sharp look, showing his distrust. Holie, approaching Cronovus from behind, asks in a fragile voice, "Who is that, babe?"

Cronovus responds, "It's an old friend."

The wind begins to pick up, forcefully pushing everyone. The dwarf says, "Before we head north, we must camp here. The wind is picking up, Sander, and it's best if we rest." The dwarf heads to the carriage, thanking everyone for helping bring it, and starts grabbing the tents.

As the group begins to set up the tents, Cronovus tells Holie, "I need to go see him." He kisses her gently on the lips, pulls up his hood, and runs fast toward the mountain where he saw the werewolf.

Meanwhile, Sander tells the group that he will start the fire. As he does, Riker begins to speak in Sander's mind. "Sander, you've gotten lucky."

Sander questions, "What do you mean, I got lucky?"

Riker replies, "You would have died if you pushed beyond your limit. Never use the purple flames unless it's night."

Sander, confidently, says, "Don't worry, with my power, I can handle it."

"Your power?" Riker retorts, angered. "You've gotten power from me when you were weak. It's not your power, it's my power. And my power is strong, but it must be used for good. I've done things in the past that still affect today, and I regret them. But you must remember who's in charge here. Listen to my advice. I don't want you to die. I don't want to die. I'll only die if Galatin dies, and that's when I choose to die. Someone showed me the light within me, that this world deserves to be ruled by neither demons nor celestials. This world is beautiful, and it should be free from both of our races."

Riker pauses, then continues, "Ashlaius wasn't born during the war, but I hope she sees what Crystal must have felt—that this world is more than just light. Do you understand, Sander? I've traveled across the world, and I've seen how humans with power often get corrupted. I don't want you to become corrupted. After all this, I want you to fall in love, to have a life. I wish I could have said this to my son. But you—live your life after your revenge. Revenge is fine, but love is more powerful than revenge."

Sander feels a pang of sadness and responds, "I understand, Riker. But my brother is wreaking havoc among the elves and dwarven kingdoms. It's time we stop him."

"Sander, your brother craves power. He and Galatin share the same goal—power. You and I are the only ones who can stop them. Let's not just be partners, let's be friends."

Sander agrees, and the two bond over the conversation. Sander lights the fire and watches the group finish setting up the tents.

"Where's Cronovus?" Gildor asks. "I knew it. He was using us for his own personal gain," Gildor says loudly.

Holie defends him, "Shut your mouths. He saw an old friend and went to see him."

Gildor, suspicious, asks, "What did they look like?"

"It was a reddish werewolf," Holie answers.

Gildor draws his sword. "Tell me the direction."

"Calm down, Gildor. We don't want to fight," Holie says.

Raymond, pulling out his sword, adds, "Or what are you going to do?"

Ashlaius steps in between them, telling everyone to calm down. "Listen, we have to stay calm. Cronovus may not have betrayed us; we don't know if he's trying to protect us. Holie, you get your own tent. Gildor and Raymond, since you guys want to fight, you'll share a tent. Kevin and his guards can share the other tent."

Ashlaius turns to Sander, "I guess you and I will share a tent, Sander."

Sander, clearly uncomfortable, tells her, "I'm not sharing a tent with you. I'm staying awake to keep watch. The tent is all yours."

Ashlaius insists, "I'll keep watch for the first night."

Sander orders her to go to the tent and leave him alone.

Meanwhile, Cronovus reaches the mountain and hears a voice telepathically. "I didn't expect to see you here," says the white wolf.

Cronovus replies telepathically, "Where is he? I know Singneus is here."

As he says this, a red werewolf and a blue werewolf appear. "Klyido, you're here too?" Cronovus asks, sitting down near the white wolf.

The three werewolves tell Cronovus they want him to rejoin their pack. Cronovus replies, "Why would I do that now? I'm busy."

"I know Riker is in that boy," the red werewolf growls. "I can feel it. I want revenge for what Riker did to me."

Cronovus asks, "What did he do to you?"

Telepathically, the red werewolf responds, "He's the one who made me this monster. He promised me revenge, but look at us now. Our tribes are gone, our family and friends are gone. I want to return to the world after the war, to see my family and friends in peace."

Cronovus explains, "The celestials won. They trapped Riker. He couldn't escape without a vessel. Now he has one, and he's going to kill Galatin. Once Galatin is dead, we can all be free."

The red werewolf declines the offer to join the group. "I'll wait until the war is over, then we'll be free."

"Will you attack the group?" Cronovus asks.

"No," the red werewolf says, "but once you're done, you'll join the pack."

The three werewolves leave, and Cronovus heads back down the mountain to the camp. Sander is waiting for him.

"I told everyone I'm keeping watch so they'll leave me alone," Sander says, approaching Cronovus.

"Where did you go?" Sander asks.

Cronovus tells the truth. "I saw the red werewolf on the mountain. I went to see him because I figured they might attack, and I was right. They were going to attack—you, Sander. They want Riker. If Riker can hear me, he'll know that the werewolves want to be freed from their curse. Only Riker can set us free from being werewolves."

Sander asks, "Why do they want to be free?"

Cronovus explains, "Once we're free, other werewolves will lose their control and kill everything they see. Only original werewolves can control their transformations. Once I'm done here, they want me to rejoin the pack. I don't know how to tell Holie."

"Do me a favor, Sander," Cronovus asks.

Sander responds, "What's the favor?"

"Don't tell Holie about the pack."

"You have my word, Cronovus. I won't say a thing."

Cronovus thanks him and goes to his tent with Holie to sleep. Sander, after watching the camp for a while, returns to his tent and sees Ashlaius awake, looking at him with lust in her eyes.

Chapter 37

Ashlaius Admits Her Feelings

Sander then begins to sit in the tent to talk to Riker in his mind as he starts to meditate. Ashlaius tries to distract Sander, but he tells her to stop distracting him from his destiny. Sander meditates, focusing on ignoring Ashlaius. He goes into his mind and sees Riker looking at him.

"Alright, tell me the truth about the werewolves," Sander asks.

Riker responds, "Listen, Sander, this was beyond your time and your father's time. This was a time of darkness and chaos. The original werewolves were created to destroy the celestial race. And yes, more of them were created afterward. But only I can turn a werewolf back to the form they were born with. I feel the magic I used a while back—when you were knocked out—I turned some black werewolves into their true forms. But it didn't work for all of them because some werewolves were born as werewolves. So, my power is limited in that respect. Also, Sander, if you haven't noticed, Ashlaius seems to have feelings for you. I think you should go for it. If she falls in love with you, you could have a queen. From a diplomatic standpoint, that would be a smart move. Your children would be powerful, and the celestials would have a good relationship with you."

Sander disagrees, telling Riker that if he falls in love, it will happen naturally. Riker then goes dormant in Sander's mind, having said all he wanted to.

Sander opens his eyes to see Ashlaius standing nude in front of him. She gets closer to him before he has time to react. Sander thinks, "What is she doing?"

Ashlaius begins to speak, "Do you like what you see?"

Sander looks straight ahead and tells her to put her clothes back on.

"Why don't you humans appreciate lust like others do?" she asks.

Sander, growing angry, replies, "We humans are more than what you describe. Some may like that, but I wasn't taught to think that way."

Sander quickly leaves the tent. Ashlaius begins to cry. Sander flies up into the sky for fresh air, thinking about the last time he saw his brother. Ashlaius, after putting her clothes back on, chases after him in the snowstorm. She crashes into him, and they both fall into a cave.

"Ouch," Ashlaius says, injured. She begins to heal herself.

"Why would you do that?" Sander asks.

Ashlaius responds, "Because I think I'm in love with you. I don't feel these kinds of emotions as an archangel. We're mostly taught to be warriors, not to have families. I don't even know what love really means," she says in a gentle voice. "Is love showing my body, Sander?"

Sander quickly says no, frustrated that she would think that way.

"The last thing I learned about humans is that they're drawn to lust, money, and power. So, I figured if I did that, you'd fall for me," Ashlaius explains.

Sander kneels down and tells her, "I can't, even if I wanted to."

"Why?" she asks.

Sander explains, "Because of my revenge. My revenge is more important than anything. I want to destroy my brother for what he did to my father and to me. He killed my father to take the throne. So, I'm sorry, but you don't want someone like me."

Ashlaius stands and looks him in the eye. "Listen, I saw what you did for Raphael. You wanted to save him so badly. Why is that? You never leave anyone behind. You show courage in battle and bravery wherever we go. You act like a leader. You're more human than a vengeful soul. So stop acting all high and mighty and just kiss me."

Ashlaius leans in and kisses Sander, but he pushes her back, looking into her eyes. "I can't. I'm sorry. It's not me. Maybe in another life when I'm not focused on revenge."

Ashlaius, angry, flies off into the snowstorm. Sander, worried she'll get hurt, starts to follow her. "Wait up! Don't fly into a snowstorm! How dumb are you?" he shouts.

She stops, then kicks him to the ground. She flies down, throwing a tantrum, and begins attacking Sander. Sander, unsure what to do, tries to block her attacks until he finally stops.

"I'm sorry, I just wanted to let you down easy. But you're strong," he says.

She kicks him in the groin, making him fall to his knees in pain.

Sander cries out, "Why couldn't you just take the compliment or something?"

Ashlaius continues to hit him until she stops, and they hear a loud howl beyond the mountains. People scream in the distance. Sander, still in pain, tries to figure out what's happening. Ashlaius stops crying and listens. She flies off toward the town.

Sander, struggling to stand, thinks, "I can't leave her. The group will think I abandoned her."

He flies after her, following the screams. When Sander arrives, he sees Ashlaius holding a child and crying.

Sander asks, "What happened?"

"What do you care?" Ashlaius snaps. "You don't care about me or my love for you. So why would you care about this town?"

Sander looks around and sees the town burning. The child in Ashlaius' arms is a baby dwarf. The night is quiet except for the crackling of fire, and the stones begin to melt.

"What happened here?" Sander asks.

Ashlaius, through her tears, says she doesn't know.

"There must be some survivors," Sander says, running into the town. He searches but finds no one, just food and toys left behind in a cave. Sander shouts, "Ashlaius! I found something!"

Ashlaius, still mourning the child, walks over to Sander. He points at a door with carvings of an ancient language.

"It's in dragon language," Ashlaius explains.

Sander asks, "What does it say?"

Ashlaius responds, "I don't know the language or how to read it."

Sander looks closer at the carvings. "It says, 'Ashlaius, this door is not to be closed unless the white shadows attack.' What are white shadows?" he asks.

Ashlaius shrugs. "I don't know, Sander. But whatever they are, they attacked this village and killed the dwarven children and people. I think we should pay these white shadows a visit."

"How will we know where they are?" Sander asks.

He examines the door, pulling out his sword.

"What are you doing?" Ashlaius asks. "There might be people in there!"

Sander looks at her, sees the gentle snow falling on her hair, and puts the sword away. He lets her handle it her way.

Ashlaius politely asks the door to open. Sander, skeptical, thinks it won't work and makes fun of her in his mind. Ashlaius gets angry but continues. "I'm here to help you, please open the door."

To Sander's surprise, the door opens, and a group of dwarven villagers comes out, bowing to Ashlaius, believing her to be a goddess. Sander, shocked, watches them.

The dwarves then approach Sander, seeing him as the guardian of the goddess.

In his mind, Sander thinks, "You've got to be kidding me. They think she's a goddess, and I'm just her guardian? Why does she always get her way? What's so special about her?"

One of the dwarves, desperate, speaks, "My goddess, a giant beast has been attacking us. We need help to fight them off. Every time we fight, we get bitten or scratched, and those beasts turn us into those awful creatures. Our village elder is dead, and we only have seven warriors left. Please, goddess of beauty, help us."

Ashlaius agrees to help, telling them, "We will help you. My guardian will kill that beast to save you."

The dwarves cheer and start to rebuild their homes. Ashlaius takes Sander by the hand and pulls him around the side of a house.

"What's next? Are you going to kiss me again?" Sander teases.

"Listen, I'm not special. I don't always get my way," Ashlaius says. "And stop making fun of me when I'm trying to do the right thing."

"Wait, how did you know I was making fun of you? I said that in my head," Sander asks, surprised.

"I can read minds," she replies.

Sander stays quiet, shutting his mouth.

"Now go along with my plan. You're my guardian, and nothing else. You're here to protect me," she says with a smile.

"Why can't you be my protector?" Sander asks.

She gives him a sharp stare. "Fine, I'll do it your way," he concedes.

Sander and Ashlaius walk back out into public.

"It's decided!" Ashlaius exclaims. "I will find these monsters and stop them."

The villagers cheer on the goddess. Then, they all go their separate ways. Ashlaius grabs Sander's hand, flies into the air, and they head back to the group.

.

Chapter 38

The Northern Dwarven Village

Ashlaius holds Sander's hand as the snowstorm stops. "Alright, Sander, now you must tell the group that you're my guardian on this quest as we hunt down the white shadows."

"I don't have to go along with this plan," Sander replies.

She stares at him with frustration. "Fine, I will do it," Sander says in fear.

Sander and Ashlaius fly back to the group. Ashlaius lands gracefully, while Sander lands hard on his feet. Ashlaius looks at him, puzzled as to why he wouldn't land softly. Sander addresses the group, "There is a village west of here. Guys, we should go there for shelter."

Gildor asks, "What race is the village?"

"It's a dwarven race," Sander replies. Raphael and the others agree to the plan. "But another thing," Sander adds, "we all have to pretend Ashlaius is a goddess."

The group begins to bicker, disagreeing with the idea.

Sander explains, "Alright, listen, they believe she's a goddess, so let's just act like she is, and we're her servants."

Kevin speaks up, "What are you, Sander, a god?"

Sander explains, "No, I'm going to be her guardian because that's what they think I am. Yeah, it's all stupid, but we have to gain some sort of ally from these people as we head north."

The group reluctantly agrees. "Fine, as long as she's not too cocky about it," Gildor mutters. The others agree, provided Sander does.

Sander looks at Ashlaius. "I trust my life in your hands."

Ashlaius smiles at him. "Alright, team," she says. "Let's go west. They have a gate, and they're waiting for us. We're there to find something called the white shadows."

Gildor speaks up, "I think I've heard that name before, but I don't remember exactly what it means."

"It's fine, Gildor. We'll find out together," Sander reassures him with a smile. "Come on, old friend, let's go to the village. It can't be that bad."

As they walk, Ashlaius tries to boost team spirit. "Alright, team, let's do this! We're going to crush those white shadows and save the village! Who's with me?"

No one responds. The group looks at her, and she stares at Sander in disappointment.

Sander awkwardly chimes in, "Yeah, guys, she's right! Let's get those white shadows!"

The group begrudgingly hypes up, and Ashlaius smiles as she begins to fly. The group watches Sander, noticing his fear of her.

Sander whispers to them, "She kicked me in the balls. It wasn't good. She's tougher than she looks."

The group, wide-eyed, looks at Ashlaius flying above them. She lands and declares, "I'm ready to take on these white shadows."

They finally arrive at the gate, where seven dwarven soldiers open it for Ashlaius, the "goddess." The group enters, knowing what role they must play. They stop in the middle of the town as Ashlaius walks forward. Sander stands behind her, slightly to her left.

"I am here," Ashlaius says to the dwarves, "with my servants and my guardian. My servants will need shelter and food for their journey to find the white shadows. May we discuss with my guardian where they come from and where they're heading?"

The dwarven leader agrees and invites Ashlaius and Sander into his small dwarven house. The rest of the group disperses to find food and shelter.

Inside the house, the dwarven leader begins to tell Ashlaius and Sander the story of the white shadows. "My goddess, they originated here. The white shadows were created by evil men with dark power. These men hated our people, and the white shadows were created to hunt us down. Our ancient elders stopped the evil from spreading by creating a gemstone in our village. But a few kids broke the gemstone, and for the past two hundred years, we've been battling those werewolves. Now we are weak and need your help, goddess, to fight against the white shadows. They're hard to spot in the snow, blending in, and they're well-hidden."

He continues, "These giant white shadows are five to six feet tall. When they bite my people, they turn into these creatures as well—giant white, wolf-like shadows. But we call them white shadows because they blend in with the snow. My goddess, will you help us against this beast?"

Ashlaius looks at Sander, then back at the dwarf. "Yes, we will help you and fix your gemstone."

The dwarf cheers with happiness and runs out to tell the town. Sander follows Ashlaius outside as the dwarves begin to cheer and throw a party. Sander walks over to Gildor.

"They blend in with the snow," Sander tells him.

Gildor replies, "So they're cold, white, and blend in with the snow. I remember now what white shadows are. Sander, they're white werewolves. They kill everything and only allow purebloods into the pack. If you're revived, you'll become a werewolf too. These creatures are incredibly strong, and since we're in their territory, their skin has thickened so much that arrows and swords won't do much damage. We're going to need bigger weapons."

Sander asks Gildor, "What kind of weapons?"

Gildor points to the militia on the wall. "We're going to have to use that."

"How many do we need to man?" Sander asks.

"At least five, depending on the size of the pack," Gildor replies.

Sander tells Ashlaius, "Goddess of love, may I speak with you?"

Ashlaius walks over. "Wow, you're really getting into character," she says.

Sander whispers, "Alright, the reason they're called white shadows is that they blend in with the snow. But they're actually white werewolves. We'll need to man five ballistas to attack them. I suggest two people for each. Me, you, and Cronovus will be on the ground to fight them."

"Wait, wait, wait," Ashlaius interrupts. "I call the shots here. This is my turn to show you that I'm a leader too."

"I never said you weren't," Sander replies.

Ashlaius takes Sander's plan and goes to the dwarven leader to relay it. Sander is confused by her behavior but stays close to her left shoulder to keep up appearances.

Ashlaius tells the dwarves Sander's plan, and they cheer and begin to set up the party. A dwarf stops to tell Sander, "The goddess is here to save us from the evil shadows." Then he continues preparing for the celebration.

"The town was so quiet when we first arrived," Sander says to himself.

Six hours later, the party starts, and Cronovus begins celebrating with Holie, treating her like a princess.

"Hey, Gildor," Raymond says, "look at Holie. Who would've guessed a werewolf and a vampire would work together?"

Gildor watches Cronovus and Holie and begins to see that Cronovus isn't such a bad guy. Gildor grabs another drink, and Raymond follows. Kevin sits with her guards, waiting patiently for their next orders. Raphael flirts with a local girl.

Meanwhile, Sander sits alone, waiting for the werewolves to arrive. Ashlaius approaches him.

"What are you doing, sitting here all gloomy?" she asks.

Sander replies, "I don't want to dance. I'd rather sit here and wait for the werewolves."

She questions him, "Why are you waiting for the werewolves?"

Sander points out, "Look at how loud they're being right now."

The band begins playing a slow dance song, and Sander feels more and more like a downcast figure.

Ashlaius asks, "Would you like to dance?"

Sander declines, but she playfully adds, "Are you turning down your goddess?"

Sander gives in. "Alright, one dance," he says as he spins her around. They slow dance, and Ashlaius tells him, "Dancers are supposed to look at each other in the eyes."

Sander looks into her brown eyes. He dips her, pulls her back up, and spins her around. Then he places a hand on her waist, and she wraps her arms around him.

From the side, Gildor says to Raymond and Kevin, "They look good together. A human and a celestial, who would've thought?"

As they dance peacefully, a loud howl cuts through the night.

"That's our time to shine," Gildor says.

Raymond, Kevin, and the guards rush to the wall. Sander shakes off his thoughts and joins them. Cronovus tells Holie to stay back, but she disagrees and follows him to the wall. The group spots ten white werewolves approaching.

Chapter 39

The White Shadows

The The howling was loud, and the people began rushing indoors as they heard the white shadows. Sander and his group stood ready to face the approaching threat.

"Well, I guess they ruined the party," said Raymond, as Gildor laughed.

Sander jumped off the wall, followed by Cronovus, as they rushed into the fight. Sander pulled out his sword while Gildor, Raymond, Holie, Kevin's guards, and Kevin manned the ballista. Raphael did his best to assist with the arrows. Ashlaius flew down, joining the battle, fighting off the white shadows. Sander ran and leaped, slicing off the head of a white werewolf, while Cronovus transformed into a giant black werewolf, with black magic surging around him. Cronovus engaged the white werewolves head-on, as Sander and Cronovus worked together to hold them off.

Ashlaius provided support by healing Sander and Cronovus during their attacks. The ballistas fired, and giant arrows pierced through a werewolf's body. Sander fought furiously, killing four werewolves in one battle, his blue flames growing brighter as he cut down the beasts.

While the front lines raged on, Raphael dragged more arrows to the ballistas.

"Guys, there are too many of them! We can't fight them all!" Raphael yelled.

Gildor responded, "If there are too many, we need to kill the alpha. It'll split the pack in two, but at least we'll stop the raiding."

"Ashlaius, Sander doesn't need healing—he needs you to fight!" Gildor shouted from the wall.

Ashlaius swiftly drew daggers from her boots, joining the battle. She spun gracefully, her face barely touched by the falling snow, her eyes glowing a brilliant brown. Sander grew frustrated, seeing that she was better than him, as the people on the wall watched in shock.

Raphael, feeling overwhelmed, ran down to the village to gather the remaining seven soldiers to help with the ballistas. He knocked on doors, calling out, "The goddess needs the soldiers of this village to come and help!"

The soldiers emerged from the garrison and followed Raphael, manning the ballistas. They fired, piercing the werewolves' chests and causing them to cry out and revert to their original forms, dead in the cold snow.

As the battle raged on in the harsh snow, a beast larger than the others emerged from the snow. Cronovus recognized it—Lintovous, a member of his original pack.

"Lintovous," Cronovus thought.

Cronovus charged toward the giant white wolf, battling him fiercely. Gildor, jealous, ran to the gate and jumped down to join the fight. Cronovus slashed and attacked Lintovous, while Sander and Ashlaius fought off the other werewolves, keeping them away from the village.

"There are too many of them!" Sander shouted. "We need to kill that giant werewolf!"

Cronovus yelled back, "He's mine!"

Cronovus and Lintovous communicated telepathically.

"You and Singnues said you wouldn't attack the group. So why attack the dwarves?" Cronovus demanded.

Lintovous responded, "Cronovus, you never understood. I recruit, or I reclaim my territory. What I want, I take. We need a bigger army for war. The celestials aren't dead. We need to kill them all. And I want that village over there under my vassal."

As the two battled telepathically, Sander, still fighting, noticed Ashlaius getting overwhelmed by several werewolves. She was injured, and Sander, furious, ignited his flames hotter than ever, burning the white werewolves as he fought.

Cronovus charged at Lintovous and bit off his head. "I'll see you in another life, brother," he said telepathically.

Lintovous reverted to his human form as he died, and Gildor felt a sharp pain in his chest, where a tattoo of Lintovous' name burned. Cronovus, turning back into his human form, walked slowly back to the village, visibly saddened. The remaining white werewolves scattered and fled.

Gildor, furious that he didn't get to kill the alpha, stormed back to the village. Raymond and the others on the wall cheered, happy with the outcome. Ashlaius smiled at Sander, saying, "I knew you couldn't let me die. You felt it, the same as I did."

Sander replied, "I'm sorry, but I can't be with you while I seek revenge. We can talk about this later. We need to get back to the group."

Sander and Ashlaius returned to the group. Cronovus sat on a bench, looking dejected. Holie sat next to him and asked why he was sad. Cronovus explained what had happened with the white werewolf. "Holie, I don't want you to tell the group this. They'll pity me."

Holie promised she wouldn't tell.

Sander and Ashlaius walked through the gate as the dwarves emerged from their homes to praise the goddess for saving them. They began a celebratory parade.

Cronovus climbed the wall to gaze into the sky as the village celebrated the disappearance of the white shadows. Ashlaius playfully forced Sander to dance.

Gildor, enjoying the festivities, approached Sander. "We need to go. We've been here too long. It's time to move on."

Sander nodded and told Ashlaius they needed to wrap things up.

Ashlaius addressed the dwarves, asking if they had any supplies before the group left. The dwarves, saddened by her impending departure, offered to build a statue and shrine in her honor.

"Praise me, the goddess of helpfulness, and my guardian of protection," Ashlaius declared.

The dwarves were thrilled, promising to always keep her in their hearts. The group gathered their supplies and prepared to leave for Orcuhan.

"Let's go," Holie said, calling for Cronovus as he walked slowly down the wall to the gate.

The group set off toward Orcuhan, heading for the lava territory. Along the way, they discussed their next destination.

"So, where are we going, Raphael?" Sander asked.

"We're heading to the lava territory, where we may encounter titans. Not just the rock titans we've faced before—lava titans. They're fiercer and will try to kill us."

"But why go there?" Kevin asked. "Isn't there another way to Orcuhan?"

Raphael explained, "There is a way through water, but you need to be a good captain for that."

The group continued on toward the lava territory, talking and learning about lava titans along the way.

Chapter 40

The Land of Cumasoom

The group finally arrived at the land of volcanoes, seeing mountains upon mountains of volcanic peaks.

"Yeah, are you sure this is the way to Orcuhan?" asked Sander to Raphael.

"Yeah, I'm sure we're heading the right way. Now I need you all to be quiet when entering through the volcano zone. Each volcano has a titan in it. A lava titan can kill us. The only ones who might survive an attack are Ashlaius and Sander. Now, let's move through quietly and follow the black paths, not the black rocks," Raphael advised.

The group followed Raphael's guidance, walking slowly and quietly along the paths, whispering and not making a sound. Even the armor and weapons in Raphael's carriage made minimal noise, not enough to wake a titan.

Sander whispered to Raphael, "Why do we have to be so quiet?"

"Because, Sander, if these titans wake up, there's no mercy. They'll kill us instantly. I hope you understand that," Raphael responded.

Suddenly, Raphael accidentally knocked a rock, causing the clinking of armor. Everyone froze, waiting for any sign that a volcano would erupt or a titan would emerge. For a moment, there was complete silence. Nothing stirred in the volcano zone.

"My bad," Raphael whispered. "Let's move quietly."

The group resumed their cautious walk. They were so quiet even a dog wouldn't have heard them.

"Why are we going so slow?" Gildor muttered. "I say we just make a run for it to the volcanic geysers."

Suddenly, they heard a loud thud in the distance.

"Ow! What the heck was that for?" a faraway voice complained.

A giant started moving toward their location. The group stood perfectly still as they heard the giant approaching.

"No one move," Raphael instructed softly.

The giant lava man approached the group by the carriage. "Yo," said the lava titan. "You know this territory is ours, right?"

The group looked at the lava titan, surprised he wasn't angry.

"Aren't you supposed to be aggressive?" Sander asked.

The lava titan replied, "No, not really. We're just territorial. You guys don't look like you're here to cause harm, and we're at peace with the phoenixes and dwarves. But if you came with an army, we'd have a problem. As long as you keep quiet and let us sleep, we're cool."

"What's your name, lava man?" Sander asked.

"The name's Secured, the warrior. I'll show you to the geysers of the land of Cumasoom."

"Wait, we never told you where we were headed," said Kevin.

"I know you're headed to Orcuhan. It's obvious," said the lava titan.

The group followed Secured toward the geysers. As they walked, Kevin asked Sander, "Sander, when we regroup with the Sirens, what's our next journey?"

"Well, cousin Kevin, our next journey is to train an army and head back home. I'll face Fergus, and the group will hold their ground. If we win, cousin, I'll give you a prize."

"What's the prize?" Kevin asked eagerly.

"It's not a prize if I tell you," Sander replied.

The group continued walking as Gildor apologized to Cronovus. "Hey, Cronovus," Gildor said, "I want to thank you for saving us. You knew what to do, and you saved the village. Thank you."

"You're welcome," Cronovus replied quietly, walking sadly.

Gildor, noticing Cronovus's sadness, asked Sander, "Why is Cronovus so down?"

Sander shrugged, also puzzled by Cronovus's mood. "Was it something we did?" Sander asked.

"I don't think so. I mean, I've given him dirty looks in the past, but I didn't do anything to him," Gildor said.

They neared the land of Cumasoom and the geysers, seeing a field of them shooting across the landscape. Birds flew overhead, practicing how to dodge the geyser blasts.

"This place is scary but amazing," said Kevin in awe. "Those birds of fire."

"I think we should cross the bridge," Gildor suggested.

The group hesitated, noticing a gray phoenix blocking the trail ahead. Suddenly, a giant blackbird swooped down from the sky.

"Let them pass," said the black phoenix.

"It's Sam, the black phoenix," Sander whispered.

The gray phoenix glared at Sam. "No, these are humans, elves, a dwarf, a demon, and a celestial. This isn't going to end well. They're on their way to Orcuhan. I can see that, Sam."

Sam responded, "Let them pass so they can fulfill the prophecy of Galatin."

The gray phoenix protested, "I don't want that prophecy to come true. I know the outcome."

Sam managed to convince the gray phoenix after some back-and-forth. "Fine, I'll let them pass if you stop talking, Sam," the gray phoenix relented.

Sam agreed, and the group was allowed to pass. As they crossed, Sam and the gray phoenix continued their conversation in the background.

"Hey, Sander, who was that?" Gildor asked.

"Well, if you don't know him, he's Sam, the black phoenix. He and another guy, Colinborn, are helping me."

"Well, I guess we should keep moving," Gildor replied.

The group made their way through the land of geysers in Cumasoom, staying alert as they continued their journey toward Orcuhan.

.

Chapter 41

The Border of Orcuhan

The group eventually made it to the border of Orcuhan, where they could now pass and enter the city. They came across a giant wall, at least hundreds of feet tall. As they approached, Raphael suggested they try entering through the door. The group agreed with Raphael but wanted a Plan B in case it didn't work. They decided that if things went wrong, they would fight their way out.

When they reached the hundred-foot gate, they were halted by a group of orcs. The orcs recognized Gildor, Kevin, his guards, and Raymond.

"I know you," said one of the orcs. "You're friends of Ares, our clan leader."

Gildor recognized the orc clan. "Sander, this is the orc clan Ares took control of. Jake is making armor for them. This clan can help us."

Sander walked up to the orc and said, "Can you take me to your leader?"

The orc agreed. "Wait up," said Ashlaius, joining Sander. The orc halted Raphael's carriage and the rest of the group while leading Sander and Ashlaius into the orc camp.

Inside the camp, Sander saw Duvessa and Scorpius.

"Sander, is that you?" Duvessa exclaimed, running to hug him. "I'm so glad you're alive. We thought you were dead."

Ares looked at Sander in surprise. "No way! You survived? Battling a basilisk usually means certain death."

"He's right," Scorpius added, smiling in the background.

"So, Duvessa, did you get better with that glaive?" Sander asked with a smile.

She beamed. "Yes! The orcs taught me some new tricks."

Ashlaius, seeing their exchange, became jealous and gave Duvessa a funny look.

Duvessa noticed and asked, "Are you okay?" with a smile on her face.

"I'm fine," Ashlaius responded angrily.

Sander, confused by the tension, turned to Ares. "So, I heard you took control of an orc clan. I never knew it was true."

Ares nodded. "Yes, when you weren't here, we made it to Orcuhan and enslaved the orcs. I challenged their chieftain and won. Now I control the whole orc clan. I also take ten percent of the merchants' gold for entering and exiting the border. I found a way to make money in Sinia."

Sander congratulated Ares on his success. "Alright, Ares, I need to tell you that I arrived here with Gildor, Raymond, Kevin, and his guards. Along with two new people: a dwarf named Raphael, who can make armor and sell it to the orcs, and Ashlaius." Sander introduced Ashlaius as Ares gazed at her.

"Sander, where did you find such beauty?" Ares asked, intrigued.

Sander explained, "Ashlaius, these are sirens—not the dark ones Riker made, but the good ones, the original sirens before they turned dark."

"There are still some left," Ares added. "We have three kingdoms of sirens and two kingdoms of dark sirens."

Ares continued, "Jake wanted to become the leader after you left, so we enslaved him to make armor."

"So where is Jake now?" Sander asked.

"He's locked away in a cave, making armor and weapons for the orcs," Ares replied.

Sander then explained that Raphael had armor and weapons for Orcuhan. Ares proposed buying all the armor and weapons for his soldiers, allowing Raphael to profit. Sander agreed, adding that his main goal was to build an army to reclaim the kingdom of Luna.

Ares led Sander, Duvessa, Scorpius, and Ashlaius to a field of orcs. "This is what I earned as chieftain," Ares boasted, showing Sander about two thousand orcs ready for battle.

"If you want to take back Luna, we can regroup, and my army is at your command," Ares said. "I'll go get my officers. You tell the officer at the border to let your group in."

Scorpius accompanied Sander back to the border, where the group waited. With Scorpius's command, they were allowed to pass into Orcuhan. When they arrived, Ares shared intel with Sander, informing him of three orc clans ready to be captured. Sander agreed to the task of claiming the clans.

"Orcuhan is a barbarian-like land," Ares explained. "You'll need to challenge the chieftains to a duel. If you lose, you die. To claim the clans, you must kill the chieftain. So, Sander, you must win."

Sander accepted the challenge. "Where do I begin?" he asked.

"In two days," Ares replied. "But for now, my army needs to know who they're following. I'll rally them. For now, here is your tent."

Sander was shown to a tent with a desk and a king-size bed. He thanked Ares and removed his armor, placing it on a stand by the desk. As he took off his shirt, revealing a scar from the basilisk, Ashlaius walked in.

"Oops, sorry, I didn't know you were changing."

"It's fine," Sander replied. "I'm just resting from this long journey."

Ashlaius then invited Sander to a party, but he declined, saying he needed to plan for the upcoming battles.

Ashlaius offered to help him think through his plans. "What do you know about war?" Sander asked with a smile.

"I know that celestials and demons have been at war for over a thousand years, and that it was a long war of great power. The demons lost because Riker fell. I also know that Galatin has been protecting Luna for a thousand years."

Sander was impressed. "Wow, you do know more than I thought. So, what should I do after I gather the orc army?"

Ashlaius suggested, "Train them. Tell them about Luna. Offer them a home there if they wish. Make your kingdom a place where all races—humans, orcs, elves, dwarves—can live together. That would be a place of beauty."

Sander thought her idea was beautiful. "Maybe I'll think about that. But right now, I need to focus on the orcs."

Ashlaius moved closer and whispered, "Why don't you just kiss me? I know you want to."

Sander hesitated. "I can't, even if I wanted to. We're from two different worlds. And I have Riker in me; he wouldn't approve."

"Who cares about him?" Ashlaius said.

"I do. You deserve someone better than me," Sander replied. "I ignore what I feel so I can carry out my revenge. You should move on. I'm not the right person for love."

Sander walked out of the tent to talk to Riker. He flew up to get some fresh air and consulted Riker. Riker awoke and suggested going to an ancient area in Orcuhan but said they could do that later. First, they needed to plan the battles with the chieftains.

Sander returned to Ares to learn about the clans. Ares told him to focus on the Sapphire Clan, the Riverland Clan, and the White Wolf Clan, the three biggest clans. Capturing them would earn Sander the title of Warlord.

Sander returned to his tent to write his plans. Once his plan was complete, he decided to fly to the Riverlands of Orcuhan to begin his mission.

Chapter 42

The Riverland Chieftain

Sander lands in a plain field of grass to see a beautiful flowing river. The water was a pure blue sapphire as it quietly flowed down the stream. Sander begins to understand why the clan is called the Riverland Clan. He follows the stream, breathing in the nature around him.

"Hey, Riker, it's nice here. Nice plains of grass and a river of pure sapphire," Sander says as he talks to Riker, walking to find the Riverland Clan. "Riker, I thought this place would be more barbaric. Why is it so nice and peaceful here?"

"Sander, just because the orcs are known to be evil or barbaric doesn't mean the world is too. You have to understand the peace in things, not just the war and destruction," Riker responds.

"This is coming from a demon?" Sander asks, confused.

"Well, Sander, the world isn't always what it seems. Best keep walking, I'm sensing the Riverland Clan is farther ahead. Enjoy the scenery while you're walking."

Sander walks miles upon miles until he finally reaches spears with giant heads on them and a sign that says "Do not pass: Riverland's Territory."

"Riker, I think we're here at the Riverland Clan."

"What makes you think that, Sander? Is it the spears with the skulls and heads, or the giant sign that literally says 'Riverland's

Territory'?" Riker teases. "Before going in there, I advise caution. The orcs are very strict with their rules. It might be a fist battle, a sword battle, or maybe an axe battle. The point is, you need to be careful because some orcs will cheat in battle. So when entering, just be cautious."

"Alright, Riker, I'll take your advice. Now for the big step." Sander steps into the territory, breathing in the fresh air. "One step closer to seeing my brother again," he says from his heart. "I think I must keep going; who knows what Fergus is doing right now."

Sander quickly begins to walk, but he's stopped by an orc.

"Who do you think you are, shrimp? Do you know what territory this is?" the orc growls.

Sander looks up at the eight-foot orc towering over him. "Yes, this is the Riverland's Territory, is it not?"

The orc sneers down at the "fragile human." "So, you think this is the kingdom of Luna and that you can walk around like you know everything? Human, I suggest you leave before you get in trouble, or end up a slave — or worse, dead."

Sander meets the orc's gaze. "I'm here to see the chieftain."

The orc laughs at Sander's demand. "Who do you think you are? A fragile human wanting to see the chieftain of the Riverlands?"

"I think I can help him with the Sapphire Clan," Sander responds calmly.

The orc continues laughing. "You think you can help us? Fine, fragile human, follow me."

"The name is Sander," he mutters.

"I don't care," the orc replies.

The orc leads Sander to a cliff overlooking the ocean, where a large fifteen-foot tent stands. They approach two ten-foot orcs guarding the tent with giant spears and shields.

"You shall not pass; this is the chieftain's tent," one of the guards warns.

"Relax, brother, let the human pass," the eight-foot orc says, allowing Sander to enter the tent.

Inside, Sander sees the chieftain, a massive orc with scars of battle across his chest. The chieftain looks up, surprised to see a human in his presence.

"What is a human doing in my tent?" the chieftain growls.

"The human wishes to speak to you, my chief," the eight-foot orc explains.

The chieftain orders the orc to leave, then turns to Sander. "Alright, human, what do you wish to talk about, trespassing into my territory?"

Sander introduces himself. "I'm Sander Helmglade of House Helmglade, son of Daniel Helmglade, and brother to Fergus Helmglade."

The chieftain's eyes widen. "You're saying your brother is the human who's growing in power, conquering the three kingdoms of the dwarves and attempting to conquer the elves. He's a threat to the world—and to orc kind. So, Sander Helmglade, why are you here while I'm at war with the Sapphire Clan?"

"I need help stopping my brother from growing in power," Sander replies.

The chieftain laughs. "You mean to say a human will command orcs? What will that look like in front of my men?"

Sander calmly responds, "When is the next battle? I'll show you why I should be in command."

The chieftain smirks. "Tomorrow, at sunrise, by the river and the plains. If you can slay the Sapphire Clan's leader, their army will become mine."

"Good," Sander agrees, walking out with pride, confident that he has this in the bag.

Sander flies up to scout the Sapphire Clan's camp, speaking to Riker along the way. "So, Riker, do you think I should double-cross the chief and help the Sapphire Clan, or should I help the Riverlands?"

Riker gives him advice. "Look, all you have to do is beat the Sapphire Clan's leader, and they'll surrender. You'll have two armies under your command, and you need three to retake your castle. Don't make an enemy of the chief—help him beat the Sapphire Clan, and you'll gain a valuable ally. Think like a general."

Sander lands near a mountain and uses Riker's power to scout the enemy. "There's the chieftain's tent, and I see the Sapphire Clan outnumbers the Riverlands. We should hurry back and warn the chieftain."

Sander quickly flies back to the Riverlands camp and enters the chieftain's tent. "You're outnumbered by the Sapphire Clan," he warns.

The chieftain eyes Sander suspiciously. "Sander, it seems you know more than you're telling me. I don't know how Fergus gained his magic to conquer the dwarven kingdoms, but I must say, those black wings of yours are quite fine. I have a theory: you have a demon inside you, and Fergus unlocked the secret book of the celestials."

Sander nods. "Yes, I have a demon inside me, and Fergus has a celestial inside him. But the celestial inside Fergus wants to conquer the world and doesn't care about you or your people. He wants the world to serve the celestial race as gods."

The chieftain looks surprised. "What makes you think the demon inside you isn't lying, trying to conquer the world and eliminate his rival?"

"Why don't you talk to him yourself?" Sander offers, allowing Riker to take control.

As Riker takes over, black flames ignite around Sander. "You wanted the truth, chief of the Riverlands?" Riker's crimson eyes blaze as the chieftain looks on in fear.

Riker explains everything about the group's journey, and once finished, Sander regains control. The chieftain is now more at ease speaking to Sander.

"Alright, Sander, if you help me defeat the Sapphire Clan's leader, I'll help you dethrone your brother. That's my offer."

Sander smirks. "Fine. Once we're done with the Sapphire Clan, I want you to meet my friend Ares at the border with your best troops. After that, we march to Luna and reclaim my throne."

Sander prepares for the next day's battle, training with his sword against a rock. As he swings and slashes with hatred in his heart, he consults Riker once more.

"So, Riker, should I walk into their camp and overthrow him by killing him, or should I challenge him in battle?"

"I think you should fight him in battle," Riker advises. "Orcs respect strength in combat. Tomorrow will be the Battle of the Riverlands. Rest now and save your energy for the battlefield. After this, we'll head back to Luna. I'll face Galatin, and you'll face Fergus. The end is near, Sander. Soon, we will part ways."

"I'll miss it," Sander admits.

"Aye, me too," Riker replies.

The two fall silent as Sander prepares for the battle ahead.

Chapter 43

The Battle of The Riverlands

A day had passed, and the orcs of the clan began grabbing their weapons and armor, saying goodbye to their families, knowing they might not return. Sadness filled the air as the looming war became more real. The chief walked out of his tent, yelling, "We best get moving! Today is the day, people of the Riverlands Clan!" The chief's voice carried the weight of the moment. "This may be our last battle, but we will not surrender. We fight until the last man. We will make sure that this fight will not be forgotten. We will show them that they are not unbeatable. If we die on the Riverlands, the gods will bless us in the afterlife. We are to be remembered in orc-kind and in history!"

The orcs chanted as they readied themselves for battle, prepared to die for their clan. "Now, let's go and stand our ground!" the chief shouted. The orcs cheered as they left the camp, heading for the battlefield. Sander followed the orcs, ready for the war ahead. The drums of war echoed through the land like thunder, the sky darkened, and the blood of two clans was about to stain the ground through terrible bloodshed.

Sander walked to the middle of the lines. Everything was silent. The chief and his officers headed to the middle as the other clan's leaders did the same. "What do you think they're talking about?" Sander asked a six-foot orc.

"I'm nearly a child, but I think they're talking about terms. Maybe they'll come to an agreement," the orc replied.

"Do you think your chief is willing to talk terms?" Sander asked as the two chiefs turned and walked back to their respective armies.

For five minutes, there was a sudden silence. Everything was peaceful. Then, in an instant, the horns sounded, like bulls ready to charge. "Show them no mercy!" the men shouted as the Riverlands Clan charged into the battlefield. From Sander's perspective, it was chaos, but to the orcs, it was a battle of the heart — a fight for honor. Blood was spilled onto the ground.

Sander moved around cautiously until an orc from the Sapphire Clan rushed at him with a giant axe. Sander had no choice but to fight. The orc swung his axe, but Sander blocked it with the Soul Absorber. Sander, using his rage as an advantage, remembered the teachings of an old general: "Use your sword as if it's a part of you. What do you fight for, Sander? Remember what you're fighting for."

Sander snapped back to reality. "I know what I'm fighting for." He counter-attacked, cutting off the orc's hand and stabbing him as he fell to the ground like a felled tree. "I'm fighting for a better kingdom. I know what my father would have wanted," Sander muttered as he flew into the sky, heading straight for the Sapphire Clan's chief. "I got you," he said as he pierced through the orc guards with his red flames, targeting the chief. The Sapphire Clan's orcs watched in horror as their leader fell.

Sander, expecting the orcs to surrender, looked around as they charged at him. "I thought if I killed the chief, they'd surrender, Riker."

"You need to kill more than one, Sander," Riker responded.

Sander, determined, fought with all his might. One by one, the orcs fell to him. In his rage, he lost control, burning trees and orcs alike. The remaining orcs knelt before him, believing he was a god. Sander floated above them, watching. Ashlaius, who had been observing from afar, flew towards him, concerned about what he was becoming.

"Sander," Ashlaius called, "is this where you are? Ares and the group are looking for you."

"Sorry, Ashlaius, but I need an army to defeat my brother," Sander replied.

"I understand, but you can't just leave without telling us where you're going," Ashlaius scolded. "Let's go back to the group."

"Before that, I need to address the orcs." Sander turned to the Sapphire Clan. "Orcs of the Sapphire Clan, I have defeated your leader. You must now join the Riverlands Clan. Meet me at the border."

With that, Sander flew away, and Ashlaius followed. "Sander, wait!" she called out.

Sander stopped mid-flight. "What do you want? I don't have time to talk. I need to find another orc clan or something strong enough to fight Galatin. I need black flames."

"What do you think I should do, Ashlaius?" Sander asked as they flew.

"I watched the battlefield, Sander. You know what your father taught you—a king must separate his emotions and do what's right for his people. You're becoming too much like Fergus. You need to watch yourself. You're turning more into Riker than you think," Ashlaius warned.

Sander glanced at Ashlaius as they flew over the lands of Orcuhan. "I need to fight my brother. If I defeat him, the war between the dwarves and elves will end. I'm all that's left for my people to enjoy peace. I'm doing what's best for my kingdom."

Ashlaius sensed there was more to it. "Sander, what do you want? To be a king or a normal person? I feel like you're forcing yourself to be king because of what your father wanted. What would your mother think?"

Sander hesitated. "I never knew my mother. She died when my brother Fergus was born. I don't know what she would think."

"You know what I think, Sander?" Ashlaius said gently. "I think you don't want to be king, but you're forcing yourself to be. My advice is to take it slow."

"Ashlaius, it's been a year since I last saw my brother, and he's already conquered the dwarven kingdoms and nearly taken the elves. I need to act quickly," Sander insisted.

"No!" she yelled. "We should take back the dwarven kingdoms he claimed, gaining allies for the war. That's what I think. Stop being reckless and listen for once."

Sander heard Riker's voice within. "Ashlaius is right, Sander. You should listen to her more often. She's an archangel, and she's wiser than you."

"Alright, Ashlaius, how long will it take for the Riverlands Clan orcs to reach the border of Orcuhan?" Sander asked.

"On foot, five days. For us, it will take thirty minutes because we're flying."

Sander landed at the border of Orcuhan, with Ashlaius following close behind.

"Sander, wait, I need to tell you something," Ashlaius said.

"Not now, Ashlaius. I'm on a mission," Sander replied.

Ashlaius slapped him. "Enough with the mission! I think we should go to a place in Orcuhan called the Ancient Ruins. It's a place of ancestor writings. I think we should go there."

"Fine, Ashlaius, I'll go, but first, I need to talk to Ares." Sander walked away from Ashlaius, heading to Ares' tent.

"Ares," Sander called out as he arrived.

"Sander, you're back! Where have you been?"

"I went to get a clan of orcs—the Sapphire and Riverlands Clans."

"Um, Sander, those two clans are at war," Ares replied.

"Not anymore," Sander said with a grin. "I've gotten the Sapphire Clan to join the Riverlands."

"That's great, but we still need one more clan to go to war with Luna. Orc tradition demands it. You already have my clan and the Riverlands. You need one more."

Sander thought for a moment. "What clan should join us?"

"I think you should head to the White Wolf Clan in the north. They're one of the strongest clans, and they're the noblest of the orcs in this region," Ares advised.

Sander nodded. "But first, I'm finally going on a date with Ashlaius."

"Well, congratulations! Where are you headed?" Ares asked, smiling.

"She mentioned the Ancient Ruins," Sander replied.

"Well, I'll leave you to it, Sander," Ares said with a chuckle. "When are you leaving?"

"Now," Sander said, bidding Ares farewell as he flew into the sky.

He spotted Ashlaius flying ahead of him. "I'm ready to go to the Ancient Ruins now," he called to her.

Ashlaius grabbed his hand, and together they flew towards the ruins. "It will be a long journey, so please wait," she told him. "The ruins tell of my brother and grandparents I've never met. It also tells Riker's story and the first war of our kinds. You're going to love it."

Ashlaius led Sander to the Ancient Ruins, located near a mountain in Orcuhan, between two dormant volcanoes. When they arrived, Sander saw words written in demonic, celestial, and reaper languages.

"If any shall enter here, they shall know the truth."

Sander walked into the cave with Ashlaius, holding her hand tightly.

Chapter 44

The Ancient Ruins

Ashlaius and Sander walked into the cave, seeing glowing names written in all languages. "It's like a library," Sander said as Ashlaius smiled, marveling at the ancient ruins. Sander let go of her hand and started walking around the ruins.

"So, what is this place really, Ashlaius?"

"Well, Sander, to others, it's the ancient ruins, but to my kind, Riker's kind, the Reapers, and the Great Phoenixes, it's the Library of Stories. It holds all the tales of heroes, wars, love, and those who did good in the world. This is a place of secrets — a place where two souls can meet."

As they walked toward each other, Sander felt a connection with Ashlaius. They shared a tender kiss, a moment of peace and unity. Ashlaius looked at him with her brown eyes and whispered, "Follow me."

Sander followed her to a ruin that bore the name "Helmglade." He read the inscription. "This is the tale of Stormand Helmglade, leader and the first of House Helmglade."

Suddenly, like a misty crystal ball, he watched the memories of his ancestor unfold — how Stormand fought against the demons and became the first king, rallying humans in their time of need. "This is your family's history," Ashlaius explained. "Stormand was the first to stand against the demons, but the truth is, he was manipulated."

She took his hand and led him to Galatin's memories. "Wait, Ashlaius, Galatin isn't dead," Sander pointed out.

"I know," she replied, "but he still has many memories here."

They arrived at the scene of the war's beginning—a celestial killing a demon. Sander watched in awe as the magic of purity and chaos collided, illuminating the room with the memories of Sinia and Calhera's greatest heroes. He saw Galatin kill Crystal in front of Riker's eyes.

"This place is more than what you think," Ashlaius said, leading him up to the top of the ruins. They entered a massive cave, so large a great dragon could fit inside. The cave glowed with the journey of Colinborn and a golden light at the end.

"What's that place?" Sander asked, surprised.

"That's the place—the one memory the gods gave us. It's the creation of Calhera."

Sander and Ashlaius flew back down together. "Is this the place you wanted to show me?" Sander asked.

"Yes, this is the place," Ashlaius confirmed, before stopping in her tracks. "Wait... this is my sister's memory."

They watched Crystal's memory, where Riker appeared happy, sharing love with her. "This is more than love—it's life," Ashlaius said softly. Together, they saw Crystal give birth prematurely.

"I didn't know she had her child early," Ashlaius murmured, as Sander wiped away a tear. "Are you crying, Sander?" she asked.

"No, it's not me... I think it's Riker."

Riker, within Sander, felt deep sadness. "If Riker's watching, who did she give the baby to?" Sander wondered aloud. They watched as Crystal handed her baby to the great dragon, Myrvus.

"She gave the baby to a great dragon to keep it safe," Ashlaius said.

Sander nodded. "Maybe Riker would understand."

"I do," Riker said within him.

Ashlaius stopped watching. "Sander, whatever you do, don't look at your own memory."

"Why not? It might bring me joy. I need to know what I'll do before I do it," Sander replied.

Ashlaius looked at him gently. "I recommend you don't. It could make you lose yourself. It's forbidden to look at what you will do next."

She urged Sander to leave, but as he turned, she took a quick peek. She saw Sander's future battle with Fergus and knew what was coming. "Wait up," she called, flying after him.

Grabbing Sander's hand, she led him beyond the clouds to watch the sun go down. "Isn't it beautiful, Sander?"

"Yeah, it's peaceful—no wars, no chaos. Just us," he said, smiling.

"You finally said it," Ashlaius teased.

"Said what?" Sander asked.

"We're finally a thing now."

"Yes, but you know you can't stop me," Sander said. "I need to fight my brother. It's my destiny."

"Let's head back to the group," Sander suggested. "We should get ready to depart for Luna."

"But wait," Ashlaius reminded him, "don't you need another army?"

Sander realized he had forgotten. "Oh, right! I need to go north to the White Wolf Clan. They're more honorable than the other orcs, so maybe they'll understand why I need to take revenge on my brother."

Just as they were about to leave, Ashlaius pointed to a tree. "There's a tree," she said.

"A tree?" Sander asked, confused.

"Yes, a tree that contains life. Let's go see it."

Sander agreed to go with her. They flew together, hand in hand, to the tree. When they arrived, they found it standing atop a high rock, with a man covered in leaves standing beside it. A giant tree man stood beside the tree.

"Who are you?" Sander asked.

"I am Leelius, and this is James, my bedent."

"An ent?" Sander asked. "What's an ent?"

Leelius explained, "An ent is a magical being, born of nature itself."

"Are there more of his kind?" Sander asked.

"Yes, there are more in the misty forest below," Leelius replied. "But enough about the ents. Tell me, why are you here?"

"Well, Ashlaius brought me here to see it," Sander said.

Leelius telepathically asked Ashlaius, "Why did you bring him here? Why do you want him to see the tree?"

Ashlaius responded telepathically, "I want him to understand how much I care for him and give him the power to fight his brother, who has Galatin, my brother, within him."

Leelius replied, "Galatin… centuries ago, he destroyed parts of the forest. He must pay. So, power is what Sander seeks. Power comes with great responsibility and can kill you if used unwisely. Why do you want him to have power?"

Ashlaius confessed, "Because after this is all over with his brother, he said he would be with me forever. I want him for myself, and no one else. If stopping my evil brother is how to do it, then so be it."

Leelius replied, "You speak the truth. I will allow him to drink from the tree's liquid. It will grant him unimaginable power, but only for three months. If he uses it beyond that time, he will die. Take this warning seriously. Many heroes have fallen because of it. Make sure this one does not fall. He is important to us all."

Leelius disappeared into the night, and the ent turned into a tree. "Why didn't he speak much?" Sander wondered aloud.

Ashlaius approached the tree and, pulling out a dagger, stabbed it. "What are you doing?" Sander asked.

"Drink the tree's liquid," she insisted. "It will give you the power to stop Galatin and his uprising."

Sander hesitated but then walked to the tree and took a sip of its liquid. Immediately, he felt a surge of strength greater than what the demon power had given him. Riker felt younger, and Sander felt wiser. The tree gifted them a power they could barely comprehend. Sander flew into the sky, overwhelmed by his newfound abilities, moving so fast that Ashlaius couldn't even see him.

Sander returned to the ground, feeling the weight of the power. "I'll meet you at the camp, but first, I need to take over the White Wolf Clan. Thank you, Ashlaius, for showing me true power."

He gently kissed her on the lips. "And I promise, when this is all over, I will make you the queen of Luna."

Sander then flew north, with a peaceful heart, to confront the White Wolf Clan, while Ashlaius headed in the opposite direction toward the border of Orcuhan.

Chapter 45

The White Wolf Clan

Sander flies through the sky and spots a snowstorm ahead. "Oh no, a snowstorm," he mutters, as the harsh winds begin to push him back. Struggling to navigate through the blizzard, he searches for shelter. "I need to find a cave somewhere," he says to himself. Suddenly, Sander hits a rock hard, knocking him unconscious.

Later, as Sander lies unconscious, a giant figure appears and carries him to a nearby camp. Sander wakes up to the sound of loud noises in the background. He opens the tent flap to see three eight-foot orcs staring at him.

"Hey, Zytrix, he's awake," one of the orcs says.

"Easy there, little guy," Zytrix responds. "You hit that rock hard, so we picked you up and brought you to our camp."

Sander, still groggy, says, "I can heal," and walks over to the large fire. "So, what clan are you guys from?" Sander asks.

Zytrix doesn't answer directly and instead says, "Why are you asking, little guy? You looking for a clan?"

"Yeah, I am. I'm looking for the White Wolf Clan of the North."

The orc sighs. "Are you a spy? If you are, we'll have to kill you."

Sander pieces the information together and realizes they are part of the White Wolf Clan. "Listen, I'm not a spy. I just need your army for the war I'm putting together against my brother."

"Well then, little guy," Zytrix says with a smirk, "you'll need to talk to my father, the leader of the clan."

Sander realizes Zytrix is the son of the White Wolf Clan chieftain. "Wait, your father is the leader?"

"Yes," Zytrix confirms. "I can take you to him, but be quiet. He hates loud noises, especially when you meet him."

"What do we do now?" Sander asks as they sit around the fire.

"We wait for the storm to pass," Zytrix replies. "In the meantime, we can talk or sleep through it. You hit your head pretty hard, so you might want to rest before we head to the White Wolf Clan."

Sander decides to talk for a bit to learn more about the new people he met. "So, does your father have any other sons?"

"Nope, just me. I came out here to scout for other orcs who might want to join us or fight us. We're one of the most powerful clans in Orcuhan, so people come to challenge my father. But truth be told, my father has never lost a battle. He's honorable and shows it everywhere he goes."

Sander responds, "I need your father's army to fight my brother. I already have the Riverlands and Redside Clans ready. I just need the White Wolf Clan to march with me to my castle and take what's mine."

"So you're a prince trying to reclaim your kingdom to become king?" Zytrix asks.

"Yes, I'm from the Kingdom of Luna, a human kingdom. But I want more than just humans in my kingdom. I want orcs, elves, and dwarves to live there as well. A kingdom where all races can live together."

Zytrix smiles. "I can agree with that. Now, the storm is getting heavier. You sure you don't want to sleep?"

Sander agrees, and Zytrix points him to one of the beds in the tent. Sander falls asleep and starts dreaming about Fergus kicking him off the cliff and into the dark pit. He dreams about the deal he made, feeling the rage inside him grow. His body begins to catch fire as his emotions take over.

Sander wakes up suddenly to Zytrix standing over him. "You alright, Sander? You were on fire and talking in your sleep," Zytrix says. "You've never told me the full truth. You can explain while we travel to my village. My father will be waiting."

Sander gets up and joins the orcs by the campfire as they prepare for the journey. Sander tells them he can fly there, but the orcs warn him, "That's not a good idea. You could get shot down by the giant ballistas on our walls."

"Your village is like a kingdom?" Sander asks.

Zytrix sighs. "It's big, but not quite a kingdom. We call it a village to avoid being attacked by the warlords. Right now, two wars are going on between the Mountain Clan and the Black Rock Clan, both fighting for dominance. Warlords to us are like kings to you."

The group of orcs finishes preparing, and Zytrix says, "Follow me, Sander. I'll take you to my village."

As they walk through the snowy forest and into the plains, Zytrix asks, "So, Sander, how did you become a demon?"

"Wait, how do you know I'm a demon?" Sander asks, surprised.

Zytrix chuckles. "I've seen many things in my life. I've read about the celestials and demons. You have black wings, an unexplained sword, and the courage to meet the chieftains of the orc clans. That sounds like someone with a demon inside them. So, are you human or demon?"

Sander explains his story as they walk toward the White Wolf Clan's village. "It all started in Luna. I was sleeping, ready for my coronation, when Fergus dragged me out of bed and kicked me into the dark pit, which contains demons. I was on the verge of death until a demon approached me with an offer to merge our souls. I accepted, and now I'm here, building an army to fight my brother."

"Wow," Zytrix says. "Explaining that to my father might get you in. My uncle did something similar to our clan, but my father won in the end, so he understands what it means to do what's best for your kingdom."

"We're here," Zytrix announces as they arrive at the gates of the White Wolf Clan's village.

Sander looks up in awe at the seventy-foot walls. "Wow, I didn't know your walls were this big."

"Yeah, we make sure no raiders can attack our village."

The gates open, revealing a beautiful village with cobblestone roads covered in snow. Sander watches as orcs go about their daily chores—bakers baking, woodcutters chopping wood.

"You said this was a village," Sander says.

"I know what I said, but truthfully, we're more like a kingdom," Zytrix admits. "But don't tell the other clans that, or they'll get angry."

Zytrix leads Sander to the chieftain's house on the mountain. "Your land is more peaceful than mine," Sander comments.

"We have a giant wall," Zytrix replies.

' Zytrix knocks on the door, and his father, the chieftain, opens it. "Hello, my son," the chief says, welcoming them inside.

"Who's this you found in the wilderness?" the chief asks.

"Father, this is Sander. He wishes to speak to you about the war."

The chief nods and gestures for them to sit at the table. "So, what's this war about? It must be important."

Zytrix tells Sander to explain everything he had told him earlier. Sander speaks nobly, recounting his entire story as the night falls. The chieftain listens intently, and after a long pause, he finally agrees.

"I will help," the chief says. "But I'm not sending my elite army. I'll send my best commander, some seasoned warriors, and five hundred recruits. My son will go with you, not me. Is that enough for battle?"

Sander thanks him and says, "Yes, that will be more than enough."

"When do you want my men to leave?" the chief asks.

"When the sun rises," Sander replies.

Sander sleeps through the night, knowing he has a long journey ahead. The next morning, he wakes to see the orcs preparing for the journey. As the sun rises, they leave the village, marching toward their next destination.

Chapter 46

The Rally

Sander and the orcs, after three days, finally arrived at the border of Orcuhan to see the Riverland clan and the Redside clan tents. "Good," said Sander. "I guess the other two clans are ready to be leaving as well." Sander walked to the large camp with five hundred men of the White Wolf clan. He walked to his tent as the other clan members gathered in line in front of the border to rally.

"Ares, what are you doing here?"

"Now good, Sander. Now that you're here with the three clans, it's time for the rally. Me, Jake, Gildor, Raymond, Duvessa, Scorpius, Kevin and his guards, along with Raphael and Ashlaius, will stand by your side."

"Alright, let's do this," Sander said, as he decided to go up to the Orcuhan border to start the speech since he had a plan. When Sander arrived, he waited for his group to come along. The group finally arrived to stand by his side when he gave the speech.

"Men of Orcuhan, men of the three clans: White Wolf, Riverland, and Redside. You are here for one purpose. You are here to help me overthrow my brother to free these lands from his raids and conquering. We are the rebels that will stop a tyrant from taking control of the world. We are the people who will not stand for his betrayal. We will be the ones who will stop him by any means necessary. We are not three clans now. We are standing as one team, one army, one nation, and one clan. Until the mission is over, we are all the same and equal. Now, let's get going and free the people from a tyrant."

The orcs cheered for Sander as if he were a king. Ares tapped Sander on the shoulder and gave him a stare.

"Are you sure you want to kill your brother, Sander?"

Sander turned around to look at Ares and told him yes, that he did want to kill his brother for what he had done to their father and the kingdom. Sander then walked alone down to his tent, telling the chiefs at the end of the stairs that they would be leaving at sunrise.

Sander arrived at the tent to see Ashlaius waiting for him.

"Did you like what I showed you and what the tree gave you?"

Sander walked past Ashlaius. "Not right now. I have to think about what my next move is. I need to head back to Luna and take my castle back."

"I know," Ashlaius said, "but why don't we have a little fun?"

"I don't have time for that, Ashlaius. If I do what my dirty mind is making me think, I won't have time to take back my kingdom."

"You know what I think?" said Ashlaius. "I think that you're paying too much attention to the kingdom, and you're forgetting about me. Is that what I am to you — a forgetful thought?"

"No," said Sander. "You're not, but I have to get some sleep. We have a big journey tomorrow."

"Wait, why don't we talk about your next move?"

Sander looked at her gentle face and told her he didn't know. He then began to look at a large map next to his tent.

"We can go through Cumasoom. Then we head towards the Black Forest, through the deep Black Forest. Once we pass through those forests, we head towards Elmus. It's like a shortcut. But before Elmus, we must head towards the Dark Forest. I've been there before, so it's not so bad. We aid the people in Elmus and help against the dwarves. Afterward, we head straight for our castle and take back my throne."

"That's a lot easier said than done, Sander. You do realize how long of a journey you just mentioned. It's like five to ten days of travel, and that's without stopping. You need to think more clearly."

"Just trust me. I think we should head towards the deep Black Forest, but before heading towards Elmus, we fight and help the dwarves. First the three kingdoms, then Elmus. We push your brother's forces back at Luna, and then we strike at that moment. So, what do you think of my plan, Sander?"

Sander looked at Ashlaius. "I guess we go with your plan," said Sander.

Sander and Ashlaius then decided to go to sleep, waiting for the right time to wake up at sunrise to head out on the new journey.

Chapter 47

A New Journey to the Northern Kingdom of Sulana.

The sun rose from the world to have the camp be shined open as Sander wakes up with Ashlaius next to him. Sander slightly got out of bed to get some water. Sander then grabs his things to get ready for the journey. "When are we leaving?" Sander said to Zytrix and the other two chiefs. Sander says, "Now. So make sure all the wagons and the baggages are set. It's going to be a long journey," said Sander with a smile on his face. Sander then goes back to his tent to see Ashlaius with an angry face. "You forgot to wake me as you are leaving."

"See, Ashlaius, look before you get mad. I woke up, got my things ready, and came back for you. See, there is no reason for you to — " as Sander was about to speak, he gets hit in the face by an angry archangel.

"Next time, wake me and we go together."

"Fine, I guess so, Ashlaius." Sander and Ashlaius begin to get the map and their things to get ready for the new journey to the northern kingdom of Sulana. The group was ready to go. As Sander sees Gildor, he says, "So Gildor, I never did ask, why is a werewolf hunter like you joining this journey?"

"You see, Sander, last time I checked there was a green werewolf leader. If I follow you, maybe I will see him again. Plus, look on the bright side, we're friends, and what are friends for?"

"You know what, Gildor? You're right," said Sander. Sander and Gildor begin to walk together as the group follows. In a long journey, the orcs then follow the chiefs and the group along the way. The group then heads off into one group. As the group was heading into the group, Zytrix asked Sander where they were heading.

"Well, Zytrix, where we're heading is south to the kingdom of Sulana, the northern dwarven city of the dwarves."

"Why would we need to go there, Sander?"

"Because, Zytrix, and you chiefs, we need to push back the troops of the Lunian force. With two more sieges like that, and one saving the elves, we head through the green forest and head towards my castle."

The orcs then agreed to go with Sander and decided to have the long journey. Cronovus then walks up to Sander. "Wait, Sander, you're saying the dwarven fortress two thousand years ago is not a castle?"

"Huh, what do you mean, Cronovus?"

"Well, back in my time, before Riker made all of us, there was a dwarven fortress. It was inside a mountain of hard, golden walls. And it contained dragan steel, in which the dragons helped make the fortress as well. They say the fortress is impenetrable. But how did you humans get to conquer it? That's my question, Sander. Now that is a kingdom. They probably got the dwarves working the mines. Sander, I pray that we're not too late to see any of the dwarves dead."

As Sander is walking, he thinks. "Hey, Riker, what Cronovus said, is it true?"

"Yes, Sander, it is true. The dwarves were smart back then. Not even a demon could get into the fortress unless you let them in. That's what Fergus did. He let himself in and then decided to take over the dwarven city using Galatian's power. That's what I fear too, Sander. We must head there quickly, free the dwarves, and get allies in this battle."

"Plus, Riker, it's the right thing to do."

As the army and the group go through Cumasoom and throughout the titans' lairs, they wind up in the north snow of the village they had once been in.

"My goddess," said the dwarves of the village. Ashlaius goes in to ask the dwarves about the northern kingdom. The dwarves then gave Ashlaius all the answers they could give them about the northern kingdom of Sulana. Ashlaius then reports back to Sander.

"Come on, guys, this way." The chiefs then order their men as the army marches south towards the kingdom of Sulana. Heading towards there, Ashlaius walks up to Sander.

"Sander, what are we going to do when we get to the kingdom of Sulana? I mean, we've got the magic, but what are we going to do about the wall? What Cronovus says—it's impenetrable."

"We're not going to do anything. I'm going in alone, and they would want me, Sander Helmglade, as a prisoner. Once I'm in, I open the gate, letting all the orcs in, taking out the Lunian soldiers, and freeing the dwarves from the cages they're in. That's the plan, Ashlaius, and I don't want you to be worried, as I can handle myself."

Sander continues to walk in silence as the army and the group make their way towards the kingdom of Sulana. Sander and the group finally arrive at the kingdom of Sulana to see a giant golden gate at the front of the mountain.

"Wow, I never knew the golden wall was that big."

The snow then gets heavy as they all look at the golden gates.

"Yeah, I thought they were just giant golden doors."

They look at the nice golden wall with two golden gates along it.

"Wait, it's too quiet. We must go hide in that cave over there."

The army then marches towards the cave near Sulana. And they decide to make a plan on how to get into the dwarven city of Sulana.

Chapter 48

The Siege in the Kingdom of Sulana

The snow got thicker; the group still sat at the campfire, trying to figure out what to do in the golden walls of Sulana. The walls thickened from the snowstorm.

"Sander, how are you going to go in? The walls are strong from dragons' breath."

"Yes, they are, Zytrix, but my fire is stronger than dragons' breath. Maybe I can punch a hole through."

"You're going to need a lot of fire," said Zytrix.

"Don't worry, leave that to me. You guys just wait for the signal."

"What's the signal?" asked Zytrix.

"You will know," said Sander.

Sander walks to the large golden wall of Sulana. "Wow, this wall is even bigger up close." Sander begins to talk to Riker. "Riker, what do I do if there is a giant wall in front of me? Is it possible that I can summon the flames within me to melt through the wall?"

Riker begins to respond to Sander in his head. "Yes, Sander, there is a way to melt the wall. But Sander, this will take most of your energy. You need to melt the golden gate for your army to walk right in and help the dwarves. Now, I believe, Sander, this may only happen once. After all, this is the northern golden gate. Then you have the silver gate and the iron gate, but those cities are far away. Right now, I want you to focus on this one."

Sander begins to close his eyes and reopen them as Riker's eyes, the crimson red eye with black surrounding it. Sander begins to concentrate. He begins to feel the flames not as an enemy but as his allies. The flames start to burn as they surround him. The flames dance around him like a dancing pony. Sander puts his hand on the wall as purple flames begin to melt and heat up the golden gate. The golden gate then heats up so hot that even the orcs feel the heat from the cave. Sander uses his rage and concentration on the gate as he burns the gate so intensely that, in his mind, he wills it to melt.

Riker then begins to respond to Sander. "Sander, don't focus on the gate. Focus on what happened to you in the dark pit. Focus on what happened to you when you were with Sofia. Focus on everything you did until now. Make sure nothing— I mean nothing—stands in your way. You are the wielder of fire. You control the flames, not Fergus, not Galatin, not anyone. Remember our deal, Sander."

Sander then begins to get angry as the gate burns even hotter. Sander lights up the gate as they see it start to melt. With all his might, Sander begins to use his rage to the point that a little black fire emerges within him. Ashlaius from the side starts to fear the black flames as Sander melts the gate. Sander slowly begins to melt the gate until there is no gate left. With all his energy, the gate finally melts in the hard, cold weather.

As the gate melts completely, Sander turns around and looks at the orcs. Sander begins to walk back to the large cave where the orcs and his friends are. Sander begins to make a speech.

"We're not going to sneak in. We're going to siege the settlement. We're going to help the dwarves that are stuck inside that kingdom. We're going to hunt every one of my kind. We will not kill all of them, but if we have to, we will. Now, enough talking, let's go inside and help those dwarves."

The orcs look at each other as they all grab arms and start to run and march into the golden gate entrance. The orcs rush into the kingdom to see a giant dwarven cabin and a battalion of humans with swords and shields.

"With a loud war cry, charge!" said Zytrix.

The orcs run down the humans as they all clash swords. The metal clashing with the swords sounded like a blacksmith hitting tools. Sander slowly walks inside the kingdom of Sulana. Sander finds his way to the dungeons to see the dwarven army and its people trapped in the dungeon. As the orcs are fighting over the settlement with a battalion of humans, Sander finds himself melting the doors of the dungeon. Sander begins to melt, one at a time, every door of the dungeon cells. Sander frees most of the dwarves as they all pick up arms—swords, shields, and axes.

The dwarves then listen to Sander. "I am Sander Helmglade, and I am the rightful king of Luna. I came here to set you free. You should not be slaves to the humans. Dwarves are meant to be free. It's time you get out there and show yourselves what you're made of. Not for me, not for you, and not for each other. Do it for your people and for the kingdom of Sulana."

The dwarves cheer as they all decide to go outside and help the orcs fight back the humans. Sander grabs his sword as he begins to fight back his own kind. While fighting, Sander feels the presence of a creature nearby, down in the deep dark tunnel. Sander wonders what this presence could be. He stops thinking about it and continues to fight back his kind.

As they push harder and harder, the humans decide to retreat back to the kingdom of Relana. "Retreat to Relana, lads! We will warn the other dwarven kingdoms we conquered!"

The orcs push them away as a couple of hundred humans run off to the kingdom of Relana. Sander then tells some of the orcs to go and free the dwarves from their own dungeons, as Sander begins to wait and talk to his friends.

Kevin begins to walk to Sander. "Sander," said Kevin, "I can't believe Fergus did this. Imprisoning the dwarves in their own kingdom. I believe he was going to enslave them and make them work the mines for his own benefit. What a selfish act."

Kevin begins to tell Sander, "Sander, you need to stop Fergus asap. Once we free the other dwarven kingdoms, we can unite to go to Elmus. Maybe the elves, Sander, can give us assistance in this battle."

Sander looks at Kevin. "Yes, cousin, you are right. Maybe they can, or maybe they can't. We all have battles to fight, even the elves."

Sander then decides to tell Kevin, "What will you do if you were the rightful king of Luna?"

Kevin begins to tell Sander, "Well, if I was king," said Kevin, "I would start to take arms. Unite the dwarven kingdoms. Save the elves from Fergus's cruelty. Then I will march to the kingdom of Luna and demand my throne back. Sander, that's what you should do. Save everyone from what's going on. A good king saves his people, Sander. If you can get Gildor Landfield, a badass werewolf hunter, Raymond, a vampire hunter, and Ashlaius, an archangel — if you can get people from different species and what they do for a living to unite under your banner — then you can be a good king. That's what your father taught you."

Sander begins to think with a smile. "You may be right, cousin. But war isn't a noble battle. We all have to do cruel things."

"I know," said Kevin. Kevin then pats him on the back and decides to move along to the orcs.

Sander walks out to get fresh air. As he steps out, Ashlaius joins him.

"You did it. I always knew you could do it," she said with a smile. "But you have a lot of work to do before confronting your brother."

She then kisses him on the cheek and begins to look into the sky.

Chapter 49

The King of Sulana

A week has passed, and the dwarven race starts to rebuild their gate that was melted by Sander. Sander begins to walk to the throne room. "The king wishes to speak to you," said the dwarven guard. Sander then begins to walk in as he needs to speak to the king. When Sander walked into the dwarven throne room, he began to talk to the king of Sulana.

"Thank you, kind soldier. But I never did ask, what is your name, and why did you save my people?" said the king of Sulana.

"The name is Sander Helmglade. I am the brother of Fergus Helmglade. I am also the rightful ruler of Luna. I'm here to help the three dwarven kingdoms gain freedom. I'm going to make my way to the elves and request their help to take back my kingdom."

"Wow, you know if I knew you were the rightful king of Luna, I would have made a banquet. So, Sander, why are you so far from home?"

Sander then tells the king of Sulana that he has been betrayed by his brother. "I'm the brother of Fergus Helmglade. I am here to help you win the war."

The king thanks Sander for what he has done. "But Sander, I will say I cannot help you with the war against Fergus. Sander, he's too strong. He has captured Cavlana and Relana, those two dwarven kingdoms of my cousin's folk. He has taken the Silver Wall and the Iron Wall."

"Alright, King of Sulana, if I can take the kingdoms and take over King Fergus's reign from those dwarven kingdoms, can you please, can you please help me take Luna?"

The king smiles at Sander. "If you can convince the elves to help us as well, then I will be happy to help you take Luna with you, King Sander Helmglade."

Sander is shocked by the name the king just called him.

"You are no prince anymore. You think like a king now. I knew your father. I must say, your father trained you well."

Sander then tells the king he is no king.

"Yes, you are, Sander," said the king. "You are. A king cares for his people. A king fights with his people, and a king stands with his people, no matter what the circumstances."

The king then tells Sander he will help get supplies for the journey to Cavlana. Sander thanks the king for what he has done and decides to leave to talk to his commanders and friends about what to do next. Sander walks outside the kingdom to see tents set up by his orc army. Sander goes and asks soldiers to go get his friends and commanders. The soldiers then went to get the commanders and friends. As Sander walked into his tent, he already sees Ashlaius there, waiting for him.

"Good, Ashlaius, I needed to talk to you about what to do next."

Ashlaius then asks, "What do we talk about?"

The group walks in, along with the commanders, into the tent. The group waits for Sander to start talking. Sander begins to speak to them about what to do next.

"So, the king requests that we go to Cavlana. This is what we're going to do. We're going on a big journey to free the slaves in the dwarven kingdoms. Push back the people in Cavlana and Relana. We're going to make sure there are no slaves in the dwarven kingdoms. We make sure these dwarves are free. Then we head to take safe passage to the elves. We get food and shelter there, and we move on to our last destination."

Sander then grabs a knife and stabs it on the table where Luna is marked.

"Now, this will take a long journey. I'm not asking for you guys to go along with all this, but I am asking that you come and help me on this journey. If you guys do, I will allow the orcs that joined to make a living in Luna."

Ares begins to speak. "Look, Sander, I'm not a king yet. But what I have seen is that you gathered an army of orcs, went through trees and forests, and went through a lot of things to get to where you are now. That's what I see in you—a king of a fallen kingdom. So I and my army of orcs will be happy to help you get your revenge on a tyrant."

Dusessa and the group begin to agree with Ares. Zytrix and the other commander agree with Sander on the journey. They all have agreed, except Ashlaius. They all decide to leave the tent, leaving Sander and Ashlaius alone.

"Why, Ashlaius? Why are you not going to agree with this?"

"Because I love you, Sander. I do not want you to get hurt. My brother Galatin is strong. He will kill you. You stand no chance against him."

"I love you too, Ashlaius. But don't you see? We have no choice. My brother has conquered two other dwarven kingdoms. He has also almost conquered the elves by now. He is probably going to conquer the rest of Sinia. I'm not doing this only for the crown. I'm doing this for the people of Luna. I'm doing this to save the people of Sinia. My brother has pushed too far. You and I will be happy. I will take my throne back. I will restore peace to the people of Sinia. I will restore peace in Luna. I need to fix everything my brother has done. Don't you understand?"

"I do, Sander, but…"

"But what?" said Sander.

"I don't want you to die and leave me alone."

Sander then hugs Ashlaius. "Don't you worry. I will not die. I will have revenge on my brother. But I will not leave you behind, for I love you too. Remember that. I will do everything in my power to live."

Sander and Ashlaius begin to kiss.

"Fine, I agree to this," said Ashlaius. "But don't think I won't let you out of my sight for just one second."

Sander smiles. "Thank you. Can you do me a favor?"

"What?" said Ashlaius.

"Can you please tell everyone around the camp that we need to leave for Cavlana?"

She then smiles back and tells him, "Yes."

Ashlaius left the tent to go tell everyone that they are leaving for Cavlana. Sander then packs his things and flies to a nearby mountain to call out to Colinborn.

"Hear me," said Sander.

Colinborn then hears Sander and flies to him.

"Sander, I hear you're going to Cavlana to save the dwarves there. Very noble of you."

Sander then asks for him to help on the journey to Cavlana and Luna.

"Look, Colinborn, I won't be able to defeat Galatin and Fergus on my own. May you please help me?"

"I'm sorry, Sander, I cannot help you with Cavlana, but I will help you with Luna."

"Why can't you help me?" said Sander.

Sander, with all his might, begins to talk to Colinborn.

"Sander, you have to understand, this walk you walk with your friends. I cannot help you in Cavlana. This is a path you must take. This path will help you own your powers to fight Galatin himself."

Sander then begins to talk to Colinborn one last time. "Alright, I can fight in Cavlana. But are you going to watch my back everywhere I go?" Said Sander.

Sander stands still as the dragon flies over him.

"Yes, Sander, I am going to look after you for quite some time until this all blows over. You are a hero now. You are a man who will take back his kingdom and begin to walk the path of a king. Sander, it's time you stop acting like a child and start acting like a king. What would your father do? What would he do in a situation like this? Start thinking more like a king. I cannot help you until you get to Cavlana. But I will give you advice—don't rush into Cavlana. Try doing this like a diplomat. If you do, maybe you'll get better results," said Colinborn as he begins to fly away.

"Wait, so I walk to Cavlana now? What would my father think?" he says as he flies off into the sky. Colinborn disappears. Sander then begins to fly off to his tent to see everyone packing up and ready to go. As Sander is ready as well, he waits for everyone to finish with their stuff. Twelve hours have passed, and Sander and the orcs are heading on the path to Cavlana to help the middle dwarven city from the humans under Fergus's reign. Sander then heads off to his new journey to Cavlana.

Chapter 50

The Journey to Cavlana

Two days have passed, and Sander begins to march with the orcs to Cavlana.

"Are we there yet?" said Kevin.

"Cavlana is a long way to go," said Raphael. "I have been there before. It's a nice place."

Raphael then continues to talk about Cavlana as the group begins to get annoyed.

"Listen, Raphael, we want to hear about the stories of Cavlana, but for right now, we are focused on the journey to it. It's a long walk, and we don't want to get bored with what we're doing. We thank you."

Raphael then understands as they walk to Cavlana. The group begins to stop as the army stops to see a forest.

"Look at that, Sinia with a forest. Not something you always see," Gildor says with sarcasm.

The forest was large and sticky. The trees were maple trees.

"Let's go," said Sander.

Sander then begins to walk into the maple tree forest. As they're walking, Ashlaius begins to speak with Sander.

"Hey Sander, are you alright?" said Ashlaius.

"No, I'm not. Every time I get closer, every time I'm somewhere near Luna, my rage begins to build up. The rage is growing, Ashlaius. I don't know what to do," said Sander.

Ashlaius then gives him some advice. "Why not use your anger for war? We're going to siege Cavlana and take it back for the dwarves. So why don't you use that rage you've been getting and use it for battle?"

The troops begin to march through the maple forest. As they're marching, a maple leaf hits an orc. The orc then freezes. Everyone stops to see the orc stop moving. They then realize the maple leaf freezes the orc.

"Don't touch the maple," said one of the orc troops.

The orc then starts to move as he begins to shake. He shakes so much he dies from the maple that touched him.

"The maple is also poisoned. Let's get out of here fast."

The orcs then begin to run out of the forest straight ahead to where Cavlana is. The rushing stampede of orcs running as fast as they can. As soon as they see light, they see a grassland stretching ahead of them. And from afar, beyond the grassland, they see the city of Luna. Sander drops to his knees.

"There she is, guys," Gildor stops running to join Sander in looking at Luna.

"She's a beauty. There will be a day that Fergus will fall, but it won't be today. I haven't seen her since Fergus pushed me into the hole when I fought him."

"That's Luna, huh?" said Ashlaius.

Everyone, after the maple forest, stops and sits down to look at Luna with Sander. For two hours, they sit, gazing at the sight of Luna from afar. The group and the troops then begin to move. Sander tells two-thirds of the orc army to head to Relana.

"How do we know where Relana is?" Gildor then tells them he will help lead the way to Relana.

"We will meet you there when we're done with Cavlana," said Sander.

Sander then begins to leave Gildor, Zytrix, and the other chieftain of the orcs of the Riverlands to go to Relana. Sander and the group decide to walk to Cavlana. Sander then talks to the group as they walk.

"When we get to Cavlana, guys, I just want to tell you, I do not have a plan for what to do."

"What do you mean, Sander?"

"I mean, guys, I literally don't know what to do with the plan to capture Cavlana."

The group then comes across a dwarven village in front of them. They see the houses burnt down.

"Dang, I feel a strange sense of déjà vu right now," said Sander.

Sander then goes and looks around to see if anyone is there. Sander sees a doll on the floor.

"There were kids here."

The Legend of Sander Helmglade

Sander then sees four strange men walking closer to the village. The men begin to speak as one. Everyone stops to look at these four men speak.

"Listen, are you Sander Helmglade, firstborn son of the last king of Luna? Are you the Sander who is the older brother of Fergus?"

Sander replies with a yes, staying truthful to his word.

"Then we must kill you."

Sander pulls out the Soul Absorber. The runes on the Soul Absorber glow as it awakens from its sleep. Riker, in Sander's head, begins to speak.

"Listen, Sander, be careful. These guys aren't like humans. They're part of the celestial race. Trust me, Sander, watch yourself. If you want, I can take control of your body and fight them."

Sander says in his head, "No, Riker, I got this."

The Soul Absorber then tells Sander what class they are.

"Sander, these are not angels nor archangels. They are Syboli," said Soul Absorber.

"What are Syboli?" said Sander.

"These guys are strong, and they fight as if they are one being. They each trust each other. Sander, best be careful in this fight."

"Guys, do not engage. These four are mine," Sander says to the group and the orc army.

Sander then ignites the flames as he gets ready for war.

"You shall not pass here. Who are you working for?" The Soul Absorber begins to speak to Sander in his head.

"Well, Sander, if you do not know, they act as what you like to call royal guards to the archangels. So, technically, they are royal guards. But they are extremely dangerous, so best be careful, Sander."

Sander then lets the flames take over as they circle around him like a light of hope. The flames then burn all over his body as if water is being poured onto him. Sander, with the demon soul inside him, is resistant to fire itself. Sander then sees that the flames turn into purple flames.

"Sander," said Riker in Sander's head, "I see you have gotten stronger. Don't you see it? These are purple flames. You're almost reaching black flames. But I will teach you how to get that later."

Sander, with quick speed, dashes at the Syboli, instantly severing one of their heads. The other three do not care and begin to engage Sander in battle. Sander turns around and blocks all three of their attacks as he sees their speed is slower than his. Everything seems to move in slow motion. Sander gets attacked by one of the Syboli as they trap him, but Sander manages to cut a Syboli in half. Sander then turns around and uses his human attacks to fight the Syboli. He attacks with all his might, stabbing one of them in the chest. Sander then loses the Soul Absorber out of his hands. The Syboli kicks Sander to the ground, about to kill him. Just as he is about to be struck down, with the speed of a lightning bolt and the swiftness of a cheetah, Ashlaius stabs the Syboli from behind, flips in front of him, and looks him in the face. Ashlaius then unleashes an attack, screaming it from the top of her lungs.

"Slashes of five hundred daggers!" she yells with all her might as she slashes him five hundred times in the chest, making the Syboli feel intense pain as he falls to his knees and dies on the floor.

"I told you to stay put," Sander says, hiding the fact that he was saved by a woman.

Sander then tells the group and the army of orcs, "Let's continue walking. We've got one more day before we hit Cavlana." Sander grabs the Soul Absorber and straps it to his back.

As he continues to walk, the group talks behind his back. "What's wrong with him?"

Ashlaius tells them, "He's got a lot going on right now."

"What do you mean, Ashlaius?"

"I mean, every time he gets closer to Luna—like Cavlana, Relana, and even Elmus—he gets angrier. Let's just hope he doesn't explode when we get to Cavlana."

"Do not fear, my dear. As I have seen on this journey, Sander has shown he will be a worthy king." Raphael then continues to walk. Ares and Duvessa begin to follow. Jake, staying silent, walks and taps Ashlaius on the shoulder. The group then begins to tap her and leave, following Sander.

As for Kevin, he begins to wait for everyone to leave. "Look, Ashlaius, I know Sander is feeling rage, but when we were kids, he wasn't, well… he was, but it's complicated. His father kept him from having fun. Yes, he made him train with a sword but didn't let him hang out with girls. His father didn't even let him go to the tavern. He made him stay in the castle at all times. So sometimes, Sander doesn't know what you're feeling. You've got to tell him what you're feeling. So stop pouting, and let's go on this last journey to Luna. Let's fight my cousin Fergus. Let's set peace to the land and to the people of Luna. And Ashlaius, if he gets out of hand, trust in the group. We'll look after him."

She then gives Kevin a hug. Ashlaius then goes and follows the group to Cavlana. As Sir Kevin looks back and sees Luna from afar, he whispers, "I will come back to you, my love." Kevin begins to go and follow the group.

Chapter 51

Cavlana

Within a day or two, the group came from afar to see the mountain that stands above the kingdom of Cavlana.

"Ah ha, here we are. You see that mountain over there, Sander? That is the mountain of Cavlana. They call this mountain Cavuna. It's stories after stories. The reason why they call it Cavuna is because of the king who founded this kingdom. Of course, it's not the king who named it Cavuna. His wife was named Cavuna, and he named it after her."

As Raphael begins to continue talking about Cavlana, Sander talks to Ares about what to do against this kingdom.

"Listen, Ares, we're not going into the kingdom like a warzone unless it's our final option. I'm thinking we should do things a little more diplomatically. I say I hail to the gates with maybe Kevin, Raymond, and you. We get into the kingdom of Cavlana and talk it out. If it's a trap, then we've got to open the gates and hail to our troops to get inside. If it's not a trap, then we can actually talk it out with the commander of this kingdom. The point in all this is to free the dwarven race. Later, they will have my support as king of Luna."

Sander then looks at Ares.

"What do you say, Ares? You ready to go on a suicide mission?"

"Look, Sander, I'm all up for a suicide mission, but if we're going to do this, how are we going to get through a battalion of humans if things go wrong?"

"Well, you see, that's what makes it a suicide mission. I don't know yet."

"Are you serious?"

As Sander and Ares are talking, Raymond hears from the other side.

"Ok, so I hear you out, Sander, but I'm just a vampire hunter. What am I going to do in there?"

"You're right, Raymond, maybe we should pick another for this job."

"Yeah, you should. Maybe Ashlaius." Raymond points to Ashlaius.

"Nah, we're good, don't need a woman to save me again."

Ashlaius then gets angry. She quickly turns away and walks to a forest to calm herself down.

"Look, maybe I can go," said Cronovus.

"Wait, my love, don't get hurt," said Holie.

"Trust me, Holie, I will be fine. Who knows, I can turn some to our side."

Cronovus then volunteers to enter Cavlana with Sander, Kevin, and Ares. The rest of the group stays with the army. The four heroes then head off on a journey to the gates of Cavlana. As the group hails to the gates, they see a long line of human archers aiming at Sander.

"I hail to the gates of the Silver Wall of Cavlana," Sander says, requesting entry to the kingdom of Cavlana. "Look, I do not wish to fight. I only want what is best for us, to talk it out with you guys. If I bring an army here, there will be lots of death and bloodshed. I'm only doing what is best for my people and what is best for yours."

The commander then walks to the top of the wall to see Sander as he looks down. The commander then begins to speak of what is going on.

"Sander Helmglade, we know what you are. We know the demon is inside of you. We know you're working with him. My question is, how do we know you're not lying to kill us all?"

"Because, commander, if I wanted to kill you right now, I would have done it by now. I only request entry to tell you the truth of what's going on in my life. May we please come in and talk privately?"

The commander then looks down at Sander with a gaze.

"Fine, if you wish to come in, you must leave your men here."

"I'm sorry, commander, but I will not do that. These men are trying to guard me," Sander says.

"Sander, I've got a bad feeling about this," Cronovus says as he looks at the commander.

"I'm sorry, Sander, but I will not let you in if you have your men. I request you leave your men here, as I do not trust you to come into the kingdom of Cavlana."

Sander requests that at least one man should come with him inside. The commander then stops to talk to his officers.

"Fine, very well then, Sander, pick a person who will come with you inside the Cavlana gates. The rest will have to turn back and wait for you."

Sander then starts to consult with his comrades on who to pick.

"Sander, I know this is bad timing, but I feel like this is a bad idea. You can only bring one of us. I suggest Ares," said Kevin.

Cronovus and Ares look at each other.

"No, Sander, me and Cronovus are not going. We both suggest Kevin. He's more noble, and well, he's a human. Along with that, he's your cousin, and he's the heir to his house. No one is more fitting than Sir Kevin Gladestone."

Sander then looks at Kevin. "Fine, but it's all on you, Kevin."

Kevin then looks at Ares and Cronovus. "Fine, I will go. But the moment something goes wrong, I will try my best to open the gates."

Ares and Cronovus nod at Kevin and start to walk back to the rest of the group.

"Wait, Cronovus," said Sander. "I suggest you tell the rest of the group the plan."

"Don't worry, Sander, I was thinking the exact thing you were thinking."

Cronovus and Ares leave to go back to the group. Kevin and Sander wait for the gate and the commander to speak. The commander looks at Sander and sees Sir Kevin Gladestone.

"Let them in," said the commander.

The commander of the battalion then heads out of the wall to the main courtyard in the mountain. Sander and Kevin then see the gates open.

"I think this is our time to go in," said Sander.

Kevin then tells Sander, "Wait, Sander, let me take the lead. I'm more used to this custom stuff in Luna."

Sander then tells Kevin to lead the way. As Kevin and Sander walk in, they see a dwarven cavern in the mountain.

"Hey, Kevin, you ever been to Relana?"

"No, Sander, never been there, but I heard of it in the library. They don't have a mountain like Cavlana and Sulana. They have a whole kingdom."

"Interesting. I guess we will find out when we get there."

Kevin and Sander continue to make their way to the courtyard. As they are being led by four squads of the battalion, they eventually make their way to the courtyard to see the commander.

"Follow me, Sander Helmglade and Kevin Gladestone."

Sander and Kevin look at each other and continue to walk with each other to the throne room. When they get to the throne room, they see that the commander turns around. The commander then looks at the four guards and tells them to stand at ease. He then begins to look at his guards and tells them to guard the entry.

"Alright, follow me, Sander Helmglade and Kevin Gladestone."

All three of them enter the throne room to see a table in the middle of the room.

"Please, you may sit."

"I'd rather stand," said Kevin and Sander, both smiling at each other.

"Alright, listen, I know you have a demon in you, and I know Kevin has the sword of light from the Order of Light."

"What is the Order of Light?" asked Kevin.

"Well, Kevin," said the commander, "it all started one thousand years ago. It happened after the demon and celestial war. Many of the knights of Luna had swords of light. There were once many of us. We decided to make an order to stop the evil demons from entering the world. So, we guarded the gate to the demon realm. Every demon that came through that gate had powers. Many of us died, but we managed to seal the gate shut. Nowadays, there are only five of us, and we're looking to rebuild the Order of Light."

"Wait," Kevin asks, "you said 'we.' Are you..."

"Yes, Kevin, I'm one of the people of the Order of Light, passed down from generation to generation."

The commander then pulls out his sword to reveal the marks of light on it. Kevin then draws out his sword to see the same markings of the Order of Light. Kevin looks at the commander as he realizes his purpose.

"Listen, Kevin, you were never trained fully on what the sword can do. It can do more than just summon light. It can bring people to life. It can heal people. We, the Order of Light, can teach you."

Kevin was about to accept the deal until he remembered that he's on Sander's side.

"I'm sorry, commander, I must not accept the deal."

"Look, you did not hear me out. I'm not on Fergus's side. I have been waiting for you guys to show up, or I was waiting for Sander to take the throne. I know who the rightful heir to the throne is. I'm loyal to the true heir, not the fake one. Fergus, with his power, showed that he was too corrupted. He went so far as to conquer the three dwarven kingdoms. He did it without diplomacy. He's more of a monster than a demon in Sander. Look, Sander, what Fergus said was simple. He said you made a deal with a demon and that he stopped you from trying to kill the entire kingdom. He said you went so far as to kill your own father. He said you wanted to have more power than your father did. He said you wanted to conquer the world. So, I led a battalion. But when I saw what Fergus was doing, everything he said looked like he did it himself. It looked like he wanted the power. He wanted to conquer the world. So, I saw a reason to take a battalion under my control. I hand-picked them myself. They all believe in the cause," said the commander.

"Wait, they believe in the Order?" asked Kevin.

"No, they don't. They believe in the rightful heir of Luna. That's what they all believe in. So, Sander, are you going to take the throne from Fergus or not?"

Sander stands up straight.

"Listen, Sander, your people are counting on you. They may think you're a monster, but Fergus is more of a monster than you are. You can do this."

Sander looks at Kevin.

"Kevin, do you want to go to the battalion's side for the time being?"

Kevin smiles at Sander.

"Thank you, cousin, but it all stands with the commander."

The commander then tells Kevin he may join.

"Welcome to the Hope's Battalion."

"Alright then, let's head out. We, the Hope's Battalion, will not leave unless Relana is taken by the dwarves. I'm going to let the king of the dwarves and the people free. Sander, you may leave."

Kevin stays with the Hope's Battalion. As Sander walks out of the throne room, in the main hall, he sees everyone in the Hope's Battalion start to kneel to the one true king of Luna.

"Hail to the king!" said the Hope's Battalion soldiers.

The soldiers then got up and began to open the gates for the army of orcs. Sander walks out of the kingdom of Cavlana. Sander walks to the orc army and the group.

"Where's Kevin?" said Cronovus.

Sander then tells the group that the mission is a success. Sander then begins to tell the group that they are on our side. They're called the Hope's Battalion. Kevin starts his training with the people of the Order of Light to help him with the sword's power. Sander then tells the group, "We must go to Relana. I'm guessing they will meet us in Elmus."

"Alright," said the group, "we guess we must take your word for it, Sander."

The group then looks towards the direction of Relana. But before Sander looks, he turns back to see the king of Cavlana with a smile. Sander then starts to walk to Relana. The group then begins to follow, along with the army of orcs following Sander. The group starts to head towards the red moonstone forest.

Chapter 52

The Red Moonstone Forest

The group came to a complete stop to look ahead at what's in front of them.

"Um, Sander, what did you take us to?"

"I do not know. Relana, I have never been there. So I'm guessing I'm heading in the right direction. Does anyone know where to go?"

Raymond points through the forest. "Once we head past this forest, we will enter Relana."

"So, what are we waiting for?"

"Wait," said Raymond. "What do you think you're doing, Sander? You're about to enter a forest we don't even know about. How about we get some answers on what we're heading into?"

"Oh, dang, look, berries," said Jake. Jake then takes off his helmet and eats some berries. "Guys, let's eat. See, Raymond, this forest has given us good news."

The group then eats first as the army waits for their orders to eat. As the group is eating, Ares tells the group he feels woozy. The group then begins to feel peace in their hearts as they feel so relaxed that they lose focus on the journey. Sander continues to eat the berries until he is done with his food.

"Sander, is that a cloud or a tree?" said Jake.

The Legend of Sander Helmglade

"Alright, Jake, stop messing with me. We both know that's a tree. We don't have time to goof off, guys."

Duvessa begins to move her head from side to side as she looks at Ares. Sander turns to look at the group losing focus and acting like children.

"What's going on? Is this magic?" said Sander.

"Sander, I think it's the berries. Look, one thousand years ago, a dwarven empire used some sort of berries against the humans. These berries make people, well, like children. They lose focus on their desires and act like children," said Riker in his head.

Sander then thinks for a second. "Wait, why don't I just knock them out?"

"Sander, good luck knocking out Ares. Ares is not simple-minded."

Ares looks at the group and sees dark sirens in his eyes. "Dark sirens!" yelled Ares.

"Orcs, hold him back!" These berries are making you think you're a child."

The orcs then decide to hold the group down as they figure out a way to cure them. Ashlaius walks up to Sander.

"So, you did something wrong. I'm not as shocked as I should be. You always tend to get someone angry or mess up. Do you need help, Sander, or are you going to get mad that a girl is helping you?"

Ashlaius then walks away and lets Sander handle it on his own. She sits down as she watches the orcs hold down Ares and the group.

"Wow, I never knew how many orcs loved me," said Duvessa.

"I see a beautiful woman in the distance," said Raphael.

Sander looks at his group and wonders why he has to figure this out. He then begins to look at the tree.

"Riker, I need your help. If these berries have a cure, how long is the cure? Tell me everything you know about these berries."

"Well, for starters, Sander, these berries have no cure that I know of. Maybe you should wait it out."

Sander then asks how long he should wait.

Riker tells him, "A couple of hours."

Sander waits for a couple of hours to see some of the group face-palming on the floor, sleeping. But Sander sees Ares still fighting, and he sees Raymond going berserk along with Raphael.

"What's going on with them, Riker? You said wait a couple of hours."

"Well, you see, Sander, these guys are fighting the berries' magic and, well, thinking that everyone is their enemy."

Raymond then stops struggling and begins to fall asleep along with Raphael. But Ares breaks out of the grip of the orcs and runs at Sander.

"I will kill you, you dark sirens!"

Sander dodges the attack from Ares and sees a whole tree fall down from his swing.

"Uh oh," said Sander.

Sander quickly rushes deeper into the Red Moonstone Forest. He pulls out the Soul Absorber to fight back. Ares then performs an attack skill he learned as a young siren. Sander blocks two-thirds of the attack before getting hit. Ares then looks at a rock.

Ares stops fighting to worship the rock. "I worship you, Red Moonstone goddess."

Sander then realizes why they call it Red Moonstone Forest—red berries equal Red Moonstone. Ares then begins to fall asleep as the berries wear off. The group wakes up feeling like trash.

"Why do I smell like berries?" asked the group.

Ares wakes up with low stamina. "What's going on, Sander? Why do I feel like sea trash?"

"I'll explain it on the way out of the forest." Sander then helps Ares to the rest of the group. The group feels a headache, along with smelling like berries.

"It feels like I fell asleep on a hard rock. Guys, do you remember anything?" said Sander. "Because when you ate those berries, you kind of went berserk. Well, by some, I mean three of you. Raphael and Raymond, you didn't put up much of a fight, but Ares, you kind of thought we were all dark sirens. I'm guessing these berries are very strong against our race. I didn't feel a thing when I ate it, so I'm going to say that for celestials and demons, it doesn't work. So you guys ate it and went wild, but I didn't, thanks to Riker's side in my body."

"Look, we can talk all day, or we can get out of here. We need to get out of this forest and meet Gildor. Sir Kevin will meet us at Elmus. So, let's go."

Sander and the group begin to gather their things as they feel sick from the berries. The orc army starts to question Sander's leadership. Sander then begins to make his way through the forest. Eventually, Sander sees the way out of the forest.

"Guys, I see the way out of the forest. Please do not eat the berries."

The group and the army of orcs then make their way out of the forest. They continue to walk down the path to Relana. When they get to Relana, they see Gildor and the two orc armies. Sander then talks to Gildor about Relana.

Chapter 53

Ashlaius Loses Control

The group just got done with the talk on Relana. As Ashlaius stays angry at Sander for disrespecting her, the group then thinks of a big plan to get into Relana.

"Look, maybe we should do the same thing that we did in Cavlana," said Ares.

"It won't work," said Sander. "The reason why I made that plan was because Colinborn told me to go diplomatic. But now I do not know what to do. We could go in, charging in and freeing the slaves and capturing the place. But I will have to go and attack my people."

"Well, whatever it is, Sander, we're all in with you," said Gildor. Everyone agreed, except Ashlaius.

"You think I should go talk to her?" said Sander.

Gildor then responds to him. "No, give her some time. I hope she will understand."

Sander then looks back to Relana. "Fine, I will give her time. Now, let's focus on that iron wall in front of us. Gildor, do you have any suggestions?"

Gildor looks at Sander. "I do, but it's a death wish."

"Well, we all got to hear it."

Gildor then starts to talk about his plan. "Well, this is what we will do. Two orc armies continue to attack the gate, while the other orc army goes to the back door. Well, it's not just a back door; it's a cave. But you got to watch out, the cave is dark."

"That's a good idea, Gildor. Maybe we can try it."

"Um, sorry to interrupt, but Sander, look behind you."

Sander begins to look behind him. Sander sees Ashlaius, mad and angry towards him.

"Ok, that's enough. I'm not going to help you anymore. Why do you have to just focus on the mission? Don't you see my feelings are hurt, and you don't do anything? Sander, why do you have to be so rude? That's not the guy I fell in love with."

As she gets angry, lightning starts to strike her, giving her the power of lightning. She then begins to attack Sander. As she hits him, he is thrown backward into the iron wall, leaving a dent in it.

"Hot and powerful. Sometimes I question why I go for certain girls."

She then jumps and decides to smash Sander. Sander begins to dodge her attack. When he dodges her attack, she makes a bigger dent in the iron wall. Sander hears the humans inside start to fear Ashlaius.

"Damn, is she trying to kill me?"

Sander then gets hit in the face so hard he flies up into the air. Sander tries to fly, but he can't when his wings are damaged.

"Um, Sander," said Riker in his head, "I forgot to leave this one note. If a celestial, reaper, or demon gets angry, we get even stronger. So technically, Ashlaius is at her full strength. Sander, I'm going to leave you to resolve this, but she can also hear this conversation right now too."

The night starts to fall, and Ashlaius's light turns blue. Sander then says, "Enough with this." Sander gets angry and lights up his purple flames. Sander dodges with his speed and continues to dodge every attack she gives him.

"Apologize!" she yells as she strikes at him, but he dodges again. As Ashlaius hits him up in the air once more, Sander says, "Enough of this." He finally gets so angry he hits her back and punches her in the face, sending her down to the ground.

"Oh no," said Sander. "Ashlaius!"

The group then looks at Sander with wide eyes. Sander lands and apologizes to her.

"Ashlaius, I'm sorry, I didn't mean it."

Ashlaius then cries as she lies on the ground.

"All I wanted from you is to apologize," she says, crying in sorrow.

"Look, Ashlaius, us humans are not used to your customs. You tried to kill me when you attacked me, so I punched you back. But look, I'm sorry that I got angry when you saved me. I'm not used to women saving me. I'm also sorry for attacking you with that punch."

She then sniffs as she tries to stop crying.

"It's ok, Sander. The punch didn't hurt. That was a weak punch anyway."

Sander thinks in his head, "Why is she crying?"

"Listen, you idiot," said Riker. "She likes you. She's crying because she loves you, and she doesn't want to leave you."

"Thanks, Riker, for the advice. I'm usually not good at these things," said Sander in his head.

"Clearly," said Riker.

"Hey, Ashlaius, want to help me get into the iron wall? Together, as partners, as friends, as my love."

Sander then turned his eyes blue, showing her his real eyes.

"Sander, your eyes... they're turning blue."

"Wait, really, Ashlaius? Usually, this takes a while for that to happen."

"Riker's eyes are red, and mine are blue. That's a funny thing, huh? But I don't know why it's blue."

"Sander," said Riker, "your eyes are turning blue because you're showing your true self. You finally found love. Plus, I also kind of lowered your power. Now, in the fight against Galatin, we won't have your eyes but mine, due to the fact my power is what you need to defeat Fergus."

"Anyways, Sander, I agree to help you take down the iron wall."

"Good, because I just thought of a good idea."

"What's the idea?" said Ashlaius.

"Well, Ashlaius, when you attacked me, I dodged the attack multiple times. But when you attacked the iron wall when you were angry, you left that giant dent. If we can break it, we can get in," said Sander.

Sander then lights up his purple flames as Ashlaius lights up her lightning around her.

"You ready, my love?" said Ashlaius.

Sander smiles back and says, "Yes."

They both begin to attack the iron wall as the archers start to shoot at them. Both Ashlaius and Sander begin to attack the iron wall with all their might, making many dents in the wall. Sander starts to sense more fear from the people inside. The gate then opens, and Sander and Ashlaius stop attacking the iron wall. A whole battalion, carrying a lightning rod with a string on it, marches out with a banner.

The battalion stops. "Who are you to attack the iron wall of Relana?"

"The name is Sander Helmglade, rightful heir to the king of Luna. I am Fergus's brother, and I wish to reclaim my throne."

"That's impossible. We were told Sander Helmglade is dead, and Fergus Helmglade said he killed the demon in you."

"Well, I guess he lied because I'm right here, and I'm right here with an army."

"If you are truly Sander Helmglade, what did the commander of Luna's guards train you with when you were a kid?" said a mysterious man in the battalion.

Sander then begins to explain to him what he was trained with. "The man trained me in a lot of things. He taught me how to use a sword. He taught me that not all battles are fought with a sword. He taught me how to make sure that a king always fights in battle with his men. That's what he taught me. He taught me how to be a fighter and a king at the same time."

The mysterious man came out of the battalion. "No way, is it really you?"

Sander then tells his orcs and his group to stand down.

"You know I have orders now to kill you."

"You can try, but Fergus was right, Commander Stinger. I do have a demon inside me, but this demon does not want the world destroyed."

"Well then, I'm glad to see the rightful heir of Luna here. Men, we're walking back to Luna."

The men in his battalion question why the commander is going to Luna.

"But sir, we're supposed to hold here until further notice."

"I do know that, young soldier, but we have to leave before Sander kills us all. My duty is to make sure you guys come back in one piece, so let's go. If you don't know how strong they are, look at the wall."

The soldiers look at the wall as they begin to fear Sander and Ashlaius.

"Alright, now it's our time to leave. Sander, look at my sword."

Commander Stinger pulls out his sword a bit to reveal the same sword as Sir Kevin. Commander Stinger then continues to march his troops out of Relana and to the kingdom of Luna. Sander, the group, and the army of orcs decide to enter Relana and free the dwarven captives. As they free the king, the king grants them access to go to Elmus. The king finds a letter to give them.

"Look, Sander, if that's your name," said the king, "hopefully you get food, shelter, and warmth in Elmus from the elves to help you. They know more about the humans than we do. And remember, Sander, if Cavlana and Sulana are safe, the dwarves have your back."

Sander then smiles at the king as he gets the passage towards Elmus. Sander then walks out of the king's chambers to tell his group and orcs that they must go to Elmus. The orcs then question what Elmus is.

"Well, you see, guys, it's the kingdom of elves."

"Um, Sander," said Zytrix, "elves and orcs do not get along. We both are different species, and we used to live in the same area."

"Well, what happened, Zytrix?"

"Well, we got kicked out for a fake war that was about to start. So, the elves kicked us out, and we moved to Orcuhan."

"I see. Well, hopefully, they let us into Elmus with this letter from the dwarves."

"Um, Sander, also note, didn't you escape the elves along with Jake?"

"I'm also banished there as well," said Gildor.

"Right, totally forgot about that. Well, let's just go there and find out what they will do."

Sander then tells the orcs to march out of Relana and head to Elmus. As the group sets off to Elmus, they both begin to question themselves if Elmus is a good place for the orcs to go. As they set off, they head back to the Green Forest and to room.

Chapter 55

The Mysterious Man

"Well, well, well. Sander Helmglade is back to sleep with my daughter again."

"King Alexander, I did not mean to do that and leave her. The demon inside me — "

"I do not want to hear it," said the king. "You left my daughter heartbroken. The second I knew you were in Dragonsteeth and escaped, I thought you would go back to Sofia."

"I was, my king, but the demon inside me erased that memory. If I wanted to go back, I would. But I can't, due to the demon erasing my memories."

King Alexander sits on his throne to listen. "Listen, I'm here now. I want to see if she's okay."

King Alexander starts to speak. "Sander, when you left, things began to go sideways. A war started brewing in the kingdom of Elmus. House Lakewood is at war with us Crimsonblades. They seek the throne of Elmus. So, I was going to offer Selena for marriage, but Sofia stepped up."

As Sander is talking about Sofia, Sofia herself walks into the castle and begins to talk to her father.

"Father, our troops are trapped. We have no way out, and if we charge, we lose. What do we do? Should we pull back our troops?"

King Alexander says, "No, I'm sorry, but we do not pull back our troops. If we do, their archers will deplete our forces. We shall hold the ground."

"Listen, King Alexander, you may not know this, but I flew here. I have three armies of orcs at the border of Elmus and an archangel at my disposal. I will gladly help you guys out against the Lakewoods if you let my troops come in."

King Alexander then thinks for a second. "Alright, Sander, I will let you prove yourself. But you have to prove yourself good."

Sofia turns her head to look at Sander. "Sander, is that you? Where have you been?"

"I have been on a long journey."

"I thought you were dead."

"Who told you that?"

She looks at her father. "You told me he died at Fort Dragonsteeth."

"Well, I didn't. I escaped from Fort Dragonsteeth. I was going to go back for you, but someone inside me erased my emotions and my memory of you. So, I didn't remember until now. I'm so sorry, Sofia."

Sofia then gets angry at her father. "Listen, I trusted you, and you're going to say he was dead? He's clearly very much alive!"

Sofia then decides to walk out of the castle.

"I'm guessing you lied to her because you were protecting her, right?" said Sander.

Sander then looks at King Alexander. "By the way, on my journey, you know I met her, right?"

"Who did you meet, Sander?"

"I met the one and only great dragon Myra. I trained and got the Soul Absorber. King Alexander, I have changed since I last saw Sofia. Things have changed between me and her, and I met someone else. So I understand why you were protecting your daughter. But I must go and get my men to put them on the battlefield. Where do you want my troops to be?"

The king then stands up to look at Sander. "I want you to put them in the middle of the battlefield at Lakewood Village."

"Wait, but what about the people?" said Sander.

"The people are just casualties," said the king. The king then walked to Sander. "Your orc army may come in, but I will run how your troops will be placed." The king then left the room and into the king's chambers.

Sander then walks out of the castle and into the tavern. Sander sees the barkeep.

"Hey barkeep, may I have a drink?"

Sander then begins to wait for the troops to come into town as he drinks his drink. Two hours pass, and the orc army, along with the group, enters the town. While the king is looking over the balcony, he spots Sander's army of orcs coming to the castle.

"By the god's name. He wasn't joking about his army of orcs, grabbing at least three clans of orcs. Sander is going to be a good king."

"Father, we are surrounded by at least five thousand troops."

"Oh my gods. Is that Sander's army, father?"

"Yes, indeed, it is, my dear Sofia. This army may turn the tide against the five thousand troops that are surrounding us."

"Well, we'd best not go meet them, Sofia."

"Wait, why father?"

"Because, Sofia, if you know the lore of elves and orcs, you would not want to intervene."

As the king and Sofia attend to their business, Sander is walking out of the tavern to talk to his army and group.

"Finally, I got you out," said Sander. "Now, are you guys ready?"

"What's going on?" said Ares.

"Well, I kinda invited you guys in, but you have to help the king with a battle."

"So, you're saying we're going to war for a little bit?"

The orcs start to get excited and pass the word to the other orcs.

"Hey orcs, set up a camp on the outer wall. We leave when we're ready."

"Yes, my warlord," said Zytrix. Zytrix grabs his men and walks over to the outer wall and sets up camp with his orcs as Sander is talking to the group.

"Look, I don't expect you to join me in this war, but if you do, I thank you."

The group looks at each other.

"I don't know about you, Sander, but I've stuck with you since I escaped prison, and now I'm back here. I'm going to fight in this battle," said Jake.

"Sander, I knew you since we were kids. I am going to fight with you," said Gildor.

Ares and Scorpius look at each other. "Listen, Sander, me and Scorpius have been fighting wars since we were kids, and we love war. So, we will fight with you."

"Aye lad, I will fight with you," said Raphael.

The group then comes to a decision that they will all fight for Sander. Sander then tells the group to go get ready as Sofia comes out of the castle. The group leaves as Gildor tells Sofia he needs access to the castle.

"Who are you going to see?" said Sander.

Gildor looks at Sander. "That's none of your business," said Gildor. Gildor then continues on his business.

As Gildor is continuing on his business, Sander is talking to Sofia.

"Sofia, I think your sister did a number on Gildor."

"Look, Sander, I know you probably moved on by now, but I didn't know a demon erased your memories. But if we were to get back together, I just want to say I am going to get married in a week. If this battle fails, I will probably be enslaved. But I will say this, if we win, I thank you for getting a giant orc army to help us win this fight."

"Don't you worry, Sofia, I will save your kingdom from harm's way. So, let's talk. Who's the lucky guy?"

"His name is Sir Alex Bloomingshine. He's a noble man from a house. His father is a legendary swordsman, and his mother is a legendary polearm user. So, you can guess where he grew up."

"I'm guessing he's a very skillful person."

Sander then asks Sofia, "So where is his army?"

"The thing is, Sander, all the other houses were trying to get me for my body, but not for noble reasons. They just wanted me, you know."

"Oh, I see. So, this is a noble house?"

"Yes," said Sofia. "Alex Bloomingshine is a noble man. He helps me with military advice and a lot of things I need to do around the castle. But I don't see his army anywhere."

"Sander, it's because we need to get married first for his army to come here."

"Oh, I see, Sofia. Your custom is very different from humans. I hope you know I really did miss you when I thought you were dead."

"Listen, Sofia, I'm seeing someone else. She's a bit much to handle, but I love her. Well, I think I do," said Sander.

Sofia then begins to speak. "Well, whoever she is, she is lucky to have you. A strong noble man that wants to save the people of Luna and Calhera."

Sander then questions, "What's Calhera?"

"Oh, right, when you were gone, I was researching in the library. The gods call this world Calhera."

"I see," Sander questions in his head. Sander then tells Sofia he must meet up with his men to discuss the battle areas.

"So, Sofia, where should I go exactly?"

She gives him a map to Lakewood Village. Sofia then says goodbye to Sander and heads back into the castle.

Sander begins to go to the camp where they are setting up camp on the outer wall. Sander enters the camp. Sander goes to his tent where he knows it's set up. Sander calls upon the officers of the orcs and the commanders. When the officers and commanders come into the tent to talk to Sander, Sander begins to speak to them.

"Alright guys, we're going to war. This battle is a one-time thing. We're going to help the Crimsonblade household attack the Lakewood household. This battle has our odds. We have more numbers than them. If we could push them back or slaughter the enemy, then the Crimsonblade household can push their castle back. Now, Sofia just gave me a map."

Sander rolls the map on the table. "Alright, so this is the area of the battlefield. We should regroup with the elven army here. Now, who's ready for war?"

The commanders and officers agreed to go to battle with Sander.

"Alright, good. Now that everyone has agreed to go to battle, let's start the strategy."

Sander then starts giving the men where their positions should be. Sander finishes the positions he's giving as the commanders and officers start to leave the tent. Ashlaius then enters the tent. Sander starts to talk to her.

"Sander, I know you and Sofia had something. I heard it from Riker in your head."

"No, Ashlaius, that's not true. Maybe I feel a little emotion for Sofia, but I truly love you. I would give anything to be with you. But I need to finish my journey to get my revenge on Fergus. In order for me to be prepared for Luna, I must go and get answers from the elves of Elmus. So, in order to get answers, I must do this for the elves."

Sander then grabs a dagger and throws it on the table, stabbing the map. "I'm going to kill every Lakewood household soldier there. I will kill them all if I have to. I need to bring my brother Fergus to an end. This is the first step to do it."

Sander then heads out to do his thing as a leader. He begins getting the plans ready and then tells the others he is going to the castle to tell the king what he is going to do. Sander heads towards the castle. He enters the throne room to see King Alexander on the throne, looking at him.

"Alright, King Alexander, I got the plans for what my troops are going to do."

"Not so fast, Sander," said King Alexander. "You do not command your troops where to go. I will tell your troops to charge into battle as my troops require cover."

"No, I will not let my troops die for your cause. This battle is a one-time thing to get answers."

The king then gets angry. "I will not have you stand here and tell me what your men will be doing. You guys are in my land, and you are under my orders."

Sander gets angry. "Shut it! I will not have any of my people die. They are my people, and they're going to stay my people. I will not send them into the battlefield, making them cannon fodder."

"Sander, you do not have a choice."

Guards start to surround Sander.

"Sander, I like how you think you're so powerful, but truth be told, you are not here. We have warden magic everywhere, and you may die."

Sander then begins to get angry. The wards on the castle start to peel off like butter. Fire starts to swirl around Sander as the guards start to fear him. The king gets mad as the wards fall.

"Fine, Sander. I will grant you access to the knowledge of the elves to find out what your brother is going to do."

Sander then stops the flames from glowing, and as he does, a strange man walks through the room.

"Alex, stand down," said the king.

"Wait, are you Alex Bloomingshine?"

"Yes, that's my name," said Alex.

"Well, I'm Sander Helmglade," said Sander.

"What's going on here, my king?"

"Nothing," said the king.

The king then looks at Sander. Sander looks at the king and walks out of the castle. He walks to his troops to give them the directions to go to Lakewood village.

Chapter 56

The Battle of Lakewood Village

When Sander arrives at his camp, he walks inside his tent and decides to go to the map. He gets so angry that he destroys the tent table. "I will kill every Lakewood soldier and get my answers for Fergus." Sander's eyes begin to turn red as he gets angrier. Meanwhile, Gildor and Selena are talking in the princess's chambers.

"Selena, I know I left you, but I'm here now. I'm only here for a little, though. But while I'm here, we can spend some time together, get to know one another."

Selena feels sad as she talks to Gildor. "Look, Gildor, I know we had fun with each other, and I really like you, but—"

"But what, Selena?"

"But I can't because of the image of the kingdom. I'm getting married to Fergus Helmglade of Luna. It's where two species will become one."

"Look, I have to go to the battle, but I will be here for you when I come back."

Gildor then leaves the room and walks to the camp with Sander. Gildor walks into the tent with Sander to see the table destroyed.

"Sander, what's going on?" said Gildor.

Sander looks at Gildor. "The king wishes to take my troops from me so he can use them against the Lakewood house. I earned those troops, not him, so to think he can take them makes me angry."

"Sander, you're not going to lose these troops. They're loyal to you and you alone. This is your fight, not theirs. Look, I don't know about leading troops, but I know what makes a good leader. Relax and take this anger out on the battlefield."

Sander calms down and thanks Gildor for the pep talk. Gildor then leaves the tent, and Sander waits until nightfall. Three hours pass, and it becomes nightfall. The troops start packing up and heading toward Lakewood Village. Jake starts to talk to Sander.

"Guys, I forgot to tell you, but Lakewood Village isn't really a village."

"What do you mean, Jake?" said Raymond.

"Well, the village is big, like city-big. The thing that's close to Lakewood Village is Lakewood Castle."

"He's right, Sander," said Gildor.

"So, you mean to tell me that we're going to be running around in the city?"

"Yep, that pretty much sets the score," said Jake.

The group and the army of orcs continue to walk through the forest and the grasslands of Lakewood.

"Sander, when we get there, what formation are we doing?" said Gildor.

"Oh, we're doing a line formation," said Sander.

Sander continues to make his way through the grasslands and into the outer side of the village.

"We're here," said Sander. As Sander sees the army of elves camped, waiting for the Lakewood house, in the afternoon the sun rises. Sander walks to the army of elves.

"Hello, commander," said Sander, "I'm here to reinforce you." Sander walks to the commander's tent.

"What do you think you're doing here, human?"

"Well, I'm here to supply my orc army for the battle."

"But what's in it for you?"

"Nothing you need to be worried about, commander." Sander walks out of the tent with no other words and heads to his orc army.

"Alright, guys, this is what we're going to do. We're going to wait until the enemy troops get here and charge in. Zytrix, you lead one army to go around and flank them on the right. Everyone got it?"

Everyone understands as the other orcs spread the word to the rest of the army. The group and the army of orcs wait as they see the Lakewood army get ready for war.

"Alright, there are no rules in war. All orcs charge!"

The stampede of orcs that decide to run down the hill into the area where the Lakewood house is horrifying. The orcs grab one elf and rip him apart as they continue to kill every Lakewood soldier there. Sander, with his flames, lights up like a burning bush and runs at the Lakewood soldiers. Slice and dice, Sander does to the soldiers, consuming the souls of the Lakewood soldiers into the Soul Absorber.

"Sander, each kill you do, the Soul Absorber absorbs their souls. Keep going, and you will be as strong as me."

Sander continues to listen to Riker as he grows darker and darker from the kills. Sander then sees a swordsman who's killing the orcs.

"Crap," said Sander. Sander knows that charging was not a good idea. Sander holds off the troops as he waits for Zytrix and his army to come from behind.

"Where are the elven troops?" said Gildor. Sander kills an elf and turns around to see the elves standing, doing nothing.

"They're making us sacrifice our lives for their cause. To think King Alexander was a good man." Sander continues to kill some elves along the way. Sander holds them off. Right when Sander is about to say retreat, he sees Zytrix with his army of orcs running towards the enemy with full velocity. The orcs clash with the elves, creating a penetration in the elven army.

"Push," said Sander. "Push," he said as he tells the orcs to push the army back. "Corner them. Do not let them pass. Show no mercy." The orcs cheer as Sander goes to the swordsman with his weapon. Sander then kills the swordsman with all his might, consuming his soul into the Soul Absorber.

Within five hours of battle, the fight is over. The orcs have slain all the elves on the battlefield, losing a quarter of their army. Sander goes to the elven army to talk to them.

"Why did you not intervene?"

"Because, human, you had it all under control."

"That's a lie. Allies help each other."

"Well, human, from this note from the king, he does not like you. So he recommended you die first, and we do the clean-up."

"So you'd rather let your king control your life?"

Sander then gets angry. "Well, it doesn't matter anyway because I'm done working for the king. It's time he gives me answers."

Sander walks back to Zytrix and the commanders. "Alright, send the orcs to the outer wall. I need to fly to the king to get my answers," said Sander.

"Yes, my warlord," said Zytrix.

Sander pulls out his wings and flies to the castle. When Sander enters the castle, he sees the king.

"Alright, King Alexander, I did what you asked me to do. I want to go and get my answers from King Fergus of Luna."

"Well, Sander, I will give you some information on the king of Luna. Fergus Helmglade is to marry my daughter, Princess Selena Crimsonblade. When we marry, he will help me get rid of the troops of the Lakewood house. I will remain king, and Fergus will be the future king of Luna and Elmus."

"But wait, only an elf can sit on the throne of elves."

"Not if the son of Selena is a half-breed. You see, Sander, Fergus and I have an agreement. But if you can take over the castle, that would be great too. These are dark times, and I need to do what's best for my kingdom. But if you want the rest of the information on the king of Luna, then you have to defeat my future son-in-law by combat without your demonic power."

"So, you want me to defeat Fergus?"

"No," said the king. "I want you to defeat Alex Bloomingshine."

Sander looks at Alex outside the castle as he sees through the window a master-skilled swordsman. Sander agrees to this term and tells the king to put his word on it. The king puts his word on it. Sander then leaves and heads out of the castle. Sander flies to the forest to go train and not use his demonic powers.

Chapter 57

The Training of the Ancestors

Sander lands in a forest to train for his trial with Alex Bloomingshine.

"Hey, Riker," said Sander in his head. "What do I do if I can't get rid of these powers?"

Riker in Sander's head begins to respond. "You can get rid of the powers by dormanting them. If you want to dormant them, I can do it for you, and you can start training on those trees on how to use a sword better. Although healing will still be able to work, just not fire itself. So, Sander, are you ready for this challenge?"

Sander agrees to the challenge. "As long as I get answers on what's going on, I've made it this far, and I'm not going back."

Sander feels his powers go dormant, like something is being taken from him. He then begins to feel dormant.

"Alright, Sander, now you're ready to attack."

Sander pulls out the Soul Absorber and wields it to attack the tree. Sander hits and hits, practicing all his stances against the trees. It was at the break when the tree was finally about to collapse. Sander fights another tree, slashes and slashes, but sees no improvements.

"Why is this not working?" Sander goes to another tree and harms more trees with his sword attacking. He slashes and sees improvements in wielding his sword.

"Yes, I got it!" Sander then trips in his stance and falls on his butt.

"Damn it," he said as he gets angry, but no flames appear. "Why don't I learn how to use a better stance?"

"Sander," said Riker in Sander's head, "you're trying too much. Make sure you take some time in peace."

"But Riker, I want to beat him as fast as I can so I can defeat Fergus and Galatin."

"Sander, sometimes you need to feel that you need to go slower than things. I know it's been a year since the happening of the Dark Pit, but now you need to realize that you and Fergus aren't far apart. Both of you have been caught up between me and Galatin. Galatin made Fergus believe in his power. Galatin made Fergus want the world. It's all on Galatin, not Fergus. So, Sander, pick up that sword, get your head together, and take down those trees."

Sander then picks up his sword, looks straight at the tree, and starts to slash the tree once. Swoosh, the sword goes. In a matter of seconds of concentration, he sees a larger cut than the others.

"Thank you, Riker," said Sander.

"You're welcome, Sander. Now, enough soft talk. Get to training."

Sander continues to train himself with the sword for three more hours.

"I'm done. Screw this. If I'm supposed to go against a master weapon user, how am I going to cut down these trees with my blade? This is an impossible fight." Sander gets angry. "Why did I accept this fight against this man? The king is a tricky bastard. Maybe he should know what power really feels like. Riker, give me power," said Sander.

Riker in Sander's head says one word. "No, Sander. I will not give you power just for you to abuse it. Relax yourself. Think of the tree falling, and think of you striking it. It's a hard concept to learn, but you will get it."

"No, I won't. There is no hope."

"Sander, wait. I sense a presence."

"Why, hello there, fellas," said a strange man in a cloak without a hood.

"Who are you, and why are you here?" said Sander with a grin on his face.

"Sander, relax. He's just a Reaper."

"A what?" asked Sander.

"A Reaper," said Riker. "Yes, Sander, a Reaper. They're rare, but they can come along to both worlds if they like."

Sander then asks, "What are you doing here?"

The Reaper responds, "I'm here because someone wishes to see you."

Sander's eyes widen as he sees a familiar face. "Father?"

"Hello, son. It's me, it's really me. Now, son, I can't stay long, but I can stay for the day to come to help you train or to tell you what I did wrong in life."

"Sander, is this really your father?" He looks like it. "Tell him something only your father would know."

"Father, is it really you? Why did you keep me away from girls?"

"Because, my son," said the father, "I wanted you to be a better king than I was, a king who did not go for a woman every time he saw one. Women are very powerful, you know, Sander. They can manipulate you into doing anything for the price they give you."

Sander then says, "Father, it is you." He tries to hug his father. "Wait, why can't I hug you?" asked Sander.

"Because I'm only a soul. The Reaper let me come here to only talk to you for one day. There are rules to follow in Purgatory. If you do not follow those rules, bad things can happen."

The father introduces himself to Riker as he knows he's inside Sander. "It is me. I am Daniel Helmglade, father of Fergus and Sander Helmglade. Nice to meet you, Riker. I will let you talk."

Riker then goes dormant in Sander as Sander walks with his father alone.

"Son, I missed you when I died, and I have also been sorry for what I did with Fergus."

Daniel Helmglade begins to talk to Sander. "Listen, I treated you like a son, but my problem is that I never treated Fergus as a son. I cast him out for what he did to your mother. I never really knew he would betray you and take the throne. But I'm going to help you train, Sander, and I'm going to tell you about Fergus. Maybe I can tell you what I did wrong with you. Now, what do you want first: the training or the bad things I did wrong?"

Sander asks for the training.

"Good. Now, Sander, do not force the sword. Let you and the sword feel as one. I'm going to teach you the secret of the Helmglade swordsman's secret art. I'm going to teach you the blade of fifty strikes. Now stop for a second, feel the air. Feel the wind. Hear the trees. Feel the nature around you. This is what you need to feel—peace—in order to use this attack."

Daniel Helmglade begins to circle Sander. "Now, grip your sword, and open your eyes and look at that tree. Stare down the target."

Sander opens his eyes, focused on the tree.

"The stance is a constant switch. Make sure you're on your toes."

Sander gets on his toes and gets ready.

"My stance was different than yours, but I was carrying more armor than you, Sander."

Sander begins to focus on the tree.

"Think of your mother, Sander. If you do not know her, I will describe her to you. She was happy, a cheerful mother who loved nature. She loved you, too, Sander. She made sure nothing would bother you—not demons, not any monsters. Now, Sander, use that rage you've been holding, and attack that tree with all your might. Always move in a circle. Now, begin," said Daniel Helmglade.

Sander begins to stay on his toes as he hits the tree constantly. The sword slashes and dices as if the sword is cutting the wind.

Sander continues to feel the sword as an extension of himself. He sees himself completing his destiny.

Daniel Helmglade smiles. "That is my son," he said in his head.

Sander continues to circle like the blade is cutting through the tree. Within a few hours, Sander learns the technique his father taught him. Sander sits down, tired.

"Father, I never knew we had this attack in our family."

"Now, my son, I have another request."

"What is it, Father?"

"I ask that you do not kill Fergus. If he betrayed you, I see that it was my fault, not yours. I was so angry that your mother died, I took it out on him. I should have never done that in the first place, so I cast Fergus out. I made him think he's an outsider. That was my biggest mistake in life, Sander. Hopefully, you'll be a better father as a king than I was."

"Father, I don't think I want to be king."

"I know what you're going to say—I have to be king—but I don't want to."

"Then, my son, I'm listening now. What do you want to do if not be a king?"

"I want to live in a big cottage with a new wife and live my life as an adventurer. I want to explore the world, not stay in a castle. That's what I want to do, Father."

"You mean to tell me, son, you want to live a normal life?"

"Yes, Father, I do."

"Then you shall go for it. Don't be like me and run away from what you want to do. Sander, if I'm not there, remember that I will always be by your side. Now, where were we?" said Daniel Helmglade.

"Hey, Mr. Daniel," said the Reaper.

"Yes," said Daniel.

"We have to go," said the Reaper, as he tells Sander.

"I understand."

"Wait, Father, what's going on?"

"Son, remember these words: even though you're going to battle your brother, both of you are still my sons. I care for both of you. I must go now, but son, I will always be in your heart."

Sander then sees his father and the Reaper disappear in front of his eyes.

"Riker, where did they go? Riker, are you there?" He went dormant as Sander gets angry. Sander then goes to another tree to practice the move his father taught him. Sander fights the trees each time and gets better and better with each move he uses. Sander then sees a tree fall down.

"I'm ready," said Sander. "My training is complete."

Sander then looks to the mountain where Alex Bloomingshine is staying.

"I'm coming for you," said Sander.

Sander then goes and walks to the pathway up the mountain.

417

Chapter 58

Alex Bloomingshine

Sander starts to walk up the path to the monastery to face Sir Alex Bloomingshine. As Sander is walking up, he sees Sofia walking down toward him.

"Hey, Sander, stop. Hear me out," said Sofia.

Sofia then asks, "How is it going?"

"Well, Sofia, I'm going up to defeat Sir Alex Bloomingshine."

"Wait, Sander, before you go, are you sure your powers aren't working?"

"Well, Sofia, all my powers are deactivated except for one single thing—my regeneration. I am not able to use the powers."

"That's good," said Sofia. "Listen, Sander, the thing about Alex is that when he has the chance to kill you, he will do it without mercy. Alex is a strong opponent to fight. Are you sure you can defeat him?"

Sander pulls out his sword, looks directly into Sofia's eyes, and says, "I will do anything I can to beat him. My life is not the only one depending on it. I have the lives of my people to think about. Their lives need saving from Fergus's reign."

Sander then walks past Sofia.

"Wait, Sander," said Sofia, as Sander's back is turned.

"Yes, Sofia?" said Sander.

"Who's the lucky girl?" asked Sofia.

Sander then glances slightly to his left. "She's Ashlaius of the Celestial Realm. She's the one I love now. I'm doing this for her and for us to live a long life together."

Sander continues walking as Sofia stands shocked by what Sander has become. Sander finally reaches the top of the mountain to see weapons on shelves and Alex Bloomingshine.

"Choose your weapon," said Alex. "Also, you can't use the weapon you're currently using, but you can use the weapons here."

Sander grabs the Soul Absorber and puts the sword down. He walks over to a human longsword, picks it up, and looks at Alex Bloomingshine in the arena. Alex, with a war cry, charges at Sander, initiating the fight. Sander blocks the attack as if his life depends on it. He counters with a sword slash, only to be blocked by Alex Bloomingshine. The two engage in a fierce duel, swords clashing.

Meanwhile, Gildor and the group, along with the orc group, start to wonder.

"I wonder what Sander is doing," said Gildor.

Ashlaius spots Sofia. "Oh, look who decided to show up," said Ashlaius.

Sofia looks at Ashlaius and points toward the tall mountain on the far south of Elmus. "If you're looking for Sander, he's up there."

Without hesitation, Ashlaius flies toward the mountain monastery to witness Sander fighting. Gildor watches the mountain.

"Guys, I will go if you guys go." The group looks at each other, wanting to support Sander in the fight. They rush after Gildor, leaving Sofia behind.

"Hey, Sofia, are you coming?" Gildor asks.

"I don't know, Gildor," Sofia replies.

"Listen, it doesn't matter who you support, but just know that Sander will always support you. I'll tell you what, if you come, I'll put in a good word with the Guild of the Werewolf Hunters that you're the best princess in the Kingdom of Elmus."

Sofia smiles. "Alright, I will go, but I'll tell you this—watch out for my sister. She's kind of a snake."

"Wait, how did you know?" asked Gildor.

"I know when my sister is seeing someone, and she's been thinking about trying to get you unbanished for a long time. So, I'm guessing you and her have something going on." Sofia winks at Gildor. "Don't worry, I will keep your secret, so you can relax," said Sofia.

Gildor smiles back and heads toward the mountain path. When the group finally reaches the top of the mountain, they see two legendary swordsmen going at it in the arena. The swords clash, and the sound of metal rings through the air as they fight fiercely. Sander, holding his own, stops for a moment and circles Alex. Then, Sander goes for a second round with Sir Alex Bloomingshine. Sander swirls and counter-attacks, catching Alex off guard.

As the fight intensifies, Sander sees his friends cheering him on, and he realizes he is not alone in this fight with Fergus. With renewed determination, Sander goes head-to-head with Alex, while

Alex uses all the tricks he learned as a child. Sander matches him, using the skills taught to him by the royal general. Both fighters have different pasts, but they are fighting for something meaningful. Sander fights for information about Fergus, while Alex fights for his beliefs.

Alex finally disarms Sander, leaving him defenseless. Sander, momentarily losing hope, stops in fear of death. But then, he sees the ghost of his father, Daniel Helmglade, from afar.

"I believe in you, my son. You are the son of Daniel Helmglade, and I believe you will become a better man than I ever was. Just remember one thing, my son—I will always be with you in your heart."

Sander looks at Alex with renewed strength, pulls a sword from his waist, and gets back on his feet, ready to face Alex with fierce determination.

"He will always be by my side," said Sander.

Alex tries to copy the unfamiliar stance Sander is using. "What stance is this? It's so uncommon," said Alex.

Sander feels the blade like an extension of himself. "The blade... it's like an extension of my arm. My body feels one with the sword," Sander thinks.

Sander looks at Alex one more time and declares, "Blade of Fifty Strikes!"

Sander goes on his toes, switching stances back and forth, attacking Alex Bloomingshine relentlessly. Alex struggles to defend himself, losing his sword in the process. Desperately, Alex pulls out a second sword, but Sander, with full force, delivers one final attack, shattering Alex's sword into pieces. Alex, shocked, loses control and falls onto his back.

Sander points the sword at Alex's neck. "Do you yield?"

Alex smiles. "I've never been beaten by anyone before, but I'm glad that you were the one to beat me, Prince Sander Helmglade."

Alex finally says the words Sander was waiting to hear. "I yield," said Alex.

Sander helps Alex up from the ground and looks toward the castle. "Looks like I have to get my answers."

Without hesitation, Sander flies to the castle in the kingdom to find the answers he seeks. Sander lands on the balcony of the king's chambers and begins making his way downstairs to the throne room. When Sander opens the door, the guards rush toward him.

"I have beaten Sir Alex Bloomingshine," Sander says boldly to the king.

The king commands his guards to kill him. With all his might, Sander is pinned to the ground by the guards as they prepare to kill him. Riker awakens from his dormant state and tells Sander to call out to the sword. Sander cries out to the Soul Absorber for help.

Meanwhile, Gildor and the group are at the mountain discussing Sander. "So, Sander doesn't really care for us if he's just flying around trying to get answers," said Gildor.

"I believe you're right, Gildor," said Ares.

As they chat, the Soul Absorber begins to move. Within seconds, it shoots out of the air and flies toward the castle. Just as

Sander is about to be killed, the Soul Absorber comes in, landing in Sander's hand. Sander flies up and attacks the guards, knocking them out. He then walks over to the king and grabs him by the throat.

"Tell me where my brother is, or so help me by the gods, I will kill you," said Sander, as his eyes turn red and black.

In fear, the king tells Sander where his brother, the King of Luna, is. "Your brother," said the king, choking, "your brother is in the Kingdom of Luna. He is in your castle. I'm sorry for attacking you. Please don't kill me."

Sander tightens his grip but then releases him, returning to normal as his red eyes fade away.

"Sander," said Riker, "we must head back to the Kingdom of Luna and finish this deal. You're turning more into a demon. Let's go," said Riker in his head.

Sander then returns to the camp, where the orcs are, and tells them to pack up. "We're going to Luna."

Sander decides to fly back to the monastery. When he arrives, he sees Alex and the group. Sander lands and tells the group, "We're heading out."

Without providing further answers, Sander begins flying back toward the orcs.

Chapter 59

The Dark Pit

Three hours had passed, and the group, along with the orc army, had finished packing and were making their way toward the elven border. The group walked in silence, with Sander leading at the front. Ashlaius began to read his mind as they walked.

"Hey Sander, are you alright?" she asked telepathically.

Sander didn't respond at first.

"Sander, are you there?" Ashlaius asked again.

Finally, Sander woke from his thoughts. "Yeah, I'm here, Ashlaius," he replied.

"What's going on?" Ashlaius pressed.

Sander told her the truth. "When I confronted King Alexander, he sent his guards after me. I called out to the Soul Absorber, and it came to me, Ashlaius, like it was bonded to me. Then, after I knocked out the guards and walked toward King Alexander... I don't know what's going on. It feels like Riker and I are merging into one body, and I'm becoming the demon itself. I attacked King Alexander, and part of me wanted to kill him. Ashlaius, I'm changing. I'm not the man you once met," Sander said emotionally.

Ashlaius walked closer to him and telepathically said, "You control the power; the power doesn't control you. I believe in you to become king," she said, giving him a supportive look.

"Thank you," Sander replied.

The group and the army of orcs finally crossed the border into the Green Forest. As they continued walking through the dense forest, they saw an army of black wolves watching them from afar. The group stopped, as did the orc army. The wolves stared down the army, and the tension mounted.

Sander instructed the group to keep walking. Cronovus stepped closer to Sander. Suddenly, the wolves charged as if preparing to attack. Everyone drew their weapons, ready to fight. As the wolves drew near, Cronovus shouted, "Stop!"

Immediately, the wolves halted and knelt before Cronovus. He commanded them to transform back into their human forms, and the wolves obeyed without hesitation. Cronovus looked back at the group. "You can all relax. These are my people, and they will be joining me in this fight."

Sander looked at him in surprise. "How can you control them?"

Cronovus explained, "Because, Sander, I am one of the kings of the werewolves. I was born as a black werewolf, meaning I can control all the black wolves — their alphas and omegas."

Cronovus ordered his people to follow them to Luna, and the werewolves obeyed, walking in line behind the group like loyal followers.

"Alright, Sander, where to next?" Cronovus asked.

Sander looked at the group and said, "We're going to the Kingdom of Luna to reclaim my throne. But I need to tell you all the truth. I'm not going to become king."

The group was shocked. "What? Why not?" Gildor asked.

"Because I never wanted to be king," Sander replied.

"Then why overthrow Fergus?" Gildor pressed.

"Because Fergus has hurt so many people. He conquered lands just to enslave the dwarves, and he spread fear across Sinia. I'm going to Luna to stop him, not to become king. But Fergus isn't the only threat. Galatin, a man who killed his own sister out of fear for the child she might bear, is just as dangerous. Believe me or not, but I will go alone if I must."

The group looked at Sander, and in unison, they all said, "We will follow you."

"We will follow you too," the orcs echoed.

"Alright then, Cronovus, Holie — will you follow me?" Sander asked.

The two looked at each other. "Yes, we will," said Holie.

"Alright, to the Kingdom of Luna, to reclaim the throne," Sander declared.

The group and the army of orcs marched out of the Green Forest and toward the dark pit. As they neared the bridge, Sander began to have flashbacks of his brother.

"I'm sorry, Sander," Fergus said in the flashback as he pushed Sander into the dark pit.

"Stop," Sander said suddenly. "We're here."

"What do you mean?" Ares asked.

"We're here, at the dark pit," Sander replied.

The group peered down into the abyss. "Wow, that's a long way down," Ashlaius remarked.

"Sander," Riker said in Sander's head. "Do you sense that?"

"Sense what?" Sander asked.

"Well, if you didn't know, I'm not the only one in the dark pit. My people are down there too. They're trapped in the cave, but I managed to escape. If you can, free my people. Half of them will leave people alone, but the other half... they'll want to kill and take souls. If we die, they'll want Galatin dead too. This could be an advantage."

"But, Riker, you said half of them want to kill people," Sander noted.

"Yes, but if we live, we might be able to command them," Riker replied.

The group stayed silent.

"Sander, are you alright?" Ashlaius asked.

"Yeah, I'm fine. Just talking to Riker," Sander said.

Riker continued, "Listen, Sander, if we win, I can command them to return home."

"But Riker, what if we die?"

"We don't think that way," Riker said. "Now, are we heading to the Kingdom of Luna, or are we going to share our story?"

Sander turned to the group. "Alright, guys. Riker and I were talking, and we're undecided. Maybe you can help. We're considering releasing the demons in the dark pit to gain an advantage in the fight against Galatin."

"I don't see anything wrong with that," Gildor said.

The group nodded in agreement. "Yeah, nothing wrong with that."

"But," Sander began, "half of the demons down there just want to eat souls and kill people."

"So, basically, normal demons," Ashlaius remarked.

"Yeah," Sander replied.

The group immediately turned on Sander, yelling, "No! We're not releasing them now that you've said that! Are you insane? Think of the innocent people who might get hurt!"

"I know it's bad, but it will help us against Galatin and Fergus," Sander argued.

"Sander, don't be stupid!" The group bickered with him for two hours until Sander finally relented.

"Alright," Sander said, and the group stopped arguing.

They turned to look at the Kingdom of Luna in the distance.

"We're ready when you are, Sander," Ashlaius said.

"I never told you the story of how Riker and I met," Sander began. "It all started when I was sleeping. Fergus dragged me out of bed and near that cliff over there."

"But that's near the dark pit," Gildor interrupted.

"I know," Sander continued. "Fergus wanted power. He said he would rule better than me, and he kicked me off the cliff. I fell into the dark pit. When I woke up, I saw Riker. Well, I didn't know it was him at first, but I met Riker down there. He shadow-dashed from place to place in the pit until he offered me a deal. I took it — the deal was to kill Fergus and get my revenge. Now, looking back, I'm not sure if I can kill Fergus, but I know I have to stop Galatin. And if I stop Galatin, that might mean killing Fergus too."

"Sander, there's one more training technique I never taught you. It will make me visible in my true form. Think of it like using your own shadow to bring me forth. I believe Fergus has already learned this, so I'm going to teach it to you now. I'll just cheat the system and give you all the knowledge of my existence."

Riker opened up the knowledge into Sander's mind, filling him with information about the world and their connection. The group looked at Sander with astonishment.

"We never knew you went through all this," the group said apologetically. "But, Sander, a person has to do what's right for the kingdom. As we see it, you need to kill Galatin and Fergus to stop the madness."

The group paused and looked at Sander as he looked back.

"Sander, we've made it this far with you, and we're not going to leave without you."

The group urged Sander to lead the way. Sander crossed the bridge over the dark pit, and they continued toward Luna. As they neared the castle, Sander instructed Ashlaius to keep an eye on him and make sure he didn't lose control.

The group and Sander made their way closer and closer to the Kingdom of Luna. The castle loomed in the distance, and Sander smiled.

"I'm coming for you, Fergus. I will get my revenge and save the people of Luna and Sinia."

Sander and the group, along with the orc army, finally arrived at the Kingdom of Luna, ready to begin the siege.

Chapter 60

The Siege of Luna

The group stopped looking at the Kingdom of Luna. "This is it," Sander said as he grabbed the Soul Absorber. Sander told the group to siege the castle when he was ready. The group then camped outside the castle, waiting for the guards to hail them. The guards then called out to Sander, "Who are you?"

Sander walked out of the shadow to show his face. As Sander emerged, the guards sounded the bell, signaling that Sander was there. More guards began to line up along the wall as Fergus stood on the balcony, watching Sander from afar. Sander locked eyes with Fergus.

"I am here to see the king," Sander said.

The guards aimed their crossbows at Sander and fired. The arrow pierced Sander's chest, but Sander healed the wound immediately. He then turned around and commanded, "Now."

The orcs rushed at the kingdom's gates and began attacking. Sander flew up into the air and headed toward the balcony where Fergus stood. Sander grabbed his sword and swung at Fergus, who blocked the attack. Sander kicked Fergus so hard that Fergus went crashing through the throne room door. Fergus's eyes turned half blue as the archangel appeared in his left eye.

"Riker," Galatin said in Fergus's head.

Fergus paused and looked at Sander as the siege continued. "Well, Sander, it looks like you've returned."

"I returned to stop you, Fergus. You pushed too far, enslaving the dwarves and trying to conquer the elves."

"Sander, that's called playing smart. The dwarves have been weak for quite some time. All it took was Galatin's power to make them believe that humans are superior."

"Fergus, this isn't you talking. This is Galatin," Sander said.

"Sander, have you heard? I made a deal with Galatin after I killed Father. I made a deal to conquer the world and be the greatest king of Luna."

Sander's eyes widened in shock. "Fergus, why would you do that?"

"Because, Sander, humans have been overlooked by the elves and dwarves. I wanted to be the king that helped humanity rise."

Fergus got into his battle stance. "Now, Sander, since you know, I must kill you."

Fergus attacked Sander, but Sander blocked with the Soul Absorber, creating a loud, shocking sonic wave that blew apart the throne room. As the tower of the throne room began to crumble, the group outside struggled to breach the gate. The orcs were being shot at by ballistae.

"How do we breach this gate?" one of them asked.

As they continued their attack, reinforcements from the Hopes Battalion arrived to help breach the gate.

"Reinforcements have arrived!" a soldier called out, just as a catapult fired and killed the guard who made the announcement.

"The Hopes Battalion has betrayed us!" the army shouted.

Meanwhile, Sander and Fergus continued their fight. "You won't stop me, Sander. Galatin's power will make us a greater race."

"Fergus, making humans superior over the other races makes you look like a dark king. You can stop this."

"Sander, now!" Riker said in Sander's head.

Within a shadow, Riker transformed into his true form, a shadowy figure with a sword, and rushed at Fergus. In an instant, Galatin emerged with the same ability. Sander shifted into the stance his father had taught him.

"There's no way you know that stance," Fergus said in disbelief.

"Father must have taught us both," Sander replied.

The two brothers clashed, each using the Helmglade technique. Their blows grew stronger and stronger, destroying parts of the throne room. Outside, the group saw their numbers dwindling.

"We're losing troops!" Gildor shouted. "We need to breach the front gate now."

The orcs created a crack in the gate but watched as it healed, as though someone was repairing it.

The commander of the Hopes Battalion approached Gildor. "I forgot to tell you — the gate is protected by magic. We need to destroy the core inside the castle for it to be breached."

"But if we destroy the core, the demons will be released," Gildor warned.

Back inside, Sander kicked Fergus again, sending him crashing into the royal library near a golden door. Sander dashed in after him, continuing his relentless assault. "Why don't you die with all your books?" Sander shouted.

The brothers fought with fury, determined to destroy each other. Above them, Riker and Galatin battled in the sky.

"She was your sister!" Riker shouted. "Why did you kill her?"

"Because she was a traitor," Galatin replied coldly. "She lay with a demon, our sworn enemy."

"That doesn't give you the right to kill your own blood!" Riker growled.

"It wasn't just that," Galatin sneered. "We were supposed to marry, to keep our bloodline pure."

"What kind of monster marries his own sister?" Riker spat.

"I'm no monster, Riker. I see the future."

Galatin rushed at Riker and slashed him. When Galatin cut Riker, Sander felt the pain on his arm.

"Ow!" Sander cried, spinning to stab Fergus in the arm in retaliation.

Galatin felt Fergus's pain and dashed toward Sander, but Riker intercepted him. "You're fighting me once and for all, Galatin. Enough running!"

As the battle between Riker and Galatin raged, the library shook from the force of their attacks. Meanwhile, the group outside was still trying to breach the wall. One of the orc commanders was struck down by the third ballista. Zytrix saw the orc chief of the Riverlands fall and caught him as he collapsed.

"Zytrix of the White Wolf Clan, take my chain and make sure we win this fight," the chief said, dying with his hands in Zytrix's.

"Kill them all!" Zytrix roared, leading a fierce charge against the gate.

Inside the castle, Sander and Fergus fought near the magical core. "What is this place?" Sander asked as he fought.

"It's the core that holds the castle together," Fergus explained. "It also holds the barrier over the dark pit."

"What do you mean, holding the castle?" Sander asked.

"This core holds everything, including the barrier around the dark pit. That's why your troops can't get through. You're alone in this fight, Sander. I'm going to win. I'll kill you and become unstoppable."

Fergus attacked Sander again. Sander swung his sword, turning it into flames, but Fergus dodged, and the flames struck the core. The magical barriers around the castle and the dark pit shattered. Demons from the dark pit began to emerge, just as the orc army breached the gate.

The orcs ran in, killing humans along the way, while the Hopes Battalion fought back against their own people. Sir Kevin led his household to fight against Fergus's army. Although outmatched, the orcs, the Hopes Battalion, and werewolves continued to battle as the gates came crashing down.

Ashlaius saw the destruction caused by Sander and Fergus's fight. As she flew toward the castle, a demon general appeared.

"Well, well, well, an angel has appeared," the demon general said, smirking. "Let's see what you can do against me."

"The war is over, general. The celestials won," Ashlaius said defiantly.

"That's not true, angel. The war isn't over until I say it's over," the demon general growled, charging at her.

As they clashed in the throne room, Gildor spotted a green werewolf with a strange essence. "Cronovus, who is that?" he asked.

"That's Cyprus," Cronovus replied. "He's one of the first eight werewolves, like me. He wants to kill everyone who isn't a werewolf. I'm guessing he and Galatin have a deal."

Gildor rushed toward Cyprus, preparing to fight him. Meanwhile, Cronovus spotted a vampire. "Raymond, that's not just any vampire. It's one of the five original vampires created by Riker. Holie and I will help you fight him."

The three of them charged at the vampire. As they fought, Ares spotted a familiar face.

"Scorpius, look!" Ares said.

Scorpius turned to see a familiar figure. Duvessa, looking confused, asked, "Who is that?"

"That's Prince Alterack," Ares said. "He's one of the princes of the Kingdom of Bumba and one of the most powerful tribes of

Bumba. His tribe is a Dark Siren tribe, and he's the one who killed my brother."

Ares killed a human in front of him and charged toward Prince Alterack, determined to avenge his brother. Meanwhile, Sander and Fergus continued their battle. Fergus blasted Sander through a wall and into the farmlands.

Fergus flew down and struck Sander in the arm. "You won't beat me, Sander. Riker is weaker than Galatin!"

"That's not true," Sander replied.

"I'll lend you my power," the Soul Absorber whispered. "There are two things I hate in this world—celestials and power-hungry fools like your brother. Now accept my power."

Sander accepted the Soul Absorber's power, and black flames began to swirl around sander. Sander gets up and fights Fergus. The kingdom and the brothers fight constantly until Gildor makes a mark on Cyprus.

Chapter 61

Gildors Mark

Gildor faced a great challenge as he battled the werewolves and Cyprus. He fought fiercely, slicing through werewolf after werewolf, but one stabbed him, halting his progress toward Cyprus. Within seconds, Cronovus ordered his soldiers to transform and attack Cyprus's forces. It became a battle of dominance between the werewolf factions.

Gildor, with help from Cronovus, pushed forward, determined to confront Cyprus. As Gildor leaped to attack, Cyprus countered, throwing him into a house. Gildor crashed through the structure, landing in the kitchen where terrified citizens huddled. He pulled himself up, shook off the pain, and charged after Cyprus again. Gildor slashed at Cyprus, only for Cyprus to flip around, disarm him, and nearly tear him apart. Then Cyprus moved on, killing orcs as he went.

Gildor, on the brink of unconsciousness, saw a light approaching. A reaper appeared before him. "Listen, Gildor, this is no ordinary werewolf. This is Cyprus, the firstborn of the green werewolves. You must be cautious. You are not just Gildor Landfield; you are Gildor, the Black-Leathered Werewolf Hunter. Now rise and use your gift to kill him."

Gildor awoke as if from a dream, fully healed, and saw Cyprus attacking the orcs. Gildor grabbed his sword and charged. "Cyprus, you're facing me, not them!" he shouted.

Cyprus turned to face him. "How are you still alive, human? Are you a werewolf hunter? If you are, I'll tear that ring from your fingers before I kill you. I've lived for over a thousand years, while you've only lived for twenty. I am immortal, and you are not. So, little werewolf hunter, run now or die."

Gildor, undeterred, stared Cyprus down. "I'd rather die slicing your head off."

A nearby werewolf lunged at Gildor, but he quickly stabbed it with a silver sword. He pulled the blade free and charged at Cyprus. Cyprus retaliated, swiping at Gildor with his claws. In a split second, Gildor remembered the voice from his dream: "Use your gifts." Trusting in his power of foresight, he blocked Cyprus's attack. Shocked, Cyprus howled, summoning more werewolves to attack Gildor before retreating into the keep.

The orcs and werewolves clashed viciously as Gildor fought his way through Cyprus's forces, slaughtering every werewolf in his path. Meanwhile, the orcs attempted to breach the second gate of the kingdom. Gildor waited as the orcs cracked open the gate. As soon as there was an opening, Gildor sprinted through and continued his pursuit of Cyprus.

He climbed over the wall alongside the orcs, reaching the third level of the kingdom. When he finally caught sight of Cyprus, Gildor used his power of foresight to anticipate Cyprus's moves. The two clashed in a deadly battle, with Cyprus using his claws and Gildor defending with his sword. In a moment of precision, Gildor stabbed Cyprus in the leg, weakening him.

Cyprus, sensing his end, spoke his final words. "Gildor Landfield, I've read your mind. I know who you love, and they will soon know too. You think I'm the only firstborn werewolf out there?

There are seven more of us: Cronovus, Lintovous, Marcus, Magnus, Klyido, Mannuel, and Singneus — the strongest of all. Each of us belongs to a different species of werewolf. Now, you must kill seven more of us." Cyprus laughed as he died.

Gildor, filled with rage, swung his sword and decapitated Cyprus. The werewolf's body crumpled to the ground, lifeless. "Five more to kill," Gildor muttered. "Not seven. Cronovus is not a threat, and Lintovous, the white werewolf, is already dead. I've only got five more."

Suddenly, Gildor felt a sharp, burning pain in his arm. He removed his leather armor to reveal a new mark: the symbol of the green werewolf. Along with the mark came a new power, the ability to ignite his sword with fire. Gildor realized that each time he killed one of the original werewolves, he gained a new ability.

He signaled Cronovus, letting him know that Cyprus was dead. Cronovus acknowledged the signal and continued his own fight, determined to kill one of the five original vampires created by Riker. Raymond, now joined by Cronovus and Holie, readied himself for battle as they embarked to face the powerful vampire.

Chapter 62

Holies Rebirth

Holie, Cronovus, and Raymond continue to fight one of the most powerful vampires to ever live.

"Wait, why does it take three of us?" said Raymond. "I can take him on my own."

"Raymond," said Cronovus, "this man is a master of the dark arts. If you attack him solo, he has enough magic to destroy the ring you're carrying."

"Is that really possible?" asked Raymond.

"Yes, it is possible. I've seen him kill a werewolf by absorbing his magic."

Raymond, Cronovus, and Holie all decide to rush him at once. The vampire begins to dodge every single attack Raymond and Holie throw at him. Cronovus manages to scratch the vampire, but the vampire grabs Cronovus and flips him over.

"You guys can't stop me. I'm too strong, and I will unite the following vampires to help me become the high vampire king. You will never stop what Gelatin has planned for you."

The vampire then starts to hunt down Raymond to kill him first. He stabs Raymond through the heart and throws him to the other side. As the vampire looks at Holie, he grabs her, and Cronovus, filled with hesitation, stops fighting and pleads.

"Please, look, I will give you my power. Just let her go."

"Oh, Cronovus, the black werewolf. I see you've fallen for a vampire." The vampire then smells what she is. "A pureblood! That sounds delicious. How about you, my dear, be my lunch? I would love to see you in my stomach. Your blood smells tasty. What is your name?"

Holie bites him to get away.

"Ow!" said the vampire. He then grabs her again and begins to absorb her magic and powers.

"No!" shouted Cronovus.

The vampire kills Holie right in front of Cronovus. Cronovus runs towards Holie, desperate to save her. He feels alone as he watches her take her dying breath.

"I never loved anyone in my life, Cronovus. It's okay to leave me. I will see you on the other side, my love," she said as she closed her eyes.

Cronovus feels devastated by his loss. He cries out to the gods to save her, but they do not answer. His anger and grief build up, and as he cries, he looks at the vampire. Cronovus' eyes turn black, and he begins to transform, driven by a desire for vengeance. His body cracks, snapping bones and joints as he transforms into his true form — a strong, black werewolf with dark magic surging from his body.

Cronovus charges towards the vampire, who quickly tries to flee. Cronovus catches him and tears him apart, limb from limb, as the vampire tries to absorb Cronovus' power. But Cronovus doesn't care, ripping the vampire into pieces until nothing remains.

Cronovus returns to his normal form and goes to Holie. He sits beside her, accepting the loss of his love. Just then, Raymond wakes up from his death and sees Holie lying there.

"What happened?" asked Raymond.

"Holie died helping me fight him," Cronovus replied.

"Where is he?" asked Raymond.

"See those guts over there? That's all that's left of him," Cronovus said, pointing to the splattered limbs and blood.

Raymond grabs his sword and slices the vampire's head in two, severing it from the body.

"What's going to happen to Holie?" asked Raymond.

"I'm going to take her home and bury her there," Cronovus said, picking up Holie and slowly walking towards Luna Keep as the war nears its end. Gildor walks next to Raymond and Cronovus.

"I'm so sorry, Cronovus. I know she loved you," said Gildor.

Cronovus looks at the mark on Gildor's chest. "Wait, there's a way to save her. Gildor, I'm going to need that tattoo. She will be reborn as a green werewolf."

Gildor shows Cronovus the mark. Cronovus places one hand on Holie's chest and the other on Gildor's mark of the green werewolf.

"Gildor, you ready?" Cronovus asked.

The mark begins to transfer from Gildor to Holie, appearing on her chest and turning her into a werewolf. She then wakes up in Cronovus' arms.

"Holie, thank you, Gildor." They are reunited, but just then, they hear a loud bang from the third level kingdom.

Chapter 63
Ares Revenge

Ares gets flung into the building.

"We will help you," said Duvessa.

"No," said Ares, "this fight is mine alone."

Ares activates his mark to increase his strength. He continues to fight for revenge on his brother, Darius.

"Why does he not want us to help him?" asked Duvessa.

"Because," said Scorpius, "this isn't our fight or anyone else's, just his. The reason he wants to fight is that it's about revenge for his brother Darius."

Ares fights with his obsidian sapphire spear as he battles Prince Alterack.

"Ares, you've never realized how powerful we are, Ares, Prince of Astra. This is what's going to happen — Astra is going to fall to the dark sirens, and Gelatin will help us win this war against your kind. If I were to tell you the truth, Ares, I loved killing your brother."

Ares' eyes begin to glow as his anger rises, and he uses his bioluminescence.

"You will not kill any more of my people or any of the siren race."

Ares starts to swing his sword as the battle intensifies. Meanwhile, Duvessa grows increasingly frustrated that she isn't helping.

"Scorpius, we have to help him! He needs it; this is an unfair fight."

"No," said Scorpius, "this is his fight and only his fight. You weren't there when they attacked the border. They all aimed for the king and only the king. When Ares saw his brother die from Prince Alterack's spear, he died in Ares' arms, Duvessa. So believe me when I say this to you — he will fight his own battle."

As they argue, Ares gets launched into a house, crashing through it. He gets up, bruised, and starts running toward Prince Alterack, determined to defeat him. Ares grabs his spear and activates all his water knight tattoos, gaining enhanced power to kill the prince. Prince Alterack uses magic, but it skims off Ares as Ares stabs the prince with his spear and then swings it to chop off his head.

Ares turns and smiles at Duvessa.

"You guys can relax now. I had it all under control."

But then Ares felt his heart stop. He had used too much of the tattoos' power. Ares falls to the ground as Scorpius and Duvessa rush to him. Ares begins to have a heart attack on the ground. Duvessa looks at him, trying to understand what's happening.

"What's going on, Scorpius?"

Scorpius grabs Ares' hand, and Ares chants the words of the ancient sirens.

"What's happening, Scorpius?" Duvessa asked.

Scorpius then tells her, "He used too much of the power inside."

"What does that mean?" Duvessa asked.

"It means he's going to die."

Duvessa starts to cry, unsure of what to do. She then decides to tell Ares to stay alive. Ares turns to Scorpius.

"Scorpius, you are the next generation of the water knight. I taught you everything I could in the water. Take my spear and use it well, as you are now a water knight."

"No!" said Duvessa.

She then kissed Ares on the lips, pouring her love into him. Ares' wounds begin to heal as he feels love for the first time. Ares kisses Duvessa back. Scorpius whispers silently, "A healer."

Ares is fully healed, and his heart starts working again. He gets up, picking up his spear, and looks toward the castle as he hears a loud crash in the throne room.

"Come on, let's go. We have to get to the castle," said Ares, hiding his emotions toward Duvessa. Ares moves towards the castle with Scorpius and Duvessa.

Chapter 64

The Reveal of Ashlaius

Ashlaius fights the demon general with all her might. The demon king then launches her into the sky as she starts flying with her wings. Things get intense, as Ashlaius knows she isn't skilled in combat flight. She can't breathe as the launch knocked the wind out of her. She feels death is near, unable to defeat this demon general. She finally gains control of her flight as he smashes her into the second level of the kingdom. Ashlaius remains on the ground, unable to get up.

The demon then grabs an innocent person and starts killing him, absorbing his soul into his body. She watches helplessly as he kills more souls to absorb.

"I totally forgot how delicious this world is," he says. "I want more humans to be a part of me."

Ashlaius looks to the sky, seeing the clouds, and remembers what her trainer taught her.

"Listen, Ashlaius, if you are ever in a situation where you can't fight anymore, make them pray and help you. Make sure you are the good person in the fight and stop him the best you can."

Ashlaius stands up and grabs her daggers, ready for another battle. The demon looks at Ashlaius after absorbing another soul.

"You can't stop me. You know you're too weak of an archangel to stop someone like me."

"It doesn't matter how weak I am," Ashlaius says with courage, "I am not going to stand here and let you absorb innocent people."

The demon, enraged, instantly flashes towards Ashlaius. With no time to react, she's smacked through the lower parts of the kingdom. The demon general charges at Ashlaius, hitting her with all his strength, and she begins to give up. He grabs her by the wing and slams her to the ground.

"You're too weak. Gelatin's sister is always weak, and I'm guessing you're not as old as the battle from a thousand years ago."

The demon starts to walk away as Ashlaius stands back up, remembering what her trainer also said.

"Ashlaius, remember, if you are trapped, always use the powers you were born with. Use your lightning and water."

Ashlaius looks at the clouds and sees it's about to rain. The people start chanting, hoping for her victory. She begins to feel the power of their prayers. She looks at the demon as lightning strikes beside her. Lightning surges through her veins as she sprints towards the demon, punching him in the chest, sending him flying toward the mountains.

Ashlaius charges after him. She begins to use her powers quickly, realizing she has grown stronger. She grabs her daggers and chops off his wings, rendering him unable to fly. The demon attacks her, but Ashlaius dodges it. She flies into the sky with him and smashes him down to the ground. She then plunges her dagger into his heart, creating a sonic wave that destroys several houses as she stabs him to death.

Ashlaius watches as the demon ignites and dies before her eyes, turning into ash. She then looks toward the farmlands and sees

Sander and Fergus fighting. Slowly, she walks away from the demon's remains as the ashes fade away.

Chapter 65

Fergus VS. Sander

Sander gets flung to the ground by Fergus and nearly gets stabbed. Sander rolls over and dodges every attack Fergus throws. Eventually, Fergus stabs Sander.

"Damn it," said Sander, clutching his head. "Fergus, why do you want to conquer? Tell me the truth."

"Because, Sander, I was always treated like I was an abomination. Now that I'm king, I can prove that I'm the rightful king of Luna, not you. You know nothing of my childhood or what Father did," Fergus replied.

As Fergus and Sander fight to see which brother will emerge victorious, Riker and Galatin talk to each other about their past.

"Riker, I've lived for more than a thousand years, and you've lived for more than a thousand years. But I fell in love with a human. We were happy until your kind absorbed her soul. Do you know who I saw doing that? It was you. You were absorbing human souls to gain power. That's why I hate you even more than I already did."

Galatin then attacks Riker, who telepathically connects with Sander.

"Sander, trust in the soul absorber to gain more power," Riker says.

Sander is engulfed in black flames as he sees Galatin and Riker settle their differences once and for all. Sander tries to reason with Fergus.

"Fergus, you've got to see reason. Luna, the kingdom, is in danger every time you start a war with another race. You have to believe me, brother. Every time you go to war, the people starve. You need to think about the people, not about yourself. The power of a king must be used wisely. That's what Father was supposed to teach us."

Sander then counterattacks and stabs his brother in the chest.

"No, no, no," said Sander as he pulled out his sword and dropped it to the ground, holding Fergus in his arms. "Wait, I didn't mean it, Fergus."

"Sander, I'm free," said Fergus.

"What do you mean, brother?" Sander asked, tears beginning to fall as he realized he was losing his brother.

"No, you have to stay with me. I didn't mean to do this. I just wanted you to see reason," Sander cried, kneeling by Fergus.

"Listen to me," Fergus said, coughing up blood. "Galatin is strong. He put all these thoughts in my head. I just wanted the people to see that I wasn't a mistake in Father's eyes. I hated him so much that I killed him. I meant to do it. Sander, you have to kill Galatin. He's the one who made me kill Father. He's the one who wanted me to conquer the dwarves. His power is too strong; he manipulated me."

Fergus looked at his brother. "I will say this, brother. You've been the best brother I've had. You should know that I will always lo—"

Fergus died in Sander's arms, unable to finish his final words. Sander, filled with rage over what Galatin had done, ignites with anger. Sander's deal finally comes to an end, and he begins to die as he reverts back to human form. As Sander lies on his deathbed, Riker continues to fight Galatin.

From afar, Colinborn speaks to Riker. "Riker, if you're losing, remember, I forgot to tell you—your son is alive. When Galatin dies, you can see Crystal. The reapers made that possible."

Riker, filled with new resolve, focuses on Galatin as black flames surround him. He calls upon the sword absorber. As the soul absorber appears, Galatin summons Fergus's sword, and the two powerful beings clash in a fierce battle.

"I will not let you win, Galatin. You've been hurting people for revenge, but Crystal was the final straw. She was your sister, your best friend, and you killed her and my child. But little did you know, my child is still alive, protected by a dragon, and I will kill you to ensure he has a better future."

Riker counterattacks and flies into the air with Galatin. With precise focus, Riker lands on Galatin and stabs him in the chest as they plummet from the sky. A massive fireball crashes into the farmlands, leaving a crater of fire and rocks.

Riker, having used all his power in that single attack, weakens to the point of near death. He sees the moment of Galatin's death and says, "Your reign has ended, Galatin of the Light."

Galatin dies in front of Riker's eyes. Riker rolls over and smiles at the sky, seeing Crystal. He reaches out as he hears her say, "Come home." Riker reaches for the sky and coughs as Sander crawls toward him.

"Looks like we're going to die together," said Sander.

"No, Sander. I'm not going to die with you. I'm going to die alone," Riker replied, looking at Sander. Riker then dies, his spirit turning to ash.

Sander briefly dies too, but Riker, in ghost form, gives all his power to Sander, transforming all the demon's power into him. Sander is reborn, and with his final goodbye, Riker departs.

Ashlaius then lands next to Sander. As Sander awakens from what feels like a sleep state, he sees the black flames surrounding him.

"Ashlaius, is that you?" Sander asks.

Sander and Ashlaius live in peace for a brief moment, forgetting that the demons have begun to escape. Together, they look toward the dark pit, realizing the demons have returned.

.

Chapter 66

The Letter

Sander flies back to the castle to send a letter to someone. He writes in his final letter:

Dear Kevin Gladstone,

This is your cousin, Sander. I have been thinking about this for quite some time, and now I believe I have made my decision. I do not wish to be king. I wish to live my own life with Ashlaius. I know I am leaving the demon situation in your hands, but I trust that you and the Order of Light will handle this. This is your journey now. I will assist with the demon problem by going after the generals. But, as King Sander Helmglade, I renounce my crown and give it to you, Sir Kevin Gladstone.

Goodbye, my dear cousin.

Sander then uses magic to send the letter to Kevin Gladstone. As the magic carries the letter to its destination, Ashlaius and Sander hold hands and fly to the high skies together.

www.ingramcontent.com/pod-product-compliance
Lightning Source LLC
Chambersburg PA
CBHW051116300726
48981CB00002B/153